D1138773

vATEER

TIM SEVERIN, explorer, filmmaker and lecturer,
has retraced the storied journeys of Saint Brendan the
Navigator, Sindbad the Sailor, Jason and the Argonauts, Ulysses,
Genghis Khan and Robinson Crusoe. His books about these
expeditions are classics of exploration and travel.

He made his historical fiction debut with the hugely successful
Viking series, followed by the Pirate and Saxon series.
This novel returns to the Pirate series, and the
world of Hector Lynch.

Visit Tim's website to find out more
about his books and expeditions:
www.timseverin.net

Follow Tim on Facebook:
Facebook.com/TimSeverinAuthor

TIM SEVERIN

✳

PIRATE

VOLUME FOUR

PRIVATEER

PAN BOOKS

First published 2014 by Macmillan

This edition published 2015 by Pan Books
an imprint of Pan Macmillan, a division of Macmillan Publishers Limited
Pan Macmillan, 20 New Wharf Road, London N1 9RR
Basingstoke and Oxford
Associated companies throughout the world
www.panmacmillan.com

ISBN 978-0-330-45830-6

A CIP catalogue record for this book is available from the British Library.

Map artwork by Neil Gower
Typeset by Ellipsis Digital Limited, Glasgow
Printed and bound by CPI Group (UK) Ltd, Croydon, CR0 4YY

Visit *www.panmacmillan.com* to read more about all our books
and to buy them. You will also find features, author interviews and
news of any author events, and you can sign up for e-newsletters
so that you're always first to hear about our new releases.

PIRATE: PRIVATEER

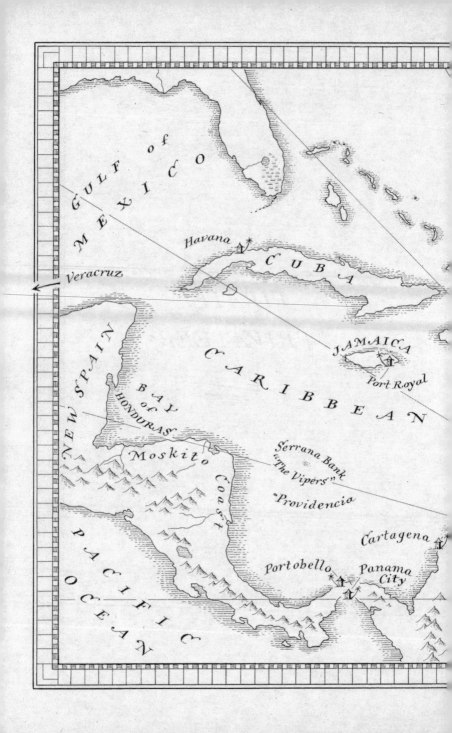

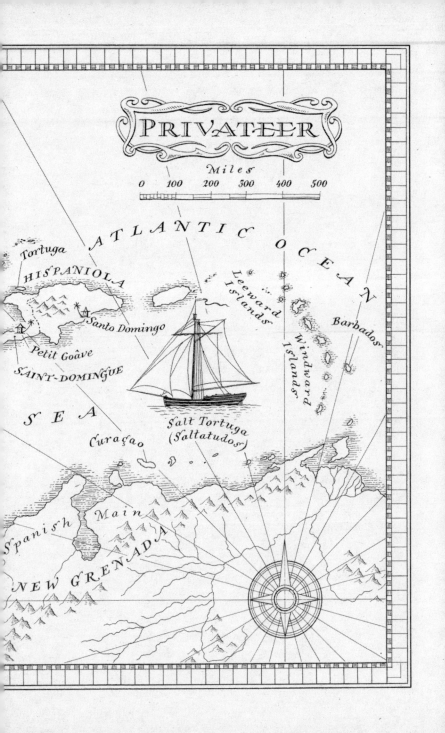

ONE

THEY BEGAN FISHING the wreck as soon as the sun's rays penetrated to the sea floor. The weather was perfect for diving: a cloudless sky and no hint of breeze to disturb the flat calm. The water was so clear that Hector Lynch, leaning out over the pinnace's rail, could make out the shape of his comrade and close friend Dan as a flickering shadow against the seabed five fathoms below. He was exploring the broken timbers of the sunken galleon. A slack tide meant there was almost no current and Dan was hauling himself from handhold to handhold, poking and prying in crevices. In another minute he would have to come back to the surface to fill his lungs with air.

Hector straightened up and took a quick glance around the horizon. The cargo of a lost galleon was still the property of the Spanish crown, and they were trespassing in an area the Spanish considered off-limits to foreign vessels. If the Spaniards got their hands on them, they would be treated as thieves and the penalty was a long prison sentence at hard labour. But there was nothing to be seen in any direction except for two insignificant islets half a mile to the east. He had already marked them on the chart he was compiling. It had taken many days to find the wreck, cautiously probing the vast underwater maze of coral, sand and rock. Now his notes on the distance and bearing to the two islets would help him return to the wreck if the pinnace was driven off her station by bad weather or the unwelcome appearance of a Spanish patrol ship. The islets themselves were unremarkable. Low humps of sand and rock, they were bald except for a few stunted bushes bleached whitish grey by the salt spray. They were all that could be seen of the dangerous zone of reefs that the Spaniards had nicknamed 'the Vipers' because their sharp fangs had ripped the bottoms out of dozens of ships. Most victims had been humble merchantmen. But a few, like the shattered galleon Dan was now searching, were the carcasses of rich vessels that had come to grief as they made their way to the annual rendezvous of the Spanish treasure fleet in Havana. In their strongrooms they had carried bags of silver coin from the mints in Peru, crates tightly packed with silver and gold ingots, sealed chests containing uncut gemstones, religious icons studded with brilliants, church plate and personal jewellery of every description. This was the glittering bait that had drawn him and his companions to take their chance in such dangerous waters.

Hector took another slow look right round the horizon. Still nothing. They were doubly lucky with the quiet weather. This was the tail end of the hurricane season. Few ships would normally dare venture out from port for another couple of weeks. That was the reason why he and Dan and the others aboard the *Morvaut* were fishing the wreck in early October. The field was clear for those willing to take the risk of a late tempest while they tried their luck, picking over what other salvors may have left behind.

There was a sudden stir in the water below him and a gasping intake of breath as Dan's head broke the surface. He was stark naked except for a net hanging around his neck into which he stuffed any small objects he found. His long, straight, jet-black hair lay plastered down to his shoulders, and the water running off his face made his dark skin glisten like oiled mahogany. A Miskito Indian from the coast, Dan was an accomplished diver and could stay down for three minutes at a time. Hector wondered if there was truth in the widespread belief that the native Americans were gifted with unnaturally large lungs. The men from the island of Margarita successfully worked pearl beds at depths no one else could attain. They were particularly in demand when it came to going underwater to patch the hulls of ships or – as now – conduct salvage operations. Thinking about them Hector briefly pictured Dan coming to the surface holding up a string of Margarita pearls originally destined to grace the neck of some beauty in Havana or Madrid. It was a wild daydream, but that would solve all his money problems.

'How does it look?' he called down to Dan.

'The Spaniards have used explosives. The deck of the galleon is blown apart. All the big cannon have been taken up.'

That was no surprise. The Spaniards kept professional salvage teams on standby at ports all around the Caribbean. Most wrecks occurred in shallow water, and whenever a valuable cargo was lost the salvage crews quickly arrived to recover what they could before the currents smothered the wrecks with sand and gravel. They concentrated on the heavier items. Cannon were valuable and accessible. The gold or silver shipments were more difficult to get at. They were stowed low down, usually beneath the commander's quarters towards the stern in a galleon. To reach them, it was necessary to blow the ship apart. The explosions often scattered smaller items that then became half buried in silt or disguised by a coating of the pale green grassy weed that grew rapidly in these warm waters.

'Any sign of the strongroom?' Hector asked.

Dan shook his head. 'They've left an anchor and chain in position so they'll be coming back.'

'Which means there's still something left worth salvaging,' interrupted a sour voice.

Hector swung round to confront a stocky, stubble-haired man who had walked up silently on bare feet. Yannick Kergonan stood with the easy balance of a man accustomed to small boats. As his name indicated, he was a Breton, and a surly expression on his weather-beaten face reinforced the suspicious look in his deep-set eyes. Hector neither liked nor trusted Yannick, and would never have sailed with him except that he was part-owner of the *Morvaut*, together with his brothers Roparzh and Yacut and their sister Anne-Marie.

'Your man needs to get a move on. There's less than an hour of slack water left,' Yannick observed. His English was heavily accented but fluent.

'Dan is not "my man",' Hector snapped. 'He'll go down again just as soon as he's ready.'

Yannick smirked. 'I thought he was your matelot. Isn't that what you buccaneers prefer?'

Hector knew the Breton was taunting him. It was true that he and Dan had buccaneered together. Twice they had gone on raids into the Pacific with bands of pirates who had looted the Spanish coastal towns. Theirs was a powerful friendship based on mutual trust and respect that dated back to the days when they had met as prisoners of the Barbary corsairs and later found themselves chained side by side on the oar bench of a French war galley. But they were not the bosom companions that Yannick was implying. Among many buccaneers it was a custom for a man to pick a companion – their matelot – with whom they shared everything, almost like a marriage.

'Dan's already been down to the wreck a dozen times today. Perhaps you should take a turn yourself,' Hector countered sharply. He knew that Yannick, like most sailors, could only flounder clumsily in the water.

The Breton sneered at him, then turned on his heel and stalked off.

'I'm surprised no one's stuck a knife into that crab,' observed Jacques Bourdon, who had sauntered up in time to overhear the exchange. A convicted Paris pickpocket and petty thief, the letters GAL branded on his cheek and still faintly visible were a legacy of the days Jacques had sat beside Hector on the galley benches. He had shared many of Hector's adventures and his skills as a cook made him welcome aboard any ship. Also he had a Parisian's disdain for provincials.

'Typical Breton numbskull. All that salt cod and cider addles their brains. You'd have thought he and his brothers would know something about provisioning an expedition. We're already running low on fresh water.'

It was true, thought Hector. He could not help wondering if Yannick and his brothers had deliberately set out to sabotage the expedition. They were only taking part in the venture because their sister had insisted they do so. Hector was increasingly aware that Anne-Marie Kergonan was a very forceful character and few people were able to stand up to her.

He shied away from that thought. Anne-Marie was another of his problems.

Something landed on the deck with a soggy clunk, spraying a few droplets of water across his bare feet. While he had been talking to Jacques, Dan had tossed an object up on to the pinnace's deck.

Jacques reached down and picked up what looked like a queerly shaped, greyish green lump of coral. At first sight Hector thought it was a fragment broken from a reef where the coral sprouted prongs like stags' horns. Then, as the Frenchman turned it over in his hand, Hector recognized a three-branch candelabrum. It was discoloured with exposure to the salt water and covered with a light coating of weed. Jacques reached for the knife in his belt and scraped at the coating of the base. Underneath was the dull glint of silver.

'At last!' he exclaimed and stepped across to the edge of the ship and looked down at Dan, who was treading water. 'Where did you find it?' he called excitedly.

'Over there, about thirty yards away,' said Dan pointing to one side. 'The gunpowder explosion split open the aft section of the galleon. The current has been scouring out the contents.'

'Should we shift the pinnace over there?' asked Hector.

Dan nodded. 'Pass me a line and a piece of wood as a float. I'll mark the spot.'

Jacques disappeared to find the materials for a makeshift buoy just as Hector became aware of a figure emerging from the tiny cabin in the stern of the *Morvaut*.

Anne-Marie Kergonan made a striking impression. In her late twenties, she had the same sturdy build as her three brothers. But what made them burly gave Anne-Marie an air of luscious sensuality. She was dressed in men's seagoing clothes – a loose linen shirt, sash and wide canvas breeches that reached just below her knees. But there was no doubting that she was very much a woman. A few unruly curls of rich dark brown hair escaped from the bright red bandana tied around her head, and her full breasts pushed generously against the shirt where it was held in by the sash that accentuated the curve of her hips. Her broad face, with its soft contours and wide-set hazel eyes, was pretty rather than beautiful and as deeply tanned as her bare arms and feet. She looked earthy, confident and luscious, and since the start of the expedition Hector had become uncomfortably aware that he and his friends had only been able to charter the *Morvaut* against the wishes of her three brothers because Anne-Marie Kergonan had taken a fancy to him.

Now she advanced across the deck towards Hector with the same easy-going barefoot tread of her sailor brothers.

'What's all the excitement about?' she asked. Her English was spoken with a husky, attractive accent. Jacques held up the candelabrum, and she took one glance at it before taking her place beside Hector at the rail, leaning forward and looking down at Dan in the water.

Hector was conscious that Anne-Marie had allowed the front of her shirt to fall open enough for him to appreciate the view.

'Dan thinks there should be more salvage in that direction,' he said.

'Then we should lose no more time. We've waited long enough for something to happen,' said Anne-Marie. She turned towards Hector and treated him to a lingering glance that left little doubt of its message.

'Give a hand here, Lynch!' her brother Yannick interrupted sharply. He would have to be blind not to notice his sister's behaviour, and clearly he did not approve. 'And get that big lubber on his feet! We'll have to put out the kedge anchor and haul across.'

The Breton was already heaving in on the painter attached to the bow of the *Morvaut*'s tender at the stern of the pinnace.

'Jezreel!' called Hector. 'We're moving. Time to get up.'

What looked like a heap of old sails on the foredeck stirred. A large hand emerged and threw aside the makeshift bedding, and a man sat up and scratched his head. The span of arms as he stretched and yawned gave an idea of what a goliath he was. Jezreel was huge. A nose broken several times and patterns of scars on his scalp were clues to his former occupation as a prize-fighter using his fists or a backsword. Years ago he had accidentally killed a man in the ring and been forced to flee, taking his chances as a logwood cutter on the Campeche coast where Hector had first met him.

'What needs doing?' he mumbled. He had been on anchor watch the previous night and, to catch up on his sleep, had been napping on the open deck on one of the few places where there was enough space for him to lie down.

'We have to move the *Morvaut*. Dan's found some salvage,' Hector explained. 'There's not enough wind to put up sail, so we'll kedge across on the anchor.'

Jezreel got slowly to his feet and went to join the second of Anne-Marie's brothers, Roparzh. He was struggling to hoist the pinnace's spare anchor from its stowage in the shallow hold.

'Here, let me take that,' rumbled Jezreel. He took the anchor with one hand and carried it effortlessly to where Yannick had brought the tender alongside.

'Watch what you're doing!' snapped the Breton. 'If you drop that, it'll smash straight through the bottom.'

Jezreel treated him to a scornful glance. He leaned out over the rail and laid the anchor gently in the bow of the tender. 'Get me a pair of oars,' he said, 'Hector and I can do the rest.'

Grateful to escape from Anne-Marie, Hector made his way aft. *Morvaut*'s tender was unusually large for her mother ship. Too big to be carried on deck, the skiff was always towed astern on a harness. Hector suspected that the Kergonans normally used the skiff to ferry goods ashore on smuggling trips.

He stepped down into the tender, and Yannick passed him a coil of anchor line. Away to his left, Dan had already set the float that marked the spot where he had found the silver candelabrum. Jezreel settled himself on the central thwart, gave a couple of powerful strokes with the oars, and the tender began to move. From the stern Hector paid out the anchor line while, on the pinnace, Yannick secured the loose end of the heavy rope.

'The Tigress, that's what they call her,' commented Jezreel cryptically as soon as they were out of earshot of Yannick and his brother. 'She's said to be a man-eater.' Hector made no comment.

'Takes after her mother, if the tales are true,' Jezreel continued.

Hector was aware of the Kergonan family's notorious history. Their mother was among the group of fifty harlots the French government had shipped out to Tortuga a generation ago. The theory was that their offspring would establish a more permanent population in the fledgling French colony. Naturally the arrival of a shipload of loose women had caused a sensation. They had been dumped on the beach, and the settlers – a lawless gang of half-wild hunters and part-time pirates – had been encouraged to take their pick.

'I can take care of myself,' said Hector.

Jezreel gave another grunt as he tugged again on the oars and sent the tender surging.

Hector knew what his friend was implying. 'I talked it over with Maria. There was no other choice,' he said and tried to keep himself from sounding apologetic. 'You saw for yourself. It takes money, lots of money to survive in Tortuga. They grow nothing there. Everything must be imported.'

'No place to leave a woman,' muttered Jezreel darkly.

'I promised Maria that I would never return to piracy. Fishing wrecks was the only alternative.'

'Much the same result if you are caught at it,' commented Jezreel pointedly.

Hector's thoughts went back to happier times when he and his friends had sailed the Pacific so that he could reach Maria, the woman he loved, and ask her to share his life. To his delight she had agreed, even though he was at risk of being taken up for piracy. For Maria, who was Spanish-born, it had meant deserting her employer, an important colonial official who was likely to be vindictive. Together they had chosen to come to remote Tortuga, hoping to find a safe haven beyond the reach of normal laws, a place where they could live together quietly. But Tortuga had been a cruel disappointment. The fort which had once defied foreign navies and given the place its semi-independence was in ruins. Most of the population had moved away, preferring the French colonies at Petit Goâve and Saint-Domingue. Those who stayed were the dregs. They passed their time in sordid drinking dens, spending the last of their booty. The settlement was reduced to little more than a cluster of squalid huts and muddy lanes where wild forest pigs roamed freely.

Hector turned in his seat and looked back at the *Morvaut*. Little about the vessel gave him confidence. She was a small boat of thirty tons with a single mast, shabby, and with only one tiny cannon. That meant she was virtually unarmed. A hostile ship of force would overwhelm her in minutes.

Yet Maria had insisted that he use the last of the money they had brought back from the Pacific to charter the *Morvaut* to go fishing the wreck of a Spanish galleon that was rumoured to be lying on the Vipers.

'We must try something,' she had said. They had been standing at the door of the two-room shack that was all they had been able to afford to rent. 'Otherwise we'll be trapped in this wretched place, living miserably. Dan and the others will agree to go fishing the Vipers. They are getting bored.'

'But you and I will be apart, maybe for months.'

'I waited three years for you to come and find me. I can endure a few more weeks' absence.'

'What if we can't find the wreck, or a gale catches us on the reef while we are searching? We ourselves could be cast away.'

She had laid a hand on his arm, looked into his eyes and said firmly, 'Hector, I've seen your skill with charts. You can bring a vessel safely through those reefs. That's what you excel at, just as Dan can dive, or Jacques can cook, and Jezreel can wield a backsword.'

He had still been doubtful. 'The Kergonans own the only vessel available. And they are demanding advance payment of the charter, plus a half share in anything we recover. They're a bunch of grasping crooks.'

She had leaned up and kissed him. 'Yesterday I happened to meet Anne-Marie Kergonan on the foreshore. She told me that you had been discussing the charter with her. She was very friendly. She told me that *morvaut* is the Breton word for a cormorant. Hector, take it as an omen – it's a greedy bird but one that gorges on its catch.'

Hector was wakened from his reverie by a slight lurch. The skiff had reached Dan's marker buoy and Jezreel was unshipping his oars. The big man picked up the kedge anchor lying on the bottom boards. 'Ready?' he asked. Hector checked that the coil of anchor line was free and nodded.

Jezreel dropped the anchor overboard, and the last few fathoms of cable ran out with a thrumming sound. As soon as the anchor had settled on the seabed, the big man waved to the pinnace. The Kergonan brothers, helped by Jacques, began taking in the slack. The *Morvaut* was too small to carry a windlass so they were hauling by hand. The pinnace slowly began to take up position over the spoil ground.

※

WITHIN AN HOUR they knew they had struck lucky. Dan came across a pile of more than a hundred pieces of eight on the sea floor where a canvas bag had rotted and burst. In the next three dives he brought up a rich haul of tableware – jugs, spoons, bowls, forks and goblets, all in massive silver.

'I wonder if any of the galleon's crew survived the wreck?' Hector asked Roparzh Kergonan. He was on the pinnace's deck, trying to divide the spoil into two equal piles, one for the Bretons, and one for himself and his friends. Roparzh was hovering over him, making sure that Hector was not cheating. Hector could smell the rum on the man's breath.

'Someone usually lives,' grunted Roparzh. 'Clings to flotsam and is washed ashore or gets clear in a ship's boat.'

Hector turned his attention to a large silver dish. Dan had found it wedged in a crevice in the coral. The dish was engraved with an ornate coat of arms, and Hector guessed that it had been the property of an officer on the galleon, someone from a noble family.

'How do we divide this item fairly?' he asked the Breton.

'Hack it up with an axe and weigh out the scraps,' came the blunt reply.

Hector winced inwardly at the thought. 'It is a match with the other pieces. They'll be worth more as a set.'

'And the first person we try to fence it to will recognize the mark and guess how we got our hands on it. Might even know the family.'

'Only if that person is familiar with the crests and emblems of Spanish families.'

Roparzh was looking at him as if he was simple-minded.

'You mean the Spaniards buy goods stolen out of their own wrecks?' Hector said.

'There's more goes on than either Madrid or London knows about.'

The Breton decided that he had said enough. He shovelled up his share of the coins and put them in a pouch. Without asking, he took the silver dish out of Hector's hand and slouched away with it. Hector decided that it was not worth making an issue of the matter and went to help Dan as he climbed out of the water.

The Miskito was exhausted. He flopped down on the deck and leaned back against the bulwarks to rest. His eyes were closed, and the water ran off his body, making dark patterns across the deck. He looked utterly spent. After a minute or two, he opened his eyes. They were red-rimmed from the time spent underwater.

'We have to watch our backs now,' he said.

'What do you mean?' Hector asked.

Dan's eyes flicked to the stern where the Kergonan brothers were huddled together. They were double-checking their haul of coins and silverware. 'One dark night when we are asleep, they may take the chance to be rid of us.'

He lifted one hand and made a cutting motion across his throat.

TWO

THE DISCOVERY OF THE silver candelabrum was the start of
their reward. In the next five days of diving on the wreck Dan
brought up nearly two hundred more coins. They were mostly
cobs, misshaped slugs of metal that scarcely looked like money.
Yet each one bore an assayer's monogram that proved it was
genuine silver. He also retrieved twenty-three gold doubloons and
an assortment of tableware and jewellery – pendants, bracelets
and necklaces. Under the mistrustful gaze of the Kergonans
everything was sorted and divided. As the value of the haul
increased, so too did the tension on board. It boiled over on the
afternoon Dan brought up a leather purse from the sea floor.
Jacques slit open the soggy purse and tipped a dozen emeralds out
on to the deck. A drunken Roparzh Kergonan gave a great whoop
of triumph and reached forward to grab the spoil. But Jacques
beat him to it. The Frenchman quietly picked up one of the jewels
and held it up to the sunlight. He had worked with a Paris fence
and knew how to spot a fake. Without hesitation he declared that
the 'emeralds' were nothing more than chunks of coloured glass.
It was as if he had blatantly swindled the Breton. Roparzh leaped
on him and seized him by the throat and would have strangled him
if Jezreel had not intervened.

That night was Hector's turn to be on anchor watch. Seated on the foredeck in the pre-dawn darkness, he knew that the salvage operation had to end very soon. Even if the Kergonans could be kept under control, less than half a barrel of drinking water remained. With no fresh water on the two nearby islands, they would soon be forced to leave the wreck site and head for home. As he was idly speculating how much his share of the salvage would be worth, he became aware of someone creeping stealthily towards him. He was about to call out a challenge when a low voice said, 'I thought I'd join you.' A moment later Anne-Marie Kergonan sat down beside him. 'It's too hot to sleep,' she said, looking along the length of the silent ship.

In the faint starlight Hector could make out that she was wearing a loose nightgown of some pale material and that it had slipped to one side, so the shoulder nearest to him was bare. There was a waft of some sort of musky scent from the perfume she was wearing.

'What are you going to do with your share of the findings?' she asked after a long pause.

Hector kept his voice as neutral as possible. 'I've no idea. Depends on how much there is.'

She turned her face towards him, and he was conscious of the shape of the soft mouth, the lips parted. Her hand reached up and caught back a strand of hair that hung loose. The movement was smooth, seductive. 'No idea at all?'

He didn't know how to answer, and she went on. 'I met that new wife of yours in Tortuga. She's very attractive. I'm sure you miss her.'

'Maria is a remarkable woman.' His reply was cautious.

Anne-Marie gave a throaty chuckle. 'And an understanding one, I would guess. Most women are when they want to keep their man.'

She shifted position, a slight movement that brought her thigh a fraction closer to him. Perhaps it was his imagination but he felt soft warmth radiating from her. 'How old are you, Hector?' she asked.

'Twenty-eight.'

'And how many women have you known?'

He was flustered, stumbling in his reply. 'A few.'

'Well before I was your age,' she said, 'I had learned to seize the opportunities that came my way. It had become clear to me that life passes by those who hesitate, and I resolved to conduct my life as I wanted, follow my instincts, and not behave as others would tell me or expect of me.'

'Is that why on Tortuga they call you "the Tigress"?' he said boldly.

A soft laugh. 'Some people find me to be fierce. Others say that I am wilful. I see it as pride in what I am and what I can do.'

The light was strengthening. The sea around them was changing from inky black to a very faint sheen of dark blue. He noticed that she was watching him closely, her eyes in shadow.

She gave a slow, deliberate smile. He read both triumph and invitation. 'Unless you take the chances that life offers, you do not taste what it is to live fully.'

She leaned towards him and stroked him gently on the bare forearm. He gave an involuntary shiver.

'Not now, and not here,' she said, glancing meaningfully towards the stern. Hector could make out the shape of her oldest brother, asleep on deck beside the binnacle.

She stood up, smoothing down the loose gown and hitching it up over the naked shoulder. Despite himself, he felt a surge of desire. He wanted to rise to his feet and put his arms around her, and press her ripe body close to him. But she bent down and laid a finger on his lips. 'Perhaps when it is more convenient,' she said quietly. A moment later she was gone, gliding along the deck in her bare feet, and ducking in through the low door of the aft cabin.

Hector sat very still. He was uncomfortably aware that from now on he would find it difficult to expunge Anne-Marie Kergonan from his mind.

It was at that moment, with his mind in confusion, that he

looked up and saw, very faintly, a tiny speck of white on the distant horizon.

*

JUAN GARCIA FONSECA moved about the deck of his urca, *San Gil*, with a dragging limp. Each time he stepped out with his right foot, he had then to swivel his lower body, heave, and lift his left foot forward. He had been sailing the triangle between Cartagena, Porto Bello and Havana nearly all his life, and in that time he had been shipwrecked four times and fought off countless attacks from English and Dutch pirates. Once he had nearly lost his ship to a gang of African slaves who had got free of their chains below deck. Firing a swivel gun down the hatchway had restored order, at the cost of one member of his own crew whom they had taken hostage. With such an eventful career behind him, it was natural that most observers imagined his pronounced limp was the result of an injury during one of his many near-escapes from disaster. Only those who had known Juan Garcia since his early childhood in Cartagena knew that his infirmity was in fact an accident of birth. He had been born with a twisted hip. When he reached his teens, he had come to the conclusion that strong arms and a good grip aboard ship would make up for awkward legs on land, and had persuaded his father, a bookish civil servant, to let him go to sea. He had prospered, saved up enough money to buy his own vessel, and shown the shipwrights where to fit plenty of handholds within his easy reach. Now, forty years later, he accepted that his urca was outdated in design, notoriously slow through the water and handled like a pig against the wind. But her broad, old-fashioned hull still provided plenty of cargo space and made her very stable. He had named her after the patron saint of cripples, and he had no intention of replacing the *San Gil*.

Juan Garcia was standing with his son Felipe, watching the swells heap up on the edge of the reef as the urca skirted south-ward along the Vipers. 'If you read the signs, you have plenty of warning,' Juan Garcia was saying. He never lost a chance to pass on his knowledge. One day, perhaps in a couple of years, Felipe would be taking over as captain.

'There.' Juan Garcia pointed to where a sudden smear of white foam showed the presence of a coral head. 'If the swell comes from a direction different from the wind and is much bigger than usual, that tells you a hurricane is lurking out to the east.'

He paused and watched the humped back of a swimming turtle appear briefly above the waves. The creature raised its head and gazed briefly at the ship, the bright eyes and hooked beak like a predatory bird. Then its flippers moved gently and it sank from view.

'And if the air becomes hot and heavy and the shirt sticks to your back even though the weather is fine and clear, be on your guard.'

Felipe Fonseca had heard his father's hurricane lecture many times. To provoke him he murmured, 'Are you not worried that the stars were twinkling so brightly last night?'

'What's that got to do with it?' his father demanded, falling into the trap.

'A sailor in Havana told me that the Philippines people believe that when the stars twinkle very brightly, it means a storm is coming.'

'Why should they think that?'

'They claim that there's a great wind far, far up in the sky. When it blows really strongly, it makes the stars flicker. Then, because it can't extinguish the stars, the wind loses its temper. It swoops down on the earth as a gale.'

'Pure superstition,' grunted his father. He was feeling guilty that he had lied to his son. He had told him that he would risk the Vipers so early in the season because it was Felipe's duty to be back in Cartagena when his son's young wife gave birth. But the true reason for haste was that Juan Garcia himself was anxious. A clumsy midwife had caused his own affliction, and he dreaded that his first grandchild would suffer the same mishap. He wanted to be at home to make sure that the midwife was the best that he could hire.

Putting the thought out of his mind, he returned to Felipe's seafaring education. 'If you are caught in a hurricane, never run directly before the wind. If you do, you'll be swamped or capsize. Instead, watch the way the wind shifts. If it backs, make sail on the starboard tack and run on a broad reach until the wind heads you. Then heave to.'

He was about to go on to say that if the wind veered, the mariner should sail as fast as possible on the same starboard tack but close-hauled. This would offer the best chance of avoiding the eye of the approaching storm. But he was interrupted.

'Father, there's a small boat on the Vipers, fine on the starboard bow.'

Juan Garcia stared where his son pointed. His eyes were not as sharp as they used to be. It was a sign of advancing age. Perhaps he should think about turning the *San Gil* over to Felipe sooner.

'Are you sure?'

'Looks like a small pinnace. Right on the reef.'

Juan Garcia shrugged. 'Could be anyone. We'll pass on by.'

Twenty minutes later they heard very faintly the sound of a cannon shot.

'They've fired a windward gun,' said Felipe.

'Bring her up two points, no more!' his father told the helmsman, who was looking at him enquiringly. A windward gun was the recognized signal that a boat wished to communicate. The unknown pinnace was too small to be a threat, but experience told him to be very wary.

'I can't see any sort of flag,' Felipe said after a while. The pinnace was close enough to make out some figures on deck. There was something untidy about her rig, the mast slightly at a slant, as if she had run aground on the coral.

More time passed, and then Felipe announced, 'There's a boat putting off. They're rowing out to try to intercept us.'

'We maintain course,' his father growled.

Felipe let out a low whistle of surprise. 'There's a woman in the skiff. She's standing in the bows and waving.'

Juan Garcia caught the look of astonishment on the face of his helmsman. The man was bending his knees as he tried to peep under the mainsail and get a good look forward at the approaching boat.

'All right then, bring her up to wind,' he ordered reluctantly. He had a crew of six, without counting himself and Felipe. They were more than enough to beat off any attack from a skiff. 'Bring a couple of blunderbusses up from my cabin and make sure the primings are dry.'

✳

ABOARD THE *MORVAUT* there had been angry words. Scarcely had Hector warned there was a ship on the horizon than the Kergovan brothers were on their feet. Roparzh and Yacut ran to the anchor cable and began to haul in the slack. Yannick hastily cleared the halyards, ready to hoist sail and flee. But a few minutes later their sister emerged from the cabin, took one look at the distant sail and yelled angrily at them. She was shouting in Breton so Hector could only guess that she was cursing them. She looked formidable. Her skin was flushed with anger, and for a moment Hector thought she was about to walk over to Yannick and slap him across the face.

Jacques and Jezreel were also poised, ready to help retrieve the anchor. She switched to English, ordering them to stop. 'We wait until we know who they are. They could be French or English.'

'They're Spanish, that's for sure. No one else in these waters,' retorted Jacques.

Anne-Marie rounded on him. 'Use your head. If that boat is indeed a Spanish cruiser, I doubt we can outrun her.' She turned to face Hector.

'Hector,' she snapped. 'You've been exploring the reef. Can you find a channel and pilot *Morvaut* through the Vipers?'

'I suppose so,' said Hector dubiously. He was astonished to see the change from the flirtatious woman who had sat beside him less than two hours earlier.

'Good. But that's only if things go wrong.' She rounded on her brothers and reverted to Breton, loosing a stream of orders.

Roparzh and Yacut stopped hauling on the anchor line. Yannick, looking surly, went to slack off the shrouds so that the mast leaned out badly off true.

'What's all that about?' asked Jacques, cocking an eye at the drunken angle of the spar.

'To make it look as though the *Morvaut* has run aground,' Hector suggested.

'That won't deceive anyone,' Jacques muttered under his breath.

Hector could see that Anne-Marie was trying to draw the foreign ship closer, but he did not understand why.

'Wouldn't it be better to let them sail on past?' he asked her.

'And miss the chance to continue fishing the wreck!' she replied sharply. Eyes narrowed, she was watching the urca. 'She's altering course to come a little more towards us. Definitely a Spaniard, a merchantman. Roparzh, get the skiff ready. You and Yannick come with me. I'm going to talk with that vessel.'

She turned to Hector. 'How good's your Spanish?'

'My mother came from Galicia.'

'I want you to interpret. We're going to get ourselves some water and food.'

Hector hesitated. There was something about Anne-Marie's belligerent confidence that made him uneasy.

'The *Morvaut* is chartered to fish for wrecks, not for piracy,' he warned.

She tossed her head dismissively. 'We'll pay the Spaniards for what we need. But they'll only deal with us if they think we have permission from their authorities to be here.'

She snapped an order at Roparzh, who shambled off and returned with a handful of silver coins that she tucked into a pocket of her loose breeches.

'Hector, I want you to tell the captain of that boat that we have been sent here from Porto Bello to make a proper chart of the Vipers.'

Hector looked at her in surprise. 'Why would he believe such a tale?'

'Show him those sketches of the reef you've been making. Flatter him. Ask him if he can add to our information. I speak reasonable Spanish, but not enough to be convincing.'

Hector glanced across at Jacques, who shrugged. 'Go ahead, Hector. If it works, we can stay here for a few more days of fishing.'

Roparzh and Yannick had already brought the skiff alongside and were seated at the oars. Satchel in hand, Hector swung over the rail and joined them. Anne-Marie Kergonan stepped into her cabin and reappeared wearing a broad sash of red silk. Then she jumped into the bows of the tender and the skiff pushed off.

✳

AS THEY APPROACHED the urca, they could see her crew lining the rail. All of them, including the two men who were pointing blunderbusses in their direction, were staring in fascination at Anne-Marie. She turned and waved, taking care to reveal her generous figure. '*Necesitamos el agua!*' she called. To Hector she hissed, 'Tell them that we are surveying the reefs and are willing to pay for food and water.'

Hector translated, and a stocky figure with a thick greying beard called out that the skiff could come alongside but only one person at a time was to climb aboard.

In response, it was Anne-Marie who promptly clambered on to the urca. Clearly this surprised the bearded man, whom Hector took to be the captain. 'You'd better come up as well,' he called down to Hector. 'But the others stay where they are.'

Hector hoisted himself up on to the urca, his satchel of maps slung across his shoulder. The bearded man looked his two visitors up and down with suspicion. 'You want water?'

'Yes, and some stores if you can spare them,' Hector answered. A young man stood next to the captain. Judging by their resemblance, they were father and son. The rest of the crew – several older mariners and a cabin boy – were unremarkable.

'It's too hot to stand here in the sun,' said the captain. He turned and limped heavily towards a door at the break of the aft deck. He stood aside to let Anne-Marie precede him, and Hector had to duck to follow them into the captain's accommodation. A curtained bunk was built into one bulkhead. There was a small table, a couple of chairs, and a cushioned bench running the width of the little cabin. 'Please be seated,' said the captain. He lowered himself on to one of the chairs and used both hands to move his useless leg into a more comfortable position. Anne-Marie took her place on the bench, and Hector, preferring to keep his distance, sat on one of the chairs.

'Felipe!' called the captain through the open door. 'Come in and join us and bring some wine.' A few moments later the young man appeared holding an onion-shaped flask of wine and four small leather tankards that he placed on the table before his father. Anne-Marie moved farther along the bench so the captain's son could sit beside her.

'Welcome aboard the *San Gil*,' said the captain. He leaned forward and splashed a generous portion of red wine into each tankard. 'I am Juan Garcia Fonseca, and my ship is bound for our home port, Cartagena.'

He looked enquiringly at Hector.

'Enrique Benavides of His Majesty's Corps of Engineers, at your service,' Hector said, 'and this is Anne-Marie Bretana, owner of the pinnace *Morvaut*.'

Fonseca gave a small bow towards Anne-Marie before addressing his next question to Hector. 'May I ask what you are doing in these waters?'

Hector hesitated. He had been given little time to practise his deception. 'I am on my way back to Madrid after a posting to Valdivia as Deputy Inspector of Fortifications.' Valdivia was three thousand miles away at the far end of Peru. It was a reasonable guess that Captain Juan Fonseca had never been there or knew any of the citizens. 'In Panama I received instructions to interrupt my journey and make more accurate charts of reefs in this region.'

'Not the best time of year to do so,' commented the Spaniard drily.

'Due to the recent heavy loss of shipping on this route, the matter was considered to be of the utmost importance.' Hector opened his satchel and began to set out his sketch maps. 'I'm hoping that you might be able to add some extra details, from your own experience of these waters.'

Juan Fonseca leafed through one sheet after another, and nodded approvingly. 'It will be a real service to mariners if we can get decent charts of this region. I am able to add some information about the currents.'

Hector heard a voice calling outside. He guessed it was a Spanish crew member trying to start a conversation with the two Kergonan brothers waiting in the skiff.

The captain picked up his tankard and raised it as a toast.

'I think it appropriate to raise a glass to the memory of Carlos Serrano,' he said.

'To Carlos Serrano,' echoed Hector cautiously. He had not the least idea who Carlos Serrano was. But Captain Fonseca obviously thought he was someone whose memory was worthy of respect.

The captain took a sip of wine and put down his tankard. 'Now,' he said casually, 'tell me the truth. Tell me who you really are and what you are doing here.'

Hector blustered. 'As I said, I am surveying the Vipers—'

Fonseca cut him short. '. . . The Vipers are marked on official maps as the Serrano Bank. They are named after the castaway Pedro Serrano who was shipwrecked there. He survived on his own for eight years, eating turtles and catching rainwater in their upturned shells. He was covered in a thick pelt of hair like a beast when they found him, so it is said. There's not a sailor in Panama who would not have told you the tale, and you would have known his name was Pedro, not Carlos.'

The captain smiled grimly. 'Señor Benavides, if that is your real name, which I doubt, I suggest that you tell me the truth about yourself and this charming lady here.'

'Here is the truth,' interrupted Anne-Marie. She reached inside her scarlet sash and produced a short-barrelled pistol. There was a click as she cocked the weapon and placed it against the head of Felipe Fonseca. 'We only want some fresh water and a little food. Nothing that you can't spare. Then you can proceed on your way.'

Captain Fonseca sat very still. Then he spoke slowly and carefully. 'It is a novelty to be waylaid aboard my own ship by a woman.' He looked completely unperturbed. 'Felipe,' he said to his son, 'do exactly as you are told. I suspect the lady means what she says.'

He levered himself to his feet and limped out of the cabin, followed by Felipe with Anne-Marie still holding the gun to his head.

The moment Anne-Marie emerged on deck, she let out a piercing whistle. In response her two brothers in the skiff rowed across and clambered aboard. It was all done with so little fuss that Hector had the feeling that this routine was something the Bretons had done before. Wordlessly Yannick and Roparzh removed the two blunderbusses from the crew of the urca and herded the sailors into a group.

As they shuffled meekly together, the Spanish cabin boy took it into his head to make a dash at Anne-Marie, trying to seize her pistol. Hector was so surprised that, without a second thought, he reached out and grabbed the lad by the collar. The boy swung round, flailing in the air with his fists, until a sharp command from Captain Fonseca made him stop.

Felipe had gone pale, but Anne-Marie's hand was as steady as her voice. 'Hector, select two men from the crew and supervise them while they fetch water jars and place them in our boat. Roparzh, see what sails there are.'

'At least leave me a jib,' said the Spanish captain calmly. He seemed to know exactly what the Bretons were doing.

Her brother prodded one of the Spanish sailors with the muzzle of his blunderbuss. '*Gouel!*' he ordered in Breton, and when the man looked blank, pointed up at the *San Gil*'s mainsail. '*Voiles! Vela!*' and followed the sailor below.

Hector picked out two of the older Spaniards, and they began to lug the heavy water jars from their stowage by the galley. As they lowered the jars into the *Morvaut*'s tender, Roparzh reappeared with the Spanish sailor. Between them they were dragging a length of canvas which they dumped near the mast. Next Yannick eased off the main halyard until the mainsail lay in an untidy heap on deck.

With her free hand Anne-Marie beckoned to the cabin boy, who stood glowering at her. 'You help the cook, don't you?' she said in slow, careful Spanish.

The lad nodded.

'Fetch me his oil,' she said.

'Do as she says,' ordered Fonseca quietly. He appeared to accept whatever was to happen next. The boy meekly went off on his errand. More sails were heaped on deck. The cabin boy came back with a greasy pan of cooking oil and was told to dump it on the cloth. As Hector brought the last water jar from the galley, he met Roparzh with a rum bottle in his hand. The Breton took a swig. 'Pity about the waste. But I've found a small keg which I'll put in the skiff,' he said. He sprinkled the remaining contents of the bottle on the heap of canvas. Hector saw growing distress on the faces of the crew.

Finally Roparzh fetched a lump of glowing charcoal from the galley and tossed it on the sails.

In the hot sunshine everyone stood and watched in silence as the fire gradually took hold. A tendril of grey smoke oozed upwards. There was a slight explosive puff as a puddle of rum caught alight. A line of flame ran up a fold of dry canvas, and suddenly all of *San Gil*'s sails were ablaze except for a single headsail which had been left hanging from its stay.

Anne-Marie pressed the pistol more firmly to Felipe's head. 'Can you swim?' she asked. The young man nodded cautiously.

She addressed his father. 'Captain Fonseca, if anyone shoots at us, you will be pulling your son's corpse from the sea.'

'I understand,' said Juan Garcia wearily.

Anne-Marie began to hustle Felipe into the skiff. 'Come on, Hector,' she said. 'It's time to go.' Hector climbed down into the boat. Roparzh handed down a small keg of rum to his brother, and the two Breton men took their places and began to row. As the gap widened between the skiff and the urca, Anne-Marie reached into a pocket, withdrew a handful of silver cobs, and flung them. The scatter of money arced through the air and clattered on to the deck of the urca. The crew paid no attention. They were busy with buckets, dipping up seawater to douse the fire.

Anne-Marie tapped her prisoner on the shoulder. 'Over you go,' she said cheerfully. Felipe, white-faced, slid over the side and began to swim back to the urca.

Hector glared at her. 'We agreed no piracy,' he said accusingly.

She showed white teeth in a mischievous smile. 'I only said that I would pay for what we needed. How long do you think it would be before they sent the *guarda costa* after us? With only a single foresail it'll take Captain Fonseca at least a week to get to Cartagena, enough time for us to finish exploring the wreck. Then we head for Tortuga.'

She glanced back at the urca. The plume of smoke was gone. The fire must have been under control.

'Captain Fonseca has suffered only a scorched deck, and perhaps an injury to his pride,' she said.

When they reached the *Morvaut* Anne-Marie climbed aboard first and, turning, held out her hand for Hector to pass up his satchel of maps. He stood up and held out the satchel at arm's length. At that moment Yannick deliberately caused the tender to tip. It was a sudden, violent lurch, intended to throw Hector into the water. Caught off-guard, Hector lost his balance and seized the proffered hand. With one smooth movement Anne-Marie hoisted him safely up to the deck. For a long moment she stood, holding his hand in hers. Then she gave a brief and unmistakable squeeze of invitation.

THREE

MORVAUT WAS FINALLY on her way to Tortuga, running comfortably before a steady north-west breeze. Hector, Dan and Jezreel had gathered on the foredeck in the last of the evening sunshine. They were looking on as Jacques weighed out their hack silver into four equal portions. He was using an ingenious set of balance scales he had rigged up from a soup ladle and pewter dipping bowl.

'Nearly fifteen pounds' weight a share,' announced the Frenchman. 'Add the jewels and cobs, and I'd say that each of us is £200 richer than when we started out.'

'Worth the effort, even if not as good as Phipps,' said Jezreel. The success of William Phipps was legendary. He had located the wreck of a great galleon, the *Nuestra Señora de la Pura y Limia Concepción*, on shoals north of Hispaniola and brought up thirty tons of silver. Phipps' success had earned him an audience with the English king and a knighthood.

'Phipps took scores of divers with him as well as a Bahamian tub,' Hector pointed out. He felt that Dan's solo effort should be recognized. Phipps' salvage team had deployed a wood-and-leather diving bell weighted with lead. It was crude but effective in helping the divers ransack the wreck. Dan had merely jumped overboard from the *Morvaut*, with a heavy stone to pull him down.

'If we brought back as much as Phipps, we could wipe clean the slate,' said Jezreel.

Hector wondered if Jezreel was secretly hoping that one day he would be able to return to London and go back to prize-fighting, as either a contestant or a manager. Watching Jacques stow their salvage portions safely into two knapsacks, he doubted that the Frenchman had similar ambitions. Returning to France would be difficult for Jacques. He would wear a galérien's brand on his cheek for the rest of his life and there was a second brand, V for voleur, on his right hand, between thumb and forefinger. As far as Hector was aware, Jacques had no family and the only women he had left behind in Paris were ladies of easy virtue. Dan, by contrast, was free to return to his people any time he chose. Yet Dan enjoyed travelling, and the Miskito people considered it normal, even desirable, for a young man to wander away from home and see the world.

Hector glanced aft.

Anne-Marie was nowhere to be seen, and he presumed she was in the cabin. Two of her brothers, Yannick and Yacut, were busy on some rope work while Roparzh was at the helm. Hector would have preferred that the brothers were not so openly hostile towards him and his companions. The Bretons made a point of speaking their own language between themselves and refused to take their meals with Hector and his friends. He was glad that the voyage would soon be over.

'Do you think we'll be able to find our way back to the wreck next year?' Jacques asked.

'Only worth it if the Spaniards haven't come back to finish the job while we're away,' said Dan. The final week of fishing the wreck had been tantalizing. Jezreel and Hector had gone off exploring in the skiff. They had spent hours rowing around the site, scanning the sea floor through a glass-bottomed bucket, looking for other debris from the wreck. The search had taught Hector a great deal more about the shape and structure of the reef, and he had noted several promising locations that looked to be worth investigating. But the sailing season was on them and there was an increasing risk of being caught by another, less gullible Spanish vessel. They had decided it was prudent time to leave the wreck site and get back to Tortuga safely with what they had found. After some grumbling, the Kergonans had agreed.

'How long before we reach Tortuga?' Dan asked Hector. The Kergonans owned and operated the pinnace, but when it came to navigation, everyone relied on Hector's expertise.

'A couple of days if this wind holds,' Hector said. His gaze was fixed on the last moments of the sunset. He never tired of watching the final moments of the gap close between the horizon and the sun. That evening the sun had turned a blazing orange red, and as the lower rim touched the sea the perfect circle began to distort, expanding and flattening to an oval, then shrinking to one last sliver as the sun slipped out of sight. He waited for a flash of green, but none came. Then the sun was gone, leaving the underbellies of the clouds a deep, fiery pink. The wind seemed to have settled, and the air was mild and balmy.

'I think I'll turn in,' he said to his friends. He had left his mattress under a tarpaulin cover near the helm. As he went to fetch it, he passed the Kergonans. Yannick spat and muttered something in Breton. Yacut scowled.

Hector spread his mattress on the deck by the foot of the mainmast and lay down. For a long time he gazed past the curve of the mainsail and up at the sky, thinking of his present situation. He had not seen Ireland since being kidnapped as a teenager by the Barbary corsairs. His father was dead these several years, and he had lost touch with his mother, whom he supposed had returned to Spain. His sister, also taken by the corsairs, had been absorbed into a Moroccan harem and no longer wished to have any contact with him. Maria and his small circle of friends were all he had.

His thoughts turned to the immediate future. The silver and other valuables he was bringing back to Tortuga should mean he and Maria could live comfortably while they decided where they might go next. For their next move it would be wise to avoid any of the Spanish colonies where his piratical past might be revealed. The same was true of Jamaica. The authorities in Port Royal were arresting former buccaneers and putting them on trial. Maybe he and Maria should move to one of the French colonies in the Caribbean, perhaps to Petit Goâve or Saint-Domingue. The officials sent there from France did not pry too closely into a settler's background, and he and Maria both spoke French well enough to get by.

He noticed that a thin veil of cloud, very high up, was spreading from the north. The stars were disappearing. As a precaution he pulled a length of tarpaulin over him. Then he fell asleep.

※

HE AWOKE TO A RATTLE of heavy rain on tarred canvas. Someone must have pulled the tarpaulin right over him as he slept. It was airless and stuffy underneath the makeshift cover, and cracks of pale daylight were seeping under the edges. The slant of the deck had increased. *Morvaut* was heeling to the wind. He rolled off the mattress and got to his feet, pulling the tarpaulin around his shoulders and holding the mattress under his arm to keep it dry.

Jezreel sat hunched at the tiller, wearing an oiled cape.

'Squall from the east. Won't last long,' he called.

It was full daylight. The raindrops were bouncing off the sea and creating a fine mist. It was impossible to see more than fifty yards in any direction.

Hector scuttled over to the shelter of the windward rail and huddled there. Someone had adjusted the sails in the night and the pinnace was close-hauled. Above the patter of the rain he could hear the hull hissing through the water.

After some twenty minutes the rain ended abruptly. The sun came out as the rain belt passed on downwind of them.

Jezreel let out a grunt of surprise. 'Where the devil did he come from!'

Hector stood up and peered upwind. About half a mile away was a sizeable vessel. It had been hidden in the rain bank and was now fast bearing down on them. Hector's gaze went to the maintop. Hoisted there was a large flag, three gold lilies on a white field, the ensign of France. At the foremast flew another, smaller flag – blue background, white cross and at its centre a single white fleur-de-lis. He did not know what it signified.

Jezreel sounded relieved. 'Thank Christ! If that had been a Spaniard we'd be running for our lives or blown out of the water by now.'

Hector was counting the number of gun ports. This was a ship of force, a light frigate of fourteen guns.

Everyone aboard the *Morvaut* gathered at the rail to watch the stranger closing in. The Kergonan brothers were grinning broadly and thumping one another on the back. They shouted something in Breton to their sister.

'What are they so pleased about?' asked Hector.

'Yannick recognizes the frigate,' said Anne-Marie. 'It's the *Sainte Rose*. A king's ship. She's based in Saint-Domingue. It's good to see a friend.'

The words were scarcely out of her mouth when the frigate yawed, brought a forward gun to bear, and there was a puff of smoke.

'*Putain!*' exclaimed Jacques, shocked. The ball had come skipping across the sea and punched a neat hole in *Morvaut*'s jib. Six feet lower and it would have shattered the pinnace's bow.

Yannick Kergonan ran to the helm, shoving Jezreel aside. He pushed the tiller across and his brother let fly the sheets.

The pinnace instantly lost speed.

'What the hell did he do that for?' yelled Jacques. He was scrabbling in the sack that contained the *Morvaut*'s collection of flags. Like most vessels of dubious origin, the pinnace carried a selection of national flags to suit the occasion – English, French, Spanish, Danish, Hollander, even a Brandenburg ensign. He picked out the flag of a French merchant ship, blue with a broad white cross. Hector noticed the resemblance to the unknown flag flown by the frigate. Standing at the taffrail, Jacques began flapping the flag frantically.

His reward was another cannon shot. This time there was a sinister rushing sound as the ball flew over the pinnace.

'Blind idiots!' Jacques yelled.

Yannick had climbed up on the rail. Clinging with one hand to a shroud, he was waving a white sheet. His two brothers ran to the halyards and let down the mainsail with a rush. Very soon *Morvaut* was at a standstill, rolling awkwardly on the waves.

The frigate came tearing on, and for a time Hector thought the larger vessel was intent on ramming the *Morvaut*. But at the last moment the *Sainte Rose* turned up into the wind, backed her topsails and brailed the courses, and took up station within hailing distance.

A man dressed in a grey and blue coat appeared amidships. He raised a speaking trumpet and bellowed that the *Morvaut* was to send across her captain and any documents that proved the vessel's nationality and a list of her cargo.

'Too lazy to send their own boarding party?' Jacques grumbled. 'Let me go. I'll tell them what I think of their gunnery.'

'Your galérien's brand won't make the right impression,' Hector told him. 'It's better that I go across with the Kergonans and explain our business. It shouldn't delay us for long.'

In no time at all Anne-Marie Kergonan appeared from the little cabin holding a sheaf of papers wrapped in oilskin, which she slid into a wallet ready to take to the *Sainte Rose*. They must be the *Morvaut*'s documents, Hector thought to himself. She was a cool customer. Not even a near-miss from a seventeen-pound cannonball knocked her off-stride.

'Have you included a copy of our charter agreement?' he asked.

'Of course,' Anne-Marie replied. She was again wearing her broad red sash and Hector saw the slight bulge of the hidden pistol. 'Not expecting to hold up the captain of a warship, are you?' he observed sourly.

She answered him with a sardonic smile. 'You never know when it might be useful.'

Yannick and Yacut rowed the two of them across in the tender. As they covered the last few yards to the *Sainte Rose*, a voice shouted down in French. 'Yannick! You little shit!'

Anne-Marie leaned forward and quietly asked her brother, 'Who's that, Yannick?'

Yannick was scanning the faces lining the rail of the frigate. 'Gaston Rassalle. We fought at Campeche together. Can't imagine what he's doing on a king's ship.' He rested on his oar for a moment, cupped his hands around his mouth and shouted back. 'Shame they haven't hung you yet.'

Hector was aware of whistles and jeers as they came closer. He was trying to recall the details of what had happened at Campeche. There had been a great raid by filibustiers, as the French called the buccaneers. Hundreds of French and Dutch pirates had overrun the town, only to find that the citizens had fled with all their valuables. The disappointed raiders had wreaked havoc, smashing the place. There had been an orgy of rape and pillage, innocent prisoners strung up. Looking at Yannick's spiteful face, it was just the sort of atrocity that he would have imagined of the Breton.

A rope ladder had been lowered so they could scramble up the side of the frigate. Yannick went up first, then Hector. As he reached the main deck, he was surprised how untidy it was. There was an unsightly clutter of ropes, tubs, odds and ends, and a coop containing several scruffy hens. The planking was stained where gobs of chewing tobacco had been spat. It did not look like a navy ship. Nor were the crew any better. The men staring at him were an uncouth lot. None of them wore uniform. They were dressed in a motley collection of clothes, and he got the impression that several of them were drunk.

He looked around, seeking an officer. A man in a greasy blue and grey coat with silver facings was holding the speaking trumpet. Hector guessed he was a petty officer.

'I am Hector Lynch,' he began to say in French. Behind him he heard a chorus of appreciative grunts and whistles from the crew. Anne-Marie must have reached the deck.

Out of the corner of his eye he saw one of the frigate's sailors step up to Yannick Kergonan and thrust his face forward to within a few inches of the Breton. The man had smudges of gunpowder on his bare forearms and unwashed clothes. Hector guessed he was a cannonier, a ship's gunner.

'Had I known you were aboard that piss pot, I'd have aimed lower,' slurred the sailor.

'You couldn't hit a sow at ten paces,' the Breton sneered.

'Wouldn't be able to tell if that sow was your sister,' retorted the gunner.

Yannick's hand dropped to the hilt of his knife.

'Steady, Yannick.' The sharp warning came from Anne-Marie. She was only a yard away.

Yannick slowly withdrew his hand.

'Taking orders from the sow then,' jeered the cannonier.

There was a sudden movement, followed by the sound of a pistol shot. Gaston looked down foolishly. A bullet had splintered the deck beside his bare foot. Anne-Marie Kergonan held the smoking pistol in her hand. 'Next time I aim for your crotch,' she said.

'What's going on?' demanded an angry voice. At the head of the companion ladder leading down from the poop deck stood an officer. Tall and good-looking, he was impeccably dressed in a long dark blue coat edged with silver lace, well-polished bucket-top boots, white stockings and maroon breeches. A pale blue sash was wound around his waist. Hatless, he wore his thick blond hair long and loose. But the most remarkable item of his appearance was his carefully brushed moustache. It was arranged in the old-fashioned Spanish style. The ends of the moustache curled upwards on each side of his nose in two luxuriant and impressive curves.

Hector would have judged the man as a dandy, but for

Yannick's reaction. It was completely unexpected. The Breton suddenly went quiet. 'I'm sorry, captain,' he mumbled apologetically. He dropped his glance. 'Don't like to hear my sister spoken about that way.'

'It seems she is well able to look after herself,' observed the officer caustically. He turned to Anne-Marie and bowed. 'Major Laurens de Graff, at your service.'

This time Hector had no need to search his memory. Laurens de Graff was the most renowned filibustier in the Caribbean. He was said to be clever, arrogant, dangerous, and prone to outbursts of violent temper. Born in the Netherlands, he had joined the Spanish Navy and risen to the rank of captain before being captured by pirates. He had promptly turned his coat and become a filibustier himself. For fifteen years he had been achieving a string of remarkable successes. Evading the squadrons that his former masters had sent after him, he had captured ship after ship and become a byword for courage, seamanship and daring. The English had tried to recruit him as a mercenary captain, offering to pay him well, but Hector had heard that Laurens de Graff had preferred to throw in his lot with the French. They had given him a commission as a major in their colonial militia and allowed him to use their harbours for refuge and re-supply. But how he came to be in command of a royal French warship was a mystery.

De Graff was treating Anne-Marie Kergonan to a frankly appraising look.

'A pleasure to welcome you aboard my ship, madam,' he said.

He turned to face Yannick. 'Yannick Kergonan, isn't it? You were with us at Campeche.'

'Yes, sir,' answered Yannick. 'Nearly got caught by the Spaniards.'

De Graff looked at Hector. 'You are . . . ?'

'Hector Lynch. I have chartered the pinnace *Morvaut*.'

'Chartered for what purpose?'

'To fish for wrecks on the Vipers.'

Shrewd grey eyes regarded Hector. De Graff's face was expressionless. 'And have you had any success?'

An impulse made Hector cautious. 'Some success, not much.'

De Graff beckoned to the petty officer and murmured something in his ear. Then he turned back to Hector. 'Let us go to the poop deck. I presume you have proof of what you claim to be.'

As they mounted the companionway, Hector noticed that the petty officer and two sailors had commandeered the *Morvaut*'s skiff and were rowing across to visit the pinnace.

'Your name sounds English,' said de Graff as they reached the frigate's poop deck. Two junior officers moved respectfully to one side.

'I was born in Ireland but am currently living with my wife in Tortuga,' Hector answered, and then corrected himself, '. . . in Tortille.'

A lift of the eyebrow. De Graff was waiting for him to go on. 'My wife is originally from Spain,' Hector added lamely.

'My own wife is from the Canaries,' said de Graff amiably, 'though I see little of her nowadays, being at sea so much. May I see your papers?'

Hector looked across at Anne-Marie. From the wallet she was carrying she produced the charter agreement that had been carefully drawn up between them.

The filibustier captain read through the document carefully. Then he looked up. 'It seems to be in order.'

Hector felt a wave of relief. He had worried that the filibustier might find some excuse to delay them on the journey to Tortuga.

'You say that you were born in Ireland?' said de Graff.

'Yes.'

'That makes you a subject of the King of England.'

Hector could not understand why de Graff was so particular on this point.

'Madame,' the filibustier captain said, turning to Anne-Marie, 'Monsieur Lynch tells me that you are the owner of the pinnace.'

'Mademoiselle,' Anne-Marie corrected him. 'I am part-owner. I have equal shares with my brothers.'

'And you are on your way to Tortille?'

'That is correct.'

'Umm . . .' De Graff was looking across towards the pinnace. Hector began to have the first stirrings of concern. There was an undercurrent of deviousness to de Graff's urbane manner.

They chatted on inconsequential matters until the petty officer returned from his inspection of *Morvaut*. De Graff took him to one side, and it was clear that he was listening to the man's report. Then the filibustier walked across to where Anne-Marie and Hector were waiting for him.

'Monsieur Lynch,' de Graff began, 'I have to inform you that you are my prisoner.'

Hector gaped with shock. 'On what grounds?' he demanded.

'As an enemy combatant.'

'How can that be?' Hector's mind was whirling.

De Graff gave an apologetic shrug. 'Perhaps the news reached Tortille after you had left on this fishing trip of yours.'

Hector felt his throat go dry. 'What news?'

'England and France are at war.'

'That's impossible,' Hector retorted. He was utterly taken aback. France and England were always wary of one another in the Caribbean but their mutual hostility towards Spain had kept them in an uneasy alliance.

De Graff smoothed his splendid moustache. He looked pleased with himself. 'I'm not a politician but I gather that the war is to do with alliances in Europe. My lord, the Sun King –' de Graff allowed himself a mocking smile – 'has aroused such envy among other sovereigns that several of the European nations have leagued against him. Even Spain.'

Hector decided his only course was to brazen it out. 'I can't see how that gives you the right to detain me—' he began forcefully.

'. . . You and your associates,' interjected de Graff quietly. 'Bring me my commission,' he said to a junior officer.

A little while later the man reappeared, carrying a large leather folder. De Graff took out a parchment. Without a word he handed it to Hector to read.

In florid, formal French with its particular spellings the document stated that 'Laurens-Cornille Baldran, sieur de Graff, lieutenant de roy en l'isle de Saint-Domingue' was appointed as 'Capitaine de Fregate legere'. He was to carry out faithfully the instructions received from his superiors. The document bore the signature of the Seigneur de Cussy, Governor pour le Roi du cote et isles de Saint-Domingue en l'Amerique sous le vent.

De Graff waited for Hector to finish reading before he said silkily, 'As you see, my instructions require me to detain enemy nationals and seize their goods and possessions.'

To Hector's surprise, Anne-Marie spoke up in his support. 'Major de Graff, you have no right to detain Monsieur Lynch. He has a perfectly legitimate contract with me, a French subject, to conduct salvage operations with a French vessel.'

De Graff turned to Anne-Marie, and though his eyes expressed admiration, he spoke with the tone of someone who would allow no argument.

'Mademoiselle Kergonan, I was coming to that. A vessel chartered by an enemy subject becomes, as it were, a ship of that nation.'

Anne-Marie's eyes narrowed. 'Are you telling me that you intend to seize the *Morvaut*?'

'The moment you entered into a contract with Monsieur Lynch, the vessel effectively became his instrument and available for hostilities.'

'Fishing for wrecks is not a hostile act.'

De Graff smiled grimly. 'The profits could be used to assist the enemy. For that reason I am also confiscating Monsieur Lynch's salvage.'

Belatedly Hector noticed Yannick Kergonan smirking up at

him from the main deck. On the deck beside him were the two knapsacks in which Jacques had stored their silver from the galleon. Hector guessed that the Breton had told the petty officer where to look for the knapsacks when he visited the pinnace.

Laurens de Graff was speaking again. 'Mademoiselle, I must ask you also to hand over your proceeds from the wreck.'

'I don't know what you mean,' Anne-Marie snapped back at him.

De Graff sighed. 'Your charter contract clearly states that half the salvage goes to you and your brothers as owners of the vessel. That half, too, must be relinquished.'

'It belongs to us, French subjects.'

De Graff's voice hardened. 'As captain of this vessel I am within my rights to confiscate all goods found on a suspect vessel.'

Anne-Marie Kergonan exploded with rage. 'That is pure piracy.'

Hands on hips, she stormed at de Graff with the violence of a fishwife. He was a crook, a cheat, and nothing better than a sea robber, and she would expose his villainy to Governor de Cussy the moment she reached Petit Goâve.

The filibustier was unmoved. 'Mademoiselle, please return to your vessel. I shall send a petty officer and some sailors as prize crew. The *Sainte Rose* will escort her to Petit Goâve. Monsieur Lynch will rejoin his comrades on your pinnace and they will be put in irons for the journey.'

'And my brothers, what are they to do?' Anne-Marie demanded, her face suffused with anger.

De Graff shrugged. 'Naturally I must replace the prize crew I'm sending with you, so I will retain them on the *Sainte Rose*. I believe they will find themselves among former comrades.'

❋

HECTOR SAT QUIETLY in the tender as it returned to the pinnace. Anne-Marie was still seething with rage. She was even angrier after they were back aboard the *Morvaut* and a gloating French

39

sailor emerged from the main hatch. He held up for them to see the heavy sacks in which Yannick had hidden the Kergonans' share of the salvage in the bilge.

'My stupid oaf of a brother,' she raged. 'If he'd kept his mouth shut, de Graff wouldn't have known about our haul.' She stormed off to the cabin, making it clear that even though *Morvaut* was in the hands of a prize crew, the cabin was her territory.

The tender made one final trip to the *Sainte Rose*, carrying away the Kergonans' share of booty and returning with four sets of leg irons and lengths of chain. These were used to shackle Hector and his comrades together at the ankle, while the free end of the chain was padlocked to a ring bolt on the foredeck.

'What are you looking so smug about, Jacques?' growled Jezreel as the ex-galérien tore off a strip of his shirt and wrapped it around his ankle under the leg iron to prevent it chafing.

'That padlock – typical government rubbish made by the cheapest contractor. Give me a spike and I could open it in less than a minute.'

'All in good time,' said Hector quietly. He was watching the prize crew tie off the tender to *Morvaut*'s stern. He counted five of them in addition to the petty officer in charge.

'Much more treatment like this, and I'll lose patience. Then someone will get hurt,' Jezreel said. He was rubbing a bruise on his shoulder where one of the prize crew had struck him with a musket butt when he moved too slowly.

'Just hold on for a while,' said Hector. Already he was beginning to wonder if there might be some way of escape.

The distant shrill of a bosun's whistle came across the water. The *Sainte Rose* was getting under way again. Her topsails were being braced around, and the main courses sheeted in.

'Goodbye to our silver,' said Jacques. 'That's already in de Graff's own pocket or shared out with his crew.'

Aboard the *Morvaut* the petty officer was telling his men to hoist the mainsail.

'You there!' he shouted at Hector's group. 'Make yourselves useful. Get the foresail up.'

The length of their leg chains allowed the prisoners to shuffle as far as the foresail halyard.

'Jacques,' Hector said under his breath, 'can you get yourself a pick-lock?'

'Nothing easier,' said the Frenchman. 'See that little runt-like fellow with the red cap. He's from Paris. I recognize his accent.' He called out a string of words which sounded French but Hector found completely incomprehensible.

The man in the red cap replied similarly.

'What's that all about?' Hector asked.

'Street beggar's slang. Told him that if they didn't have a decent cook, I could do the job.'

'And his reply?'

'He said he would check with his boss.'

Some time later the Parisian came to the foredeck, unlocked Jacques' chain, and led him to the cook box. The boy looped the chain through the handle of a large iron cauldron and closed the padlock. 'Let's see if you can cook as well as you claim,' he said to Jacques. 'The last time I was on a prize crew, it was aboard a Dutch fluyt, and I got sick of bean soup and stockfish stew.'

'I'll do better than that,' Jacques assured him, and within the hour had served up a gratin of peas, biscuit and crumbled cheese. When he was returned to the foredeck, he silently pulled a fork out from his shirtfront. 'Any time you want us free of our chains, Hector, just let me know,' he said with a grin.

Hector waited until well after dark when everyone was settled for the night. The moon was showing through rents in the cloud cover and gave enough light to see the outline of the *Sainte Rose*. The frigate was under reduced sail and half a mile upwind, keeping pace with the pinnace. Whatever happened aboard the *Morvaut* would have to be done without alerting the warship.

The petty officer and three of his men, their stomachs full of

Jacques' gratin, had gone to sleep on the main deck. Two men were left on watch, one as helmsman and the other as lookout. From time to time they were passing between them a bottle that Jacques had taken care to half-fill from the small keg of looted rum and leave on view. Anne-Marie was not to be seen. The only time she had opened the door of the cabin was to accept a plate of food.

Around him Hector could sense his friends awake and ready for his word.

'Let's go,' he whispered.

Jacques wriggled across to the ring bolt and, using the fork, worked at the padlocks, one by one, until all the prisoners were free. Dan wrapped a length of chain around his hand, slithered away to the rail and crouched there, waiting. Without raising his head, Hector watched the two sailors at the helm. The next time he saw the bottle pass between them he reached out and tapped Dan on the ankle. In one quick movement the Miskito half rose, slid over the windward rail and disappeared overboard.

Along her entire length *Morvaut* was girdled with a rubbing strake, a thick plank that acted as a fender when she was docked. This plank protruded nearly two inches from the hull, and Dan had said it was enough for him to get a purchase with bare feet. Now, with one hand grasping the rail to prevent him falling into the sea, he was invisible from the helm as long as he stayed crouching down. Only if the lookout walked right to the edge of the vessel and looked overboard would the Miskito be seen.

Hector watched the rail. Once or twice he had a brief glimpse of Dan's hand, moving like a crab as the Miskito inched his way aft, using the rubbing strake as a ledge.

Minutes passed, and Hector could only hope that Dan had successfully reached the stern, and was hanging there waiting for his opportunity.

After what seemed like an age, the helmsman's comrade left his post. The rum bottle was empty and he came aft to pour a refill. He reached the cook box and bent down to remove the bung from the rum keg. At that moment Jezreel rose and in two strides he was above the sailor. He smashed his clenched fist down on the back of the man's head. The stunned sailor toppled forward; Jezreel caught him and eased him gently to the deck.

The commotion had not caught the attention of the helmsman when Dan dropped quietly over the gunwale behind him. In a single smooth movement the Miskito whipped a loop of chain around the helmsman's neck and choked off any sound. The man thrashed from side to side in anguish. Grimly Dan tightened the garrotte. Now was the most dangerous moment. The tiller swung free and the pinnace, unchecked, swung up into the wind. There was a lurch and then a slap of canvas loud enough to wake a light sleeper. Stepping closer to his victim, Dan twisted the noose more fiercely until the choking helmsman's legs gave way. Even as he collapsed unconscious to the deck, Dan grabbed for the tiller and hauled it towards him, steadying the pinnace and bringing *Morvaut* back on course. The little boat sailed on quietly.

Hector's attention had been focused on the petty officer and his three men. If they awakened now, the plan was to overpower them. But none of them moved.

Already Jezreel was filling a sack with some hard tack, a piece of dried fish, the remainder of the peas. Jacques and Hector tiptoed across and joined him. Each of them lifted a jar of water. Silently they edged their way along the deck with their loads, cautiously skirting past the sleeping men. Once on the poop deck, Hector laid down his burden and took over the helm from Dan. He kept the boat on course so the Miskito could stuff a dirty rag into the mouth of the unconscious helmsman and tie the gag in place. Jacques and Jezreel were at the stern and hauling in the tender by its painter.

Not a word had been spoken since Hector had given his first order. Everything had gone exactly as the four friends had discussed that afternoon.

Jacques lowered himself into the tender, and Jezreel began handing down the food and water. Hector looked anxiously towards the *Sainte Rose*. As far as he could tell, the frigate was continuing on her way as before. She was too far away for a lookout to have seen the scuffle, but he feared that someone might notice that the pinnace's tender, normally towed on a long painter, was now fastened close under her stern.

In another couple of minutes they were ready to leave. Jezreel had joined Jacques in the tender, and Dan had passed down the oars and a roll of tarpaulin.

All that remained to do was to lash the tiller so that the pinnace stayed on course for as long as possible and allow them to get clear. Dan found a length of line and took a loop around the windward rail and then two turns around the tiller. Carefully he adjusted the tension to his satisfaction and tightened the knots. A moment later he was gone, climbing lightly over the taffrail and dropping into the waiting boat.

Hector turned to follow him, and had not taken two paces when he heard a muffled grunt. It came from the helmsman lying where he had fallen. The moon appeared from behind the clouds, and the sudden flood of moonlight showed the man was about to spit out his gag. Hector could see his jaws working. Another moment and he would raise the alarm.

Hector spun round, knelt, and brutally crammed the wad of cloth deeper into the man's mouth. Then he tightened the gag fiercely. He was about to rise to his feet when a shadow fell across him.

He froze.

Someone was standing on the deck above him. It took a moment for him to realize that it was Anne-Marie. Her cabin was directly below the poop deck, and the commotion overhead must have disturbed her. He wondered how long she had been standing there, and why she had not cried out.

He got slowly to his feet and faced her.

The shadow stepped closer. 'Here take this,' Anne-Marie whispered. She was holding out something in her hand. Hector reached out and felt the butt of a pistol. 'Like I said, it might come in useful.'

'But why . . . ?' Hector began. He was too stunned to say more.

'Go!' she hissed. 'There's someone waiting for you on Tortuga. I'll make sure that the *Morvaut* stays on course.'

Hector's legs were shaking as he stumbled to the taffrail and lowered himself into the tender. Dan had found a knife and was in the bow waiting to cut the rope. He was reaching forward, blade in hand, when a bundle – a roll of tarpaulin – dropped from above and into the boat with a soft thud.

He jerked back in surprise. The towrope then went slack and the free end, unfastened from the *Morvaut*'s stern, dropped into the water.

Outlined against the sky was the figure of Anne-Marie standing at the taffrail, a hand silently raised in farewell.

Released from her tether, the tender fell away rapidly as the pinnace sailed on. Hector waited for a shout of alarm, but none came. He looked away to his left. The *Sainte Rose* was maintaining her course.

Jezreel had seated himself on the central thwart and set the oars in place and was ready to begin rowing. 'Which way?' he enquired in a whisper though already the pinnace was far out of earshot.

Hector looked up at the sky. He stood up in the little boat, extended his arm to full stretch and turned to face the Pole Star. He clenched his fingers and placed the lower edge of his fist on the horizon beneath the star. His hand spanned the gap between star and sea almost exactly. It was a trick he had learned from an Arab merchant captain who showed him how to measure the height of a star by the width of his hand or fingers. They were in 16 degrees north or thereabouts. After weeks exploring the Vipers he carried a chart of the area in his memory. Jamaica must be north-west, some hundred and fifty miles away. Saint-Domingue and the French colonies would be twice that distance in the direction that the *Morvaut* and the *Sainte Rose* were now disappearing in the darkness.

If he had judged de Graff correctly, losing his captives would hurt the man's pride. Driven by an angry captain, the frigate would turn around and hunt down the fugitives. Logic would dictate that they had fled north-west towards Jamaica, and that was the direction where de Graff would search.

Hector swivelled round and faced the opposite horizon. Sirius was clear and bright, low in the sky. 'Towards the Dog Star,' he said to his companions. Jezreel dipped the oar blades in the water and began to row south-east.

FOUR

THE GOVERNOR OF SAINT-DOMINGUE, Pierre-Paul Tarin de Cussy, stood loitering in the shade of a palm tree on the beach of the French settlement at Petit Goâve. A frail-looking man with a head that seemed too large for his body, he was dressed as usual in a light coat and loose breeches of white cotton, and wore a broad-brimmed straw hat. As a tobacco planter on the island for twenty years, he was accustomed to the climate, but today was exceptionally hot and it would be at least another hour before Major de Graff came ashore. Besides, the Governor enjoyed watching the *Sainte Rose* work her way into the anchorage. De Cussy was not a sailor himself, but he could appreciate competent ship handling when he saw it, and he was relieved that the frigate was back in port. He worried every time *Sainte Rose* set sail, fearing that de Graff's opportunism would get the better of him and the filibustier would end up losing the ship in a rash battle with the English or Spaniards. An even worse nightmare for the Governor, though he never breathed a word of it to anyone else, was that de Graff would steal the ship and go off on his own account with his crew, half of whom had earlier served with him as sea robbers. As far as de Cussy was concerned, de Graff was still a pirate at heart.

The frigate was now almost on top of her mooring in a

sheltered cove at the western side of the bay. De Cussy saw the splash as her main anchor went down. Squinting against the glitter of the sun on the water, he tried to identify the small pinnace that accompanied the frigate. Something about the boat was familiar. Then he recognized it as the *Morvaut*, owned by the Kergonan family on Tortuga. The Governor knew the Kergonans by reputation. It was common knowledge that they ran illegal cargoes to the Spaniards and perhaps traded with the English in Jamaica as well. But he had yet to catch them red-handed. For a moment he wondered if de Graff had intercepted just such a smuggling run and arrested them. The thought gave de Cussy a brief glow of hope. But on reflection he decided it was unlikely. The captain of the *Sainte Rose* would actively encourage smuggling, not prevent it, if there were a profit to be had.

An eight-oar launch pushed away from the *Sainte Rose* and set off across the bay towards the landing stage on the near side. The Governor left the shelter of the palm tree and began to stroll along the beach towards the wooden jetty to greet his frigate captain.

Anne-Marie, seated beside de Graff in the launch, recognized the figure of the Governor moving along the shoreline. Occasionally he had come on an official visit to Tortuga, which was nominally a French possession, but he never stayed on the island for long. She had met him once, and very briefly, because her brothers tended to make themselves scarce whenever the Governor was around.

The hard shape of the small pistol hidden in her sash brought her thoughts back yet again to Hector. The weapon was the pair of the one she had given him, and she had been regretting for the past four days that she had allowed Hector to slip through her fingers. He was a most unusual young man. There was a quality about him that she had rarely encountered – a sense of honour. She smiled to herself as she recalled the shocked look on his face when she had put a pistol to the head of that young Spaniard on the urca. He had genuinely believed that it was an underhand way of getting the food and water they needed. Yet, according to his friends, Hector was no faint-heart when it came to a crisis. Jacques had told her something of their adventures in the Pacific and how they had survived as prisoners among the Moors. The loyalty of his three friends had impressed her greatly. They were a remark-ably assorted bunch – prize-fighter, galérien and Miskito. Yet they accepted Hector as their leader and looked to him as a man they trusted to lead them in difficult times. Anne-Marie had seen for herself that he was level-headed and clever. And, besides, he was rather good-looking in a finely drawn sort of way, though he did not know it.

She stole a sideways glance at de Graff on the thwart beside her. He too was handsome, though in a very different manner. The filibustier had a strong beak of a nose above the luxuriant moustache, and he carried himself with a swagger that had a definite appeal. Also he could turn on the charm at will. In some ways he reminded Anne-Marie of her former husband. She had been married for less than a year to an engagé, an indentured man who had come out to Tortuga from France hoping to make a new life hunting wild cattle and selling their hides. At first he had seemed affable and charming, but had quickly turned into a drunk and an idler, given to outbursts of violence. That was when she had learned to keep a pistol in her sash. She had not been sorry on the day he had died of the black flux.

She wondered how Captain de Graff treated his wife. He also had a violent temper. She had seen it on the day Hector and his companions had escaped. The petty officer in charge of the prize crew on *Morvaut* had woken to find the pinnace sailing along by herself, the tiller lashed, the helmsman and lookout tied up and gagged, the prisoners and the skiff gone. There had been shouts and yells, the petty officer kicking his men awake, a great deal of running to and fro, a musket fired to attract the *Sainte Rose*'s atten-tion. She had emerged from her cabin at the sound of the musket, pretending not to know anything, and asked what was going on. She was fairly sure that she had fooled the petty officer, but when she was brought across to the frigate and questioned by de Graff, she looked into his grey eyes and saw mistrust and suspicion.

She had noticed spots of blood on the frigate's deck as she left that interview. Later Yannick told her that de Graff had already interrogated the petty officer. The filibustier captain had repeatedly slashed the unfortunate man about the face with a cane as he screamed his questions. Then he had ordered a flogging for every man on the prize crew.

She could still sense de Graff's anger at the prisoners' escape now. He was staring straight ahead, his back rigid and jaw set, his face shaded by the wide brim of his hat with its flamboyant white ostrich plume. He was dressed in the full uniform of a frigate captain and she wondered if perhaps he had chosen this dashingly impressive wardrobe for her benefit.

'The *Sainte Rose* makes a splendid sight, captain,' the Governor called down from the wooden jetty as the crew of the launch caught hold of the pilings and steadied the craft. He watched Anne-Marie appreciatively as she came up the wooden steps. She had put on a simple working dress and a pinafore which accentuated her generous bosom.

'Allow me to introduce Anne-Marie Kergonan of Tortille,' said de Graff.

'Perhaps we have already met briefly,' replied de Cussy. It would have been difficult to forget such a shapely figure, he thought. 'How are your brothers? Yannick and, er . . . ?'

'Roparzh and Yacut,' she said. 'They are well, thank you.'

'I've added them to my crew,' interrupted de Graff.

De Cussy raised an eyebrow. He had noted that Anne-Marie looked less than pleased. 'I'm sure you had good reason,' he said.

'A waste of prime seamen otherwise. I intercepted their boat, *Morvaut*, in questionable circumstances,' de Graff continued. 'They had four suspicious strangers aboard – a big Englishman, and a Miskito Indian, as well as a Frenchman renegade. Their leader was a young man. Calls himself Hector Lynch.'

'The name means nothing to me.'

'I arrested them and impounded the *Morvaut*. But they escaped.'

'In the middle of the sea?'

'Stole the ship's tender and made off.'

'And you followed?'

'Of course. We turned back and spent two days searching for them. They couldn't have got far. But they had vanished. I decided to bring the *Morvaut* into port without wasting any more time.'

'And what were they doing aboard the *Morvaut*? You think they were spies?'

'No. The Kergonans had taken them out to the Vipers.'

De Graff shot the Governor a knowing glance, which made de Cussy pause for a moment.

'Perhaps we should discuss this matter privately.'

While the others were talking, Anne-Marie had been observing several small boats putting out from the frigate. Crowded with sailors, they were heading directly for the landing in front of the cluster of wooden houses and thatched huts that made up the settlement of Petit Goâve. The crew of the *Sainte Rose* were obviously on their way to the drinking dens and brothels for which the place was renowned.

'If you will excuse me, Your Excellency. My brothers are coming ashore and I should go to meet with them. Naturally we will be contesting the seizure of our vessel and will seek the return of our property. You will grant us justice, I hope.' She faced de Graff and treated him to a withering glance. 'Captain, I bid you goodbye. I shall remember your company.'

Her remark produced a flicker of amused interest on de Graff's face as he watched Anne-Marie stalk off the jetty.

'A fiery young woman,' commented de Cussy.

'Carries a pistol in her sash, if you hadn't noticed,' said de Graff.

'I'd say she'd be more than most men could handle, however much they wanted.'

Together the two men made their way to where de Cussy had

set up an office in a tobacco warehouse he owned on the outskirts of Petit Goâve. The colony he governed was a string of isolated settlements dotted around the western fringe of the island the Spaniards knew as Hispaniola and, in practice, its capital was effectively located wherever he happened to be at the time. His tobacco warehouse was one of the few buildings in Petit Goâve which had an upper storey, and the two men mounted a set of outside stairs that led to the Governor's private quarters. Once inside, de Cussy waved his visitor to a chair and despatched a servant to bring them some refreshments. He waited until the man had left the room before saying, 'You mentioned the Vipers. Tell me more.'

'When we searched the *Morvaut*, we found a considerable quantity of valuables aboard. Mostly silver, but some gold and jewellery too. The Kergonans said it was salvage they had taken from a Spanish wreck on the Vipers.'

'And you confiscated this haul?'

'Yes. I used the excuse that they and their vessel had been hired by this Lynch fellow. He's Irish born so a subject of the King of England. But, by the look of him, I would say that he's a free agent.'

The Governor smiled thinly. 'And where exactly is this booty now?'

'Safe in a strongbox in my cabin on the *Sainte Rose*.'

'You realize, of course, that His Majesty is entitled to a ten per cent share of its value. That is the rule for all prize taken at sea by a royal ship.'

'I was coming to that,' said de Graff. 'I propose to hand over half to you as His Majesty's representative rather than the usual ten per cent.'

For a split second de Cussy stared in open astonishment. Then his good sense quickly got the better of him. He was being offered a bribe.

'Very generous. His Majesty will be pleased,' he responded drily, and waited for de Graff to continue.

The frigate captain leaned forward. 'This wreck may well contain far more treasure than the *Morvaut* was able to salvage.'

'And what gives you that idea?'

'The *Morvaut* is too small a vessel to fish a wreck properly. I understand there was a single diver aboard, this Miskito Indian. If the wreck was searched with a full team of divers, the rewards could be immense.'

The Governor understood what de Graff had in mind. 'You want me to authorize you to go there with the *Sainte Rose* and use her for salvage work, is that it?'

The frigate captain said nothing. His silence was enough.

De Cussy looked out of the window for a full minute without saying a word. From where he sat, he could see over the broad sweep of the bay. The frigate lay at anchor against a backdrop of intense tropical green where a headland covered with lush vegetation sheltered the anchorage. A lone heron was gliding down towards the near shoreline and, as he watched, the bird landed. The broad outstretched wings gave a final slow shake and flap, and it stalked briskly into the shallows. It came to a halt, the snake-like neck curved back, and the eyes scanned the water, the beak ready to stab. The heron, he thought to himself, knew where the fish tended to gather. That is how he ought to deploy de Graff and the *Sainte Rose*.

He swivelled in his chair and faced the captain. 'What you ask is impossible. We are at war. The *Sainte Rose* is the only ship of force with which to protect the colony. It would be madness to send her off on a salvage adventure.'

'Yet His Majesty would be delighted if we recovered so much treasure,' said the filibustier. 'There would be promotion and honours for those concerned. The royal dividend would be enough to finance this colony for several years.'

De Cussy returned his gaze to the distant warship. The wind must be shifting for she was swinging to her anchor. He had to admit that the frigate captain was very shrewd in dressing up his proposal as being in the interests of France. He decided to test de Graff a little further.

'If the rewards will be so immense, why is it necessary to use the *Sainte Rose*? Could you not persuade investors to equip another vessel for salvage work?' he said.

De Graff shook his head. 'Proper salvage will take many weeks. As soon as the Spanish know that an interloper is working the wreck, they will send vessels to drive off the intruder. Only a well-armed ship is able to see out the task.'

Governor de Cussy chose his words carefully. 'This can only be done with authorization from Paris.'

De Graff sensed that the Governor was tempted by his proposition. 'You will not regret it if you recommend to Paris that the *Sainte Rose* is assigned to this task.'

'I agree only to ask for permission to despatch the *Sainte Rose* to intercept enemy trade by sea.'

'How will that help?'

The Governor stood up and went over to the window. The heron had just speared a fish. It was holding its victim up in the air. The fish wriggled, flashing silver, frantic to escape. A swift movement, and it was nothing more than a bulge in the heron's throat. Keeping his back to his guest, de Cussy spoke slowly and precisely. 'To inflict the greatest damage on the enemy, the frigate must be at the heart of their shipping routes, not here on the fringe where her presence is known and can be avoided.'

'And you have a location in mind?'

'The island of Providencia, formerly an English colony, has been abandoned. I will suggest to Paris that you establish a temporary base for the *Sainte Rose* there.'

De Graff could picture exactly what the Governor had in mind. The island of Providencia commanded the sea routes between Cartagena, Havana and Porto Bello. From there the *Sainte Rose* could pounce on all the passing shipping.

The frigate captain shook his head in admiration. 'Governor, you would have made an excellent admiral.'

What the Governor had left unsaid – and de Graff knew full well – was that Providencia was less than a day's sail from the Vipers. If the *Sainte Rose* was based on Providencia and unsupervised, de Graff would be able to conduct salvage operations whenever he wanted.

De Cussy turned and held up a hand in warning. 'You must be patient. It will take some months before I receive an answer from Paris. I presume you know the precise location of the wreck?'

The filibustier's expression hardened. 'That is why I added the Kergonans to my crew. I'll make sure they tell me.'

The servant entered with a tray of wine and some cheese, and the two men quickly dropped the subject. For some time they chatted amiably about other matters – the prospects for the tobacco crop, the recent hurricane that had devastated the eastern end of the island, rumours of military reinforcements arriving from England and being deployed on Jamaica. Eventually, when the heat had gone out of the day, the Governor suggested that they should take a stroll through the town.

✻

MEANWHILE ANNE-MARIE had located her brothers. They had chosen the nastiest tavern in Petit Goâve. It lay right on the waterfront, a down-at-heel shed with a reed thatch roof weathered to a dingy grey. Several half-starved dogs dozed against walls of planks warped by sun and rain. Chickens scratched the dirt around the open doorway, and by the corner posts were patches of damp in the dust where the customers had relieved themselves. From inside came the sounds of loud conversation, bursts of tipsy laughter, and someone playing clumsily on a fiddle. After a childhood spent on Tortuga, Anne-Marie knew what to expect as she stepped in through the open door. The floor of the tavern was grimy beach sand stained with spilled drinks and scuffed by boot heels. Shafts of sunlight entered through the unglazed windows and struggled to penetrate thick clouds of tobacco smoke. Along the far wall were rough wooden shelves stacked with bottles and tankards. Below them, on stands, were several kegs and a battered serving counter. The smell was of rum, beer, unwashed bodies and stale tobacco. The place was packed with customers. They sat on benches and stools around tables set far enough apart for the serving women to push their way through with more drinks. Occasionally one of the drinkers got up to accompany a serving woman. The two of them disappeared behind a length of sailcloth hung over a sagging rope which screened off the far end of the room. The tavern did double duty as a brothel.

Anne-Marie's entry attracted several glances. Most of the drinkers were men from the *Sainte Rose* so they recognized her immediately. Free of shipboard constraints they ogled her and there were several catcalls of approval. Near the counter a heavy-set man in a stained apron was staring at her in a calculating manner. She guessed he was the tavern owner and wondering if her presence would cause trouble. But the shrewdest appraisal came from the serving women. There were about a dozen of them, and their ages could have been anything between fifteen and forty. A few paused briefly in their work and looked her over carefully, then went back to attending to the customers. Others glared, not troubling to conceal their hostility. These were dressed in brightly coloured skirts that had been chosen to set off the colour of their skins which ranged from jet black to a pale coffee. Every one of them was naked from the waist up.

Anne-Marie looked around the press of drinkers, searching out her brothers. The three of them were at a table some distance into the room and seated with a couple of men she did not recognize. Unwilling to force her way through the crowd she stood waiting until they noticed her presence, and then she beckoned. Yannick scowled and deliberately raised his tankard to his lips before slowly getting to his feet. Roparzh and Yacut stayed where they were.

As he slouched towards her, she saw Yannick was very drunk. He staggered, swerving between the tables. He was passing one group when someone put out a leg and deliberately tripped him.

He fell forward, reaching out, and dragged down one of the other drinkers. Immediately there were angry shouts and several curses as drinks were spilled. Then Yannick was back on his feet and looking round to see who had tripped him.

The fiddler stopped playing. Suddenly there was a silence as half the room waited to see what the sullen Breton would do next.

With an oath Yannick lunged, clawing for his victim. But he had mistaken the man responsible for his fall. Within a heartbeat the scuffle was threatening to turn into a general brawl. Bystanders were knocked off their seats, pushed and shoved, took offence and began to fight amongst themselves. Several of the serving women dodged behind the curtain. The others withdrew to the side of the room and looked on, arms folded under bare breasts. It was a scene they had witnessed many times.

The tavern owner was quick to intervene. He charged through the crowd with several of his regular customers at his back to help him. They seized Yannick and the other struggling men and bundled them towards the door and out into the street. Anne-Marie beat a tactful retreat before them.

Outside, only Yannick and his real tormentor wanted to keep up their quarrel. Anne-Marie saw that it was the same sailor, Gaston Rassalle, who had insulted her on the *Sainte Rose*. Both men were in an ugly mood, glaring at one another. Rassalle spat on the ground contemptuously. He reached behind his back and pulled a knife from its sheath on his belt.

'I should have gutted you at Vera Cruz,' he sneered as he crouched in a fighting stance.

There was a glint of steel as a knife also appeared in Yannick's hand. 'Then it's time you tried your luck,' he replied, and jabbed the blade towards his opponent.

Anne-Marie knew it was futile for her to intervene. More and more men were emerging from the open door of the tavern. They hurried up to form a ring around the two fighters. Shouting encouragement, they urged the contestants to get on with their fight. The air was thick with blood lust.

Rassalle began to circle to his right, shuffling across the sand. Yannick kept pace, moving sideways so that he kept facing square to his opponent. Whenever Rassalle changed direction and moved in the opposite direction, so too did the Breton. They stared at one another, eyes locked in mutual hatred.

Abruptly Yannick hurled himself across the gap, slashing with his blade. But Rassalle had seen the Breton gather and tense before he sprang and anticipated the attack. He skipped away as the crowd hurriedly fell back to give him room. Now it was Yannick's turn to jump out of arm's reach.

'Get on with it!' someone shouted from the crowd. 'If you want to dance, I'll call for the fiddler.'

The spatter of laughter from the onlookers goaded Yannick to try again. This time he stabbed rather than slashed with his blade. He extended his arm forward like a swordsman and thrust, aiming for Rassalle's chest.

Rassalle was too quick for him. He turned his body sideways and avoided the point of the knife. Grabbing the Breton's wrist before Yannick could withdraw, Rassalle stepped forward, forcing Yannick's knife hand downward and closing with his opponent. The two men collided with a thud. For a couple of seconds they stood, chest to chest, grunting and straining against one another as Rassalle maintained his grip. Only when Yannick used his free arm to launch a punch at his enemy's head did he succeed in breaking clear. By then Rassalle's knife had done its work. He had slid the blade deep into the Breton's stomach, low down on the left-hand side.

Yannick stepped back, apparently untroubled. He was breathing deeply, his chest heaving. For a long moment he stood upright, still glaring at his opponent. He raised his left arm and wiped the back of his hand across his mouth, then gave a slight cough. A look of puzzlement crossed his face. He made as if to step forward but seemed to lose control of the movement. He let go his knife and clutched at his side. Then he dropped to his knees on the dirt.

A tremor ran through the watching crowd. Rassalle remained standing where he was. He looked down at his victim with narrowed eyes, knife in hand and waiting.

Yannick coughed again and tried to get back on his feet. He pushed himself half upright with one hand, the other still clutching his belly. In that instant the crowd could see the stain of blood spreading across the front of the shirt. Then the effort was too much for him and he slumped forward face down.

There was a commotion to Anne-Marie's right. Her two other brothers were pushing their way through the crowd, which opened out to give them space. Roparzh and Yacut were even more drunk than their brother. Their eyes were bloodshot and they could barely stand. They came to a halt at the edge of the ring of spectators and looked down stupidly at Yannick on the ground. Yacut gave a great, rum-sodden belch as he turned towards Rassalle. Something in his addled brain urged him to take revenge. He shook his head as if trying to clear his vision and let out a low growl of anguish. With his hands held out like claws in front of him he began to advance on Rassalle, who watched him come on, his bloodied knife at the ready.

A shot rang out.

Rassalle snapped forward, folding in half. He screamed in pain. He took a pace backwards. Then he too sank to the ground and curled up in a ball, whimpering with anguish.

The startled crowd turned their gaze on Anne-Marie. She stood with the pistol still held out in front of her, the barrel at the same slight downward angle as when she had pulled the trigger. A wisp of gunpowder smoke hung in the hot tropical air.

Rassalle was moaning, writhing from side to side. 'Gut shot,' someone in the crowd said.

'It was meant to be his groin,' said Anne-Marie calmly. 'Now someone call a surgeon.'

*

KNIFINGS AND SHOOTINGS were sufficiently common in Petit Goâve for no one to bother reporting them to the authorities. Governor de Cussy learned about the fight while on his evening stroll through the settlement. He and de Graff had reached the spot where the fight had taken place when one of the idlers outside the tavern brazenly called out, 'Will you hang her, Governor?'

The owner of the tavern was hurrying over, wiping his hands on a soiled cloth. 'What's that fellow talking about?' snapped de Cussy.

'The Kergonan woman,' said the innkeeper. 'She shot Gaston Rassalle in the guts. Surgeon says he'll not live.'

'Why did she do that?'

'Rassalle had knifed her brother,' said the man.

De Cussy was taken aback. He had been expecting a sordid tale of one of the tavern whores engaged in a brawl.

'It didn't happen in my place, but out here,' the innkeeper added defensively.

'And where's the woman now?'

'She and her other brothers carried off the injured one. They took him to the house of a distant kinsman. Cousin of that ne'er-do-well she was married to.' The tavern owner grimaced. 'Those worthless Bretons always stick together.'

'Did you see the fight yourself?'

The innkeeper shook his head. 'No. But plenty did. And some of them will stand witness. Yannick Kergonan had few friends.'

The Governor was quick to note the past tense. 'What do you mean, *had* few friends?'

'Surgeon says that he's as like to die as is Rassalle. Neither will live out the week.'

De Cussy dismissed the tavern keeper. Taking de Graff by the elbow, he walked on casually as though the fracas was no more than a minor disturbance. He waited until they were halfway back to his office before he said quietly to the filibustier, 'Looks as though you've lost one of the men who could locate that wreck for you.'

De Graff sounded irritated. 'A pity. Yannick Kergonan was the sharpest of the three brothers.'

'What about the other two? Will they know where to look on the Vipers?'

'Can't say. I'll take them to Providencia aboard the *Sainte Rose* and tickle up their memories.' He swung a savage cut with the cane he was carrying. His target was a wild shrub with red flowers growing at the side of the path. Petals fluttered to the ground.

'The sister was aboard the pinnace too,' suggested the Governor softly.

De Graff came to a halt and turned to face the Governor. The filibustier's eyes were hard and probing. 'And how would I get her to cooperate? I draw the line at taking a cane to a woman.'

'You won't have to,' the Governor assured him. 'Mademoiselle Kergonan will soon be on a charge of murder. I will make it clear that if she cooperates, her case will be dropped. She and her surviving brothers might even get their pinnace back.'

De Graff pursed his lips. 'A woman aboard a warship. The men won't like it.'

The Governor chuckled. 'That's the first time I've heard you worry about the opinions of your crew. You could make it evident that you are smitten by her charms. Captains have been known to smuggle their mistresses aboard.'

De Graff tugged at his moustache. He was clearly intrigued by de Cussy's suggestion. 'Is that a challenge?' he asked.

De Cussy allowed himself a sly smile. 'A challenge that most men would like to take.'

❉

THREE HUNDRED MILES to the south Hector sat in the skiff and waited for the sun to sink beneath the horizon. Just a week ago he would have been happy for the superb spectacle of a Caribbean sunset to linger in the sky for as long as possible. Now all he wanted was for the blazing red circle to drop out of sight. The sides of the boat and the thwarts were scorching to touch, and though their skins were toughened by years of living in the tropics, he and his companions were suffering burns and exposure. Gingerly Hector ran the tip of his tongue over his lower lip. It was painfully cracked. He could feel the sores beginning to develop on his arms and legs and buttocks. His hands and feet had puffed up, his bowels had blocked, and he was afflicted by an occasional headache and increasing lethargy. Dan seemed to be affected the least. Perhaps his dark Miskito skin was less delicate. Jezreel, on the other hand, was in trouble. Weeping sores had broken out on his face, even under the thick beard, and his bare shins were blistered. Jacques doled out their ration of drinking water each day, and with a full jar remaining, fresh water was not yet a worry. But there was none to spare to wash and clean their wounds and oozing scabs.

Dan gave a grunt and stood up. For a moment Hector thought his friend had seen a ship on the horizon. But Dan was looking up into the evening sky. A lone seabird was flying towards them, gliding on outstretched wings. The creature was curious about the tiny boat all by itself on the sea. Dan faced towards the bird, quietly raised both his arms parallel to the water and stood motionless. The bird swooped closer. It made several passes, flying in lazy circles down one side of the little boat, then turning and coming again. Dan waited patiently. Finally, with a slight clatter of wings, the bird settled. It gripped Dan's outstretched right arm with bright blue web feet. The Miskito's left hand flashed across and he grabbed the creature by the neck. A quick wrench and a sound like someone cracking their knuckles and the bird went limp, its neck broken. Without a word, Dan handed the carcass to Jacques. He stripped away the feathers, and while the flesh was still warm tore the breast into four parts and shared them out. The four friends chewed quietly.

'You'd think those birds would learn not to land on us,' said Jezreel. It was the third time it had happened.

'They've got to live up to their name,' said Hector.

'You mean "boobies"?'

'*Bobo* is Spanish for stupid.'

'We call them *fou à pieds bleus* in France: blue-footed maniacs,' added Jacques as he tossed the carcass overboard. 'Hector, how long do you think before we see land?'

It was a question they debated several times a day. They could not be certain that they were heading in the right direction all the time. There might be currents against them or in their favour, and they had to take their leeway into account. Whenever the wind suited, they hoisted the tarpaulin as a simple square sail. One oar was used for the mast, the second was the yard. If the wind died or turned against them, they took it in turns to row; Jezreel on his own, the others in pairs. But even by the most generous calculation they were making no more than two or three knots through the water. That was scarcely walking pace.

'My guess is that we could sight land in another two to three days,' said Hector. The calm competence of his friends was heartening. They were accustomed to the sea and had the steadfastness needed to make the voyage. Should bad weather hit them, they would handle the little boat well. The rest was up to fate. He hoped that Maria, waiting for him back in Tortuga, was being as patient. He was grateful that none of his companions had mentioned her. They all knew that he was worried. As the days passed and he became more and more overdue, she would become concerned. Yet there was nothing he could do except wait until they reached land and he could find some means of sending her a message.

The light was nearly gone. Hector looked up into the heavens and located the Fish's Mouth, the star the Arabs called Fomalhaut. It lay in the constellation of Pisces and it always showed him whether the skiff was still headed in the right direction. By day he steered by the position of the sun in its arc and by observing the pattern of the wind and waves. But these were vague and uncertain guides. Only the stars were reliable. Now he was pleased to see that Fomalhaut lay almost directly in line with the skiff's makeshift mast and that meant they were still on course. Since early afternoon they had enjoyed the advantage of a light breeze in their favour and were making good progress. If the breeze held steady throughout the night, it would allow the four of them to rest, each man judging his two hours at the helm by heaven's clock – the eternal swing of the Wain around the Pole Star.

There was a sound of splashing water. Dan was bailing out the bilge, using a wooden scoop they had found fastened by a cord in the skiff. The little boat was chronically leaky. They had tried to staunch the leaks by stuffing strips of cloth into the cracks. But the hull was so fragile that the planks threatened to split farther apart. Only regular bailing was keeping them afloat. At first it had taken only five minutes in every hour to tip the water back into the sea. Now it was taking twice as long.

They had sighted several sails at a distance since evading the *Sainte Rose*, but had not sought help. There was always a chance that it was Captain de Graff coming back to look for them, and if they were Spanish or English ships, four men found in an open boat in time of war would be hauled off to Jamaica or Cartagena for weeks of interrogation. After a brief discussion they had agreed that their best choice was to head for the Dutch free port in Curaçao. There no questions would be asked and they could quietly slip back into a normal life. Hector had even been toying with the idea of arranging for Maria to join him there.

That night passed as usual. Under a starry and cloudless sky the air cooled quickly, and by the time Hector came on watch shortly before dawn, he was shivering from the chill. He had left the *Morvaut* dressed only in a shirt and breeches, and he huddled at the tiller waiting for the sun to rise and bring warmth to his bones.

When the sun did finally climb up out of the sea, he became aware of a faint smudge on the horizon to the south-east. It was barely noticeable and lay off their course so he waited until the sun was fully up before he nudged Dan awake.

'Do you see land over there?' he asked the Miskito.

Dan shaded his eyes. He had the keenest eyesight among them. 'An island, a smallish one. Do you know which it is?'

Hector tried to visualize the chart of the Caribbean. Along the coast of South America extended an irregular chain of islands. He knew little about them. Most of the larger ones were claimed by the Spaniards, and it was safe to assume that the smaller ones were uninhabited.

'It can't be Curaçao. It lies too far off our course.'

Jezreel had woken up. He joined them in staring at the distant sea mark. 'How far away do you think it is?'

'Ten or fifteen miles,' said Dan.

'I could row us there by early afternoon,' Jezreel offered. 'We could find a quiet landing place, go ashore and mend our boat. Even if the place is inhabited, we would be on our way again without anyone knowing.'

Hector looked at the others, seeking their opinion. Dan and Jacques both nodded their agreement, and Jezreel promptly began to dismantle their jury rig. Within minutes he was seated on the central thwart and rowing powerfully towards the distant land.

Slowly, very slowly, the island began to take shape. It was desolate-looking, low and nearly flat. The interior rose only a few feet above the level of the sea. Towards the eastern end a couple of white sand beaches were backed by dunes. But otherwise the place was featureless. There were no hills or trees, and from a distance no hint of human occupation.

It was a desert island.

As the sun rose higher, the glare from the sea made it more and more difficult to pick out even those few details. Then a thick heat haze arose, and as the skiff crept nearer, the shoreline distorted into an indistinct shimmering blur.

'We'll be lucky to find fresh water in a place like that,' said Jacques. The outline of the island was dancing and wavering in the hot air. Hector joined Dan on the oar bench so that they could take over from Jezreel and row the final mile.

TIM SEVERIN

All of a sudden Jacques called out in surprise.

Hector turned in his seat and looked forward.

Emerging from the haze a boat was coming straight towards them. It was a piragua, a large canoe of local design. The long, narrow hull was carved from a single huge tree, and the sides were built up with planks to make it fit for coastal passages. For a brief moment Hector thought they had blundered on a native tribe. But then he saw that one or two of the men rowing the piragua were wearing large hats to shade them from the sun. He had never seen Indians who wore such hats, and they rarely rowed. They preferred to use paddles.

'Who in God's name are they?' breathed Jacques.

'Whoever they are, there's no escaping them,' said Jezreel.

The piragua was coming on apace, rapidly closing the gap. Some instinct made Hector reach for the pistol that Anne-Marie had handed him. He hid it inside his shirt.

'*Saludos!*' shouted the leading man in the piragua.

The canoe was thirty yards away, and Hector could get a good look at its crew. There were a dozen of them, and all were so heavily bearded and unkempt that it was difficult to tell whether they were white men or native. Two wore greasy leather caps with long visors to shade their eyes. The rest favoured either broad-brimmed hats or coloured headcloths.

The piragua was turned and slowed so the oarsmen could inspect the skiff, and a shiver of apprehension ran up Hector's spine. Never in his life had he seen such a gang of cut-throats. They were like a pack of starving wolves sizing up their prey.

'*Saludos!*' called their leader again, and then he switched to English. 'What happened to you?'

Hector thought quickly for a plausible answer. 'Castaway!' he shouted back.

'Then welcome to our camp!' came the reply, and the captain of the piragua waved them towards the shore. It was not an invitation, but a command.

As they were escorted towards the beach, Hector caught a

glimpse of a musket barrel protruding over the gunwale of the piragua. Judging by its length the gun was one of the old-fashioned but deadly muskets favoured by sharp shooters who hunted wild cattle on remote islands. Such men were reputed to be as untamed and dangerous as their prey.

'Brigands,' muttered Jezreel under his breath.

'Let me do the talking,' Hector said, just loud enough for his companions to hear him.

The piragua beached alongside them as he and Dan ran the little skiff on to the sand. Several of the brigands hurried across to lay hands on the little boat and drag it up above high water mark. It gave them the chance to look inside and check its contents. '*Nada*. No weapons, Lucas,' one of them shouted to their leader.

The man they called Lucas walked over to interview the new arrivals. He had hard, cunning eyes whose calculating look failed to match the smile on his face.

'So what brings you here?' he asked with false geniality.

Hector tried to place the man's accent. His voice had a slight burr. He could originally have been from Scotland.

'Bastard of a captain set us adrift,' Hector lied. The beach seemed to sway beneath him. He had yet to regain his land legs and was feeling unsteady on his feet.

'Why?'

'We didn't like the way he treated us, the stupid sod,' said Hector.

'So you mutinied.'

'We had no choice. If he had kept doing things his way, we'd have gone to the bottom.'

Hector hoped that the sour tone he had adopted would be convincing. The brigand's false smile puckered the scar which ran up from the corner of his mouth and vanished into the tangle of filthy black curls which emerged from under his hat.

'Where did it happen?'

Hector waved vaguely out to sea. 'Four days back. He gave us some water and a little food and sent us off.'

Lucas was looking at him calculatingly. 'You were lucky to arrive here when you did. We were just heading off.' He paused, his eyes shrewdly assessing the four men. 'Maybe you would like to join us.'

Hector was at a loss as to how to reply. He had worked out exactly who the piragua men were. They were sea bandits, butchers who preyed off local villages and passing ships. They obeyed no laws and had no scruples. Runaway indentured men, escaped felons, murderers and thieves, they came together in small bands and roamed the coast. They descended on small undefended villages to rape and loot. If they came across a small ship at anchor they went aboard and slaughtered the crew, then stole the cargo. They were enemies of all nations and were hunted down like vermin. Beside such villains, men like Major de Graff were saintly.

'We're exhausted,' Hector temporized. 'We need to rest and gain our strength.'

The brigand's expression did not change but he stiffened slightly, as if insulted by Hector's lack of enthusiasm to join his band. 'You mean you would prefer to remain on this godforsaken lump of rock and sand?' he asked.

Hector did not reply, and Lucas turned towards Hector's companions. 'What about you,' the brigand asked. 'Any of you want to join us?'

Jezreel shook his head, and Jacques looked away. Dan stared back silently.

'So be it,' rasped Lucas. His hand dropped to the butt of the pistol in his sash. For a moment Hector thought he was about to be shot. But the brigand turned to shout at his men. 'Take anything useful. Then smash up their boat.'

While Hector and his friends looked on helplessly, the brigands removed the rope, oars and tarpaulin from the skiff and put them aboard their piragua. They also stole the two water jars and all the remaining food. Then they rolled the skiff upside down on the sand. Two of the ruffians fetched hatchets from the piragua and splinters flew as they hacked a great hole in the bottom of the upturned boat.

Once the skiff was ruined, Lucas waved to his crew to go back aboard the piragua and announced waspishly, 'This place has no people, and few ships pass by. You'll wish that you'd stayed out at sea in that cockleshell.'

With one last look at the splintered wreckage, he strode off down the beach and waded out to where the piragua was waiting. He climbed aboard and his crew began to row.

'God help any village they come across,' said Jezreel grimly as he watched them leave.

'Why would they want to strand us here?' Jacques demanded.

'So we cannot warn others of their presence. We should be thankful that they did not murder us out of hand,' Hector answered.

❋

THE BRIGANDS' abandoned camp was a scene of squalor. A blackened pit and scorch marks showed where they had lit their cooking fire. Nearby were the shells of dozens of turtles that had provided their main diet. Broken bottles and filthy rags lay scattered about. Judging by the smell, they had not troubled themselves to go very far for their latrine.

'Ugh, they lived like animals,' mumbled Jacques, trying to avoid breathing through his nose.

Dan sifted through the rubbish and came across the remains of a broken musket. Its firing lock was damaged beyond repair.

'This will come in useful,' he said, rubbing away the rust with his thumb.

'To beat someone to death?' commented Jacques.

'With the flint we can start a cooking fire,' explained the Miskito patiently.

'If the bastards had left us anything to cook,' objected Jacques. 'I don't fancy living off blue-footed maniacs from now on, if that's what you are about to suggest.'

'I have something else in mind. Just stop complaining and get that cooking fire started, I'll be back with some food soon enough,' Dan told him.

The Miskito walked off along the beach to where a ledge of rock projected into the sea. There he waded out until knee deep in the water. He could be seen stooped over, searching the loose rocks beneath his feet.

Meanwhile Hector had located the well that the brigands had dug. It was a shallow drift excavated into the hard-packed sand at the back of the beach. Water was oozing into the shallow basin. He scooped up the contents in the palm of his hand and tasted. The water was brackish but drinkable. There was more than enough to satisfy their needs.

Jezreel took on the chore of sweeping up and burying the worst of the filth of the brigand camp. Then he used timber salvaged from the skiff to build a frame which he covered with some abandoned flour sacks. 'It's nowhere near watertight but at least it will keep off the sun,' he said, as he completed the humble shelter.

Within half an hour Dan returned with an ample haul of limpets and other shellfish that he had gathered among the rocks. Jacques roasted the catch in the ashes of the fire, and after they had eaten the meal, which Jacques had to admit was very tasty, the four of them sat on the sand and gazed out on the sea. It was a balmy evening and there was a perfect calm. A flock of pelicans flew laboriously past, not more than six feet above the water, their wings beating in solemn unison.

'Tomorrow we explore the island,' said Hector.

Jacques had cheered up considerably now that he had a full stomach. 'We could be worse off. A few days' rest will be time enough for our sores to heal.'

'Have you been able to work out exactly where we are?' Jezreel asked Hector.

He shook his head. 'Somewhere quite close to the mainland. That piragua was not designed to go very far out to sea.'

But he knew that they could no longer plan on going to Curaçao. The loss of the skiff had changed everything. He doubted they would find materials on such a barren island to build a replacement boat. They would have to survive until a passing vessel rescued them, and there was no way of knowing when that might happen, or where the vessel might take them. In the meantime Maria would be wondering why he had not returned. Yet he did not regret refusing Lucas' invitation to join his murderous band. He had kept his promise to Maria that he would do everything to avoid returning to a life of piracy.

FIVE

NEXT MORNING THEY SET OUT inland to investigate their new home. The day was scorchingly hot under the bowl of a cloudless pale blue sky, and there was no breeze. The still air carried the chirping and clicking and buzzing of a myriad of unseen insects as well as the distant sound of the sea receding behind them as they walked. Everything that met the eye was bleached pale yellow or tawny brown. They picked their way across a barren landscape where thin plates of loose rock clattered and shifted awkwardly beneath their feet. Twice they disturbed flocks of small dun-coloured birds that looked like sparrows. Otherwise the place was a wilderness. Low thorny bushes tore at their clothes and strange bulbous plants sprouted from the stony soil. Each was the size of a man's head and armed with fearsome arrays of three-inch-long spikes. The plant had a fluffy topknot and inside was a small pink fruit which tasted and smelled like wild strawberry. But collecting the fruit was hazardous. The ground was littered with the fallen spikes, sharper than any needle. Soon both Jacques and Hector were limping from puncture wounds in their feet.

The island sloped very gently upwards until after a couple of hours they crested a low ridge and found themselves looking once again at the sea. They had arrived at the centre and found nothing.

'Might as well go the whole way across now we are here,' said

Hector. They went on towards the farther shore. As they approached, the ground turned soft and boggy and they came to an area of reeds. Beyond it, the hot air shimmered over a dreary expanse of saltwater marsh. It was here that they found the only evidence of human activity. Four artificial conical mounds stood on a dike. About four feet high, they were a dirty brown.

'Salt piles,' said Jezreel. 'I came across them on the Mexican coast. The salt rakers scrape up the salt in heaps which they cover in dry grass and then set alight. It makes a hard shell to protect the salt against the rain.'

He picked up a stone and walked over to one of the mounds and struck it hard. The outer shell of the mound cracked and he peered inside.

'Nobody has attended this in a long time,' he announced. He dropped the stone and looked at Hector. 'Do you think we should shift our camp here and wait for the salt rakers to return?'

Hector thought for a moment. 'I don't think so. It could be weeks or even months before they come back, and we have to stay near our well. I doubt there's any other fresh water in this wilderness.'

They turned aside and began following the shoreline, heading back for their camp. On the way Dan spotted a treasure that made their entire journey worthwhile. They were clambering over a stretch of slippery, seaweed-covered rocks when he noticed something trapped between two sea-washed boulders. Wading into the sea he found that the receding tide had exposed the rotting remnants of a small broken barrel. It must have drifted ashore, carried by wind and currents after someone jettisoned it as useless. Dan wasted no time in freeing his find and carrying it on to land. He gave a grunt of satisfaction as he pulled off the rotting staves and held up the two rusty metal hoops that had once held them together. 'Now we can make ourselves some decent knives,' he said.

Carrying their trophy they arrived back in camp in the late afternoon. There, Hector smoothed a patch of sand and traced a wavering line with his finger.

'I believe I know where we are,' he said. 'This is the coast of the Main.' He made some small circles to one side. 'And these are the offshore islands. I can't remember how many there are but one of them about halfway along is known as Salt Island. That, I think, is where we are stranded.'

His companions all gazed down at the sketch. 'What are the chances of a ship passing this way?' asked Jacques.

'Only fair.' Hector made a mark at each end of the line. 'Here and here are Curaçao and Cartagena. One is Dutch and the other Spanish. They are not supposed to trade with one another. But there must be an occasional ship between them, a smuggler perhaps.'

'So you think we could be here for some time?' said Jezreel.

'I'm afraid so. We'll prepare a signal fire and light it if we see a passing ship. But we'd better be prepared for a long stay.'

He looked up and searched the faces of his companions. Jezreel was resigned. Jacques seemed a little disappointed. As usual Dan was expressionless. Hector had a sense that in the weeks to come they would depend on their Miskito comrade.

*

ON TORTUGA a shopkeeper had told Maria that *Morvaut* had arrived in Petit Goâve and was being held there. The shopkeeper had a brother on the main island, and when she asked about Hector, the man was more interested in providing a lurid description of the knife fight between Yannick Kergonan and Rassalle. He told her that Yannick's sister was forbidden to leave the settlement, pending her trial for murder. 'She's lived up to her name as the Tigress,' he commented with more than a hint of local pride. He had no news of Hector.

Maria waited for another few days and when Hector still did not appear, she decided she would take passage to Petit Goâve. There she would ask Anne-Marie Kergonan what had happened to her husband.

It was another week before she found a supply boat heading in the right direction, and there were many stops at plantation landing stages along the coast before she was finally set ashore at Petit Goâve. It was midday and the settlement looked deserted. Most of the inhabitants were indoors, sheltering from the heat. So she was lucky that the first person she met was a serving woman who worked in the tavern where the fight had taken place. She was told that if she was looking for Anne-Marie Kergonan she should follow a cart track that led out of town, through a coconut grove and past several smallholdings. After half a mile she couldn't fail to recognize the cabin where the Breton woman was staying. It was the one with a white goat tethered in the front yard.

The cabin was in remarkably good repair. The palm thatch roof had been replaced recently, and someone had planted rows of vegetables in the front yard. A double line of large seashells marked the edges of the path leading to a freshly painted blue door. Maria knocked and waited while the goat regarded her balefully. She had always dismissed the superstition that goats were agents of the Devil. But the creature's black rectangular pupils did appear diabolical against the yellow of its eyes. She gave a shiver of apprehension at the thought she was visiting a killer.

After a short interval Anne-Marie opened the door. She was wearing man's clothes of baggy breeches and a long, loose shirt of linen. Both were freshly washed and pressed. Maria was conscious that her own petticoat and skirt were stained and crumpled after the long journey. She felt dowdy and uncomfortable.

'I've come from Tortuga to ask about my husband, Hector . . .' she began.

The Breton gave her an appraising glance.

'He and his friends should have returned by now,' continued Maria.

Anne-Marie stepped to one side. 'Why don't you come in,' she said. 'It's easier to talk inside rather than standing out in the sun.'

Anne-Marie led her guest to a seat beside the scrubbed table in the middle of the room. She set two bowls before them, and took down an earthenware jug from a shelf.

Maria looked around. The interior of the cabin was as spruce and well-ordered as the exterior. The earth floor had been swept. Everything had been neatly put on shelves or hung from pegs on the walls. Through the open back door she could see a raised hearth under an open-sided shelter where the cooking was done. A garland of white flowers was draped around the neck of a tall water container in one corner. The only item which jarred with the peaceful domestic setting was a long-barrelled musket hanging from its leather straps on one wall.

The Breton noted her glance. 'The gun was the only item of value from my husband's estate,' she said.

'I'm sorry. I had no idea you have been widowed.'

Anne-Marie gave a dismissive shrug. 'He was no loss.'

On her way to the cabin Maria had wondered if she should raise the matter of Yannick's death. Already it was clear to her that Anne-Marie was someone who preferred to get straight to the point. 'In Tortuga I heard the news about your brother. I'd like to offer my sympathies.'

Anne-Marie poured a steady stream of goat's milk from the earthenware jug into the two bowls, sat down and took a sip from one, before pushing the other across the table to Maria. 'My brother Yannick was destined for an early grave,' she said quietly. She put down the bowl and looked straight at Maria. 'You were asking about your husband.'

'I haven't had any word from him, nor his friends. I beg you, please tell me what has happened to him or where he might have gone.'

Anne-Marie regarded her visitor for several seconds before replying. To her surprise she found herself envying the tired-looking, resolute young woman seated in front of her. Maria was plainly in love with her husband and determined to find him. The Breton wished that she herself felt so strongly for someone that she had the same courage and sense of purpose.

'I believe that Hector and his friends are safe. But I have no idea where they might be.'

'Then at least please tell me all you know.'

Anne-Marie took a deep breath. 'What I am about to say must stay between us. I am in enough trouble already.'

Maria gave her a look full of pleading. 'You have my word that I will tell no one.'

In a calm voice Anne-Marie described everything that had happened on the *Morvaut*, from the time spent fishing the wreck on the Vipers until her interview with a furious de Graff after the loss of his prisoners. The only part she omitted was how she had helped Hector and his friends to slip away. She did not want to be asked her reasons for assisting Hector to escape.

'Surely Captain de Graff turned back and tried to find the skiff?' Maria asked.

'He did. But the boat had vanished. There was no trace of it.'

'Had it sunk?' There was a tremor in Maria's voice.

The Breton shook her head. 'The weather was fine. Your husband and his comrades are good sailors. I don't think they would have drowned.'

'Then what happened to them? Where did they go?'

'I've asked myself the same question many times. The obvious answer is that they set course either to Cuba or to Jamaica. Which of the two do you think more likely?'

'Jamaica. All four of them have had their troubles with the Spanish authorities.'

Anne-Marie collected up the empty bowls and was about to get up from the table when she saw the tears beginning to well up in Maria's eyes.

'Did Hector ever talk about me?' Maria asked.

'Of course. He told me that he was looking forward to getting back to Tortuga because you were waiting for him.'

It was a lie, but the Breton saw how her visitor was drooping with exhaustion, emotional as well as physical. 'Do you have somewhere to stay in Petit Goâve?' she asked gently.

Maria shook her head. 'I came to Petit Goâve to seek you. What I would do next depended on what you told me.'

'Well you've found me and heard my story, and now you are welcome to stay. I'll be pleased to have your company. I don't see my other brothers. They've been forced to join de Graff's crew and are not allowed ashore for fear they might run off.'

Belatedly Maria remembered that Anne-Marie had to deal with her own difficulties. 'What about you? Is it true that you are to be tried for shooting your brother's killer?'

'The Governor isn't in a hurry to set a date for a court hearing.'

Maria detected the scepticism in the Breton's reply. 'And you think he has a reason?'

Anne-Marie allowed herself a world-weary grimace. 'Every time I'm summoned to the Governor's office for questioning, I find Captain de Graff also there. He seems to be taking a close interest in my well-being.'

'Perhaps he's there as a witness.'

'He makes a great effort to be charming.'

'And is he?'

The Breton shrugged. 'He has a certain allure. But I suspect his attention may have more to do with what your husband and his friends were doing on the Vipers.' She paused as a fresh thought occurred to her. 'Maria, you say that Hector and his comrades most likely headed for Jamaica.'

Maria nodded. 'Hector sometimes said that Jezreel might want to return to London. If that's the case, then the four of them would have gone to Port Royal. From there Jezreel could easily find a ship to England.'

'Would you be willing to go yourself to Jamaica in the hope of finding Hector?' said Anne-Marie slowly.

Maria sat up straighter, a spark of hope in her eyes. 'Of course. There's nothing keeping me in Tortuga except to wait for Hector's return. The place is a den of thieves.' She stopped abruptly, embarrassed as she remembered that Tortuga was home for the Kergonans.

But the Breton took no offence. 'You may be glad of those thieves. My brothers were smugglers, and *Morvaut* wasn't the only boat to land illegal cargoes into Jamaica. I can speak with some of their associates.'

'You mean you can arrange for them to take me to Jamaica?'

'Not to Port Royal. More likely they will drop you off at some deserted spot on the coast.' Her voice grew serious. 'You'll be taking a risk. If you do get to Port Royal, you'll discover it is as much a thieves' den as Tortuga.'

'I can take care of myself,' said Maria stubbornly.

'Suppose you don't find Hector? What will you do then?'

The young Spanish woman set her jaw. 'I'll continue to look for him. Make enquiries. Someone must have news of him.'

'And how will you support yourself?'

'I still have a little money from what he left with me. When that runs out, I'll find work. I've looked after children and I am a capable seamstress.'

Anne-Marie leaned forward and laid a hand on Maria's arm. 'I'll make enquiries among the smugglers. But in the meantime I suggest that you keep out of sight. It would be a disaster for both of us if Governor de Cussy or Captain de Graff hears that Hector Lynch's wife is within their reach.'

✳

ON SALT ISLAND the weeks passed slowly. The lives of the castaways became routine. Before sunrise each day they set out from camp in pairs and headed in opposite directions along the beach. They scouted quietly, keeping a lookout for the humped back of a turtle, black against the shadowy sand as the creature crawled laboriously back to the sea after laying its clutch of eggs. The strength of two men was needed to turn a turtle. Grabbing the creature by the flippers, they heaved it upside down and dragged it to the camp to be butchered. On their best morning they captured four of the animals in this way. When Hector objected that this was needless slaughter, Dan reminded him that the turtle nesting season would soon be over. It was better to catch as many as possible while they could. They had plenty of salt at hand to cure the meat and they were building up a reserve of food for the future.

Jezreel set himself to stripping the leaves of desert plants and rolling their fibres into cord to make fishing lines while Dan extracted iron nails from the wreckage of the skiff and turned them into hooks. They roasted the catch – chunks of barracuda and sea bass – on the skewers over their camp fire. To vary their diet, Jacques tried out various plants to see if they were edible. If they were, he baked the roots and stems in the ashes though many of the results were tasteless and stringy. He buried any rejected vegetables in shallow pits and waited for them to rot in the heat. Eventually he succeeded in pressing out a fermented juice, cloudy white, which smelled and tasted foul, but at least had the tang of alcohol.

Towards the end of the second month, just as Dan predicted, the number of nesting turtles began to dwindle. Fewer and fewer came ashore and those that made the journey returned to the sea while it was still dark. The castaways had to content themselves with following the deep tracks the flippers had gouged in the sand until they reached the nest. There they dug for the eggs. They retrieved so many that Hector was tempted to try his hand at pottery. Hoping to make the bowls or jars which they lacked, he made his clay by mixing fine sand and the yolks of turtle eggs. But each time he baked the moulds in the ashes of the fire, they cracked and fell apart.

So the weeks dragged by, and the four castaways fell into the regular habit of sitting together at sunset on a sand dune behind their campsite, close to the spot where they first came ashore. It was a convenient place from which to watch the empty horizon and at the same time observe the setting of the sun and the rhythm of life around them. The same squadron of pelicans flew past in the same direction at much the same hour. The same two pairs of white terns wheeled and called in the sky above them. The same armies of tiny crabs emerged from their burrows and scurried across the wet sand after each retreating wave. It seemed that nothing would ever change.

'It's now three months without the sight of a sail,' observed Jezreel one evening. He placed his hand gently down on the sand so that a tiny grey-brown lizard could crawl on to his palm. The creatures had become their pets. They showed no fear, running up the humans' arms and legs, crawling in their hair.

'Let's see how far the little rascal can jump,' said Jacques. The Frenchman extended his arm towards Jezreel. Obligingly the lizard leaped across the gap. 'Bravo! Now go back the other way!' Jacques exclaimed. On cue the lizard sprang back to where it had come from.

'We'd make a fortune if we could train a whole troupe of these and take them back as a sideshow in the circus,' said the Frenchman.

'Or rent them out in the mosquito season,' said Jezreel. The lizard, now on his shoulder, had snapped up a flying insect.

'I'd advertise them as pygmy crocodiles,' said Jacques. 'That should bring in the crowds.'

Hector lay back on the sand and stared up at the sky. He was beginning to doubt his decision to stay at their original campsite. Perhaps it would have been better to have based themselves on the southern shore, looked for water there, watched that side of the island for passing ships or the return of the salt rakers. Or maybe they should be taking turns to patrol the coast rather than meeting together for the evening ritual. A ship might make a brief stopover, just for an hour or so in a neighbouring bay, and they would be none the wiser for it.

The light was fading fast. The first evening stars were appearing in the sky. He wondered if Maria was looking up at them, and he pictured her, still waiting for him in Tortuga. Every evening at the same time he treated himself to this moment of imagination. It allowed him to leave the island behind, to see the expression in her eyes as she saw him return, and to recall what it was like to hold her in his arms. He was never in doubt that she was waiting for him. They had been apart for far longer in the past, and he knew in his bones that he would find his way back to her. It was a moment of comfort and reassurance.

'Goodnight,' he heard Jezreel say. The big man rose to his feet and headed off for their little hut. Jacques and Dan preferred to sleep out on the sand.

Hector felt a slight tickling sensation as one of the little lizards ran across his face and jumped off. The creatures always disappeared at dusk and came back the following afternoon. A few feet away, Jacques began snoring softly.

For perhaps an hour Hector lay awake, watching the stars wheel slowly across the sky and thinking about Maria. Then, unable to sleep, he got up and quietly made his way down to the shoreline. There he stood for a long while, watching the wavering path of moonlight on the waves and listening to their sound as they lapped the strand. There was enough light for him to see his way so he turned and began to walk slowly along the shore. It was a familiar path that he and his companions had taken every dawn searching for turtles. He knew every inlet, every cluster of rocks, every undulation of soft beach sand.

He must have gone about half a mile when a movement ahead of him and farther along the beach caught his eye. He stopped short. The hair on the back of his neck rose up. In the distance something black and formless was coming towards him, weaving from side to side. Hector was so accustomed to the notion that he and his companions were the only large living creatures on the island that he felt a sudden tingle of fear. His heart thumped wildly as he tried to make sense of the advancing shape. Sometimes it was almost the height of a man. Then suddenly it halved in size. Now it was coming towards him, the next instant it had halted. Occasionally it veered off as if about to plunge into the sea, but then came back and was advancing in his direction.

Hector stood stock still, his throat dry. He considered making a quick dash for cover. There was a low sand dune to his right and if he crouched down behind it he would be out of sight and away from the creature's path. But as he hesitated, he understood what he was seeing in the moonlight. Coming towards him was a man moving at a staggering run. He had his head down and was able only to see the ground just in front of him. Occasionally he fell to his knees, and once he tripped and sprawled on the ground. Each time he got unsteadily back on to his feet and came on, lurching from side to side. As he came closer, it became clear why he was bent forward. His hands were tied behind his back.

The running man was now near enough for Hector to hear his laboured breathing. When he was five yards away, he tripped again and came crashing down on his knees. He must have sensed Hector's presence, standing motionless just in front of him, for he raised his head and looked up. His face was stark, the eye holes black and the lips distorted by the moon shadow. '*Ayudame!*' he wheezed, and then again in English, 'Help me!'

Hector saw a young man, slightly built, with dark hair, and dressed in a torn white shirt and breeches. He looked shocked and desperate, and there was an ugly, ragged streak down one side of his face, black in the moonlight. Hector guessed it was blood.

'*Ayudame!*' repeated the stranger.

Hector stepped forward. Putting an arm round the young man's waist, he helped him back on his feet. 'Come,' he said. 'I'll get you back to camp, but let me undo that rope first. Stand still a moment.'

As Hector worked at the knots, he felt the young man's wrists trembling with exhaustion. Finally the rope was loose, and the stranger was able to lower his arms to his sides. He gave a moan of pain.

'Who are you?' Hector asked.

'Baltasar Corbalan, until very recently the master of the bark *Los Picos*.'

Hector noted that he spoke educated Spanish. 'What happened to you?'

'My crew mutinied. They intended to kill me. But I managed to escape.'

'Let's get you to camp. Put one arm over my shoulder, and I'll help you along.'

Haltingly they made their way along the beach, Hector holding up the young man whenever he stumbled.

Dan heard their approach long before they arrived at the camp and had woken Jacques and Jezreel.

'This is Baltasar Corbalan. I met with him about a mile along the beach. He's in a bad way,' said Hector to his friends as he eased the young man to the ground. Corbalan sat gazing around him, clearly confused. The unexpected sight of his rescuers, heavily bearded and wild-looking in their ragged clothes, must have seemed almost as terrifying in the moonlight as Hector's first glimpse of the young ship captain.

'We have been stranded here for the past three months,' Hector explained, switching to Spanish. 'You are the first person we have seen in all that time.'

Corbalan lifted a hand and touched the side of his head. He winced with pain. 'I hope you can assist me,' he said in English, heavily accented but clear.

'Tell us exactly what happened,' said Jezreel.

'I was outward bound on a trading voyage when my crew seized the vessel and stole the cargo. They attacked me and my sailing master and brought us to this place—'

'Your ship is here now?' Jacques broke in, a note of excitement in his voice.

'Anchored just along the coast, in a small cove.'

Hector knew the place. It was a little more than two miles away. He and his friends had visited it regularly on their turtle-hunting trips. Normally there was no reason for a ship to anchor there because it lacked any source of fresh water nearby.

Baltasar was speaking again. 'My sailing master was on watch when the crew knocked him down. They grabbed me when I came on deck to see what all the noise was about.'

'How many of them are there?' asked Jezreel.

'Just four. We were sailing short-handed. If it had been my regular crew, we would have had no trouble. But these were men hired at short notice.'

'What do they intend now?'

'I heard them discussing their plan after they had overpowered us. They decided that they would come ashore here, bury the valuables taken from the ship, and kill me and the sailing master as the only witnesses.'

'It would have been simpler to have dumped you overboard and sailed off,' said Jacques.

'Two of the mutineers have family back in Cartagena, our home port. They want to be able to return there. They were going to claim that the ship had been attacked by brigands operating in this area. They would say that my sailing master and I were killed in the fight, and the pirates had made off with the cargo. Later the mutineers would return here and retrieve the loot.'

Hector thought back to Lucas and his crew of cut-throats. The mutineers' tale would have had the ring of truth.

'Yet you managed to escape,' prompted Hector.

'We dropped anchor late in the evening. Two of the men brought me and the sailing master ashore intending to murder us. But they had helped themselves to the ship's stores and were drunk. They amused themselves by saying they would give us a chance to live. They would let us make a run for our lives, one after the other. But first they tied our arms behind our backs.'

'Did you both get away?' asked Jezreel.

Baltasar shook his head. 'My sailing master, Pedro, went first. They shot him in the back before he had gone five yards. They took a few more drinks before it was my turn. By then the light was fading and they missed their aim. One bullet just creased my head. It knocked me down and they thought I was dead, so they went back to the bottle.'

'They will come after you in the morning when they've sobered up and can't find your body,' said Jezreel. 'They can't afford to let you get away.'

'I know that,' said Baltasar. 'So I beg you to attack them first. Help me get back my ship.'

'I'm afraid we have no weapons,' said Jezreel heavily. 'We are unarmed. We were stranded here without even a decent knife between us.'

Baltasar looked stunned.

'You're forgetting we have a musket,' said Hector. 'The one we found when we first got here. We've been using the flint for lighting our fire.'

'But the gun itself is broken and useless,' Jacques pointed out.

'The mutineers don't know that.'

Dan was quick to grasp what Hector had in mind. 'So we bluff them.'

'There's a risk. The bluff won't work if all four of the mutineers go searching for Baltasar as a group.'

'Only the two men who brought me ashore will come looking for me,' said Baltasar. 'I'm certain of that. They won't report to the others that they have made a mess of things.'

Baltasar paused for a moment as a wave of nausea overcame him.

'Their ringleader is a vicious bully. If he thinks the two of them are trying to cheat him or are incompetent, things won't go well for them. He might even abandon them here.'

'Then we had better get going,' said Hector, putting an end to the discussion. He had the details of his plan clear in his mind. 'Dan, see if you can bind that broken musket together with fishing line to make it look in working order.'

He turned to Jezreel and grinned. 'You're the biggest and ugliest of us. You'll be the one holding the gun.'

'And where's this bluff going to take place?' asked Jacques.

'As close to the ship as possible,' said Hector. 'The crew think the island is uninhabited. If they come across our camp or any trace of us, they'll be on their guard. We need to carry the attack to them, not let them come to us.'

'I must accompany you,' said Baltasar.

Hector regarded the young man doubtfully. He looked about to faint.

'I want to have my revenge on those murderous swine,' insisted the Spaniard.

'All right,' Hector agreed. 'But we need to be in position well before first light.'

✳

ALL TOGETHER they set off along the beach. Half a mile from where *Los Picos* was at anchor, Hector turned aside. He led his little party up behind the crest of a low dune that overlooked the shoreline. Here he placed his ambush. Dan and Jacques were the first to take up their positions, well back where they would be out of sight. He stationed Jezreel, with the musket, closest to the anchorage, the direction from which they expected the searchers to arrive. Twenty paces away, farther on along the dune, a straggly patch of beach grass offered some slight cover. Hector scooped out a hollow in which he and Baltasar could lie concealed and from where he could see Jezreel and also have a clear sight of anyone approaching along the shore.

Prone on the sand they waited. When the first streaks of dawn appeared, Hector was pleased to see the line of footprints in the soft sand which Baltasar had left behind him as he fled from his enemies. His trail was easy to follow.

For some time the only sign of life was a flock of a dozen seagulls. They landed on the foreshore directly below the ambush and began to hunt for food. Baltasar lay with his eyes closed, fighting off the pain of his wound. The blood oozing from the deep gash in his head had begun to crust. A few flies settled on the feast. Every few minutes Hector parted the stems of the grass and gazed along the length of the beach towards the anchorage.

After about an hour he saw what he had hoped for: a lone man was trudging along the beach towards the ambush. He was wearing a broad-brimmed hat and carrying a musket. Hector nudged Baltasar, who struggled up far enough to take a quick look.

'That's Julio,' he whispered. 'It was his bullet that hit me.'

Baltasar slumped back on the sand, and Hector looked across towards Jezreel. The big man lay pressed against the ground, his face turned towards him. Hector gave a slight nod, then turned his attention back to the beach and kept very still.

The man with the musket came on. He was walking casually, feet sinking deep into the white sand as soft as sifted flour. He held his musket in both hands across his body, his attention fixed on the ground ahead of him. It was clear that he was following the track that Baltasar had left behind.

He passed the place where Jezreel was hidden. The flock of seagulls, alarmed by his presence, lifted off from the sand, flew a few yards downwind and settled again ahead of him.

Hector quietly raised his right hand.

Jezreel stood. In a couple of strides he was on the crest of the dune. He brought the useless musket to his shoulder. Unaware of the giant aiming a gun down on him, Julio had paused for a moment. He reached for the leather strap which held his cartridge box, and adjusted it so that it sat more comfortably across his chest. He was close enough for Hector to see the dark patches of sweat staining his shirt at the armpits. Irritably the mutineer swatted an insect that had settled on his cheek.

'Stay right where you are,' growled Jezreel, just loud enough to be heard by his victim.

The sailor spun round. The sight of Jezreel, wild and savage, pointing the musket at him made him freeze.

Hector sprang to his feet and careered down the slope of the dune. He snatched the musket from Julio's grasp. The mutineer gaped at him in astonishment. Hector stepped back to give himself room, cocked the musket, and pointed the gun at the man's stomach. 'Down on your knees,' he snapped.

The terrified sailor did as he was told, even as Hector became aware that Baltasar was limping down the slope towards them. 'You treacherous bastard,' the Spaniard spat at their captive as he arrived in front of him. 'Next time shoot straighter.' Baltasar turned to Hector. 'The swine tried to shoot me with my own gun.'

Hector glanced down at the musket in his hands. The polished stock was of fine walnut and the brass fittings were engraved with filigree patterns. The gunsmith had stamped his initials on the lockplate.

'Where's Luis?' demanded Baltasar, glaring down at the kneeling sailor.

Their prisoner cringed. 'I wanted no part in this. The others forced me. Luis is back there, waiting.'

Baltasar was bitter. 'Waiting for what? For you to report back that you had shot me down like a dog. My father and grandfather were good to your family. And this is how you repay us.' He turned away in disgust.

Hector prodded their captive with the muzzle of the gun. 'On your feet!' He took the pistol hanging from a hook on the man's belt. 'And hand over that strap and cartridge box.' The man did as he was told, and as Hector slung the belt over his shoulder he noted that the cartridge box was also particularly fine. Riveted to the leather flap, a large silver medallion depicted a hunting scene – a shooter aiming at a wild boar.

Jacques arrived and lashed the man's wrists together with a length of their home-made fishing line. 'Take him away and stick a gag in his mouth,' Hector told the Frenchman. 'I expect his comrade will soon come looking for him.'

Dan went off to scout and came back within twenty minutes to report that *Los Picos* was lying at anchor very close to the shore. There was no sign of activity on the boat. Julio's companion was sitting on the beach waiting for him to return.

They reset the ambush.

Once again they waited, and an hour later their second victim walked straight into the trap.

'Just two more mutineers to deal with,' said Hector. He tried to sound confident but he knew that he would have to improvise from now on. 'Baltasar, if you're feeling strong enough, I'd like you to come along with Dan and me. I may need your advice.'

Leaving Jacques and Jezreel to guard their prisoners, Hector, Dan and Baltasar circled inland so they could approach the landing beach without being seen. They crawled the last fifty yards across the dunes until they had a clear view of the anchorage.

A small skiff was drawn up on the beach where Julio and his comrade had come ashore with their prisoners. Some seventy yards farther out a bark rode at anchor, her sails neatly furled. *Los Picos* was similar in design to the *Morvaut* but newer and sleeker. A figure was leaning on the rail, idly staring down into the brilliant turquoise water.

'That's Miguel Roblandillo. He's the ringleader,' said Baltasar. There was an edge of pure hatred in his voice.

The figure looked up and gazed towards the shore. For a moment Hector had the feeling that the mutineer was looking directly at him. 'Can he and his companion handle *Los Picos* on their own?' he asked. He found himself whispering though the bark was far away.

'Miguel's a competent sailor,' Baltasar replied reluctantly.

They cautiously made their way back to where there was no risk of being seen from the ship.

'I fear that if the two men on the bark take fright, they will sail away, leaving us all stranded,' Hector said.

Dan nodded in agreement. 'Without their jolly boat, I doubt that they'll attempt to come ashore. More likely they'll simply wait for their companions to return. And then, if no one shows up, they'll head off.'

There was the sound of a musket shot. Dan's head jerked up. 'There! They're trying to attract the attention of the shore party now.'

The strap of the cartridge box which Hector was wearing was too tight. As he reached for the buckle to adjust it, he noticed for the first time that the figure of the shooter in the hunting scene on the flap was picked out in gold.

'Baltasar, how good is this musket of yours?'

'My father gave it to me on my twenty-first birthday. He ordered it from Brachie, the gunsmith in Dieppe. He wanted to give me a Spanish-made gun but Brachie's weapons are said to be the best there are. It cost a small fortune.'

'Do you know how it shoots?'

The Spaniard smiled grimly. 'I've hunted with that gun for three years. I know exactly how it shoots.' He gave Hector a level stare. 'But I'm in no condition to aim straight.'

Hector looked across at Dan.

'You are as good a marksman as I am,' said the Miskito quietly.

Hector turned back to Baltasar. 'I estimate the range at about a hundred paces.'

'Aim between five and six feet above your target.'

'Anything else?'

'No. The gun shoots straight.'

Hector hefted the musket and put it to his shoulder. The weapon was beautifully balanced. It was already loaded but he could not afford a misfire. He opened the cartridge box. As he had expected, it contained a dozen cartridges neatly arranged in their slots as well as everything needed to service the gun – extra flints, a turn screw for adjusting the lock, a tiny flask of oil, squares of cloth, beeswax, a priming wire. There were also two attachments for the ramrod. One, a tow worm, was for holding the strips of cloth when cleaning the barrel. The other, a ball screw, was for extracting the bullet after it had been inserted in the barrel. He fitted the ball screw to the musket's ramrod and hooked out the wadding and bullet. After he had then shaken out the loose powder charge, he carefully cleaned the empty barrel. He thumbed back the frizzen, took a fresh cartridge from the box, tore it open with his teeth, and sprinkled a small quantity of powder on to the flash pan. Before he closed the frizzen, he pressed his fingertip on the powder and held it up for inspection. The grains were dry and even.

'Don't worry,' said Baltasar, who had been watching the ritual. 'My father ordered a hundred pounds of best Normandy powder to go with the gun.'

Hector set the hammer to half cock. He tipped the remainder of the powder out of the cartridge and down the musket barrel, dropped in the musket ball and was about to push down the paper of the cartridge as wadding when Dan stopped him. The Miskito had opened a second cartridge and taken out the bullet.

'Two would be better,' he said, holding up the lead ball.

Hector glanced across at Baltasar. 'Aim another couple of feet higher,' said the Spaniard.

Hector dropped the second ball down the barrel, and seated everything firmly home with the ramrod.

'Wait at least five minutes,' he said to Dan. Holding the musket carefully before him, he crawled off to his firing position.

Below him nothing had changed. There was still the peaceful scene of the jolly boat drawn up on the beach, the bark riding at anchor beyond it on the calm sea. The same man was standing on the deck of *Los Picos*.

Hector reached forward and scooped together a little mound of sand. He patted it down firmly, placed the gun on the rest, and sighted down the barrel. There was no wind, and the bark lay on her anchor with the full length of her hull exposed.

He pulled back the hammer and waited.

The minutes dragged past. The man on the deck of the bark strolled away to the base of the mast, where he was part hidden. Hector saw his head tilt back and guessed that he was drinking from the tub of water normally kept there.

All of a sudden there was the loud crack of a musket shot. It came from directly behind Hector. Dan had fired the second gun. The man on the bark immediately stepped back into view. He still had the water dipper in his hand. He walked quickly to the near rail and gazed expectantly towards the beach.

Hector aimed six feet above the target, took in a half-breath, and held it. Then he gently squeezed the trigger.

SIX

THEY BURIED THE BODY OF Miguel Roblandillo among the
sand dunes that evening. The musket ball, an ounce of lead
fired from a hundred paces, had shattered his lower jaw, killing
him instantly. His companion surrendered meekly as soon as Dan
and Hector rowed out in the jolly boat to take possession of the
bark.

'I am forever in your debt,' said Baltasar. He had a cheerful
boyish face below the bandage wrapped around his head. Tufts of
curly dark brown hair sprouted from the top of the dressing and
made him look even younger. 'You must tell me what I can do to
help you.'

'We were headed for Curaçao when we were marooned,' said
Hector. After the burial he and his friends had transferred to
Los Picos to discuss their plans. The three surviving mutineers
remained on-shore. It had not even been necessary to discuss their
fate. They would be left behind when the bark sailed. They could
fend for themselves.

'Jezreel is thinking of returning to England,' continued
Hector. 'Jacques and Dan have not yet decided on their plans.'

'And you?'

'I intend to rejoin my wife, Maria. She's waiting for me on
Tortuga.'

'And after that?'

Hector shrugged. 'I'll make a living somehow, find a home for us.' The truth was that he had no idea what to do next. The loss of the salvage from the galleon had put an end to his hopes of moving somewhere where he could start a new life with Maria, perhaps even leaving the sea.

'Maria is a Spanish name.'

'Her family comes from Andalusia. She was employed in Peru and later in the Marianas.'

'So she might consider returning to the colonies.'

'I suppose so.'

Baltasar brightened. 'I have a suggestion. Instead of continuing to Curaçao and an uncertain future, why not accompany me back to Cartagena? Remember, England and Spain are no longer enemies. I can make sure you are welcome.'

Hector glanced at his friends for their reaction. They were listening carefully, but their faces gave nothing away. Spain's Caribbean colonies had been out of bounds to them for so long that venturing there at the suggestion of this enthusiastic young man might seem foolhardy.

The Spaniard pressed on eagerly. 'My family has much influence in Cartagena. My father is a leading merchant, a member of the advisory council, and greatly respected. When he hears how you saved my life and this ship, he will do everything to assist you.'

Hector phrased his next remark carefully. 'I don't understand why your crew mutinied. They had little to gain.' Coming aboard *Los Picos* he had noted the absence of any goods in her hold, and he found it odd that a small, empty merchantman had such a well-educated and affluent captain as Baltasar.

'I'll show you why they took the ship,' said the Spaniard. He ushered them into the small cabin in the stern and rolled back the red-and-white checked canvas which served as a floor covering. He levered up several planks to expose a hidden locker. Stacked inside the cavity were small canvas bags. They were instantly recognizable as the bags used for transporting coin, and they filled the space entirely.

'A little over seven thousand pesos in silver,' announced Baltasar.

Jacques gave a low whistle of astonishment.

'Every few months my father sends a large payment to his trading partners,' said the young Spaniard. 'He settles his accounts with them in cash. The transfer is my responsibility.'

'And your crew got to know of the money?' asked Jezreel.

'That's right. I think Miguel Roblandillo heard that I was to be in charge for this voyage and worked out why. Somehow he managed to interfere with the regular crew and get himself aboard. When Julio said he was persuaded into the mutiny he was probably telling the truth.'

Hector had been thinking over Baltasar's explanation. 'Doesn't your father believe in normal letters of credit?'

There was a worldly-wise twinkle in Baltasar's eyes as he replied. 'Hector, half the business done out of Cartagena is under-cover. Laws passed far away in Spain forbid us to trade with foreigners except under strict licence. Yet we need the foreign goods and we have the bullion to pay for them.'

Hector looked down at the nest of sacks, row upon row of pesos. *Los Picos* was carrying more silver than they had been able to salvage from the Vipers. 'And your father could arrange a passage to England for Jezreel?' he said.

The Spaniard's grin grew broader. 'There's not a port in the Caribbean where my father does not have excellent contacts and can call in favours. He can even arrange for Maria to come from Tortuga to Cartagena, if that's what you want.'

Hector was warming to Baltasar. Despite his initial concerns, he found the young Spaniard to be refreshingly honest and open. It occurred to Hector that perhaps he should think of setting up as a merchant-smuggler himself. It would be a way of provid-ing for Maria without resorting to outright piracy or plundering wrecks. If it was done discreetly, he and Maria might even live a more normal life.

The Spaniard seemed to guess his thoughts. 'Hector, I've been thinking of establishing my own trading house. Of course my father must agree and I would need him to loan me the capital to get me started. But what would you say to the idea that you and your friends enter a partnership with me.' He made a sweeping gesture. 'Our base could be in Cartagena and we would trade from one end of the Caribbean to the other. Dan would be our agent among the mainland peoples. And Jacques our contact with the French colonies.'

'France and Spain are at war,' objected Jacques. 'So how would a Frenchman be treated in your city? Especially one who bears a mark like this.' He touched the galérien's brand, faintly visible on his cheek.

Baltasar was undeterred in his enthusiasm. 'We turn it to advantage. We'd say that you were sent to the galleys after being found guilty, though you were innocent of any crime. This made you renounce your allegiance to France. Besides, provided you don't come to the attention of the Governor or the authorities, no one will even question your presence in the city.'

'Then I'm happy to take my chances in Cartagena,' said Jacques.

'I'll go along with that,' added Jezreel, and Dan nodded his agreement.

Baltasar slapped Hector on the shoulder. 'Soon you'll be seeing your Maria again. She'll persuade you that a life in Cartagena is so pleasant that both of you will wish to stay.'

✳

BALTASAR WAS still bubbling over with optimism as *Los Picos* steered into Cartagena's anchorage five days later. As the vessel passed before the seaward rampart he pointed out the natural features that made the city impregnable to any attack from the sea.

'An enemy would be crazy to try to land troops directly on the beach. His ships would wreck on dangerous shallows, and if men did manage to get ashore, the ground is so waterlogged that they would drown in their trenches.'

Hector suppressed a twinge of anxiety. He and his friends were entering the stronghold of what had once been a feared enemy. In his mind's eye he could imagine the lookouts on the battlements now gazing down on the little bark as it crept under the muzzles of their cannon.

They turned to port, committing themselves to the channel that led into the great six-mile-long lagoon behind the city, where an entire fleet could lie safely at anchor. 'And should his squadrons try to force the entrance to the harbour,' Baltasar was saying proudly, 'they must run the gauntlet of Santa Catalina, San Lucas, Santo Domingo, Santiago and La Cruz.' He rattled off the names of the forts and bastions, batteries, curtain walls and watch towers which defended the city.

The bark eased into the anchorage and Hector's attention was caught by the spectacle of three huge galleons moored in the inner harbour. Built like floating castles, they were the largest ships he had ever seen.

Baltasar noted his interest. 'There lies a reason why Cartagena prospers,' he said, gesturing towards the galleons. 'As soon as the treasure galleons have loaded their cargoes of silver and gold at Porto Bello, they come to Cartagena. Here they lie in safety, protected from storms and pirates as they wait for the sailing season and their return to Havana.' He continued in full flow. 'Just think of it! Cartagena is the only port in South America where the flota, the annual fleet from Spain, stays for any length of time. Everything from the interior – the gems, the timber and hides, the coffee and chocolate – must pass through this port. That is why four generations of my family have stayed here and prospered. We are Cartagena-born and proud of it.'

Looking around, Hector could tell that Baltasar was right. Cartagena was indeed thriving. He could see merchant ships of every size and type, from substantial ocean-going vessels to small coasters. Some lay at anchor waiting to move to the wharves. Others were already alongside the quays, taking on or discharging cargo. As his gaze swept past the mass of shipping, something stirred faintly in his memory, just as the young Spaniard called across to Dan, who was at the helm, 'Head for that jetty on the far side! That's where we dock.'

Hector thought it odd that he could see no sign of any officials waiting at the quay where *Los Picos* was to tie up. The coastguard at the harbour entrance must have reported their approach. There should have been men sent by the usual authorities – the collector of customs, the port office, and the magistrate responsible for checking the papers of any passengers.

There was no one. The bark was ignored. *Los Picos* might as well have been a ghost ship.

It was evident too that Baltasar was careful not to draw attention to their arrival. 'I suggest Jezreel and your two other friends stay on board until after dark,' he said as soon as the bark had made fast. 'Later this evening my father will send some of his staff to remove the silver and carry it to our vaults.'

He jumped nimbly on to the dock.

'Come on, Hector,' he said, 'I want to introduce you to my father.'

They set off at a brisk pace through the city. Hector was impressed by what he saw. The usual dockside clutter of warehouses and sheds soon gave way to well-paved streets of two-storey houses with neat wooden balconies and freshly painted shutters. They passed across several small plazas. Each had a fountain in the centre, and along the sides were arcades of shops selling food, clothing and housewares. At portable stalls one could buy fruit juice and other drinks. The most popular beverage, according to Baltasar who was enjoying playing the guide, was a milky grey drink made from fermented plant sap and imported from New Spain, where it had long been a favourite of the native peoples. Hector could see for himself another contribution of those earlier inhabitants of the continent. Many passers-by had copper-coloured faces, high cheekbones with narrow slightly slanting eyes, and long straight black hair. The citizens of Cartagena were of every mix of race and colour – from the darkest black of Africa to the pasty white of immigrants recently arrived from Europe.

The farther that he and Baltasar advanced into the city, the taller and more impressive the buildings became. They passed a number of convents and large churches – Cartagena seemed to be a city of churches – until eventually they reached what was evidently the wealthiest quarter of the city. Here the houses bordered on the palatial. They were three or even four storeys high, with ornate ironwork gates and balconies swathed in flowering shrubs. In this sector the majority of the people were white and richly dressed. Liveried servants held parasols to shield them from the hot sunshine and, if they had been shopping, carried their purchases for them. Occasionally a coach rattled past, door panels gleaming and a driver, usually a black man, handling the reins.

Finally Baltasar turned into a street broader than most and came to a halt in front of a particularly imposing mansion. Its outer wall was decorated with patterns of blue and white tiles. At his knock the massive double door with its huge iron studs and a spy hole was opened by a footman wearing a uniform of white and burgundy. Beyond was a large entrance hall floored with marble. It was expensively furnished with carved chests, a couple of small bronze statues, a tall clock. Everything looked as though it had been shipped in from Spain.

Baltasar hurried across the hallway. The far door opened on to a large courtyard laid out with flowerbeds and shade trees and a long ornamental pond. The buildings overlooking the courtyard were so immaculately whitewashed that the glare made Hector's eyes hurt. Without a pause Baltasar escorted him up a wrought-iron stairway that brought them to a gallery running the full length of the building. He threw open the first door they came to and announced in a loud voice, 'Father, I'm back! And here's someone I want you to meet!'

Hector stepped inside and found himself in a large and spacious office. The ceiling with its exposed beams was a full fifteen feet above his head and two enormous windows stood open to let in a cool breeze. Someone had taken care not to fill the room with unnecessary clutter: apart from two large chests ranged against the wall and a carved armoire, the only major item of furniture was a massive oak table. It was placed where the light fell across the neat stacks of paper arranged on its surface. Seated at the table on an old-fashioned Spanish chair with a leather backrest was a middle-aged balding man dressed in a plain lead-coloured tunic with a lace collar. He had a deeply lined face, hooded brown eyes, and an expression of guarded surprise as he looked at his visitors.

'This is Hector Lynch,' said Baltasar breathlessly. 'My crew mutinied and set me and Pedro ashore on the Isla del Sal. They killed Pedro, but I escaped, thanks to Hector and his friends.' He was about to plunge into a full description of all that had happened on Salt Island when his father held up his hand to stop him.

'I am glad to see you are safe. Where is *Los Picos* now?'

Hector looked between the two men. He was unable to see a family resemblance. That is until the father spoke. Both of them had exactly the same intonation and phrasing though the father spoke more softly and quietly.

'At her usual berth in the harbour,' said Baltasar. 'And the silver is still on board.'

Hector thought he detected a flicker of relief on the older man's face.

'I am delighted to make your acquaintance,' said Baltasar's father, turning to Hector. 'I am Alfonso Corbalan. You are welcome to my home. I hope you will stay as my guest.'

His son interrupted. He was still exuberant. 'Father, Hector has three companions aboard *Los Picos*.'

'Of course they too will be my guests.' The merchant eyed Hector, who was still dressed in the ragged and patched clothes he had worn on the island. 'I am sure that Señor Lynch would like to bathe and rest. It sounds as if you have all had a considerable ordeal.' He reached for a small silver bell on the table and rang it. 'Baltasar, we should leave your full account of what happened until dinner this evening. Your mother and sisters will also want to hear the details. And by then Señor Lynch's companions will have joined us.'

A servant appeared in the doorway.

'Miguel, make four guest rooms ready. And send for the tailor. He is to measure Señor Lynch for a new suit of clothes, which must be ready by the time we dine. The tailor is also to send his assistants to the dock to do the same for Señor Lynch's companions.'

He waited until the servant had left the room, and turned to his son.

'There is another matter, however, which needs immediate attention.'

'What is it, Father?'

'You say that your crew mutinied?' asked the merchant mildly, though Hector detected a steely undertone to the question.

Baltasar sounded apologetic. 'Not Pedro the sailing master, of course. The ringleader was a man called Miguel Roblandillo.'

'I remember him. Hired at the last moment,' said his father quietly.

'Roblandillo persuaded the others to mutiny,' said the son.

'And what happened to him?'

'Hector shot him.'

The merchant gave Hector a quick, approving glance. 'And the others?'

'We left them on the island.'

'Then they must be hunted down.' The merchant's mildness had vanished. His face was hard-set and bleak. 'Tomorrow morning as soon as the office of the Alcalde del Crimen is open you will swear a deposition identifying them as pirates and mutineers. Then we can act.'

'What do you propose, Father?' asked Baltasar obediently.

'No one flouts the authority of the house of Corbalan. I want the mutineers picked up before they have a chance to escape and brought back here to stand trial. By tomorrow evening a government coastguard vessel will be on her way to Isla del Sal. I am sure the Governor will agree to my request.'

The merchant's gracious manner returned just as quickly. 'Baltasar, why don't you show Señor Lynch around our home. I hope that he will be staying with us for some time.'

Baltasar was beaming as he left the office with Hector. 'My father likes you,' he said cheerfully. 'Tomorrow after we get back from the magistrate's office, I'll put to him my idea that I should have my own trading house in association with you and your friends.'

As Hector was shown the splendours of the Corbalan home, he allowed himself to be swayed by his guide's infectious optimism. He admired the elegant ballroom with its glittering chandeliers and panelled walls, the dining room with a mahogany table that seated twenty-four, the twin reception rooms, one for formal occasions, the other for private meetings, and a collection of paintings that would not have looked out of place in a ducal palace. All this luxury, he reflected, had been purchased with profits from trade and commerce, much of it conducted on the very fringes of legality, yet so subtly that it avoided the risks that sent men to prison at hard labour or the gallows. For the first time in many months he saw a way out of his difficulties.

✳

IT WAS PITCH DARK when the Petit Goâve smugglers put Maria ashore in Jamaica. Sunrise revealed that they had left her on an open beach. The place was deserted. There were no buildings, not even a fisherman's shack, and no people to be seen. The only sign of human activity was the faint trace of a footpath which came down to the shore through the featureless rough scrubland that stretched inland. Feeling helpless and betrayed, she found a patch of shade under a stunted palm tree and sat down to wait. Sooner or later, she reasoned, someone would appear. Then she would ask the best way to get to Port Royal.

The entire morning passed with nothing happening but the breeze strengthening. The sea, which had been calm that night, gradually became rough. The waves built up, crashing steadily on the strand. She found a hypnotic satisfaction in watching their rhythm, so it was with a start that, shortly after midday, she noticed a small boat sailing slowly along the coast towards her. She drew back farther into the shadows and kept still, waiting to see what would happen. The boat crept closer and she identified it as a humble barge of the same type that had brought supplies out to Tortuga. When it drew level with where she sat, the single sail was lowered and a crewman threw the anchor overboard. The boat came to a halt no more than fifty yards off the beach. Moments later there was a long echoing moan. It was the sound of a conch shell being used as a trumpet.

Soon afterwards a black man emerged on to the beach from the footpath. He was young and muscular and wore only a pair of ragged pantaloons. He hefted a small barrel on his shoulder. Judging by the way he walked down the slope towards the sea, the keg was heavy. He did not pause when he reached the water's edge, but waded out into the waves. When he could no longer stand, he dropped the barrel – it barely floated – and began swimming out to sea, pushing the barrel ahead of him. Frequently the larger waves broke over his head. Maria watched the man struggle, trying to keep moving forward. Occasionally he was rolled right over in the surf still clutching the barrel. Once or twice it was swept out of his grasp, and he had to swim to retrieve it. Yet he persisted, and eventually she saw him reach the anchored coaster. There, two crewmen looped a rope around the barrel and hoisted it aboard.

The man swam back to the beach and disappeared up the path. A few minutes later he returned with a second barrel on his shoulder. This time he was followed by half a dozen other men, similarly burdened. They were all black except for a mulatto with greying hair who looked on. Maria guessed he was the overseer of a slave gang. She got to her feet and went over to speak with him.

'How do I get to Port Royal from here?' she asked.

'Port Royal is no place for a woman on her own,' he replied in a deep, drawling voice. He must have already noticed her earlier for he did not seem surprised.

Tiredness made Maria short-tempered. 'I've lived in Tortuga on my own,' she retorted sharply.

'Maybe. But Port Royal far outstrips Tortuga in villainy. Wickedest city in the world, and proud of it.'

'I'm expecting to find my husband there,' said Maria stubbornly.

The mulatto turned his gaze on her. 'Before you go wandering the streets of Port Royal in search of him, you'd be wise to find yourself somewhere to live. Else you could find more than you bargained for.'

'I don't have anyone to turn to,' said Maria. 'I'm willing to find work.'

She sensed a weakening of the man's indifference. After a pause he said, 'When we've finished loading that drogher out there, you come with me. That's Captain Blackmore's rum we are hauling, and I can set you down at his place. He might give you work.'

'Who's Captain Blackmore?' asked Maria.

'He's in thick with the Spaniards,' said the mulatto. He gave Maria a sideways look. Maria was discomfited to realize that her accent had betrayed her. She was well aware that Spaniards, the long-time foe, might not be welcomed in Port Royal.

✳

THE SAME THOUGHT was uppermost in her mind the following morning as she turned in through the imposing gates of Captain Blackmore's plantation. The mulatto's mule-drawn cart had dropped her on the rutted approach road. On the approach they had passed field after field where men were clearing weeds, cutting, trimming and stacking cane, loading carts with the stalks. Most labourers were black slaves, though there were a few desperate-looking white men, whom she guessed were indentured workers. To her right she could see the simple thatched huts of wattle and daub where the black slaves lived. Ahead, about a quarter of a mile away, the great house stood on the crest of a knoll. She could smell the faint aroma of boiling sugar and knew that somewhere out of sight was the boiling house and all that went with it – the crushing mill, curing house, trash house, and the distillery.

The great house itself was not what she had expected. An austere, square-built building, it had walls of grey stone. The original two storeys had been extended upward by inserting windows into a steeply pitched roof of red tiles. The result was to make the place look functional rather than elegant. Cotton trees and palms had been planted in an attempt to soften the severity of the site, but Maria had the impression that the greenery was added as an afterthought.

She walked towards the house. Three children were playing noisily on the dusty space which passed for a lawn. Two were boys, one about eight years old and the other a year younger. The third child was a girl who must have been about five. Doubtless they were brothers and a sister. All three had flaxen hair, pale skins and loud voices. The older boy, in particular, was shouting at the top of his lungs, giving orders to the others. The little girl must have been slow to obey because her brother suddenly lashed out. He swung an arm at his sister and smacked her across the ear. He was six inches taller than his victim, and beefy, and the blow knocked her off her feet. She fell to the ground with a wail of pain. To Maria's dismay, the younger boy then ran across and kicked his sister as she lay on the ground. He stood over her, preparing to deliver another kick.

Without thinking, Maria darted forward, seized the younger boy by the shoulder, and hauled him back. 'Stop that, you little brute,' she said fiercely. The boy glared at her, his face red with anger. He tried to twist out of Maria's grasp, but she held on more tightly. 'That hurts!' he shrilled and threw a punch at Maria. She held him away as he continued to struggle. His sister lay curled up on the ground, bawling. The elder brother made no move, a slight smirk on his face.

Maria looked round. She could not imagine that the children had been left unattended. A black woman, dressed in a dingy cotton pinafore and with her hair tied up in a bandana, was slouching towards them without urgency. Maria guessed that she was meant to supervise their play.

'Get her off me,' yelled the child in Maria's grasp. He managed to reach Maria's shins with a kick.

'Stop that!' she snapped and shook him.

'What's all the commotion about?' said a voice.

Maria turned to see a white woman, who must have come out from the great house. She was thin and bony, with straggly reddish hair and skin blotched by the sun. She was too old to be the children's mother. Maria guessed she was an elderly aunt or, more likely, their grandmother.

'I was just calming things down,' Maria said. She released the boy, who backed away, glaring at her. The little girl got back on her feet. 'Charlie kicked me,' she sobbed theatrically.

'Charles, how many times do I have to tell you that you are not to attack your sister,' scolded the woman. She rounded on the older boy. 'And Henry, you are not to allow it.'

Maria waited for a lull in the screams of the little girl. 'Please could you tell me where I might find Captain Blackmore?' she asked.

'The captain's gone to Port Royal. He won't be back for several days,' replied the woman. She brushed back a strand of loose hair. 'I am his mother. I can speak for him.'

'My name is Mary Lynch,' said Maria. 'I am recently arrived in Jamaica, and hoping to find employment.'

The older woman was eyeing her, sizing her up. 'What sort of employment?' she asked in a neutral tone.

Maria drew herself up straight. She realized that she appeared dusty and bedraggled but she did not want to seem desperate. 'I've looked after children,' she said firmly. She knew that her statement risked being taken as a criticism of the scuffle.

Fortunately Mrs Blackmore ignored the inference. 'And where was that?'

Maria decided to risk revealing her Spanish connections. If what the mulatto overseer had said was correct, Mrs Blackmore's son was on good terms with certain Spaniards he dealt with. 'In Peru. I was with the family of a senior judge.'

Mrs Blackmore threw a quick glance towards the black woman. She was out of earshot.

'The captain has spoken of having his grandchildren learn to speak Spanish,' she said. 'He believes it would prove to be a most useful accomplishment should they continue with our plantation.'

'I could certainly teach them to speak good Spanish, and their letters as well,' said Maria.

Mrs Blackmore gave a slight sniff. 'Do you carry any sort of written recommendation from the judge?'

'My luggage has not yet arrived,' Maria lied.

The older woman treated her to a glance full of disbelief. 'In that case the most I would be willing to offer is a trial period as a governess. Just board and lodging. If you prove satisfactory after, say, four months, I will consider some sort of payment.'

'That is very kind of you,' said Maria quietly, though she thought the captain's mother was quick to take advantage of another's weakness.

'However,' continued Mrs Blackmore, 'the captain must agree.'

Maria's heart sank. Her good fortune was about to desert her just as she thought she had found a place to stay while she searched for Hector. But Mrs Blackmore's next words caused her hopes to revive.

'As I said, the captain is now in Port Royal. I am going there with the children this afternoon. You can come with us and meet him.'

It was a joltingly uncomfortable carriage ride to reach Port Royal. During the four-hour journey, Maria learned that the children's mother, Mrs Blackmore's daughter-in-law, had died of fever two months earlier. After a suitable interval the captain would be travelling to England 'to look for a new bride as there's no one here remotely suitable', as his mother put it haughtily. In the meantime the children were being looked after by household staff until a governess could be found who was satisfactory. Judging by Mrs Blackmore's supercilious tone, finding a tolerable governess on Jamaica was as unlikely as finding a suitable wife. With every sentence the old woman made it clear to Maria that the Blackmores were extremely rich and snobbish, and regarded themselves and their fellow planters as the rightful rulers of Jamaica. The captain, Mrs Blackmore was at pains to state, was a leading member of the Assembly, the island parliament. 'London has sent yet another appalling man as Governor!' she exclaimed. 'He's forever meddling in our affairs, without understanding them. Not like dear Sir Henry.'

Seeing that Maria had not the least idea whom she was talking about, the old woman added, 'Sir Henry Morgan. He was one of the best Governors we ever had, and a brave soldier. A close friend of my husband.'

Maria knew of Morgan only by his Spanish reputation. To them he was Morgan the Pirate. She said nothing.

'It was a sad day when they buried him,' continued the older woman.

'Was he killed in action?' asked Maria, feigning innocence.

'Heavens no! Died in his bed. Probably drunk, mind you. Had a tremendous send-off. Carriage and horses, and a twenty-two gun salute. We buried him over there in the Palisadoes.' Mrs Blackmore pointed out of the carriage window. In the distance, across a lagoon, Maria could see the outline of a sizeable town. She realized that they had reached the coast and that Port Royal was built on a long, low spit of land that projected out into the Caribbean.

The carriage drew up at a stone jetty where a ferry was waiting. As Maria shepherded the three children on to the boat — young Charles shooting her a look of pure hatred — she felt a quickening excitement. She had already decided on her course of action. As soon as she had completed her interview with Captain Blackmore, she would visit the docks. There she would ask if anyone had seen a group of four men — among them a Miskito and a big powerful man who looked like a prize-fighter.

The arrival in Port Royal itself came as a shock. The ferryman had to roar and shout to force his way through the swarm of skiffs and small boats blocking the landing steps. The quays themselves were black with people. Ships lined the wharves two or three deep. More vessels lay at anchor, waiting to take their places. Everywhere was noise and bustle. The chance of tracking Hector down in this confusion was remote.

On shore Maria found her surroundings even more daunting. Everyone seemed to be in a hurry. People were picking their way through the clutter of barrels and boxes and bales. They pushed past her rudely and to her dismay she could hardly understand the snatches of conversation she overheard. She spoke fluent English, but on the dockside there were so many accents and strange words that she was often at a loss to know their meaning. Only the frequent curses were unmistakable. The sudden boom of a cannon made her jump. Mrs Blackmore noted her alarm. 'That'll be a newly arrived ship,' she said. 'The captain is letting everyone know that he has a cargo for auction, slaves probably.'

They left the waterfront and Maria felt even more bewildered. Mrs Blackmore was a person of sufficient importance for two burly porters to be hired to shepherd the little party through the scrum. Even so, they were jostled and pushed. Maria was accustomed to the orderly layout of Spain's colonial townships and she was dumbfounded by the higgledy-piggledy arrangement of the streets. It seemed to her that a ramshackle European town had been uprooted and dumped on the sandspit. The houses were jammed up so close to one another that the only room for their expansion was upwards. Many were tall and narrow, four storeys high, and they seemed to be ready at any moment to topple forward into the street. Every few yards there was a tavern, and trade was brisk. Drunks accosted the little party, and the porters were kept busy fending them off. Maria's head whirled. Her eyes and ears were battered by the hubbub and bustle. She wondered with increasing desperation how she would ever manage to track down Hector in this disarray and tumult.

In due course Mrs Blackmore stopped in front of a house, located in what was evidently the wealthier part of town. Although as tightly squeezed together as elsewhere, the buildings were all of recent, fashionable design with their mullioned windows and lower floors built of brick, which must have cost a small fortune to import. She rapped on the door with the brightly polished knocker in the shape of a dolphin and a black manservant answered. Maria followed the old lady and the children into the dark hallway. At the far end was a flight of stairs, and the three children broke away and scampered up them, pushing and shoving as they raced one another to what was evidently their customary room.

'Where's the master?' enquired Mrs Blackmore brusquely.

'In the parlour, ma'am,' responded the servant. Without pausing, Mrs Blackmore pushed open a door immediately to their right and strode inside, taking Maria with her. The 'parlour' was a poorly lit reception room which smelled of damp and tobacco. In its centre three men were gathered around a table covered with a stained white tablecloth, on which were some glasses and a decanter of wine. One of them, dressed in a dark suit and wearing eyeglasses, was some sort of secretary. He had a pen in his hand and was seated with an account book on the table before him. Standing beside him was a fat, florid man of middle age with a goatee beard and moustache. He was in the process of reading aloud from a list he was holding. At the interruption he stopped in mid-sentence and looked round in surprise. Also seated at the table was the man Maria knew instantly was Captain Blackmore.

He was about forty years old and dressed in pale buckskin breeches and an embroidered waistcoat and was wearing a turban of purple velvet. He was smoking a long thin pipe. A black servant was standing behind him, dressed in an imitation of his master, with a velvet cap and surcoat with a row of shiny buttons. He too was smoking a pipe.

'Richard!' began Mrs Blackmore. She spoke to her son abruptly, in the manner of someone accustomed to getting her own way. 'I'm sorry to interrupt your meeting, but I need to ask you about Mary Lynch here.' She drew Maria forward so she could be seen clearly. 'She says she can instruct the children to speak good Spanish and I think she can also teach them some manners.'

Captain Blackmore took the pipe stem from his lips and deliberately looked Maria up and down. She thought to herself that the knowing expression on his face must be the same as when he assessed an indentured man recently set ashore or a slave on the block. To her surprise the man with the goatee beard spoke first.

'Are you a peninsular?' he asked.

'From Andalusia,' Maria answered. Immediately her interrogator switched to Spanish. He spoke so fast that Maria could barely answer one question before the next was flying at her. Where had she been educated? How old was she when she left Spain? What made her leave? Where had she lived in the colonies? Evidently she passed the test, for he turned to the man with the pipe and gave a slight nod.

The captain's teeth were stained with tobacco. 'Martha,' he said in a slow drawl to his mother, 'she'll do. Show her where she can sleep above with the other servants.'

The interview was over. Maria made a small curtsy and followed her new mistress out of the room. As she turned to close the door behind her, she cast a quick look into the room. The man with the goatee beard had returned to reading the list in his hand. The secretary was reaching out to dip his pen in the inkwell. Captain Blackmore had taken another puff at his pipe and was staring after her. Maria had an uncomfortable feeling that there was a hint of lust in the heavy-lidded eyes partly obscured behind the curling plume of smoke.

＊

HECTOR WOKE TO FIND himself staring up at an embroidered and fringed canopy. He was lying in an enormous four-poster bed. The mattress was so soft that he had sunk into a hollow so deep that he would have to make an effort to climb out of it. The sheets were of the finest cotton, smooth against his skin and faintly perfumed. He stretched luxuriously and turned his head to look around. All the bedroom furniture was made of massive dark wood, heavily carved: the uncomfortable-looking upright chairs, a prayer desk, a vast hanging cupboard, a clothes chest, even the frame of the mirror on the wall. Dust motes danced in the bars of bright sunshine shining in through the slats of a shuttered window. He could hear the distant cries of street vendors. He lay still for a moment, gathering his thoughts. Last night there had been a lavish dinner with his host Don Alfonso. Jezreel, Dan and Jacques had been there, as had Baltasar's two sisters and his dignified mother. Baltasar had enthralled the company with tales of his escape from the mutineers. Hector had been called upon to describe life as a castaway on a desert island. The evening had ended late.

Hector sat up and swung his legs over the side of the bed. It was such a grandiose piece of furniture that his feet did not even touch the tiled floor. He had remembered Don Alfonso's words as the meal came to an end. 'Baltasar will take you to the Alcalde's office first thing tomorrow morning,' the merchant had said. 'He will need someone to confirm the deposition stating the details of the mutiny.'

He dressed. The clothes tailored for him the previous afternoon were a good fit – a white shirt, light silk hose, a collarless over-vest of black wool closed with a sash, shoes of fine soft leather. He admired himself in the mirror as he adjusted the muslin neckcloth, then slipped his arms into the sleeves of the mulberry-coloured coat. The Spanish costume suited him, and for a moment he preened, imagining himself as a prosperous merchant of Cartagena.

The illusion continued as he descended the stairs to the court-yard. Breakfast fruit was laid out on a side table – guavas, papayas, sapodillas, custard apples. A footman held his chair, and as soon as he sat down, another servant was at his elbow offering fresh white bread accompanied by a sweet preserve. The frothed choc-olate came in a blue and white china cup. Judging by the empty place at the head of the table, his host, Señor Alfonso Corbalan, had already breakfasted and gone to his office. The ladies of the household had not yet appeared, nor had any of his friends. Baltasar was his only companion. The young man was prattling on eagerly about his schemes for his own independent trading house. He saw opportunities for profit in indigo, the price of quinine was sure to rise, there were rumours of a new commer-cial agreement with the Dutch. Eventually he ran out of his list of projects and said, 'Hector, we should go to the office of the Alcalde whenever you are ready. If we get there early enough we can see him straight away. Otherwise we may have to wait there for a while. He's a busy man.'

Hector swallowed the last of the chocolate and rose to his feet. 'Have you discussed your plans with your father?' he asked.

'Not yet. It's better to wait until this little chore is out of the way. Then he'll listen.'

Together they left the house, Baltasar continuing to chatter gaily. Hector was happy to listen to him in silence. As they walked, several passers-by greeted Baltasar by name, and the young man introduced them to his companion. Hector felt himself slipping contentedly into his new role as a well-to-do confidant of a scion of an influential merchant family, perhaps a business partner.

The office of the district judge, the Alcalde, was in the main government building, a grandiose edifice built of huge coral blocks, with a broad flight of steps and heavily barred windows. Baltasar confidently led the way past the sentries at the entrance and spoke with a clerk seated at a desk in the main lobby. They were assigned an usher who escorted them down a long cool corridor and brought them into a large anteroom. There Baltasar explained to yet another clerk that he had come to make a deposition relating to an act of piracy.

'You need to speak to a relator,' he was told.

Baltasar was impatient. 'I'm in a hurry. Can't an ordinary scribe take down the details?'

The functionary notary treated him to a withering look. 'Señor, only a relator may draw up a deposition for forwarding to a judge. If you would be kind enough to wait.'

With a sigh of exasperation Baltasar turned to Hector. 'So much for getting here early.'

They returned to the corridor and for a full hour the two of them paced up and down restlessly. Finally the door of the anteroom opened and a small, fastidious man in a sombre black suit put his head around the door and beckoned. They followed him into an office where he went behind a large desk and sat down. They were left to stand like schoolchildren before a teacher. The relator arranged some papers meticulously on his desk before looking up expectantly at his visitors. 'You wish to make a deposition concerning an act of piracy?'

Excitedly Baltasar began to describe his adventures. The relator interrupted him. 'No, no,' he said testily. 'There is a formula for such a deposition.'

He searched in a folder on his desk until he found the paper he needed. Hector saw it was an old legal document, the ink beginning to fade. The relator found a fresh sheet of paper, scrupulously cleaned the nib of a pen with a small rag, dipped it into the inkwell and began to write. The room went silent except for the slow scratching of the nib on the parchment and an occasional dry cough from the relator as he copied out the time-worn phrases.

Baltasar glanced across at Hector and raised his eyebrows in a gesture of exasperation. Head down, the relator kept writing, gradually working down the page with his flawless script. Finally he had finished copying out what Hector supposed was the legal preamble. At that point the relator paused. He looked up, his pen poised. 'Now I need to fill in the names of the accused,' he said.

'Miguel Roblandillo,' said Baltasar immediately. 'He was the ringleader. He lives in the Getsemani district.'

The pen scratched on the parchment.

Hector became aware that the door of the office had opened behind him.

'The other man was Julio. His family name is Almagro,' said Baltasar. 'He used to work for my family.'

The clerk's expression told him that this extra detail was unnecessary.

'Anyone else?' he asked.

'The third man is Jose. I don't know his family name.'

Impassively the clerk wrote down 'Jose' then left a blank.

Again the pen was poised. 'Anyone else?'

'You have left out one name,' said a voice behind Hector. 'Enrique Benavides – though I doubt it is the correct one.'

Hector swung round and found himself looking into the weatherbeaten face of Captain Juan Garcia Fonseca. With a sudden sharp twinge of memory Hector recalled that he had seen the *San Gil* moored in the harbour when arriving in Cartagena. But he had failed to recognize the urca.

Fonseca had shifted his attention to Baltasar. 'Hello, young man,' he said. 'I didn't expect to find you in the company of pirates. Or perhaps your father has new friends.'

From the tone of the remark Hector suspected that Fonseca and Baltasar's father were commercial rivals.

'What do you mean?' demanded Baltasar. He was looking annoyed. The relator was staring at the three men. He appeared to be both astonished and puzzled by the sudden interruption to his bookish routine.

'This man,' said Fonseca, pointing a stubby finger at Hector, 'robbed my vessel off the Vipers. If the relator cares to look into his files, he will find my report of the incident. The value of the stolen goods was negligible. But he and his associates also set fire to my ship and that I resent. It lost me a whole week of the sailing season.'

Baltasar was gaping at Hector. 'Is this true?' he demanded incredulously.

'It was unfortunate,' Hector admitted. Silently he was cursing himself for forgetting that Captain Fonseca was based in Cartagena. 'I had no idea what would happen.'

'Perhaps he should have consulted his lady friend,' suggested Fonseca grimly.

'But, Hector, I thought you said Maria was on Tortuga,' exclaimed Baltasar.

Hector shook his head. 'No, that wasn't Maria. It was someone else.'

Baltasar shot him a look full of disappointment. Hector could feel the disillusion setting in. Baltasar had been so admiring of his love for Maria; now he felt that he had been duped.

Fonseca was speaking again, this time to the relator, his voice gravelly and firm. 'I suggest that you call the constable and have this man arrested,' he said.

The relator looked flustered. He could never have expected to meet a pirate face to face in his own office.

'Wait a moment!' pleaded Baltasar. 'I'm sure that there has been some sort of misunderstanding.'

'No misunderstanding,' growled Fonseca. 'I can summon my son Felipe to act as a witness. He will swear to an act of piracy by this man.'

Baltasar was stammering with confusion. 'Just give me time to consult my father. Hector is a guest in our house. I will stand surety for him that he will not abscond.' He looked pleadingly at Fonseca.

'Very well,' grunted the captain. 'I will expect your father to hold you to your promise.'

He turned and stumped away, dragging his useless leg behind him.

Baltasar had panic in his eyes. 'Hector, my father will know what to do.'

They left the building and hurried back towards the Corbalan mansion.

'Let me tell you what really happened on the Vipers,' Hector began. He recounted the unfortunate incidents of that day and how he had never expected the Kergonans to be so ruthless. He took care to stress that Anne-Marie was the joint owner of the *Morvaut* and that he had no idea she was carrying a pistol. By the time he had completed his explanation, he could tell that Baltasar's good opinion of him had largely been restored.

Fortunately Alfonso Corbalan was still in his office. After his son explained what had happened, he asked Hector for a detailed account of the events aboard the *San Gil* on the Vipers. When Hector finished speaking, Señor Corbalan sat quietly for several moments, his face expressionless. When he spoke, it was softly and without any emotion. It was as if he was discussing the terms of a business loan.

'Juan Fonseca will not withdraw his charge of piracy against Hector,' he said.

'Can't you try to persuade him?' said Baltasar.

His father shook his head. 'Fonseca is a man of strong principles. I respect him for it even though he is my commercial rival. Besides, Hector admitted his part in the pillaging of the *San Gil* in the presence of the relator.'

'Then why don't we approach the relator? Make it worth his while to bury the matter in his files?' said Baltasar.

'A bribe might be wasted,' said his father calmly. 'The relator could take the money and still forward the charge to the Alcalde. Besides, Fonseca would insist.'

Baltasar looked despondent. His boyish enthusiasm had gone. 'There must be some way out of this mess.'

'There is,' said his father. He rose to his feet. 'The Governor, Don Martin, has the power to intervene. I have no wish for the garrotte to be put around the throat of the man who saved my son's life.' He looked at Hector with profound sympathy and was rewarded with a flicker of wary hope in Hector's eyes. The merchant went to the door and called for his carriage to be made ready. Turning to his son he said, 'Baltasar, it's now nearly noon and I don't have an appointment to see Don Martin. He won't be receiving anyone until the worst of the day's heat is over, and even then I'll have to wait my turn. You and Hector will have to be patient.'

It was nearly midnight when Alfonso Corbalan finally returned from his mission. Baltasar and Hector were still up, waiting in the central courtyard. Everyone else had gone to bed. The household servants had left a few lanterns burning, and their lights reflected in the black sheen of the ornamental pond. They heard the noise of an approaching carriage, and a few moments later the merchant came striding briskly through the shadows.

'I'm sorry to have kept you waiting so long,' he said as he laid his hat and cane on a stone bench. 'There was a ball at the Governor's palace and I had to wait for an interval when I could speak with Don Martin privately.'

Anxiously Hector tried to read the merchant's expression. But as usual the man's face gave nothing away.

'The best he could offer was to reduce the death sentence to ten years of hard labour.'

Because he was so tense, Hector's senses were all the more acute. He became aware that the still night air carried a faint scent of jasmine.

'I reminded him that Spain and England are now allies, though recent ones, and piracy is a scourge for both our nations.'

Listening to his dry voice, Hector failed to see where this argument was leading.

'I pointed out that we had caught a confessed pirate who is a subject of the English king. Instead of executing him out of hand, we could send him to Jamaica for the English to deal with. They would see it as a friendly act, implying that we trust the English to exact punishment on our behalf. In addition we win over their public opinion. The English mob always enjoys a public hanging.'

'But how can that help Hector?' Baltasar broke in, shocked. 'He will be choked by a rope instead of by a public garrotte.'

'For a start Juan Fonseca is not in Jamaica,' answered his father. 'He will not be on hand to give direct evidence. His testimony will not be so strong. Besides –' and here the merchant paused – 'I have a friend in Port Royal who might nudge English justice off-course.'

'And the Governor agreed?' asked Baltasar.

'He did. A frigate from Jamaica, the *Swan*, is due in Cartagena in the next few days, bringing a delegation from the newly appointed Governor of Jamaica. It's both a courtesy visit and to confirm the alliance between Spain and England. When the *Swan* returns, Hector will be aboard. If he gives his parole, he will not even be in irons.'

'What then?'

'He will be handed over to the authorities in Port Royal. It will be up to them to decide his fate.'

The merchant looked at Hector. There was compassion as well as regret in his final words. 'I'll send a message to my friend in Port Royal, alerting him to your difficulties. It is the best I can do.'

'Señor Corbalan, I am grateful,' said Hector.

But he was thinking that even the help of the merchant's mysterious Jamaican friend might not be enough. If the Jamaican authorities checked their records, they would find that one Hector Lynch was already on their wanted list for piracies committed in the South Sea.

SEVEN

THE COMMANDER OF His Most Christian Majesty's frigate *Sainte Rose* was in an unusually good humour. Seated at his dining table in the great cabin he watched his guests working their way through a lavish luncheon. They were now on their fourth dish: fricassee of fresh-caught amberjack prepared with sorrel sauce. It was exceptionally succulent, even by the standards of his personal cook, and there were three more courses to follow, culminating in soursop flan. Captain Laurens Cornelis Boudewin de Graff was particularly fond of soursop. Its slightly tart, delicate flavour reminded him of the quinces he had eaten as a child. He recalled being told that the quince had been a symbol of fertility for the ancient Greeks and they dedicated the fruit to the goddess of love. Laurens de Graff wondered if soursop might have the same significance in the Americas. That line of thought was in response to the presence of the woman seated opposite him.

Anne-Marie Kergonan was wearing a low-cut dress of russet-coloured material. For practical reasons she had cut her hair short and it was a close mass of unruly dark brown curls. De Graff was finding the result very attractive and he doubted that Anne-Marie had any idea that she was in the height of Paris fashion. According to an ensign recently arrived from France, arranging your hair in this way was all the rage among the young women at the Sun King's court. They called the style 'hurluberlu'.

Laurens de Graff beckoned to his steward and murmured a quiet instruction. The man left the cabin. Anyone at the table who had sharp hearing might then have detected the noise of shuffling feet outside the cabin door. There was a pause, and a voice said softly, '*Un, deux* . . .' A moment later the sound of music came wafting into the cabin. Three violas, two trumpets and an oboe – Captain de Graff's private band of shipboard musicians – were playing a passepied, a Breton dance. The captain hoped that his special guest recognized the compliment in the choice of tune.

A look of astonishment appeared on Anne-Marie's face. The officers on the *Sainte Rose* already knew of their captain's penchant for carrying a band on his ship, but this was the first time the band had performed since the Breton woman had come aboard. De Graff concealed a smile of satisfaction. Persuading her to join the ship had not been easy. It had required weeks of pressure from Governor de Cussy. He had given broad hints that his enquiry into the shooting of the sailor Rassalle would be set aside, even forgotten, if Anne-Marie would agree to sail on the *Sainte Rose*. She had negotiated shrewdly, wanting to know what lay behind the Governor's innuendos. Eventually she had wormed out of him that the frigate might go fishing for a Spanish wreck, the same ship she and her brothers had investigated on the Vipers. Her advice on the position and working of the wreck would be invaluable. If the salvage was a success, she and her brothers would be well rewarded, and the murder charge forgotten. Although she was cautious about putting her trust in the Governor's promises – and well aware that there was more to de Graff's interest in her than as someone who could identify the location of the Spanish wreck – she was confident of out-manoeuvring both men.

De Graff's gaze shifted to the centrepiece on his table. The handsome silver candelabrum was the only item he had kept back from the valuables seized from the *Morvaut*. The remainder he had handed over to de Cussy, as promised. He wondered if Anne-

Marie Kergonan recognized the candle holder now that it had been repaired so cleverly. The silversmith was a gifted craftsman who had been sent to Petit Goâve to serve the last years of a sentence for handling stolen goods. He had reshaped the bent and twisted sticks, restored the detailing and fine scrollwork on the stem and base. Now, lovingly polished, the candelabrum stood on the white tablecloth, points of light glinting where the sunshine reflected from the surface of the sea below the stern windows. The candlestick revived a worm of doubt in de Graff's mind. There was something suspicious about the escape of the prisoners on the *Morvaut*. The way they had slipped from his grasp had been too slick, too improbable. And there was something about that young man, Lynch, which made him uneasy.

Captain de Graff's eyes slid back to Anne-Marie. She was talking animatedly to the man seated on her right, the young ensign who had spoken about the Parisian hairstyle. To his surprise, de Graff felt a stab of jealousy. He decided that he would put on a musical soirée the very next evening. At dusk he would assemble his musicians on the quarterdeck. Anne-Marie Kergonan would learn that Captain Laurens de Graff was more than just a patron of the arts. He would reveal that he was himself an accomplished performer on both the trumpet and the viola.

His musings were cut short by the officer of the watch. The man had served for years as a filibustier under de Graff and held the courtesy rank of second lieutenant aboard the frigate. So there was no hint of naval formality as he barged into the room.

'Within cannon range soon,' he said brusquely.

De Graff pushed back his chair and got to his feet. 'Please excuse me for a few moments while I attend to my duties. Then I shall rejoin you.' He treated Anne-Marie to a slight bow and was a little irritated that she failed to acknowledge his gallantry. Pointedly, she looked down at the tablecloth and toyed with a fork.

He followed the officer up to the quarterdeck and crossed to the leeward rail. The ship they had been chasing for the past six hours was now less than a mile away and still desperately ploughing ahead under all sail. But the *Sainte Rose* was gaining steadily. In less than an hour he would have taken another prize. A gust of wind combined with a sudden heave of swell to make the frigate lurch and swoop. De Graff reached up and grasped a shroud to steady himself. He was calm, almost bored. The taking of prizes had become routine over the past few weeks. Governor de Cussy had ordered him to patrol the shipping lanes off Tierra Firme and disrupt the enemy's commerce. He had done exactly as he was asked. He had captured a dozen of their merchant ships and sent the prizes back to Petit Goâve for sale.

The task had been easy enough. The *Sainte Rose* was one of very few ships of force in the region. The English had a pair of frigates but they seldom ventured this far west. The only real threat was the three warships of the armada de barlovento, the squadron tasked to defend Spain's interest in the western Caribbean. But he had seen no sign of them and very soon he and the *Sainte Rose* would vanish. He would head for the secluded anchorage on the island of Providencia and hide there while he careened his vessel. De Cussy had promised to send him a store ship with supplies.

De Graff released his grip on the shroud. The palm of his hand was sticky with black tar that had melted in the sun. He noted with irritation that several spots of tar had also dripped on the immaculate white breeches he had worn for the luncheon. It would mean changing his clothes before he returned to the table. He decided he would rather stay on deck and see out the capture of the Spanish merchantman. Slapdash maintenance of the frigate was the price he paid for having so many of his ex-filibustiers on his crew. But it was worth it. In action they were twice as aggressive as regular navy men. He clicked his fingers at the helmsman's mate. 'Have my steward send a clean cloth soaked in turpentine,' he snapped. The man ran to obey. The only sure way to control filibustiers, De Graff thought to himself, was through a mixture of fear and respect. It helped that his men knew their captain had a violent temper.

'Captain! I know that ship,' called one of the deck watch as he came over. He wore the leather cap which marked him as a former cattle hunter.

'How so?' demanded de Graff.

'Four years ago, off Porto Bello. She fought us off until nightfall, then escaped in the dark.'

De Graff took a closer look at the chase. He could tell from her lines that she was locally built, perhaps in Cartagena. Sturdy and plump, she was no greyhound of the sea. Indeed if the *Sainte Rose* had not been so heavily fouled with weed, the frigate would have overtaken her several hours ago.

The watchkeeper was speaking again. 'We tried to board and carry the ship. But her captain was a tough old bird. He stood by the rail with a cutlass and hacked the fingers off the first man who laid a hand on his ship. Fearless he was, though a cripple. Moved like a crab.'

'Well there won't be any lost fingers this time,' said de Graff. 'Run out all our starboard guns and show we can smash him to splinters if we want. And put a shot into his hull for good measure.'

It took the frigate's crew ten minutes to carry out his order. The frigate was upwind of her target and heeling to the wind. The lids on her lower gun ports had been kept closed to keep out the sea. Now helm and sails had to be adjusted so that the frigate sailed on a more level keel, and the gun ports freed.

Above the sound of the wind and waves and the creaking of the ship de Graff heard the lids to the gun ports swing open, one by one. They would be made fast while the guns were used. Then, like trapdoors, they would drop back to seal up the hull when the guns were retracted. Next came the squeal of blocks and the grumble of the truck wheels as the cannon were hauled forward until their black muzzles emerged from the ship's side. To the Spanish sailors on the merchantman it would be a chilling sight.

His steward appeared at de Graff's side with the turpentine-soaked rag he had demanded. Fastidiously the captain wiped his hands clean of the sticky rigging tar, making sure that nothing soiled the lace cuffs of his shirt.

A single cannon shot and a hole appeared in the mainsail of the merchant ship. The gunner on *Sainte Rose* had either aimed too high, or he was loath to damage the target, which would reduce its value as a prize.

In response the Spanish vessel suddenly luffed up, and a ragged sequence of four cannon shots came back. Her entire broadside. None of the cannonballs struck the frigate.

'Fools,' muttered de Graff. He had no wish to exchange cannonades. It was a waste of gunpowder which he could ill afford. Only three barrels of powder remained on the frigate – another reason to head for the careenage at Providencia and wait for the re-supply that de Cussy had promised.

De Graff took a speaking trumpet from the officer of the watch. As he raised it to his lips, he saw out of the corner of his eye that the gunfire had brought his lunch guests out on deck. Anne-Marie was standing in the waist of the ship. She was with two rough-looking sailors, whom he recognized as her brothers. Like everyone else, they were watching what the Spanish ship would do next.

'Main deck gunners only! Aim for her mast,' de Graff called down. It was a way of conserving powder. The gun layers on the open main deck had a much clearer view of the target than their comrades peering through the gun ports a deck below them. The Spaniard had a single mast. If that came down, the vessel would be crippled, and the fight would be over.

At ragged intervals the frigate's guns fired, each cannoneer trying his skill. One round shot struck splinters from the merchantman's rail. More holes appeared in the rigging. De Graff wished the frigate carried some chain shot: the two cannonballs linked with a short length of chain stood a better chance of taking down the mast as they whirled through the air. But his cannoneers had only round shot at their disposal, and most of the balls flew overhead and skipped across the sea beyond their target. All the time the gap between the vessels was narrowing. Now and again the Spaniard would yaw ponderously and lose off a shot or two at her looming tormentor. One shot even struck the frigate's hull, but it was lightweight, a four-pound ball and did no damage. The men on the *Sainte Rose* jeered.

Finally the captain of the merchantman must have realized the hopelessness of his position. The vessel suddenly let fly its sheets, and the sails spilled wind. The ship was surrendering.

'Bring her close enough to board,' de Graff growled at the helmsman. The frigate was much the taller ship and loomed over her victim. Standing on the quarterdeck as the two ships came together, he found himself looking down on the merchantman. He looked for the limping captain that the watchkeeper had spoken of. But he could not see him. The vessel appeared to be commanded by a younger man. He stood on the aft deck, holding a sword and glaring angrily up at the frigate. On deck his men were milling about. They looked cowed.

The gap between the vessels narrowed. Grapnels flew. A web of ropes began to bind the ships together as the boarding party assembled on the frigate. De Graff took a quick glance amidships. The Kergonan woman was still there, watching. She had been undeterred by the gunfire. She was clearly a woman with courage.

Laurens de Graff decided to lead the boarding party himself. He knew that he looked splendidly dashing in his blue and white uniform. He descended the companionway to the frigate's main deck, and made his way to the rail. 'Do you surrender?' he bellowed across the gap.

The young captain cupped one hand around his ear as if he had not heard clearly.

'Surrender!' shouted de Graff.

There was a heavy grinding thump as the hulls of the two ships touched in the swell and rebounded apart.

'Do you surrender?' repeated de Graff. The two ships were again coming together. He waited for the precise moment and jumped across the gap, coat tails flying, and landed deftly on the merchantman's deck.

The young man had left the aft deck and was coming towards him.

'In the name of His Most Christian Majesty, I declare this ship to be a prize of war,' de Graff announced in Spanish as the man stood quietly across the deck from him.

'I am Luis Felipe Fonseca,' the young man replied calmly. 'The title of this vessel is *San Gil*. May I know your name and rank?'

It was an unexpected reply, spoken in heavily accented, clumsy French. For a brief moment de Graff was at a loss. 'Captain Laurens de Graff,' he answered. He could hear the thuds of feet landing on deck behind him as his men began to jump down on to the merchantman. 'This ship is a prize of war,' he repeated, this time in French. Then he added, 'You are my prisoner.'

The young man stood only a couple of yards away, a look of incomprehension on his frank, open face.

All of a sudden de Graff became aware of a familiar smell. It took a moment for him to identify what it was. Then he recognized the distinctive stench of turpentine. For a moment he thought the smell came from his hands where he had just cleaned them. Then he noticed a large, damp stain on the deck by his feet.

He whirled about and looked at his own ship, even as there came a muffled crash and someone shouted, 'Fireballs! Fire below!' There were cries of alarm from the frigate and a volley of curses.

Too late he understood. The young Spaniard had duped him. Out-gunned, the Spaniards had prepared balls of oakum and hemp and rags, soaked in tar and turpentine, and hidden them. They had waited until the *Sainte Rose* was close enough, then they had lobbed the burning fireballs and pots of tar into the frigate.

There was a much louder explosion, this time from within the frigate's hull. A spout of black smoke shot up from the forward hatch of his own ship. De Graff swore. His crew had left the frigate's lower gun ports open. The carelessness of his filibustiers had put his ship at risk. The Spaniards had succeeded in tossing at least one firepot through an open gun port. If the fire spread to the frigate's powder, his ship would be blown apart.

He spun round to face the young Spaniard. Felipe Fonseca had a recklessly triumphant expression. He was proud that his ruse had succeeded. Seldom in Laurens de Graff's long and lucrative career as a filibustier had he been hoodwinked, and never by someone half his age. With murder in his heart he drew his sword and advanced on the young Spaniard, intending to run him through like a chicken skewered on a spit.

His furious lunge was directed straight for the young man's heart. There was no skill to it, just a straightforward thrust, delivered in white-hot fury. Felipe Fonseca took a half-step back. His own sword swept up and deflected the lunge to one side. De Graff sprang forward again and lunged once more, this time a downward slant. He aimed for the thigh. He wanted to cripple his tormentor and then deal with him at leisure. Once again Felipe flicked aside the attack with his own blade. As steel clashed, then slithered on steel, a sudden sobering awareness penetrated de Graff's boiling anger. He was attacking a trained swordsman. He felt it through his hand and wrist and along his sword arm to his shoulder. The young man facing him knew how to wield a weapon. De Graff dropped his glance to his opponent's feet. The young Spaniard had shifted to a duellist's stance, one foot pointing towards his opponent, the other slightly at an angle, the leading knee bent. His entire body was in balance, ready to advance, retreat, or step aside.

De Graff made a huge effort to control his anger. He backed away as he sized up his situation. Immediately Felipe Fonseca took two quick paces forward and his sword darted at the captain's face. De Graff jerked his head back just in time. He retreated still farther until he was safely out of killing range. The boarders from the *Sainte Rose* who had followed de Graff were standing in a ring around the two men. They had to shuffle back hastily. It occurred to de Graff to shout to one of them to pistol the upstart Spaniard where he stood. But a spirit of pride flickered long enough to make de Graff reject the idea. He had a reputation to protect. Laurens de Graff was known throughout the Caribbean as a crack shot and an outstanding swordsman. His enemies sometimes surrendered without a fight because they feared him so much, and because he was known to be chivalrous and to treat his opponents well. Such notoriety was priceless. It would be lost if the story spread that when de Graff found himself challenged to a sword fight, man to man, he had his youthful opponent shot.

Carefully de Graff eased his left arm out of his close-fitting dress coat. The fashionable long skirts, extravagant lapels and pocket flaps were nothing but an encumbrance now. He had to be rid of it. He transferred his sword to his left hand in order to free his right arm and there was a moment when the young Spaniard had him at a disadvantage. Felipe Fonseca could have struck but instead he merely flicked his sword tip from side to side, almost playfully. His opponent's confidence and sense of fair play annoyed de Graff still further.

The weapons held by the two men were much alike. Both were rapiers. Fonseca's had curling counterguards and knucklebow of steel. Like all rapiers, it was primarily designed for thrusting. But the thirty-six-inch blade also had cutting edges for slashing blows. De Graff's weapon had an ornate handle of carved ivory as it was partly for show. Yet it was also a killing weapon, and though the blade was shorter by two inches than the Spaniard's, the disadvantage was cancelled by the frigate captain's longer reach.

For several seconds the two men faced one another. Then to de Graff's astonishment, his opponent stepped forward boldly, rapped his blade firmly against the captain's sword, and as the metal rang and quivered, launched a deadly attack. The flickering point of his rapier first menaced the captain's throat, then changed direction in mid-air and was aimed at his stomach. De Graff gave ground, springing back, beating the blade aside. He had almost forgotten how to fight like this. Shipboard combat was very different. It was crude and bludgeoning. The weapons of choice were cutlass, boarding axe, club and dagger, used hand to hand, chest to chest, in tight, close-packed brawls. Now he was faced with a rapier at arm's length and fast-moving but just as deadly. He dredged up from his memory the lessons he had learned from a fencing master when he had ambitions to become a naval officer. That was long ago, before he had turned his coat and become a filibustier captain.

Lunge, parry and riposte – the rhythm of the rapier duel came back to him. High guard, low guard, the muscles of his sword arm seemed to have a memory of the moves and counter-moves. Yet he was obliged to give ground all the time – stepping backwards, circling slowly, fending off the attacks. His fencing master had told him to watch his opponent's feet. They would signal the direction of the next attack. But Fonseca was so lithe and he moved so quickly that it was difficult to anticipate his next on-slaught. Again and again, his sword only just missed his target. De Graff was sweating with effort, hard put to maintain his defence though he was the bigger, stronger man. He tried to break Fonseca's rapier with a smashing sideways cut, knowing that the young Spaniard would block the blow with his blade. But the clash of metal told de Graff that Fonseca's rapier was forged from good Toledo steel, almost impossible to splinter.

Fonseca kept probing for his enemy's weakness. Then he found it. He made as if to strike at de Graff's face. But it was a feint. As de Graff moved his sword to ward off the thrust, the young Spaniard dropped his sword hand low and to the right, pivoted on his leading foot, and lunged. The tip of his rapier pierced de Graff's left hip. An inch closer to the belly and the fight would have ended there and then. De Graff felt the lancing pain and knew he had been hurt. In desperation he counter-attacked, delivering a slash at Fonseca's neck, and when that was blocked, lunged at full stretch, hoping to take advantage of his longer reach. His target was Fonseca's leading leg, fully extended and vulnerable. Like a dancer, Fonseca drew back, rose on tiptoe, and then a moment later his sword point was descending towards the back of de Graff's neck as the bigger man was still leaning forward. It was only by chance that de Graff was not skewered. He slipped and canted sideways, saving himself with a grunt. As he straightened up, he knew that he was losing the fight. It would not be long before he received a mortal hit from Fonseca's deadly swordplay. He threw aside all caution and made an all-out thrust at the young man's chest. As Fonseca's blade came across to parry, de Graff stepped forward. As blade met blade with a clash he pressed down on his sword with all his weight until the hilts of the two rapiers slammed together. In that same moment he grabbed the Spaniard's sword arm with his free hand and forced it aside, twisting his sword point up into the young man's face. He felt the tip enter the eye, and then suddenly the fight was over. The young man pitched backwards and crashed to the deck.

Panting with exertion, de Graff stood over the body. A dull pain was spreading from his injured hip, and he was aware of the blood seeping down his breeches. A whiff of smoke in his nostrils reminded him that the *Sainte Rose* had been attacked with fire-pots and was in danger of burning. He turned. To his relief there were only a few wisps of smoke curling up from the main hatch. There was no sign of panic. The fire must have been extinguished. His gaze traversed the length of his ship. Standing at the rail was Anne-Marie Kergonan. She was looking down at the deck where the fight had taken place. She was staring straight at him, her face set. But he could not tell what she was thinking – whether she was appalled at what she had seen, relieved at the outcome, or indifferent.

✳

PORT ROYAL'S provost marshal was in a sour mood. He scowled at the young lieutenant from the *Swan* who had walked into his office and announced that he was leaving Hector in his marshal's custody. 'And what am I supposed to do with him?' the marshal demanded. 'The gaol is already full.'

'There's no need to lock him up. He's given his parole,' answered the lieutenant. He was pink-faced and overweight and breathing heavily though it was only a short walk from the docks. '*Swan* took a week to get here from Cartagena. We have to go back out on patrol immediately.'

'I can't accept the prisoner without a warrant signed by the civil authority.' The provost did not bother to get up from behind his desk, and scarcely glanced at Hector standing off to one side with his three friends.

The lieutenant was keen to put an end to the exchange. 'Where can I find someone to provide that warrant?'

The provost marshal glowered at his visitor. 'There's a war on. The French have raided the coast four times in as many weeks. Burned plantations, seized slaves. Half the government is away serving with the militia.'

'Surely there must be someone?'

'You could try asking Mr Reeve. He's the secretary to the Governor. Came out from England with His Lordship.' The provost marshal picked up a document from his desk and ostentatiously began looking through it. Clearly the meeting was over.

The lieutenant pulled a face. He nodded at Hector to follow him, and the little group went out into Port Royal's main thoroughfare, the High Street. Hector had been in Port Royal some years earlier, and from what he could see the town had got busier, more prosperous, even more dissolute. Many more of the shops were now selling luxury goods – jewellery, perfumes, imported wines and expensive furniture, fine clothes. From one such shop a well-dressed woman emerged followed by a black manservant with a pile of three hat boxes balanced on his head. At the western end of the street the stallholders in the meat market had already cleared their counters before their produce spoiled in the tropical heat. Farther on towards the intersection with New Street, the vegetable sellers were still trying to get rid of the last of their yams, coconuts, potatoes and plantains. A few even had displays of imported apples, cabbages and pears. But the crowds were thinning as the shoppers headed home for their customary three-hour break at midday. For most of them this was to avoid the worst of the heat, though others took it as an excuse to make for one of the taverns located every few yards along the street. Knots of drunks and down-and-outs already loitered near these drinking dens. And of course there were parties of rowdy sailors. They were ogling and catcalling the women, though the common townswomen of Port Royal were a rough-looking lot. They wore neither shoes nor stockings, and their usual dress was a dirty smock or coarse linen petticoat and a straw hat. Many puffed at red clay pipes. Hector observed that almost as many women as men frequented the ale houses.

King's House, the official residence of the Governor, was less than a five-minute walk away. The building had twice the frontage of other houses in the High Street, but was rather shabbier. The brickwork was in need of cleaning and repointing, and the yellow paint on the window frames was peeling. There was no sentry the door and the place had a deserted air. Balchen, the naval lieu-tenant, was obliged to ask a bored-looking clerk in the gloomy entrance hall how to get to the Governor's secretariat. He was directed up a flight of stairs to an office at the back of the building. There was no answer to his knock so the lieutenant pushed his way in, followed by his little group. Hector and his companions found themselves in a small, dingy room containing several large cupboards that stood open, revealing shelf after shelf of files neatly tied with twine. By the window a large, plain table was heaped with more bundles of papers. In the far corner stood a church lectern. Barely visible behind it was the top of a lawyer's wig. Just as Hector realized that the lectern was a stand-up desk the wig moved and a small, rotund man darted into view. He reminded Hector of a robin briskly hopping out from behind a bush. He stared at his visitors through thick round glasses and asked what they wanted.

'I've come to find Mr Reeve, the Governor's secretary,' said the lieutenant.

'You've found him.'

The lieutenant was taken aback. 'My apologies, sir. I had not meant to disturb you without first being announced,' he stammered.

'No matter,' said the man brusquely. 'I am George Reeve. What can I do for you?'

'With respect, sir, the provost marshal is asking for an official affidavit before he will accept one of these men into his custody. I would be grateful if your staff could prepare such a document.'

'I have no staff,' said Mr Reeve sharply. 'They are either sick or malingering.' He peered at Hector and his friends, reminding Hector more than ever of a robin, this time inspecting newly turned soil for the presence of worms. 'Who is it you want to lock up?'

The lieutenant pointed out Hector. 'This man, sir. Hector Lynch.'

'And what is he convicted of?'

'He is not yet convicted, sir. The Spaniards in Cartagena sent him to be tried as a pirate.'

'And the others?'

'They are his friends. They insisted on accompanying him.'

'I see. Then I will prepare the affidavit myself. If you would step out of the room for a few moments and take Mr Lynch's friends with you, I will set down Mr Lynch's details.'

Clearly relieved, the lieutenant ushered Jacques, Jezreel and Dan out of the room. The Governor's secretary darted back behind his lectern.

'Mr Lynch,' said his disembodied voice. 'Your name, age, and place of birth, please.'

'Hector Lynch, twenty-eight years old, born in the County of Cork, Ireland.'

'And how long is it since you left that place?'

Hector needed a moment to calculate. 'It's some five years since we were taken.'

'What do you mean by "we were taken"?'

'My sister and I were both kidnapped by Algerine corsairs. Carried off to North Africa. I have not been back to Ireland since.'

'How extraordinary!' Mr Reeve popped out from behind his lectern.

'The Algerines raided for slaves, sir. They took the entire village.'

'No, no. That's not what I mean. Do you know who the new Governor of Jamaica is?'

'I'm sorry. I have been out of touch.'

'His Excellency the Governor is William O'Brien, the second Earl of Inchiquin. Does the name mean anything to you?'

'The family is Irish aristocracy, is it not?'

'Indeed. But there are many Irishmen in Jamaica. It is the coincidence that is extraordinary.'

'I don't understand.'

'Lord Inchiquin was also a prisoner of the Algerines for some years. Captured by Barbary corsairs. He will be most interested to hear your story.'

Mr Reeve was positively beaming. 'Only this morning he told me he needed something to distract him, if only for a little while, from his present duties. He finds them both tedious and taxing.'

The Governor's secretary was already halfway to the door. 'Mr Lynch, your visit could scarcely be better timed. His Lordship is spending the siesta here in his apartments. If you would wait here a moment I will see if he will receive you, informally of course.'

With that, the little man darted out of the room.

As Hector waited, he strolled over to the window. To one side the rear of King's House looked out over the neighbouring backyard. He could see the roof of a cookhouse, the square box of the latrine standing on stilts, and various sheds and outhouses. A black washerwoman was hanging out clothes on a line. As he gazed down on this domestic scene, he recalled that the only Earl of Inchiquin he had ever heard of had earned the nickname 'O'Brien of the Burnings', from the ferocity with which he had behaved during the recent civil wars. It was said that the Earl had fled to the continent and become a mercenary soldier. He could only suppose that the current Earl and Governor of Jamaica was his son.

Mr Reeve came back into the room. 'His Lordship will see you immediately,' he announced brightly, and led Hector across the landing. The room opposite was much grander than the secretary's poky little office. It was a high-ceilinged salon, expensively furnished with heavy velvet curtains, a Turkey carpet, an escritoire inlaid with ivory, and gilded chairs arranged around a large mahogany conference table. Also it commanded a fine view over the High Street. On the window seat and eating an orange was a heavy-set man dressed in a long, loose dressing gown. His fleshy face was covered with beads of sweat, and there was an underlying grey pallor which spoke of ill-health. Hector put his age at about fifty. As the Governor turned to inspect his visitor, Hector saw that the man's left eye was concealed under a black patch.

'So, Reeve, this is your Barbary captive!'

'Yes, Your Excellency. He is Hector Lynch. He was a prisoner for some years in Algiers.'

The Earl regarded Hector with interest. 'As a slave?'

'Yes, Your Excellency. Though I was well treated by my master. He was an educated man.'

'More than can be said for these tiresome Jamaican planters,' observed Inchiquin. He waved his orange. 'We are fellow unfortunates. I was captured at sea by corsairs while on my way with my father to serve the Portuguese.'

He prised off a segment of the orange and popped it into his mouth. 'My father was quickly ransomed, but I was left to kick my heels in captivity for another couple of years until the funds were raised. Who paid your price?' It was common knowledge that almost the only way Christian slaves emerged from the slave barracks in Barbary was if their families or charities paid for their release.

'I wasn't ransomed, my lord. My master's ship was sunk in a naval action while I was aboard her. I was taken prisoner by Christians.'

'And who was your master?'

'His name was Turgut Reis. He was head of the taifa, the league of corsair captains.'

The Earl paused in his eating. 'I spent long enough in Algiers to know what the taifa is,' he said. 'Are you telling me that you sailed with a Captain of Galleys?'

'Yes, as his assistant.'

'And then . . . ?'

Hector explained how he had been captured after a sea battle with an English warship, sold as a galley slave in the French Navy, wrecked on the coast of Morocco and had then managed to escape. He glossed tactfully over his more recent adventures with the buccaneers in the South Sea, fearing that it would only strengthen the charge of piracy against him.

By the time Hector had finished his tale, the skin and pips of the Governor's orange lay in a fine porcelain dish beside him. Inchiquin turned to his secretary. 'Reeve, you say that our new-found allies the Spaniards want this man tried for piracy?'

'That is correct, my lord.'

Inchiquin got to his feet and walked over to the conference table, on which lay a map of the Caribbean.

'Lynch, come over here.'

Hector joined the Governor and stood looking down at the map. The Earl waved a plump hand over the details.

'Lynch, you've served a Captain of Algerine Galleys. So you know how sea brigands operate. There's a French warship on the loose. It is interfering with traffic between Havana, Porto Bello and Cartagena. Merchant captains are frightened to sail. Our trade is badly hurt.'

The Governor belched gently. His breath had a fetid smell. As he leaned over the chart, a drip of sweat fell on the paper. Once again, Hector sensed that Inchiquin was a sick man.

'We know that the French warship hasn't returned to Saint-Domingue, and there are reports of store ships leaving Petit Goâve and heading west. So the French must have set up a secret base somewhere closer to the trade routes. Where do you think that is?'

Hector recalled his days with Turgut Rais. The Algerine galley had lurked at the cruciero, the maritime crossroads between Spain and Italy, ready to ambush its prey. There had been a friendly port nearby on the Sardinian coast where the galley had taken on food and water. In the South Seas the buccaneers had done the same. They had set up a base on an uninhabited island where they could careen their vessels and keep a stock of food. He scanned the chart.

'Your Excellency, my guess would be that the French warship is based here.' Hector placed his finger on the small speck of an island some hundred miles off the coast of Central America. The island lay within the triangle of ports that Inchiquin had listed.

'On Providencia! Exactly what I thought myself,' exclaimed the Governor triumphantly. His eyes bright, he turned to Reeve. 'I think we can do better with Mr Lynch than put him on trial for piracy. *Swan* also brought a letter from Don Martin, the Governor of Cartagena. He asks for urgent help in tracking down this French raider.' The Earl's voice was rising with excitement.

'What do you propose, my lord?' asked Reeve. Hector detected a note of caution in his voice.

'You mentioned earlier that Mr Lynch has three companions. Do they look like seafarers?'

'They do, my lord.'

'Then let's not waste them! The Spaniards can wait a little longer for their piracy trial. I'll give Mr Lynch here a chance to prove his worth. He and his friends can go after that Frenchman and find where he is cowering so the Spaniards can send the armada de barlovento to smoke the rogue out. That's just the task for someone who has sailed with the Barbary corsairs.'

The secretary sucked his teeth. 'In what capacity will you send Mr Lynch? It would be unfortunate if it was said that you were abetting a pirate.'

'Write out a privateer's commission for him.'

'But, my lord, I must remind you that the Board in London has discouraged the granting of privateer licences.'

'These are exceptional circumstances,' Inchiquin said firmly. 'Jamaica is stripped of good men. Here are four active seamen, experienced and available. There is no need for delay. Write out Mr Lynch's privateer commission now. Send a copy to London for the Board's approval. Meanwhile Mr Lynch and his colleagues can get on with the job.'

'He will need a ship for the task,' said the secretary. Once again Hector had the impression that Reeve was seeking to restrain the Earl's enthusiasm.

'There's that smugglers' vessel we captured just last week. Mr Lynch can use that.'

'Yes, my lord.' Mr Reeve seemed resigned to accepting his master's instruction. 'But I would be remiss in my duty if I did not remind you that if the planters get to hear of this, they will be quick to complain to London that they were not consulted.'

'Then let it be done discreetly. On my own sole recommendation.' The Earl sat down heavily in a chair, mopping his face. The underlying greyish pallor was very noticeable.

'Yes, my lord, it will be done,' murmured Reeve and, taking Hector by the elbow, steered him out of the room.

The secretary did not utter a word until he had re-entered his office. 'Mr Lynch, I'm afraid the Governor sometimes gets carried away by his schemes. He is difficult to deflect,' he said apologetically. 'He does not realize that there are limitations on his authority and that the planters here will seek to undo him. Alas, he is not popular with them.'

'So you will delay the commission?' asked Hector. His hopes had risen while hearing the Earl's scheme.

'I must of course carry out His Lordship's instructions,' said Reeve. 'But I warn you that our resources are overstretched. Our able-bodied men are already in the militia. The Navy has taken the best of the sailors. You will have to recruit your own crew from what is left over.'

'And what is this about a smugglers' ship?'

Reeve spread his hands dismissively. 'The *Speedy Return*. We captured her from some smugglers very recently. I am not a seafaring man myself so I cannot say whether it is suitable for the task. But she is all there is.' He searched through a file until he found the writ for the seizure of the *Speedy Return* and disappeared with it behind his writing desk. Moments later, he reappeared. 'Careful how you handle it. The ink is still wet. I've endorsed the warrant to say that you have charge of the vessel.'

'I am truly grateful to you. I will not disappoint His Lordship's trust in me,' said Hector as he accepted the document. Events were moving so fast that he was only just getting over the fact that he no longer had to wait in Port Royal for a trial to begin.

'Think nothing of it. If you call back here tomorrow in the morning, I will have your privateering licence drawn up and signed by His Excellency.'

The secretary gestured towards the piles of documents awaiting his attention. 'I hope you will excuse me, Mr Lynch, but I must ask you to see your own way out. Please ask that navy lieutenant to step into my office. I will tell him that the Governor has personally accepted your parole and he may return to duty on his ship.'

Hector found Balchen waiting with Dan and the others in the gloomy entrance hall. He told the lieutenant that the Governor's secretary wished to speak with him, and as soon as the lieutenant was safely out of earshot he informed his friends of the extraordinary turn of events.

There was a stunned silence. Then Jacques spoke up. 'Hector, you astonish me. We came here expecting to leave you in civil custody awaiting trial for piracy. An hour later you tell us that you are about to be commissioned as a privateer and have been given a vessel.'

'Not so fast,' said Hector. 'The Governor didn't say who commands that mysterious French raider we are chasing after. Maybe he doesn't know. But from everything I heard I can guess who it is. Our old friend Laurens de Graff.'

EIGHT

THE FOUR OF THEM decided to celebrate. The Three Mariners, a waterfront tavern, was only a few paces from King's House and Don Alfonso had generously provided them with a purse of silver pesos for their expenses when they reached Port Royal. The taproom was packed with noonday drinkers, and the hubbub of conversation was so loud that Jacques had difficulty making himself understood when he insisted on a glass of claret rather than the beer the others chose. The four of them settled down at a table with their drinks.

'What sort of vessel are we to use?' asked Jezreel.

'All that Reeve told me is that the ship is called the *Speedy Return*,' said Hector. He had to raise his voice above the raucous singing of a party of dock workers. They had lurched into the tavern already drunk after deliberately breaking open a barrel of spirits they were loading.

'Let's hope that she's as fast as her name. If we manage to find de Graff's hideout, we'll need to get away quick if he spots us,' said Dan.

'She could be quick . . . in the right hands,' said a voice. All four of them turned to see the stranger. He sat by himself at the next table, a man of about forty, burly, hard-bitten and with the indefinable air of a mariner. He had short, dark, tightly curled hair, bloodshot eyes, and a deep tan which, on closer inspection, proved to be his natural skin colour. Hector guessed that the Spaniards would have called him a 'terceron', the son of one white parent and a mulatto.

'Have you sailed on her?' asked Dan.

'One trip only,' answered their neighbour. 'I'd have screwed a couple of extra knots out of her, but her captain was a dolt. Now his crew will suffer for his stupidity.'

'You don't think much of him.'

The stranger shrugged. 'The idiot put up a fight when the Navy intercepted him on a smuggling run. One of the boarding party was killed in the scuffle. Chief Justice Barnard will decide the sentence, and he's a hard one.'

'Where can we find the *Speedy Return* now?' asked Hector. 'My friends and I would like to take a look at her.'

'You'll find her tied up at King's Wharf. She's the brigantine-rigged pink.'

'I'll buy you another drink if you'll come along with us and tell us what you know about the ship.'

The stranger gave him a disdainful glance. 'Hoping to buy her cheap as a condemned prize?'

Hector shook his head. 'No. My friends and I will be sailing on her soon.'

'And who's to be the captain?'

'I am.'

The bloodshot eyes regarded Hector shrewdly. 'So you might be needing a sailing master?'

Hector felt he was being rushed. There was something about the stranger which was vaguely unsettling. 'Maybe. Depends if he's the right man.'

'Then you don't need to buy me another drink. I'll take you to see the *Speedy Return* just as soon as you're ready. My name is Henry Bartaboa.'

✳

A SHORT WHILE LATER Bartaboa was leading them along the quay. As they threaded a path through the bustle of porters and wharfingers and the clutter of sails, ropes, boxes, barrels and general litter, Hector managed to extract a few more details about their guide. Bartaboa was Jamaican born and his father had once owned an ale house in Port Royal. At an early age he had gone to sea and served in the Navy. For some unspecified demeanour – Hector suspected ill-discipline – he had been dismissed and gone to work on the sloops that traded up to Boston and New York. One thing was clear: with every sentence Henry Bartaboa revealed an intimate knowledge of ship handling and Caribbean sailing conditions.

They reached the farthest point of the quay where it ended at the foot of the curtain wall of Fort James.

'There she is,' said Bartaboa. He nodded towards a small two-masted vessel tied to the dock. To Hector's eye the *Speedy Return* had an odd shape. Her hull narrowed to a very thin stern, and on top of it the shipwrights had built a broad poop deck, which extended out sideways over the sea and made her look out of proportion.

'Built in Curaçao for sure,' Bartaboa was saying. 'That's a pink's hull. No mistaking the skinny tail. Typically Dutch. But the brigantine rig doesn't suit her. Would be better to have a second set of square sails instead of that gaff and boom.'

'And what would that achieve?' asked Jacques. The ex-pickpocket from Paris was utterly bemused by the nautical jargon.

'It would turn her into a brig, of course,' answered the Jamaican. His tone indicated that he thought the Frenchman was an ignoramus.

'We'll take a closer look,' said Hector. There was no watchman to be seen, and no one aboard the pink, so they clambered on to the ship. Everything about her appeared to be in good working order – ropes, sails, ground tackle. It was what Hector had expected. A smuggling vessel needed to be kept in good trim if it was to escape its pursuers, and the *Speedy Return* had only recently been captured.

'How come she was taken?' he asked Bartaboa.

'That blockhead of a captain agreed to pick up a cargo of rum from the arse end of a bay, not thinking that he could find himself trapped.' The Jamaican slapped the breech of one of the dozen six-pounder cannon lined up on deck. 'As if these were enough for a gun battle against a frigate.' He looked Hector straight in the eye. 'Well, what do you think, captain? Are you going to need a sailing master for your new command?'

Hector let the question hang. 'You haven't told me why you want to ship out, and you haven't even asked where we are headed.'

'No need to,' said Bartaboa. 'If I stay around Port Royal I'll be conscripted into the militia or made to serve on one of the Navy ships. I've had enough of that already.'

Hector came to a decision. 'I would be glad to have you join my crew. But I don't yet know what I can pay. I'm promised a privateering licence and the details are unclear.'

Bartaboa smiled sardonically. 'The war with the French must be going badly. The planters won't be happy to hear the government is handing out privateers' papers. They think a privateer is just as likely to turn pirate and steal their cargoes.'

Hector heard the echo of Reeve's warning. 'For that reason you are not to speak about the commission to anyone. We sail as soon as we have found sufficient crew.'

The new sailing master glanced towards the quayside. 'Then you could also take on my friend over there.'

Hector had been aware that a tall scarecrow of a man dressed in a clerical garb of long dark coat and low-crowned black hat had been following them at a distance ever since they had left the Three Mariners. Now he was standing on the quay.

'Simeon, come over!' shouted Bartaboa. Lowering his voice, he added, 'Don't be put off by his manner of speaking, captain, nor by his cloth. Simeon Watson was once an artillery man.'

The gangling stranger scrambled on to the deck of the pink. Hector noticed that the soles of the man's scuffed buckled shoes were coming apart from the uppers, and that his stockings were torn.

'The Reverend Simeon Watson at your service,' said the newcomer. He swept off his hat and bowed, exposing a scalp mottled with brown patches and draped with a few long strands of grey hair. His voice was rich and mellifluous, each word beautifully enunciated. It must have suited the pulpit.

'The captain is taking on crew,' Bartaboa told him.

'Then I am even more at your service, sir,' said this strange creature, bowing again.

Hector recovered from his astonishment. 'Mr Bartaboa tells me that you were once a gunner.'

'Sakers and demi-culverins were my wards before I took the cloth,' intoned the clergyman. His eyes flicked towards the pink's modest armament.

'Don't you have parishioners to look after here in Jamaica?' asked Hector.

'Sadly I am no longer able to minister to them,' Watson replied.

Bartaboa interrupted. 'His sermons cause some resentment. He would be well advised to stand for the offing.'

'As my good friend so nautically puts it, it would be in my best interest to leave the island for a while,' said the clergyman.

'This ship does need a gunner. But as I've explained to Mr Bartaboa, any payment is doubtful until I have received further instructions,' said Hector.

'Even the slightest recompense will be an adequate stipend,' said the clergyman. He replaced his hat and turned to look along the length of the little ship.

Hector wondered exactly what sort of trouble made the Reverend Simeon Watson so keen to find his berth immediately. But the chance to add a gunner to his fledgling crew was too good to ignore. Besides, he recalled that he himself and his friends had nowhere to stay while in Port Royal. It made sense to start using the pink as their base immediately.

'Then it is settled. From this moment we regard the *Speedy Return* as our home. Mr Bartaboa is to prepare a list of naval stores he may need. The Reverend Watson will do the same for gunner's supplies. Dan can help me obtain what is required by them. Jacques, I am putting you in charge of victualling.'

'And what about me?' asked Jezreel.

'I'm giving you a more delicate task. We need at least ten more men if we are to serve all the guns and handle the ship to best advantage. Go about the town and see if you can persuade the right men to join us. But do it very, very quietly. Try not to attract attention to yourself.'

＊

IT WAS DIFFICULT for someone over six foot tall and with a face battered by years of prize-fighting to remain inconspicuous. But Jezreel persevered at his task for a full week. On Hector's instructions he avoided the taverns for fear of getting into the sort of amiable conversation which would end up with him being asked awkward questions about what he was doing in Port Royal. Instead he loitered at the various markets, hung about the dockside, mingled with congregations as they left church. He was hoping to strike up casual conversations with men who looked as though they might join the *Speedy Return*. But the results of his efforts were meagre. He enlisted just three men. The first was a tailor's assistant disgruntled with his master's failure to pay his rightful wages. Jezreel hoped he might be useful as a sailmaker once he was on board. The other two were discharged sailors. However, one of them had lost all the fingers on his left hand as well as the thumb of his right hand. He could scarcely grasp a rope.

It was on the eighth day of his search for recruits that Jezreel left the ship soon after daybreak aware that Hector was growing increasingly fretful. Mr Reeve, the Governor's secretary, had written out his privateer's commission, though he had been worryingly vague about its terms. He had also provided an order which allowed Bartaboa and the Reverend Watson to draw on the Navy stores for gunpowder and shot, provisions, cordage and spare spars. All was ready and loaded. The pink only lacked crew.

The morning was hot and sultry and there was a heaviness in the air which warned of a thunderstorm later in the day. Jezreel paused in front of a vintner's shop window in the High Street, taking advantage of his reflection in the glass to adjust his neck-cloth to sit more loosely. Through the thick, distorting glass panes he could see bottles of Rhenish wine, Madeira, sherry, port, Canary and half a dozen types of brandy. There was a slightly different atmosphere in the town that day. The gangs of street children were more agitated than usual. They were darting here and there and seemed readier to fight and scuffle, quicker with their taunts and quarrels. They reminded Jezreel of terrier puppies with their nasty high-pitched yapping and needle-sharp teeth.

Reaching the central market, he noted that the shoppers also appeared to be on edge. They were hurrying as if they wanted to complete their purchases as quickly as possible. He watched a woman whom he guessed was the housekeeper for one of the wealthy merchant-planters as she bought two parrots at a poultry stall. Doubtless she would wring the birds' necks, pluck and prepare them as a meal for her master's family. She paid as if the coins in her purse were hot to the touch and did not even pause to double check the change. A little farther on a widow who he knew ran a boarding house was haggling over the price of yams. The widow always bargained, but it seemed to Jezreel that today she negotiated more briskly than usual. He was about to saunter off towards the waterfront, hoping to encounter another out-of-work sailor, when he heard the distant beat of a drum. It came from the direction of the parade ground at the farthest end of the High Street. Here the military engineers had built a fort and palisade across the neck of the sand spit on which Port Royal was built.

For a brief moment Jezreel thought that the French had landed and the drumbeat was a call to arms. Then he recognized the regular steady tapping. It was the sound he had heard so often at fairgrounds in the days when he gave exhibition fights with backsword or fists against all comers. It was a drummer announcing an event.

'What's going on?' he asked a passer-by.

The man, a butcher's assistant judging by the streaks of dried gore on the front of his apron, stared at him in surprise. 'It's the tune for the hempen jig. You'd better hurry if you want a good view,' he answered cheerfully.

'Who's to be hanged?' Living quietly aboard the *Speedy Return* he and his friends had been cut off from the town gossip.

'Two brace of pirates,' said the man with some relish. 'Haven't had such a good show since the Navy took to stringing them up while still out at sea. It's not the same if they are already dangling at the yard arm when brought into port. All the fun is gone.'

The man rushed off, and Jezreel followed at a more deliberate pace. He knew now why the street urchins had reminded him of terrier puppies. Terriers were bred for rat fights in front of howling audiences.

The tapping of the drum grew louder as Jezreel approached the parade ground. He joined the steady stream of townsfolk all heading in the same direction. He saw tradesmen, clerks, apprentices, shopkeepers, sailors, potmen, off-duty soldiers, idlers and storemen. Men far outnumbered women. Nevertheless there were a number of Port Royal's sluts. They were tying on their sun hats as they headed for the entertainment. The more fashionable among them hoisted gaily coloured parasols. Everyone was in a holiday mood, exchanging greetings and swapping jokes.

When he had first arrived in London as a prize-fighter, Jezreel had attended a public execution. It had been a mass hanging, five men convicted of crimes ranging from murder to repeated larceny. He had gone with a couple of toughs from the prize ring, and on the way they had stopped off for several glasses of gin. By the time they had reached the Tyburn gallows, the five condemned men were already standing on the back of an open cart, which was drawn up under a triangle of heavy beams supported on thick upright posts. The men had nooses around their necks, the end of each rope fastened to a stout bar above their heads. As Jezreel and his companions jostled to get a good view, the prison official gave an order, and the carter had whipped up his horse. The cart moved away, leaving the victims dangling. Jezreel could still picture them kicking and struggling, hear the awful gurgling sounds as they fought for breath, and see the dark urine stains spreading on their breeches.

So he was puzzled on arriving at the parade ground of Port Royal to find that a wooden stage had been erected instead of a gallows. It was as though the crowd had come to watch the performance of a play. Only when he studied the structure more closely did he see that the platform was not deep enough to be a stage, and what he had taken to be the rail for the front curtain was in fact a heavy timber bar.

The crowd was growing thicker, forming a close-packed mass which could advance no farther. With his great height Jezreel was able to see over their heads. A line of soldiers sweating in their heavy red coats was holding back the spectators from coming too close to the stage. Off to one side the drummer was still tapping away steadily. Occasionally he allowed himself a rapid tattoo. After perhaps ten minutes a low cheer went up, and the onlookers parted enough to allow a small group of men to walk towards the wooden scaffold. Jezreel recognized the provost marshal. He led the way, followed by four men with their arms bound in front of them. They were bare-headed and dressed in dirty canvas breeches and loose shirts. One of them wore a moth-eaten officer's jacket, flapping open as the buttons were missing. They all had halters around their necks, the loose ends of the ropes looped around their shoulders. On each side of the prisoners walked guards carrying staves.

'Bloody villains!' shouted someone in the crowd. There was some half-hearted hissing and booing. An urchin darted out of the crowd and flung a stone at one of the prisoners. A guard dealt the boy a sharp blow with the butt end of his stave. The crowd laughed.

Several paces behind the little group walked a priest. For a moment Jezreel was startled to think that it was the Reverend Simeon Watson. The man wore the same black clothes and low-crowned hat. The white collar tabs were bright on his chest. But this priest was shorter and not so thin and spindly. Also he had chosen to wear a short wig under his hat. He held a Bible in one hand, and was fanning himself with a palm leaf fan with the other.

The little group reached the stage and halted. There was a brisk final tattoo by the drummer. The crowd fell silent except for some rude noises from a group of urchins who were pretending to be choking. The marshal faced the crowd and read out from a document in his hand. Jezreel was too far away but he presumed it was the sentence of death passed by Chief Justice Barnard.

'If Sir Henry could see this, he'd be turning in his grave,' said an old man on Jezreel's left. He was addressing his equally ancient companion. By the look of them they had both been at sea for most of their working lives.

'Balderdash! You forget Morgan turned his coat and hanged his former crew mates,' retorted the second man. Both men spoke in the querulous tones of those who habitually disagreed and bickered with one another as a way of passing time.

'Why are the men to hang?' Jezreel asked, though he had an uncomfortable feeling he already knew the answer.

'Did for a Navy tarpauling, the wantwits.'

Now that it was confirmed that the condemned men were from the previous crew of the *Speedy Return*, Jezreel was in two minds whether to stay or not. Then he decided that among the spectators might be men whom he could recruit. So he watched the four prisoners climb up a short ladder and on to the stage. From their unsteady walk, he guessed that some kind soul had filled them up with strong drink. He presumed the one who wore a shabby officer's coat was the smuggler captain whom Bartaboa despised. There was little remarkable about the others. They looked to be in their twenties, unshaven and unwashed and they had the crushed look of men who were accustomed to a harsh life. Accompanying them and the priest on to the platform were two sombrely clad bruisers with grim, set expressions. They had to be the hangman and his assistant. The latter was holding a grubby canvas bag.

The prisoners shuffled together into a little group and faced the priest. He read from the Bible, then offered up a prayer. Now Jezreel saw why the men had their arms bound in front of them. It allowed them to clasp their hands during the prayer. The priest, his duty done, left the platform and carefully made his way back down the ladder. On the stage the hangman's assistant delved into his bag and pulled out some soiled white cloths which proved to be hoods. The hangman placed them over the heads of the prisoners, one by one. Then, with the help of his assistant, he took each of the condemned men by the elbow and manoeuvred him until all four of the prisoners were standing in a line at the edge of the stage. They faced the crowd, nooses around their necks. It took another ten minutes for the free end of each halter to be uncoiled, tossed over the bar above the men's heads, made taut, and then fastened to the rear of the stage. When all was ready, the hangman and his assistant climbed down the ladder. Now the condemned men were by themselves. They stood awkwardly, still fuddled with drink but just sober enough to try to keep their balance. They knew that the slightest misstep would mean a premature death. Jezreel found himself wondering that they would wish so desperately to prolong their lives even at this final moment.

The crowd had fallen silent. There was a collective intake of breath, a quivering eagerness to witness the climax of the event. Then the shocking thump of a hammer blow made Jezreel jump. Then another blow. Jezreel rose on tiptoe, straining to see what was making the noise. At the base of the scaffold the hangman and his assistant were wielding mallets, knocking away the props which held up the front of the stage. Another double thump, and this time the right-hand edge of the platform suddenly sagged a foot or more. But the opposite end held firm. The prisoner farthest to the right toppled sideways but he was held up from falling by the noose around his neck. It tightened, but not fatally. The wretched man spun slightly, held up by his halter. The crowd let out a cross between a great sigh and a groan.

'Whoreson carpenters couldn't make a tight coffin for their own mothers,' grumbled one of the old men next to Jezreel.

Three or four more mallet blows boomed as the hangman and his assistant hurried to finish the job.

Abruptly the entire front edge of the stage collapsed. This time all four of the prisoners were left dangling, their legs kicking frantically as the nooses tightened around their necks.

Jezreel felt a nudge on his ribs and looked down. One of the old men was trying to attract his attention, his eyes shining with excitement. 'Anyone on the heels?' he demanded.

When Jezreel hesitated, not knowing what was meant, the old man prodded him again sharply. 'Take a look and tell me,' he said. 'If there's someone pulling down to the captain's legs, I'm three pesos to the better.'

'But only if it's the captain, not the others,' added his companion. 'That's our wager.'

Disgusted, Jezreel turned aside and began to push his way through the crowd. He had not gone far when there was a terrific clap of thunder. While the execution had been taking place, no one had paid attention to the dark storm cloud boiling up over the baking land. Now the thunderhead rolled in over the town with peal after peal of thunder followed moments later by the sudden onrush of torrential tropical rain. The crowd scattered, running for shelter. Raindrops bounced off the brick surface of the parade ground. A Port Royal bawd ran past Jezreel, her parasol useless as an umbrella, sodden clothes sticking to her body, revealing sagging breasts and bloated thighs. There was a glimpse of the parson scurrying for cover, one hand clamping his black hat more firmly on his head, the other holding his Bible, now wrapped in the palm leaf fan.

Jezreel let the crowd disperse. He ignored the sluicing downpour and waited on the parade ground until he was almost alone. Across the now-deserted square most of the soldiers had vanished. Half a dozen of them had taken shelter under what remained of the dripping execution stage. They were peering out from behind the legs of the hanged men, now motionless and twisting slowly in the air. Among them was the drummer. He had stretched an oilcloth cover over his drum skin and was drinking from a rum bottle. In front of the scaffold, exposed to the rain, waited a bedraggled group of half a dozen men. They were chained at their ankles and wrists. Beside them was a two-wheel cart. As Jezreel watched, the rain eased as suddenly as it had begun, and one of the soldiers emerged from his shelter. He mounted the scaffold and went to the rear of the stage. There he untied the ropes and, one after another, the hanged men dropped to the ground like ripe fruit. The waiting gang of prisoners gathered up the corpses and stacked them on the cart after another soldier had carefully removed and coiled the ropes that had hanged them.

'Ready to use again,' croaked a voice. Jezreel glanced round to see that the two old men had reappeared like ghouls.

The prisoners began to wheel the loaded cart away.

'Where are they to be buried?' enquired Jezreel.

'Buried!' The old man gave a toothless grin. 'They'll be kept in the yard at Marshalsea until nightfall and then taken out to Deadman's Cay. There they'll be hung up until they rot, like game.' He gave a phlegmy laugh.

Jezreel left the parade ground and began to make his way back towards the harbour and the *Speedy Return*. He walked with long, quick strides so as to outpace the gruesome old men. There was another clap of thunder. The rain was not entirely over. He could see almost the entire length of the High Street, empty of people except for those who had been taking shelter in the shops. Now, taking advantage of the break in the rain, they popped out like rabbits flushed from cover and began to scurry towards their homes. In the far distance, Jezreel caught a glimpse of a woman moving away from him and, for a moment, he thought he recognized her. The set of her shoulders and the way she walked put him in mind of Hector's wife, Maria. But it was a far-off view, and of course he must be mistaken. Maria was in Tortuga. Besides, the woman in the distance was a mother. She was shepherding her three children to get them home before it began to rain again. Dismissing the thought as a coincidence, Jezreel turned aside and took the shortcut through a lane which would bring him to the waterfront. Five minutes later he was back aboard the *Speedy Return* and greeted with relief by Hector.

'I'm glad you came back early, Jezreel,' he said. 'We're setting sail tonight.'

'What about the extra crew? Have you decided to sail short-handed?' Jezreel asked, surprised.

'Bartaboa and the Reverend have solved our problem for us. They have promised that they'll have enough skilled seamen aboard soon after dusk.'

Jezreel suppressed a snort of disbelief. It was galling that someone else had done his job for him. 'I'll believe that when I see it.'

But he was wrong. As darkness fell, Bartaboa and the Reverend Simeon Watson left the ship briefly and reappeared within a quarter of an hour leading a group of fit-looking men. Jezreel counted eight of them as they came aboard and, without a word, disappeared below deck. Moments later Bartaboa was asking Hector for permission to unmoor the *Speedy Return* and leave the dock.

Jezreel and Hector exchanged glances. There was a slight pause, then Hector nodded. Dan went to the helm. Bartaboa, Jezreel and the others hoisted the jib and a deep-reefed mizzen. None of the new crew members appeared on deck to help. The first stirring of the off-shore breeze pushed the *Speedy Return* away from the quay and within a few paces the pink was gliding under the guns of Fort James. Above her the crenellations were black against the starry night sky, so close that when the sentry called down to wish them a fair voyage, his voice seemed to come from their own masthead. As the little ship headed into open waters, Jezreel felt the vessel come alive beneath his feet, the deck heaving softly to the rhythm of the swell. A tight cluster of several lanterns came in view. They were no more than a pistol shot away, close on the port side. At first Jezreel mistook them for the lights of a fishing boat working its nets by night. But then, in the yellow glow cast by the lanterns, he made out the figures of a dozen men. They were on the islet known as Deadman's Cay, putting the finishing touches to the gibbets on which to hoist the four corpses in full view of every vessel entering Port Royal. What remained of the cadavers after carrion seabirds had pecked away the rotting flesh would serve as a warning to those who dared to challenge authority.

Jezreel felt the hairs prickle on the back of his neck. He was uncomfortably aware that something was not quite right about Hector's privateering commission. It had been given out too easily and quickly, almost furtively. If it proved to be invalid, everyone aboard the *Speedy Return* was acting outside the law. The eight new crew members that had come aboard so furtively were all black men. He knew for sure that they must be runaway slaves. Anyone found guilty of helping their escape would face the death penalty and finish up suspended from gibbets on Deadman's Cay.

＊

ON THE DAY OF THE HANGING, Maria had taken the children shopping as a diversion. Her occasional visits to Port Royal depended entirely on Mrs Blackmore. They took place whenever Mrs Blackmore wanted to call on her friends or attend one of the balls and receptions given by the wealthier merchants and planters or, less frequently, by the Governor. For however much Mrs Blackmore resented Lord Inchiquin, she was not averse to attending one of the official gatherings. On these trips to Port Royal she usually brought along her three grandchildren so that their father could see how their education was progressing. The captain himself spent very little time at the plantation. He preferred to live in the family's town house in Port Royal. There he attended to his commercial interests and dabbled in local politics.

That morning, Charles, the younger boy, had got to hear about the hanging. Over breakfast he had kicked up a fuss and pleaded to be allowed to see it. To silence his constant nagging, Maria had hurried the children out of doors and walked them briskly down to the foreshore at Fort Charles. Then she had taken them into a pewterer's workshop to show them how the mugs and plates were made, and finally brought them to a pastrymaker's on the High Street to buy sweet cakes. They had emerged from the pastry shop and were walking towards the Blackmores' town house on York Street when the first torrential rain caught them in the open. Maria had ducked with them into the nearest shop, a cordwainer's, to take shelter from the deluge. They had stayed until the worst of the rain was over, with Charles complaining of the smell of curing hides and whining that he should have been allowed to see a man hang, while Maria wistfully examined a pair of fine grey leather shoes in the French fashion which she knew she could not afford.

They emerged from the shop when the rain stopped and set off towards York Street, Maria holding the little girl by the hand. She was busy keeping an eye on Charles, making sure that he did not double back and evade her. So she did not see Jezreel.

That afternoon came the ritual inspection of the children by their father. Maria smartened up her charges to look presentable and brought them into the front room which Captain Blackmore used as an office and to entertain. As usual the fat man with the goatee beard was also present. Maria had learned that he was Señor Pimiento, the commercial agent sent from Cartagena to oversee the operation of the asiento, the licence to trade with the Spanish colonies. His role was to question the children in Spanish to see what progress they were making in learning the language.

Henry, the elder boy, was proving himself to be a dunce. On this occasion he stared back mulishly at his questioner, barely able to utter a single phrase. Charles stumbled through a few stiff sentences. Fortunately the little girl, Mary, had an ear for languages and she chattered away, charming her interrogator. Maria hovered discreetly in the shadows, puzzling about the Spaniard. She detected an undercurrent of understanding between him and the captain which she found difficult to fathom. She was careful not to catch Captain Blackmore's eye for she was aware of the covert glances he made in her direction. Every night, when staying at the Port Royal house, after she had put the children to bed, she locked her bedroom door.

At daybreak next morning, while the children were still asleep, she quietly left the house to search for Hector. Yesterday's thunderstorm had cleared the air, and the sky was a pale sapphire blue. She headed directly to the waterfront, her spirits lifted by her sense of purpose. It was less than a five-minute walk, and she had got to know several of the nightwatchmen during previous visits on the same quest. It was to them that she would direct her questions, asking if they had seen a party of four men, one of them a big tall man with a scarred face who looked like a prize-fighter, and another a Miskito Indian.

But yet again she was disappointed. None of her informants could help. Afterwards she stood on the edge of the quay, gazing out over the mass of shipping waiting at anchor until there was space alongside at the dock. She wondered if perhaps Hector and his friends were asleep on one of those vessels. She felt frustrated that she had so little time to spend searching for him on each visit to Port Royal. She had a recurring worry that Hector might come ashore in Port Royal only long enough to take passage to Tortuga to join her, and arrive there to find her gone and with no clue as to where to look for her. Sometimes she feared that she had made a mistake in setting out to search for him. Perhaps she should have stayed in Tortuga.

She took a deep breath and told herself not to be defeatist. She would find an excuse to come back to the waterfront later in the day. There were plenty of idlers hanging around the docks who had nothing better to do than watch the comings and goings. She would ask them. A bout of heavy coughing drew her attention to two old men rummaging through the rubbish on the dock. She guessed that, like many elderly people, they got up early, and they came to the waterfront on the off-chance that they could scavenge something worth keeping. She could hear them bickering, their voices raised in dispute.

'You owe me three pesos,' one of them was saying.

'You've no proof!' said the other. 'That big fellow never said he saw a heel hanger.'

'He didn't know what to look for. You saw the scars on his knuckles. Probably had his brains rattled loose.'

Maria came alert. 'Excuse me. Who are you talking about?'

'Big, ugly ruffian. Watched the execution with us yesterday,' replied the old man, eyeing her suspiciously.

'Do you know his name?'

The old man shook his head. 'No, but I reckon he was friends with those hempcracks, though he acted as if he didn't know them. Looked a right villain himself, as if he had been in any number of fights.'

Maria kept her hopes in check. 'Where is he now?'

The old man shrugged. 'We saw him go down the High Street. He turned down Sweetings Lane, maybe he was on his way to have a drink. You could ask that fellow over there.'

A bleary-eyed servant had just emerged from the door of the nearby tavern. The faded sign had a badly drawn image of a fully-rigged ship and the name of the ale house – the Three Mariners. He crossed to the edge of the quay and dumped a bucket of slops into the already foul water. Maria hurried after him.

'Excuse me, I'm looking for a big man, well over six foot. I'm told he came here yesterday. He looks as if he might have been a prize-fighter. Broken hands and some scars on his head. Have you seen him?'

The servant put down the bucket, hawked up a gob of phlegm, and spat it into the water. 'Can't help. James was serving yesterday evening, he might know. You'll find him inside, sweeping up.'

Maria went into the tavern. The place reeked of sweat and tobacco and strong drink. A man in an apron was pushing a broom around the filthy floor.

'Are you James?' Maria asked.

The man nodded.

'I'm told you were working here last night. Did you see a big man with the looks of a prize-fighter?'

The servant treated her to a long, calculating inspection. Maria thought he was probably wondering if she was trying to track down an errant husband. She hoped she did not look too vengeful.

'This man might have been in the company of three others,' she coaxed. 'One of them a Miskito Indian. And another would be speaking with a French accent.'

James leered, showing broken teeth. 'Didn't see him yesterday. But he was here with his friends more than a week ago. The mounseer ordered claret.' He used the broom to rearrange the little pile of sawdust he had accumulated. 'Typically Frenchified, putting on airs.'

Maria could feel her heart pounding. Hector was here in Port Royal. 'Do you know where I can find them now?' she asked.

James turned and shouted into the back of the room. 'Herbert! Do you know what happened to that foursome who were here the other week? One of them was a bruiser you wouldn't want to meet on a bad day, another an Indian.'

'I saw the big fellow a couple of days ago,' came back a disembodied answer. 'He was coming off that smugglers' pink anchored up by James Fort. Next to the government warehouse.'

Maria spun round and hurried from the tavern. Abandoning all pretence of composure, she ran the length of the quay, passing the line of moored ships. 'What's the hurry, darling!' she heard someone shout. 'Hope he's worth it!'

She reached the end of the dock, the blood pounding in her ears. A watchman was sitting on a pile of lumber, smoking a clay pipe.

'I'm looking for the smuggling boat,' she blurted.

He removed the pipe from his mouth, and blew out a stream of smoke. 'You mean the *Speedy Return*,' he said.

'Where is she now?' asked Maria breathlessly.

'She was moored here for almost a month,' said the man. 'But she left last night. All very odd. No one seems to know where she's headed, or when she'll be back.'

NINE

JACQUES HAD PREPARED a stew to be eaten on the first day at sea. He had boiled beef, ham and capon together, then added onions, peppers, okra and sweet herbs, and the flesh of a dozen land crabs.

'It won't last in this heat so might as well finish up the lot,' he said, doling out the concoction for the crew's breakfast. Bartaboa's recruits had emerged on deck and, except for Dan still at the helm, the entire complement of the *Speedy Return* were gathered round the Frenchman's galley.

'If the fodder and weather continue like this, it'll be a pleasant voyage,' commented Bartaboa. He picked a speck of crab shell off the tip of his tongue and held it up for inspection. The pink was gliding along comfortably under plain sail, drawing a clean wake across a sea which sparkled with myriad points of early morning sunlight.

One of the black men muttered something in his own language. 'He says it's very good crab pepper pot,' Bartaboa translated.

'You speak their language?' asked Jacques curiously. He looked round at the circle of black faces. The men ranged between twenty and forty in age, and appeared able-bodied and fit. They wore the usual slave costume of a coarse cotton shirt, loose trousers and straw hat or, more frequently, a headscarf. He noted that several had small ritual scars carved on their cheeks.

'They're Coromantees, from the same tribe as my grand-mother. She taught me the lingo when I was very small,' explained the sailing master.

Hector decided this was the moment to tackle Bartaboa directly. 'You and the Reverend Watson owe an explanation,' he demanded.

Bartaboa was not the least put out. 'These men had already decided to run. They were planning to join the rebel maroons in the hills—'

'How did you know that?' interrupted Hector.

The parson spoke up. 'Through me. I was their minister on their plantation. Some of them speak enough English to explain their plan.'

Bartaboa's mouth twitched in amusement. 'The Reverend is known for his scandalous ideas. He believes that all men are equal before God.'

'Have you explained to them the purpose of our voyage?' asked Hector.

'Only vaguely. They're just glad to be off the plantation.'

Hector struggled to control his irritation. 'And what do they think will happen to them when we return to Port Royal?'

'They really don't care. The way I see it, we may never get back.'

Hector was blunt. 'Make it clear that I am the captain, and they must obey orders. Tell them that we are in search of a French ship far more powerful than ourselves, a ship that could destroy us if we make mistakes.'

The sailing master turned to the Coromantees and spoke at length. They listened carefully, their faces expressionless. When he had finished, the oldest man, who appeared to be their leader, responded slowly and deliberately. The others nodded in agree-ment.

'They will follow your orders until such time as they decide to go their own way,' Bartaboa told Hector.

'And do they understand the dangers of this voyage?' Hector insisted.

'They do,' said the sailing master seriously. 'And don't worry. I'll make it my responsibility that they learn the ropes.'

✳

THE SAILING MASTER was as good as his word. Within a day the Coromantees could name in English the different parts of the rigging and understand the words of command. They were coastal people, born seamen, and Hector had seldom seen such a competent crew. After Bartaboa set them to shaping two new square sails, they showed themselves equally good with needle and thread. The sailing master had already obtained two suitable spars from the government stores in Port Royal and was still determined to re-rig the *Speedy Return* as a brig.

'Do you think you could teach them to be as good at gunnery as they are at needlework?' Hector asked Reverend Watson. The two of them were watching the former slaves stitching away industriously.

The parson's long thin face gave him a lugubrious expression. 'It would take considerable time,' he replied.

'And what happens if we get into a gun battle before then?'

The minister pursed his lips. 'I'd have all our cannon ready loaded before the battle began. You and your friends could aim and fire them one by one. But there'd be no chance of delivering a broadside.'

'And after that, when all the guns are fired?' Hector prompted him.

'I'd pray to the Lord.'

'Then let's hope he hears you,' said Hector. Out of the corner of his eye he saw that Dan, who had been at the masthead as lookout, was sliding down the back stay. He must have seen something.

'We've got company, about eight miles to the north of us,' said the Miskito.

'What sort of ship?' Hector asked. From the deck it was impossible to see that far.

'Difficult to say, but about our size and sailing the same course. I'll take another look at mid-afternoon when the sun is lower, that should show up some extra details.'

Four hours later he climbed back to the masthead and shouted down that the unknown vessel was a brigantine similar to the *Speedy Return*. The two boats were heading on almost parallel tracks, and travelling at the same pace. The stranger was flying no flag.

Hector called to Bartaboa, who was busy showing the former apprentice tailor how to work a cringle into the edge of one of the new sails. 'Maybe you know that vessel. She could be one you've encountered before.'

'No use my climbing to the masthead,' confessed the sailing master. 'My distance eyesight is gone. I'll have to wait until she's closer.'

'I'll ask Dan to show you.' Hector beckoned to the Miskito, and Bartaboa looked on in open astonishment as Dan descended to the deck and went to Jacques' cooking fire. He picked up a lump of charcoal and drew the outline of a sailing ship on an off-cut of sail canvas.

'Didn't know you were an artist,' the sailing master commented admiringly.

'Can you identify her?' asked Hector. For some time he had been wondering if the presence of the unknown ship was more than a coincidence.

Bartaboa studied the drawing for a moment. 'If I knew more about her rig . . .'

With a few strokes of his charcoal Dan added more detail of the sails and spars.

Bartaboa's brow cleared. 'French! No doubt about it. Only the French would think of setting a jib when the wind is nearly astern, though it does them little good.'

Hector recalled his conversation with Lord Inchiquin. He

pictured the chart on which he had pointed out to the Governor that the island of Providencia was the most likely base for the French frigate. A vessel which had set out from, say, Petit Goâve for Providencia would be following much the same route as the *Speedy Return* starting from Port Royal. There was a real possibility that the two ships had the same destination.

He spoke to the sailing master. 'If we convert our vessel into a brig as you propose, how much more speed can you get out of her?'

'Depends on the wind direction,' said the sailing master. He glanced up at the gaff sail. With the wind from nearly directly astern, it was eased far outboard. 'I'd say we could sail one or two knots faster.'

'And how long to make the change?' Hector asked.

'A couple of hours as soon as we have the canvas finished. The spars don't require any shaping.'

'Can you manage the changeover in the dark?'

Bartaboa grinned. 'With this crew, easily.'

'Then as soon as dusk falls, I want you to switch the rig.' Hector turned to Dan. 'When we are no longer visible to that ship, adjust course. Slant up towards her so that at dawn we are within gunshot.'

'Do you mean to sink her?' asked the Miskito.

'If her captain guesses we too are bound for Providencia, he might get there ahead of us and warn the French frigate. But it would be better if we board and take her. We know very little about the island, and he might be persuaded to talk.'

At nightfall the pink's crew lowered the big gaff sail, rove fresh halyards and repositioned blocks. Then they hoisted the two new cross-spars in their slings with the new-made square sails held furled with sailmakers' twine. When Bartaboa was satisfied that all was in place, a powerful heave on the sheets snapped the twine. The sails dropped open and in the starlight Hector looked up to see them belly out and fill, capturing the following breeze. He felt the *Speedy Return* gently accelerate, thrusting through the water. Already Jacques had doused the galley fire, and forbidden lanterns and candles. At the helm Dan shifted the tiller a fraction to alter course, steering by the stars and the direction of the wind. Without lights and in silence the pink ran across the blue-black sea.

They spent the night peering through the darkness. Caught up in the excitement of the pursuit, those who slept did so in short snatches. Bartaboa roamed the deck, laying a hand on the sheets one by one to feel their tension, muttering instructions to his men to haul in or ease out. The Reverend Watson went from cannon to cannon with Jezreel and the two Port Royal sailors, and they loaded the guns with powder and shot. Hector fretted that he might have made the wrong decision. Bartaboa could have been mistaken: the vessel they were pursuing might not be French, or it might not be headed for Providencia. Worse, it could prove to be heavily armed and well manned. The result would be disastrous.

The first glow of dawn appeared astern, and as the light strengthened, Dan, who had been at the helm all night, let out a sigh of satisfaction. Fine off the starboard bow and no more than half a mile ahead was the mysterious vessel, sailing steadily onward.

'Definitely French,' Bartaboa confirmed. 'That flag is false.' Two men on the poop deck of the ship had seen the approaching *Speedy Return* and were running up a large ensign, a red eagle on a white field.

'What are they pretending to be?' asked Jezreel.

'Brandenburgers. The Danes have given them a licence to traffic in slaves.'

Hector was debating his next move. Even as they hoisted false colours, the crew of the French ship were dragging extra sails up from below deck. They had been taken by surprise and were intending to spread more canvas, hoping to escape their pursuers.

That was encouraging. They did not feel sufficiently confident to offer a fight. On the other hand, the French captain must have noted that the *Speedy Return* was now rigged as a brig and would sail best before the wind. By changing course so that the wind was no longer from astern, the French might yet draw clear. There was no time to be lost.

'Can you put a shot across her bows at this range?' Hector asked the Reverend Watson.

'If you will follow me, I will hope to demonstrate that I retain the art of cannonry,' answered the parson. Under the shadow of his low-crowned black hat there was a gleam of excitement in his eye. With long, gangly strides he led the way along the line of half a dozen cannon on the starboard side. Reaching the foremost gun, he patted the breech affectionately. 'This one should shoot true,' he said.

He gestured towards a row of half a dozen round shot lying neatly in a tray. 'I took the liberty last night of preparing for just such an eventuality, captain. These are the nearest to a perfect sphere. Jezreel has already loaded the first.'

A satchel of greased leather was hanging from the gun carriage. Watson reached in and took out a length of matchcord wound around a short stick. 'Run out the gun, if you please,' he said to Jezreel, who had joined them. Helped by three of the Coromantee sailors, Jezreel hauled on the tackles until the muzzle of the gun projected through the gun port. Meanwhile Watson had knelt down in the shelter of the gunwale. For a moment Hector thought he was about to say a prayer. But then came clicking sounds as he struck a steel and flint, out of the wind, and set fire to the matchcord. He straightened up and handed the glowing linstock to Hector. 'Please hold this for a moment while I set a quill,' he said.

From the leather satchel he produced a thick quill cut from the wing feather of a large bird. 'Old-fashioned but effective,' he commented as he held it up to check that the hollow shaft was filled with fine gunpowder. 'I am accustomed to use a swan quill, but this would seem to have been cut from a seabird's feather, a pelican perhaps.' To Hector he sounded like a pedantic schoolmaster.

He stepped across to the breech of the gun and removed the small lead plate which covered the touch hole. With a sharp knife he trimmed the end of the quill to a sharp point and, as soon as the fine powder began to dribble out, thrust the quill firmly into the touch hole. 'Now the linstock, if you please,' he said, taking the lit matchcord from Hector. Removing his black hat, he bent over the gun, standing slightly to one side and sighting along the barrel. Nothing happened for several moments and Hector found himself with nothing to do but stare patiently at the parson's mottled scalp. He refrained from looking back towards Dan at the helm. The Miskito knew that he should be keeping the vessel as steady as he could. The *Speedy Return* was moving with a regular, slight corkscrew motion in the following sea. She pitched and rolled gently.

The parson brushed back a long strand of hair that was dangling down and interfering with his vision. Then, abruptly, he brought the linstock towards the gun. The powder in the quill ignited. There was a loud explosion and the gun fired and sprang back against the restraining ropes. Positioned upwind of the cloud of grey-black gun smoke which belched out, Hector was able to follow the brief flight of the six-pound round shot. To his disappointment it struck the sea short of the French ship and went skipping across the water three or four times before it vanished harmlessly into the sea.

The parson was unruffled. 'It seems I must make allowances for the deficiencies of naval gunpowder,' he said calmly. Jezreel was already busy with sponge, rammer and ladle, preparing the gun for the next shot.

Twice more the *Speedy Return*'s foremost gun fired, and the fall of shot crept closer to the target. It took three or four minutes each time to fire, swab and reload, and the pink had come closer to her target. There was no answering cannon shot from the French.

After Watson had observed the fall of his third shot, he blew gently on the glowing end of the linstock and asked Hector calmly, 'Would you prefer that I aim for the ship itself? Now that I have my ranging.'

Hector thought that the parson was remarkably confident. Gunnery at sea was never precise.

'Anything to make the French heave to and surrender,' he said.

'With the help of Our Lord and the Saints,' replied the parson and stooped over the breech of the gun once more.

Again there was the deafening explosion. By a fickle eddy of the breeze the cloud of gun smoke drifted back across Hector's face. He shut his eyes. There was a burnt smell and an acrid taste on his tongue. When he looked again at the French ship, he saw that the parson had achieved the near impossible.

The shot had smashed the jib boom. The shock on the fore-stay had caused the foretopmast to carry away. It was tumbled sideways in a tangle of fallen shrouds and canvas. The jib itself was trailing in the water, causing the helmsman to lose control. The brigantine was slowing down and yawing wildly. Half a dozen men were scrambling frantically to get at the damage.

Now was his chance.

'Run out our starboard guns,' he shouted. His crewmen hesitated. This was an order that had not been explained to them. But they saw Jezreel heaving on a gun tackle and followed his example. In no particular order the starboard gun ports were raised, and the muzzles of the pink's broadside appeared. Dan put up the rudder, and the *Speedy Return* bore down on her opponent, showing her teeth. She must have made a terrifying sight, for there was frantic activity on the poop deck of the French vessel. Hector saw the man he took to be the captain cup his hands around his mouth and call forward to his men. Moments later, the remaining topsail was let fly. It was the signal of surrender.

*

ANNE-MARIE KERGONAN was coming to the conclusion that her voyage with the *Sainte Rose* was turning out far better than she had expected. She was comfortably seated in a tent erected for her sole use in a grove of coconut trees close to the beach. Through the open flap of the tent she could see the pleasant sickle-shaped bay where the frigate had almost finished careening. The island of Providencia was such an idyllic spot that she wondered why the English settlers had abandoned it. Its remoteness was its only drawback and that was precisely why Captain de Graff had made it his base, and in doing so had done everything to make her stay comfortable. She looked around the furnishings of her tent – a fine Turkey rug spread on the sand, a washstand of pear wood, two delicate chairs with gilded backs and embroidered seats, a full-length mirror in its ebony frame, the escritoire which was doing duty as a table for a range of scents and powders. Of course everything was loot, right down to the matching pair of ivory-backed hairbrushes and the phials of costly perfume. De Graff had taken them out of the hapless merchants' ships which the *Sainte Rose* had intercepted these past few weeks. He had given his men strict orders to preserve any items that might make her life more agreeable. The rest of the loot had been divided up if it was ready bullion or, if normal merchandise, carried away by one of the supply ships which occasionally met up with the *Sainte Rose*. They ferried the booty back to Petit Goâve, where it was auctioned off to the shippers. Sometimes Anne-Marie imagined a particularly fine item – say, a chest inlaid with mother of pearl – making a complete round trip: fashioned by craftsmen in Spain or France, purchased by a wealthy Creole on a visit to Europe, shipped out for the Indies but intercepted, bought by a middleman in Saint-Domingue, and shipped back to Europe to be resold at a handsome profit.

Her dead husband's long hunting rifle struck a discordant note among all the feminine items that decorated her tent. She had insisted on bringing the gun with her from Petit Goâve. She kept it as her sole link with the past. Learning to shoot the rifle was one of the very few occasions when she had felt genuinely close to her husband. Philippe had been a good teacher, patient and careful, utterly unlike the rash, loud-mouthed bully he had been otherwise. The only occasion she could remember when she had enjoyed his physical touch was when he stood behind her and put his arms around her and showed her how to hold the gun steady, aim and fire. It had been a unique interval, when she had felt they were genuinely together in a partnership. That was before his heavy drinking meant that his hands shook and his eyesight blurred until he could no longer hit the target.

The sight of the hunting gun brought her to the difference between Philippe and de Graff himself. Both men had been daredevils, but in Philippe's case his bravado had been scarcely more than show and bluster. De Graff was different. She still did not quite know what to make of him. Most of the time he was attentive and pleasant. He never thrust his company upon her and he was gracious. Yet she was very aware that he could be arrogant, and more than once she had had a glimpse of his ferocious temper. On the surface he was intelligent, amusing and civilized. But underneath was a darker nature that she found troubling. At times he seemed to be foolhardy, deliberately courting danger as if waiting for the day when his phenomenal luck ran out. She had watched the sword fight between him and that young Spaniard Felipe Fonseca on the ship they had captured, and she observed how close de Graff had come to losing his life. The thought caused a momentary chill to run up her spine, and she was surprised to find herself contemplating what she would do if her protector – which is how she had come to think of de Graff – was killed.

A shadow moved across the canvas of the tent. She recognized it as de Graff. His feet had made no sound on the sand as he approached, but he had banned any of the ordinary sailors from coming near the tent. It was another of his courtesies, though at first it had made Anne-Marie angry because it would give the impression that the captain was saving her for himself, like some rare and luscious fruit.

'I trust that you are not getting bored,' said de Graff. He had coughed discreetly to let her know he was there, before he stepped into view. 'We've finished the careening, and it remains only to shift the men back aboard, re-rig, and bring our guns off.'

'And what do you propose then?' Anne-Marie asked, though she had guessed the answer.

'We will visit the Vipers reef and go fishing for salvage,' said de Graff.

So now the time has come, Anne-Marie thought. This is when de Graff reveals his true motive. She had long suspected that all the pampering had only been to make her agree to assist in the search for the Spanish wreck. Suddenly and unexpectedly she found herself wishing to remain in this pleasant limbo with de Graff, and for him to keep the spell unbroken for another day or so.

'If we are to leave this island soon, I propose we enjoy a last walk together,' she said.

'With pleasure, as always,' said de Graff. He stood waiting politely until Anne-Marie emerged from the tent, and the two of them strolled down through the coconut trees and turned along the beach. It was a walk that they had made many times, usually in the evening when the air had lost its noon-day heat. But today, at the earlier hour, the sand was still hot to the touch, and Anne-Marie took care to walk on the cooler rim of hard wet sand where the tide had just begun to recede. They would turn back at the far end of the beach where it ended in a mangrove swamp. Before then they would have to pass the makeshift camp set up by the men from the *Sainte Rose*. It was an untidy straggle of bivouacs with no semblance of order. Shelters had been made by throwing a length of sailcloth over stacks of boxes. Some of the crew had merely strung hammocks between the trunks of palm trees, while others had cut down palm fronds and woven low flimsy shacks. Scattered on the ground were odd lengths of spare timber, coils of rope, kegs, blocks, bundles wrapped in sacking, ballast stones, netting, all the paraphernalia normally stowed aboard their ship.

Today, in the centre of the camp, the cooks were boiling up the midday meal, and the blue smoke from the cooking fire drifted down towards the shore. It carried the smell of the wood they were burning mingled with the odour of spices in the pot – a scent which Anne-Marie could not identify. It was exotic; tempting yet peppery. Like de Graff himself, she thought.

'Will the men be sorry to leave the island?' she asked.

De Graff gave a sardonic laugh. 'They will be delighted, for they are growing restless. They know that a clean ship is essential to catch the prey in a chase, but resent the work that is involved.'

'And what do they think of fishing a wreck?'

'They are happy to do anything that might fill their pockets.' He laughed again, without humour. 'Our supply of grog is running out and that makes them all the more eager to be gone. Without strong drink to divert them, the men need the prospect of loot to spur them on. They dream of spending it on more rum and brandy and women.'

'And you? Why do you seek riches?' she asked.

A serious look appeared on the strong face with its splendid moustache. 'Wealth allows me to surround myself with the luxuries I appreciate – music, fine food and wine, an elegant wardrobe.'

'You did not mention women?'

'For at least ten years I've not laid eyes on my wife. Nor do I know where she is. We have gone our separate ways, and I have little wish to see her again. Doubtless she has changed. Perhaps she does not wish to see me.' He turned to face her. 'My perspective on women has changed. I look to the future.' He smiled, showing white teeth.

Anne-Marie was left wondering quite what he meant.

TEN

LESS THAN A quarter-mile away Hector and Dan were crouched ankle deep in the black ooze of the mangroves. Five days had passed since they had captured the French vessel and found she was the *Meteor*, a store ship bound for Providencia with supplies. After shifting the French captain and his men to the *Speedy Return*, Hector had put a prize crew on the *Meteor* and the two vessels continued to Providencia and were now hove to off the west coast. On their approach they had steered well clear of the bay at the north end of the island which, according to the chart found on the *Meteor*, was where *Sainte Rose* was based.

'If Laurens de Graff is still in command, it's no wonder that frigate has been so troublesome,' said Hector, squinting through the tangle of mangrove stems. He and Dan had rowed themselves ashore in the cockboat to scout, and approached the bay under cover. The two men had recognized the *Sainte Rose* instantly.

'She's almost ready for sea after careening. Another couple of days and we would have missed her,' said Dan.

A launch had set out from the frigate and was heading directly across the bay towards the far headland.

'De Graff's yet to bring his guns aboard, but that shouldn't take long,' said Hector. The headland overlooking the entrance channel was such an obvious spot for a shore battery that they had detected the defensive works without difficulty.

'So you can now tell Lord Inchiquin where he can find the raider,' replied Dan.

There was a whiff of marsh gas and a wet squelching sound as he pulled one foot out of the sucking slime of the swamp. Dan was about to begin making his way back to the cockboat when Hector laid a hand on his arm. 'Wait a little while longer. I think there is a way we might repay de Graff for robbing us of the salvage from the Spanish wreck.'

Dan treated his friend to a quizzical look. 'Hector, I hope you are not planning anything rash. Those guns up on the hill will smash to splinters any ship that tries to force the entrance.'

'It would also be in our interest if we made sure that the *Sainte Rose* stays in Providencia long enough for the Spanish flota or the Navy to get here and deal with her,' said Hector.

'That's not what Governor Inchiquin expects. He only asked us to locate the raider.'

'True. But he's only postponed our trial for piracy, not cancelled it. If we can come back to Port Royal and say that we've crippled the *Sainte Rose* and she's there for the taking, I doubt that the Spaniards would continue to press charges against us.'

The Miskito searched his friend's face for clues. 'Cripple the *Sainte Rose*! And how do you propose to do that? Even if we ambush her as she leaves harbour, it would be matching French culverins against our little sakers. Simeon Watson is a remarkable gunner, but we would be reduced to matchwood inside an hour.'

'I'm not thinking of a naval battle. We can damage the *Sainte Rose* even before she leaves the anchorage,' said Hector thoughtfully.

He was about to explain further when he noticed that Dan was staring towards the beach. Usually impassive, the Miskito had a startled expression. 'There's Anne-Marie Kergonan,' he said.

Hector was so taken aback he thought he had misheard his friend or that Dan's eyes were deceiving him. But there was no mistake. The Breton woman was strolling along the beach. Hector needed a moment to recognize her because she was wearing a skirt and blouse and a bonnet, and he was accustomed to seeing her dressed in men's clothes. But there was no doubt that it was her. Even more astonishing was that Captain Laurens de Graff was at her side. Yet the last time Hector had seen Anne-Marie she had helped him and his friends escape the *Morvaut* and thwart the French filibustier.

'That's de Graff with her!' he burst out in surprise.

'I thought so,' commented Dan drily.

Hector was utterly bewildered. He racked his brains, trying to find an explanation for Anne-Marie's presence on Providencia. The island was so seldom visited that the Breton could only have arrived aboard the *Sainte Rose*. Watching her walking alongside de Graff, Hector found it was impossible to tell whether she was there willingly or as a prisoner. From time to time she appeared to engage the Frenchman in amiable conversation, but then again there were long intervals when she ignored her companion completely. Hector was so absorbed with this puzzle that only a low warning hiss from Dan alerted him to the approach of a party of sailors from the *Sainte Rose*. Carrying axes they were coming in the direction of the mangroves to cut firewood. Dan and he risked being discovered. Stealthily Hector crept away, following the Miskito as he picked a path through the mangroves and then across the scrub-covered neck of land which divided the careenage from the beach where they had left their jolly boat. An hour later they were back aboard the *Speedy Return*.

✳

'WE SEND IN a fireship,' Hector announced. He had assembled everyone on the pink's aft deck to hear his plan of action. Only Allgood, the sailor with the missing fingers, and three of the Coromantee sailors were absent. They were on the French supply ship now hove to in the lee of the *Speedy Return*, and both vessels were far out of sight of any lookout on Providencia. On the deck in front of his audience Hector had laid a length of rope to illustrate the coastline of the island. A deep loop in the rope represented the bay where the *Sainte Rose* had careened. Using the ramrod from a musket as his pointer, Hector tapped the spot in the bay where the French frigate lay at anchor.

'De Graff has placed his ship exactly opposite the entrance to the bay. Tomorrow afternoon when the sea breeze is strongest, I propose sailing the *Meteor* through the entrance, then setting her alight and letting her drift down on the French frigate.'

Bartaboa, the sailing master, nodded approvingly. 'Even if the *Sainte Rose* has re-rigged her spars and sails, de Graff can't shift her fast enough nor can he beat out of the bay. The wind will be against him. He's trapped.'

Hector went on. 'The *Meteor* carries combustible naval stores including large quantities of gunpowder and tar—'

'—and dozens of barrels of brandy and rum,' added Jezreel. 'De Graff's crew must be a gang of tosspots if that's what they asked to be sent to them. That ship will blaze like a firework.'

With the tip of the ramrod Hector traced a line on the deck. 'This will be the *Meteor*'s route. She makes a direct approach from the sea, the breeze dead astern. Only a minimum of sail handlers are needed, three or four at most. Here –' he tapped the end of the rod on the narrow entry to the bay – 'they set fire to the cargo and leave the ship in the cockboat. They row clear to be picked up by the *Speedy Return*. The fireship sails on, unmanned, and collides with the frigate.'

Jezreel spoke up. 'Surely de Graff knows that his careenage is vulnerable. He must have placed a shore battery to protect the entrance.'

Hector exchanged glances with Dan. 'You are correct. De Graff has landed some of his guns and set up a battery at this point.' Another tap of the rod. 'On the slope of the hill which overlooks the harbour entrance from the west.'

The parson, Watson, gave a snort of disappointment. 'Even a drunken gunner's mate couldn't miss at that range. He'll be shooting from a steady platform. Your fireship will be blown to bits before she's halfway through the entrance.'

'De Graff's gunners won't know that she is a fireship,' said Hector quietly. He had their full attention now. 'He's expecting a supply vessel to arrive. Indeed he may even know that it's the *Meteor* from Petit Goâve. When his gunners see a ship heading boldly for the entrance and recognize her as French by her rig, they will let her sail in.'

'And what happens if de Graff is not expecting a supply ship?' objected the sailing master. 'He'll smash the *Meteor* to splinters with his first salvo. The plan is suicidal.'

'We make sure that he thinks the *Meteor* is friendly. And at the same time we give those who are aboard the fireship their best chance of getting away.'

He paused and looked round the circle of faces. He thought someone else would have seen how to fool de Graff. But he was met with bemused silence.

Hector took a deep breath. Now came the key part of his plan. 'De Graff is unaware of our presence and that the *Meteor* is in our hands. Around noontime tomorrow his lookouts on the hill will see a ship, a French vessel judging by the look of her. She is heading straight for the entrance to the bay, tearing along at full speed, every sail set, clearly in an emergency.'

Jacques gave a cackle of delight. He had guessed. 'And not far behind her is the *Speedy Return*, guns firing, chasing the *Meteor*, apparently trying to catch her before she reaches safety.'

Hector grinned. 'Exactly. De Graff's shore battery allows *Meteor* to race into the bay. The gunners concentrate their attention on the *Speedy Return*, waiting for her to come in range. Meanwhile, below them, in the entrance to the bay, the men aboard the *Meteor* put torches to the combustible cargo, abandon ship and row out to the *Speedy Return* to be picked up.'

'Hector, you're as cunning as Captain Drake!' exclaimed Jezreel.

'Does anyone have any questions?' asked Hector.

'Just one,' said Jacques. 'Who will be aboard the fireship?'

'I will, and I need four volunteers to come with me,' said Hector.

Jezreel, Dan and Jacques immediately raised their hands. Hector had expected them to do so. 'Dan, I'd be glad if you would come along. This is a job for good swimmers should anything go wrong.'

Then he hesitated. Jezreel and Jacques both knew how to swim but they were clumsy in the water. He did not want them floundering in the sea under gunfire. The sailing master was speaking rapidly to the Coromantee sailors. He must be explaining the plan. When he finished, his listeners asked a few questions and then four of them stepped forward.

'Captain,' said Bartaboa, 'these men would like to join you on the fireship. It will be their way of repaying you for agreeing to help them. On the African coast they worked on the boats that run the surf. I can assure you that they are excellent swimmers.'

'Just three men will be sufficient. Please thank them for their bravery.'

He felt light-headed now that he had committed himself and his volunteers to the adventure. 'Tonight we stay well clear of Providencia. In the morning we prepare the *Meteor* for burning. Then, as soon as the on-shore breeze picks up, we set sail for the entrance.'

Suddenly he was tired, very tired, and with exhaustion came the realization that he would have to hand over command of the *Speedy Return* during his absence. 'Jezreel, I'm placing you in charge until I get back. If for some reason neither Dan nor I return, you and Jacques must decide jointly what is best.'

✳

THE *METEOR* REEKED OF tar and rum. They had hoisted two barrels of ship's pitch from the *Meteor*'s cargo and softened it to a bubbling sludge in kettles over the supply ship's galley fire. They had cut up the spare sails and dipped the canvas strips in the sticky liquid before stuffing the rags in cracks and crevices around the vessel. Knocking in the top of a hogshead of rum, they had taken dippers and splashed the liquor around the hold. The gunpowder kegs they left sealed. Loose powder could lead to a premature explosion which would shatter the *Meteor* before she was along-side the French frigate, and ruin their plan. It was enough to shift the powder kegs from their safe storage in the bowels of the ship, and position them at intervals within the hull so they would detonate one after another when the conflagration reached them.

On deck everything still appeared normal. The preparations that had turned the brigantine into a floating bomb had to be invis-ible to sharp-eyed lookouts on Providencia. Hector walked around the deck, checking for any suspicious signs. He could see none. The little skiff they would use to escape the burning vessel was chocked on deck close to a gap they had sawn in the bulwark. He doubted that this unorthodox arrangement was enough to arouse the suspicions of observers on the island. The crew of the fireship had only to cut two lashings, then slide the skiff through the gap and into the sea.

The day was full of bright sunshine with only the faintest smears of high gauzy cloud. Already the sea breeze had begun to blow towards the land. The *Meteor*, all sails set, was travelling at her best pace straight for Providencia. The low hill at the entrance to the careenage was two miles ahead and plainly visible. Hector himself had dressed in a rust-red coat taken from the French captain's wardrobe, and at the stern flew the same Brandenburg ensign which the *Meteor* had shown when she had tried to escape the *Speedy Return*. In every detail they were trying to repeat the appearance of that earlier chase, and once again the *Return* was in hot pursuit. Bartaboa, the sailing master, was handling the pink skilfully, and there was no doubt that she had been gaining on the *Meteor* yard by yard. If she kept up the blistering pace, she should overtake her prey before the *Meteor* reached apparent sanctuary in the bay.

A cannon boomed, and the ball threw up a spout of water thirty paces to one side of the fleeing *Meteor*. Hector looked astern. The *Speedy Return* had yawed to one side so that her forward gun could be brought to bear. She was well within range. Inevitably the manoeuvre slowed her down, and when she came back on her course the gap between the two vessels would have widened again. Hector allowed himself a moment's satisfaction. Everything was going as he had intended. For the past ten miles, whenever the *Speedy Return* began to get too close to the *Meteor*, she had made that deliberate swerve. Simeon Watson aimed off and fired a useless shot, and the chase went on. To the observers on Providencia it must seem that the *Meteor* was fleeing for her life, and it would be a close call if she reached her refuge before she was captured.

He turned to look at the island ahead. In that short space of time the details of the landscape had become much more defined. Over the starboard bow rose the hill that commanded the entrance. Halfway up its flank he could make out the ledge where de Graff's men had cleared away the vegetation, levelled the ground, and placed their artillery. It must have been hard work to haul the heavy culverins up there through the matted bushes and tangled undergrowth that covered the slope. The opposite shore was much lower and more open, a promontory where the coconut palms tossed and waved in the breeze. Straight ahead through the entry he could already distinguish the three masts of de Graff's frigate. She was still anchored where he and Dan had last seen her. At that distance it was difficult to be sure but it appeared to him that the *Sainte Rose* already had her yards crossed. The filibustier captain must have been driving his men hard to have re-rigged his ship so quickly. In a day or two he would be ready to sail.

Hector's gaze returned to the *Meteor*'s deck. The supply ship must now be in clear view of the gunners on the hillside. He was suddenly uneasy that they would wonder why so few people were on the deck of the approaching vessel. But there was nothing he could do about it now. He could only hope that the drama of the chase unfolding below them would distract their attention.

The *Meteor* raced on. Dan, at the helm, was steering the vessel into the middle of the entrance channel. Hector stole another glance at the shore battery on the hillside. He was close enough now to see the individual cannon, four of them, their black barrels sinister against the green foliage around them. The gun crews would have had ample time to load and prime their weapons from the time they first saw the *Meteor* and the *Speedy Return* hull up against the horizon. He could see the gunners standing poised, almost motionless. They were waiting for the command to open fire.

A darting movement caught his attention. A man was running down from the summit of the hill, where de Graff must have placed his lookouts. The undergrowth was so thick that Hector could only see the man's head and shoulders as he sped towards the battery. The slope was very steep, nearly a precipice, and the man had to double back and forth in a series of zigzags, following a hidden track. Hector watched his progress, saw him arrive among the gun crews, and then a flurry of ant-like activity as they responded to the message he brought. They were adjusting the angle of the guns.

Once more he looked back at the chasing pink. In a matter of moments the *Speedy Return* would come within range of the shore battery. He hoped that Jezreel would not be rash and bring the vessel dangerously close. De Graff's gunners had to be made to think that they could destroy the *Speedy Return*. But at the same time Jezreel should stay far enough out to sea to make it unlikely that they would hit their target. It would require fine judgement and skilful sail-handling.

'Another two or three minutes,' called Dan from the helm. The *Meteor* was in the jaws of the entrance. Hector was conscious of the land closing in on either side, and the gun aimers on the hillside above him looking down, watching his every movement. He strode purposefully towards the cook's hearth near the forecastle. Stowed there were half a dozen firebrands, twists of oakum wound around short lengths of stick. He would light them from the wick of the lantern they had taken from the binnacle and hidden within the cook box, then distribute the flaming torches to his crew. All pretence cast aside, they would hurry about the vessel and set fire to the tarry rags, wood shavings and dry kindling they had prepared.

He arrived at the cook's hearth and knelt down. He reached for a bottle that was wedged there, drew the cork and sprinkled a generous dose of the contents on to the yarn of the firebrands. The sweet smell of rum filled his nostrils. He was relieved to see that the lantern was still burning. He did not relish fiddling with flint and steel to light the firebrands. Every second was vital.

He swung open the flap of the lantern and at that same instant felt an intense rushing, rippling sensation in the air. A split second later there was the unmistakable thud of cannon fire. Instinctively he ducked. The lantern fell on its side, and he had to grab it and set it upright again. But the flame in the wick had gone out. He cursed and fumbled in his pocket for his tinderbox. From behind him he heard Dan shout, 'Hector! Stand clear! Look out, above you!'

He glanced upwards. To his stupefaction he saw that the *Meteor*'s foretopmast was askew. It was leaning at a weird angle. A severed shroud was dangling free. In another few moments the strain of the topsail would bring the topmast down. Shocked, he looked towards the hillside and de Graff's shore battery. A cloud of pale grey smoke was blowing away, dispersing across the green slope. In its wake the gunners were working furiously, reloading.

Hector had a sudden sick lurch in the pit of his stomach. De Graff had not been fooled. He had seen through the ruse and guessed that the *Meteor* was in hostile hands. The man who ran down from the hilltop must have told the gunners to aim for the supply ship, not for the pursuing *Speedy Return*.

In the tense silence which followed the first salvo from the shore battery, Hector distinctly heard the high-pitched creaking sounds of twisting timber. The topmast was drooping farther to one side. In another moment it would come crashing down where he stood. He sprang to his feet and bolted. Two of the Coromantee sailors were already crouched on the edge of the deck, sheltering beneath the bulwark, looking upwards, terrified. The third had been on the foredeck and now he was scuttling aft. But he was too late. There was a loud crack and the topmast folded like a snapped fishing rod. The mast top came swinging down on the deck and struck the running man. He was hurled to one side by the force of the blow, his head at an unnatural angle. Moments later the topsail settled over his corpse as a shroud.

'They're firing at our rigging!' Dan shouted. Hector looked up at the battery in time to see a bright yellow tongue of flame leap out from the muzzle of one cannon, then the spurt of smoke. Immediately came the dreadful rushing sound as the shot tore through the air. The gun aimer had overcompensated for the downward angle. A thick gout of water burst up a few yards to starboard of the *Meteor*, showering the midships with spray.

'They're using chain shot,' bellowed Dan.

Two more of the cannon on the hillside fired in a ragged sequence, and this time they found their mark. The *Meteor* shuddered down her entire length as a pair of round shot joined by three feet of iron links whipped across her deck and scythed away the mainmast. Now the brigantine was utterly crippled. She slowed abruptly and began to turn sideways to the breeze.

Hector heard the snap and pop of musket fire. The range was extreme but the gunners on the shore battery had also taken up small arms and were shooting down on the deck of the helpless ship.

The little skiff so carefully prepared for the escape was half buried under the wreckage of the mainmast. There was no chance of freeing it.

'Save yourselves!' Hector yelled at the two Coromantees still crouched behind the bulwark. He waved them to go overboard. One man gave a final glance towards where his comrade lay crushed under the topsail. Then he joined his companion and both men swarmed over the rail and launched themselves into the sea.

Hector crouched, eyeing the mess of ropes and spars and canvas draped across the ship. He was looking for a path through the tangle that would bring him to the cook box. If he could get there and light a torch and set fire to the ship, there was still a chance that the

Meteor would drift down on her target and burn de Graff's frigate.

He heard a thud as a musket ball fired from the hillside struck the deck beside him. Then came a queer ringing sound in his head and a stab of pain. He blinked, trying to focus on the chaos of wreckage ahead of him. Defeated, he had to accept that he would never be able to get through to reach the firebrands.

Bending low, he scrambled back towards the stern. He was seeing everything through a mist. It was difficult to keep his balance. He was staggering from side to side, his legs wobbly underneath him.

Another musket ball went whirring away past him and rapped the tiller head. Dan was beckoning to him urgently. 'The port side,' he said, 'keep the ship between us and the marksmen.'

The hem of Hector's borrowed coat caught on a hidden snag, and he was held fast. He scrabbled furiously, lunged, and felt the fabric rip. He seized the rail and tumbled over it, cartwheeling through the air. He landed awkwardly. The sea closed around him and he took a choking gulp of seawater. Spluttering, he came to the surface, the heavy coat already soggy and clinging around his shoulders so that he could barely swim. He trod water, struggling to get his arms out of the sleeves, when he felt someone grab the collar of the coat and peel it off his back. He turned in the water. It was Dan who had saved him.

'It'll be a long swim,' said the Miskito.

Hector looked away to the north. There, almost a mile distant, was the *Speedy Return*. The pink was tacking through the wind. As she came broadside on, he saw the spurt of smoke that told him that she was firing cannon towards the shore battery. But it was a single gun, a mere gesture.

'Pray that Jezreel doesn't come in too close. He'll lose the ship,' he said to Dan.

'He'll do what's right,' said the Miskito grimly. His long straight black hair was wet and plastered tight against his head. For a second Hector was reminded of how his friend had looked when he was diving on the Spanish wreck.

Together they struck out for the *Speedy Return*. Behind them they could hear de Graff's cannon still firing. Now there were longer intervals between the shots. They were taking their time, aiming carefully at the distant ship. He was aware of an occasional splash in the water nearby, and guessed that the musketeers were still taking potshots at the heads of the four swimmers who had abandoned the *Meteor*, relying on luck to make a lucky hit. Once he turned over on his back and looked at the disaster he was leaving. A longboat, probably the same one he and Dan had seen when they were spying from the mangrove swamp, was alongside the crippled *Meteor*. De Graff's men had rowed out to take the crippled supply ship in tow. Now they would haul her into the careenage and unload the stores they had been waiting for. The catastrophe was complete.

*

IT MUST HAVE BEEN the best part of an hour later when Hector accepted that he would not be able to reach the *Speedy Return*. The blow to his head had weakened him, and a deathly tiredness was setting in. The muscles in his shoulders ached. There were moments when a thick dark veil blotted out his vision, robbing him of sight. His head ached viciously. He raised one hand and touched where it hurt most, and felt the gash in his scalp. With increasing frequency his mouth and nose dipped below the surface. He knew he was using his strength to keep afloat rather than move forward. Everything was hazy and indistinct.

Then he was conscious that Dan was at his side, helping him as best he could. But he had no idea how long the Miskito had been there. In a moment of clarity he knew that Dan was also tiring. The Miskito was a powerful swimmer, but supporting his friend in the water over such a distance was sapping his strength.

'Save yourself,' gasped Hector. A wave splashed into his open mouth. He choked and coughed, another sliver of energy wasted.

'I stay by you,' answered Dan.

Hector was too tired to argue and too feeble to insist. They were now beyond the range of the musketeers but the sea breeze had built up a small choppy sea, and he could no longer make out the *Speedy Return*. Dispirited, he wondered if they had been swimming in the wrong direction.

'I can't go on,' he murmured. His throat hurt from so much salt water, and there was a ringing sound in his ears. A profound lethargy overcame him and he closed his eyes; the sea was welcoming him.

When he opened his eyes to take a final despairing look, his vision was blurred and there was a racking pain in his head. A seal was approaching, its sleek black head and liquid brown eyes coming directly towards him. He knew that he was hallucinating. Seals did not live in those waters. Unexpectedly, two strong hands gripped his wrists and pulled his arms forward. He reached out and at last there was something to hold on to. Its surface was smooth and slippery but it was a support that kept his face above the water. With slow comprehension he realized that his arms were clasped around a man's neck, and that he was riding on a swimmer's back. The wet, rough sensation against his cheek was a mass of tightly curled hair.

One of the Coromantees was towing him forward. He closed his eyes again and hung on.

Time passed, he had no idea how long. He was dimly aware that the swimmer changed. Another replaced the man supporting him, and again he felt the powerful movements of someone underneath him swimming forward.

He continued to slip in and out of consciousness until a painful blow on his shoulder jolted him out of his stupor. He was looking directly up at the bow of a rowing boat. The keel had struck him. There was momentary confusion as the rowers spun the boat, the blade of an oar banged him on the ear, and then he was being hoisted aboard, the gunwale scraping his ribs. He heard someone shouting an order in a French accent, urging the rowers to get the boat back to the ship. He knew that the speaker was Jacques, and that the cockboat from the *Speedy Return* had saved him.

ELEVEN

STANDING FACING HIS audience in the waist of the *Speedy Return*, Hector swallowed gently to clear his throat, still sore from taking in so much seawater twenty-four hours earlier. His headache had subsided to a dull throb which he could ignore. All the dizziness and blackouts had gone, and Dan had stitched up the gash in his scalp left by a flying splinter. Watching the ring of expectant faces waiting to hear what he proposed to do next, it occurred to Hector that an outsider would scarcely have been able to tell that the attempt to launch a fireship had been such an utter disaster. The weather was just as sunny and pleasant as it had been every day for the past week, and if there was an air of disappointment aboard the *Speedy Return*, it was very muted.

'Yesterday I had hoped that we would damage the *Sainte Rose* so badly that she would be unable to set sail. Today I propose we sink her.'

An astonished silence greeted his words. Then came the strange guttural sounds of Bartaboa translating his statement to the Coromantees. Allgood, the sailor with the missing fingers, was looking at him as though he had taken leave of his senses. 'Captain,' he asked, 'if you are so sure you can sink the frigate why did we not try that yesterday? Instead we've handed the *Meteor* to de Graff and made him stronger.'

'It is because de Graff and his men have got their hands on the *Meteor* that we can now destroy his ship.'

A general look of puzzlement spread among his listeners.

Jezreel spoke up. 'You'll have to explain, Hector. Maybe I'm being slow but I can't see how that changes anything.'

Hector's head wound had begun to itch. He resisted the urge to reach up and scratch. 'What do you think de Graff and his men will be doing over the next few days?'

'Celebrating their victory and getting the frigate ready for the sea with the help of fresh supplies from the *Meteor*,' said Jezreel immediately.

'Precisely. They will not expect another attack.'

'And what sort of attack do you have in mind?' asked the Reverend Watson cautiously.

Jacques already knew the answer. 'It's all that rum and brandy on board the *Meteor*, isn't it, Hector? You think that de Graff's men will be drunk and incapable for the next few days.'

'That's right, Jacques. We saw the sort of men who sail with de Graff on the day he put a prize crew aboard the *Morvaut*. They were hard drinkers, every last one, always at the bottle. Imagine what they will be like now that they've got their hands on the *Meteor*'s cargo, with all that rum and brandy. They probably had their tongues hanging out for it.'

The parson was still unconvinced. 'Even if de Graff's gun crews are blind drunk and the *Return* manages to get into the anchorage, we can do little harm to the frigate. Our sakers may inflict some damage but they're unlikely to sink her.'

Hector allowed a moment to pass before he responded. Then he said slowly and deliberately, 'I don't intend to take the *Speedy Return* into the bay. We can dispose of the *Sainte Rose* without firing a shot.'

Now even Jezreel was beginning to look at him as though his head wound had done damage to his brain. He ploughed on. 'De Graff is renowned for his boldness, courage and cunning. But what are his weaknesses?'

No one replied, so he answered for them. 'He is also known for his high opinion of himself, his gallantry, and his vicious temper. It is these that I intend to exploit.'

He paused and looked across at Jacques. If anyone could guess his plan it would be the Frenchman. Besides, he would need Jacques' help. But Jacques was silent, a slight frown on his face as he tried to puzzle out what scheme Hector was hatching.

'Two days ago when Dan and I went ashore to spy out de Graff's camp we saw a woman walking the beach with him. We recognized her as Anne-Marie Kergonan. She's from Tortuga.'

'You think this woman can help us?' interjected Bartaboa. There was deep scepticism in his voice.

'Indirectly. I don't know if she is willingly with de Graff or whether she is some sort of prisoner,' Hector told him. 'But one thing is sure: de Graff will fly into a rage if an enemy or a rival whisks this woman away from him.'

Bartaboa was still doubtful. 'That would be true if she is his wife or mistress. But you admit that she may only be some sort of prisoner.'

'You miss my point,' said Hector. He looked round the faces of his audience, trying to judge whether his listeners were open to persuasion. 'It's de Graff's reaction that counts. He would be mortified if the story came to be told how a woman was filched from under his nose. It doesn't matter whether she was his mistress or his captive. His pride will cloud his judgement.'

'So you propose to steal this woman, and then what?' asked Bartaboa.

Jacques supplied the answer. 'De Graff will try to get her back, at any cost.'

'And that's when we will arrange to have his ship destroyed,' added Hector.

The parson's brow cleared. 'You mean we take this woman, and lure de Graff out of the careenage. Then we lead him to some place where the Spanish flota can deal with him,' said the Reverend.

'That is one way of doing it,' said Hector, though it was not what he had in mind.

✳

THE TEMPTATION TO scratch at the wound in his scalp was almost impossible to resist. This time it was not the stitches which were tormenting him, but mosquitoes. He could hear their whine and, from time to time, felt a piercing needle stab of pain as one of them settled on his bleeding scalp and began to feed. Hector gritted his teeth and tried to ignore the ordeal. It was close to midnight and he could see de Graff's camp fires between the trees. He and Dan had landed from the cockboat, not on the same beach as before, but on the low spit of land across the channel from the shore battery. This time Jacques accompanied them. They had made a wide circle, staying a safe distance inland. Then they had crept through the coconut groves which fringed the bay until they were some hundred paces from the filibustier's camp. Judging by the sound of drunken singing and loud voices, Hector had been right to assume that de Graff's men would celebrate the capture of the *Meteor* with a debauch.

'Where do you think we find the Kergonan woman?' whispered Jacques.

'Dan and I saw a separate tent set back among the trees. That's probably for her,' replied Hector softly.

Treading carefully, the three men crept towards the isolated tent. Its shape reminded Hector of the small pavilions that hucksters set up at fairs. De Graff must have found it in the cargo of some merchant vessel. The tent was bulky enough to shield them from the main campsite, and they reached it without trouble. There was no one on guard, and for a few moments the three of them stood quietly listening. All they could hear was the background noise of laughter and braying voices from the main camp. There was no sound from inside the tent, and Hector feared it might be unoccupied. He knelt down on the sand and began to cut a slit in the rear panel. The material was unexpectedly tough, and he had to saw with his knife blade to slice through the fabric. From time to time he paused and listened again, but still could hear nothing to suggest he had been discovered. A succession of musket shots made his heart leap into his mouth, but it was only de Graff's rowdies shooting off their guns into the air in drunken celebration. Finally the slit was large enough for Hector to crawl through.

On hands and knees he entered. The door flap of the tent facing the bay was open, fastened back to let in the air. Slowly and carefully he rose to his feet, holding his breath. Enough light came in through the opening for him to see that the tent was comfortably furnished and a hammock was strung between two of the tent poles. Disappointingly the hammock hung limp and unoccupied. The light from the distant fire glinted off the barrel of a long hunting gun, propped against a chest, and he decided that he had made an error. The tent was occupied by a man, not by Anne-Marie Kergonan. Perhaps it was de Graff's own tent. Hector let out his breath. His plan had miscarried. He was about to crouch down and wriggle out through the slit in the back of the tent when he felt something hard and blunt pushed into his back.

'*Tourne-toi*,' said a voice he recognized.

He turned and looked into the face of Anne-Marie Kergonan. She had a pistol in her hand and it was levelled at his stomach. Astonishingly, she did not appear to be in the least surprised.

'I thought it was you,' she said quietly, this time in English, 'even in the dark and on your hands and knees. But I needed to be sure. Otherwise I would have pulled the trigger.'

Hector had recovered from his astonishment. 'Did I make that much noise?'

She shrugged. 'Not so much. But when a woman lives among so many men, not all of whom are gentlemen, she sleeps lightly and keeps a pistol close to hand.'

'I've come to take you away. There's a ship standing by,' said Hector. He kept his voice low.

'And why should I want to go with you?' asked the Breton.

'I thought that de Graff might be holding you as a prisoner,' ventured Hector.

'And what made you think that?' There was a mocking tone in her voice.

Hector was confused. He was aware that Dan and Jacques were standing behind the tent, waiting for him. They could hear the conversation.

'When we last met, you were furious with de Graff for seizing our salvage from the Vipers.'

'So now you want me to run away with you and your friends, who, I presume, are waiting outside?'

'That's right. And we must move quickly . . .'

Anne-Marie held up her hand to silence him. 'I need a moment to think.'

Hector's eyes were fully used to the dim light inside the tent. The Breton was dressed in a light shift, her shoulders bare, her hair cut short. Her expression was impossible to read, the lustrous eyes were deep pools of darkness.

'Tell me more about this ship of yours, and where you are going,' she demanded.

'She's the *Speedy Return*, based in Port Royal.'

'Not a place that would welcome a French woman,' she said drily.

'I could arrange for you to get back to Tortuga, if that is what you want. I'll be going there myself to find my wife, Maria.'

There was an odd note to her voice as she replied. 'So you've not heard from Maria recently?'

Hector was puzzled. 'No.'

'Then I have to tell you that she's no longer in Tortuga.'

Hector was taken aback. He had thought to rescue or even kidnap Anne-Marie Kergonan. Instead they were discussing Maria.

He heard Jacques hiss from outside the tent, 'Hector, hurry up! We can't stay here all night.'

Anne-Marie gave a low throaty laugh. She seemed to have made up her mind. 'All right. I'll come with you. But first I gather a few things together.'

Hector moved to stand just inside the door of the tent where he could keep watch, looking towards the camp fire. The sounds of revelry were dying down. He guessed that de Graff's men had drunk themselves senseless or were beginning to settle down for the night.

There was a rustling at his elbow and there was Anne-Marie. Under one arm she had a bundle, presumably of clothes. With her free hand she was carrying the long-barrelled musket he had seen propped against the chest.

'A souvenir of a previous life,' she answered, seeing his surprise.

He touched her on the shoulder, feeling the smooth skin, and pointed the direction she should go. They slipped out of the tent and Dan and Jacques appeared from the darkness. Together they began to retrace the path to where they had left the cockboat.

They had gone only a short distance when someone belched loudly. They froze. A man was urinating against a tree trunk not twenty yards away. He was standing with his back towards them, and must have come up from the beach to relieve himself. He had only to turn and they would be seen.

Jacques reacted quickly. He stumbled forward as if tipsy and took up a position on the far side of the sailor. He fumbled at his belt, humming under his breath.

'*Bordel de merde! Fous-moi le camp vite faite,*' snarled the sailor.

'*T'énerve pas,*' muttered Jacques. He hiccuped and moved a few yards away. There he dropped his breeches, squatted down and broke wind noisily. The sailor hurriedly adjusted his clothing and stalked away in disgust and without another glance.

As soon as the sailor was gone, Jacques pulled up his breeches and hurried back to join the others.

'I'll soon be qualified to be a sailing master.' He grinned. 'I remembered to fart from upwind.'

*

Anne-Marie was beginning to wonder why Hector and his companions were wasting time. They had reached the beach where they had left their cockboat and launched the little boat without the alarm being raised. Now, instead of rowing off to rejoin their ship, they were drifting aimlessly in the entrance to the bay. Dan and Hector were at the oars, and Jacques was seated in the stern beside her. She could see a scar crusted with dried blood on Hector's scalp. Someone had shaved away a patch of hair and done some neat stitching. The wound looked fresh.

'There'll be some fierce hangovers on-shore,' observed Jacques to no one in particular.

'Let's hope it spoils their aim,' Dan answered. The Miskito gave a gentle pull with his blade to keep the cockboat pointing out to sea. Anne-Marie noted that his gaze kept returning to the hillside overlooking the channel.

Hector was asking her a question. 'Anne-Marie, did de Graff mention when the *Sainte Rose* would be ready to sail?'

'He wanted it to be last week. He was cursing the men and threatening to punish any idlers. He cheered up, though, when he got his hands on the store ship.'

'Is there a lot still to be done on the frigate?'

'Only some rigging and getting the rest of her guns aboard. The men have already started to bring their gear back on to the ship. The plan was to dismantle their camp after last night's celebrations.'

'There's someone up there now!' Dan broke in quietly. The first rays of the early morning sun were turning the hillside a vivid green. Tendrils of mist curled up where the overnight dew was burning off the foliage. Anne-Marie could make out the figure of a man standing beside the muzzle of one of the guns. He looked down at them and then ran off.

'Here comes their launch now. Time to be on our way,' said Hector. He and Dan bent to their oars and began to row the skiff seaward. Anne-Marie turned in her seat and saw the frigate's launch in the distance, coming towards them. Her absence must have been discovered and they were giving chase.

'Excuse me, madam. Perhaps you would prefer to look the

other way,' said Jacques. The skiff wobbled as he rose to his feet, dropped his breeches and exposed his buttocks towards the hillside. Anne-Marie saw there were now half a dozen men standing beside the gun battery.

'They're beginning to recognize that side of you,' said Dan as Jacques pulled up his breeches and sat down again.

'Just to make sure,' Jacques replied. Hector and Dan were rowing steadily now, moving the skiff purposefully through the water. Some distance up ahead, a ship was sailing down towards them. Doubtless it was the *Speedy Return* coming to pick them up.

'De Graff will kill you if he gets his hands on you,' she warned Hector.

He gave her the ghost of a smile. 'And the hangman in Port Royal will probably string me up.'

Anne-Marie had a sudden urge to shatter the young man's calm self-assurance. 'So let us hope that Maria does not watch you dangle there,' she said meaningfully.

She was pleased to note Hector missed a stroke. He went pale. 'Is Maria in Port Royal?'

The Breton shrugged. 'When I last spoke with her, she intended to go there to look for you.'

Hector appeared dumbfounded, even paler now. 'You spoke with Maria? How did that happen?'

'She came to Petit Goâve, looking for you. She had heard that the *Morvaut* was taken, and wanted to find out what had happened to you.'

'And you told her?'

'Not everything. I helped her find a boat, a smuggler, who would take her to Jamaica. She thought that was where you were most likely to be found.'

Hector had stopped rowing. He stared at her. 'When was that?'

'About three months ago. Maybe more.'

He began to row again, his expression thoughtful. Unexpectedly, he said, 'Why did you decide to come away with us?'

'I've been asking myself the same question,' she replied. Then, feeling ashamed of the way she had been treating the young man, she added, 'It was a decision on the spur of the moment. But I have been feeling vulnerable for some time.'

He looked at her questioningly. 'Vulnerable? That doesn't sound like the person they call the Tigress?'

She grimaced on hearing her nickname. 'Captain de Graff was becoming a hazard. His constant attention was wearing me down. I needed breathing space.'

'Then you shouldn't have sailed with him,' he said flatly.

She shook her head. 'The Governor of Petit Goâve made sure that I went to Providencia. De Graff needs me to help locate the place where we found the Spanish salvage when we were on the *Morvaut*.'

'And how did the Governor persuade you?'

'You remember my brother Yannick?'

Hector nodded.

'I shot and killed the man who knifed him. I could have been tried for murder. The Governor agreed to delay my trial.'

Hector smiled thinly. 'Then we have that much in common. I went in search of de Graff only because the Governor of Jamaica postponed my trial for piracy if I did so. The Spaniards are keen to have me hung for that incident when you and your brothers robbed the *San Gil*. I was an accomplice, you may remember.'

He lapsed into silence. Anne-Marie felt a pang of remorse. 'I'm sorry if you are in trouble for that reason. I hope you will set it against my help when you and your friends escaped from the *Morvaut*.'

Jacques, sitting beside her, uttered a bark of frustration. 'Will you two please stop discussing the past! Hector, if you don't pay attention to your rowing, that launch will catch up with us and then de Graff can carry out whatever punishment he thinks we deserve.'

TWELVE

HAGGARD AND FROWZY, the crew of the *Sainte Rose* had seldom seen their captain so angry. De Graff came storming through the camp early in the morning, roaring that he wanted the frigate to be under way within the hour. Rapier in hand, he slashed through the cords of hammocks so their occupants crashed to the ground. Then he kicked them savagely until they rose to their feet. One slow-witted sailor groaned, rolled over on his face, and went back to sleep. The sword point prodded two inches into his backside.

'What's eating him?' asked a carpenter's mate. His guts were rumbling with a mix of rum and cheap brandy, three flagons of it from what he remembered of the night before.

'His Breton woman's run off,' said his colleague. 'The lookout reported she's on a skiff and heading out to sea.'

'Let's hope that bastard brother of hers has gone with her,' muttered the first man. His comment ended with a quick gasp of discomfort and a gush of yellow-green vomit as he threw up.

The longboat sent in pursuit of the fugitives was recalled. It was obvious that it could not catch the runaways before a small brig picked them up. It was the same vessel that had attempted to send in a fireship two days earlier. The *Sainte Rose*'s petty officers had caught their captain's evil humour. They were bawling orders, cuffing and cajoling the bleary men to get on board the frigate and prepare to weigh anchor. Unwisely the master gunner asked for permission to send the longboat to retrieve the cannon from the shore battery. De Graff snarled that the guns could stay where they were. The frigate would return and pick them up later.

The longboat picked up a towline and began hauling round the frigate's bow so her sails could catch the last of the land breeze. A lucky fluke of the wind and the *Sainte Rose* overtook the longboat and would have sailed away without stopping if the coxswain had not grabbed a dangling rope and taken a turn around athwart. With a clatter of spilled oars and a slew of oaths the longboat crew scrambled up the side of the frigate. De Graff raged at them, shouting that the longboat was a hindrance and they should hoist it on board at once.

The frigate's crew went about their tasks, heads down, not daring to catch the eye of their fuming commander. De Graff had somehow found time to dress in his usual immaculate costume – dark blue coat lined with silk and edged with gold braid, white breeches and stockings, and tall bucket-top boots. He took up his position on the poop deck, scowling as he surveyed the crew's frenzied activity, his lips clamped together under the extravagant blond moustache, with his rage subsiding to a cold, vicious anger.

'Excuse me, captain,' said a diffident voice. It was the first mate, a regular officer from the Navy. 'This man has something to say that may be important.'

De Graff wheeled round and glowered down at the sailor. A small scrawny man wearing a red cap, his ingratiating smile showed a mouthful of bad teeth. 'What do you have to tell me?' the captain demanded.

'The men in that skiff, Your Excellency. I know them,' said the sailor.

'How?' rasped de Graff.

'I was with the prize crew you put aboard the pinnace we captured some months back. They were on that boat.'

'How can you be sure?'

'I've been with the gun battery these past few days. Two of

those fellows were on the fireship, and again in the skiff this morning. I got a good look at them.'

His words struck deep. De Graff could recall every detail of the capture of the pinnace. It was the first time he had laid eyes on Anne-Marie. He could still picture how attractive she had looked. He even remembered the name of the young man who had come aboard the frigate with her to be interviewed – Lynch, Hector Lynch, that was it. Half Irish, or so he claimed. There had been something unlikely and all too slick about the way Lynch and his companions escaped the next night, vanishing into the darkness from the pinnace. De Graff's suspicions came flooding back. Anne-Marie Kergonan had claimed to know nothing about that escape. Now she was running off with the same man. The fili-bustier gritted his teeth with fury. The Breton woman had played him for a fool. He felt duped and, just as bad, he knew that he was jealous. He had always told himself that jealousy was an emotion reserved for weak people who could not control their emotions. To admit to himself that he was prey to jealousy made him even more ill-tempered.

The first mate was trying to be tactful, humouring him. 'We should catch that brig before nightfall. There's no chance that she can outsail us.'

De Graff treated him to a look of pure contempt. When it came to dealing with Anne-Marie Kergonan or Hector Lynch, nothing was a foregone conclusion.

❋

'How long before the frigate has us within cannon range?' Hector asked Bartaboa aboard the *Speedy Return*.

'Normally, five or six hours. But she's not fully rigged and can't carry all her canvas.' The sailing master had been observing the *Sainte Rose* for the past three hours as the frigate chased after the pink.

'Can you stay clear of her until nightfall?' Hector said.

'Certainly.'

'I'm counting on you to do so. We change course as soon as it is dark, as if to throw her off our track.'

Bartaboa hesitated. 'There's nearly a full moon. I doubt that we'll escape de Graff that easily. He could see our manoeuvre.'

'I hope so,' said Hector, and before the sailing master could say anything more, he hurried down the companionway to the chart locker in the stern cabin.

He selected a map of the Caribbean. It was a match of the one that he had discussed with Lord Inchiquin, but faded and stained with much use. The *Speedy Return* had no chart table so he cleared a space on one of the bunks and laid out the map. Taking a pair of dividers, he walked them across the parchment, measuring the distance between Providencia and the graveyard of the Vipers. If the wind held, the pink should reach the reefs by noon the following day.

He laid aside the dividers, found a clean sheet of paper and a pencil, and sat down. For a long while he sat motionless, eyes closed, seeing pictures in his head. Then he began to draw. First he marked a small circle off-centre. To the left of the circle and close to it, he added a few faint lines. He reviewed the result, was not satisfied, and corrected what he had drawn. After several false starts he became more confident. The pencil strokes were more certain. They extended farther and farther across the page. Gradually a random pattern of wavering lines emerged. He shaded in some of the empty spaces. Other areas he left plain, or inserted a question mark. With a ruler he marked several straight lines radiating from the first small circle he had drawn. Finally he went to the cabin door and called for Dan.

When the Miskito appeared, he showed him the sheet of paper. 'Do you recognize this?'

Dan needed only one quick look. 'That's where we fished the galleon,' he replied.

'Have I left anything out?' asked Hector.

The Miskito picked up the sketch and inspected it for several seconds. 'Not that I can think of. But I only know the area around the wreck itself.'

'The rest is what I remember from when I rowed out with Jezreel looking for more wrecks,' Hector told him.

'You seem to have identified some channels,' said the Miskito. 'I intend to take the *Speedy Return* through them.'

'And hope that de Graff tries to follow you?'

'Exactly.'

Dan handed back the sketch. 'The Vipers earned their nickname. Let's hope their fangs can snag another victim.'

'I'll need you at the masthead,' Hector told him. 'You'll have a copy of this drawing. When we try to run the reef, you con us through. I'll stay by the helm.'

As always, Dan was unruffled. 'You'd better explain your plan to the rest of the crew. I doubt if they can imagine anyone piloting his way through the Vipers without putting his ship on the reefs.'

※

ALL THAT DAY the chase had gone on, the gap between the two ships steadily diminishing. The sun was already slipping below the horizon when an anxious-looking Bartaboa came to Hector with an apology: 'I didn't make enough allowance that the frigate is newly breamed. She's gaining an extra knot from that clean hull.'

'Keep us far enough ahead so our change of course looks credible,' Hector told him. There was half an hour of daylight left. 'If de Graff thinks he's about to catch us, it will make him all the more eager. He'll want to cripple and board so as to get his hands on us. He's not interested in sinking the *Speedy Return*.'

As he spoke there was an orange-yellow flash in the gathering gloom. De Graff's gunners had tried a ranging shot. No one saw where it landed. The minutes crawled past and the night came on. The outline of the chasing frigate became increasingly difficult to see against the darkening surface of the sea. There was no more cannon fire.

Hector waited until he was satisfied that the *Speedy Return* was almost invisible. 'East by north,' he said to the helmsman quietly. The crew of the pink adjusted the set of the sails, and when their ship had settled on her new track, he summoned them aft. They were little more than dark shadows as they clustered on the aft deck.

'We wait until dawn,' he told them. 'Until then there is nothing to be done except keep a good lookout. By morning we will be close upon the reefs, where I intend to lure the frigate to her destruction.'

'On to the Vipers?' asked a sceptical voice he recognized as Bartaboa.

'Yes. There are channels that we can slip through. Narrow but passable.'

'Let's hope de Graff doesn't know about them too.' This time it was the parson, Simeon Watson, who spoke from the darkness. There was a low murmuring as the plan was translated for the other sailors. Hector became aware of someone standing apart from the others, close to the windward rail. It was Anne-Marie Kergonan. She had been listening to his plan. He wondered what she was thinking of his makeshift crew and their chances of success. For a moment he considered asking her about de Graff. She might know whether the filibustier was familiar with the reefs and what he was likely to do. Then he rejected the idea for fear that she would answer that de Graff was well acquainted with the Vipers and had sailed the *Sainte Rose* across them safely. If so, his plan was worthless and he was leading his men into another debacle. But he no longer had a choice: he had committed his ship and his men. He alone would be responsible for what happened next morning.

Before first light he was already perched high on the topmost main spar, watching the dawn slowly seep up from the eastern horizon, the sea turning from black to darkest indigo. He faced aft, straining his eyes for a glimpse of the *Sainte Rose*. To his disappointment it seemed that the frigate was no longer there. Then, as the light strengthened, he saw her hull down to the south-west.

He felt a surge of relief. De Graff must have suspected that the *Speedy Return* could change course in the night, or his lookouts had seen the pink alter direction. He had kept his options open, shadowing the probable route of the pink, but keeping slightly to one side just in case he was in error, careful not to commit himself entirely.

For some time Hector continued to scrutinize the distant vessel. After a while he saw the *Sainte Rose* spread more sail and begin heading towards the pink, resuming the direct chase. It was an unhurried, deliberate manoeuvre, and it reassured him. He climbed down the shrouds and regained the deck.

'De Graff knows that the Vipers lie ahead,' he told Bartaboa, who was waiting beside the helm.

'What makes you say that?' asked the sailing master.

'Because he took his time in altering course to follow us. He thinks the *Speedy Return* is headed into a dead end and when we reach the Vipers we will either have to turn and fight or we run our ship on the reef. He sees no need for haste.'

'What are your orders?' asked the sailing master.

'The same as yesterday. Draw him on. I want him close, yet not so near that his cannon disable us before we run the Vipers.'

'How soon will that be?'

It was a question that Hector could not answer with certainty. From the masthead there had been no sign of the reefs, and he had no way of establishing just how far eastward the pink had sailed in the night. The angle of the sun would tell him how far north or south he might be, but there was no known means of measuring a position east or west. He could only make an educated guess by calculating the course he had sailed since leaving Providencia and the pink's speed through the water. But this took no account of the currents and the amount of sideways drift.

He answered with more confidence than he felt. 'Within three hours we should be in sight of two small islands at the southern edge of the reefs. I will use them as my marker.'

Bartaboa nodded. 'I know them. Waterless places, the haunts

of seabirds. You can go ashore to gather their eggs when the tide is right.'

His mention of the tides reminded Hector how easily his plan could go wrong. If it was low water when the *Speedy Return* reached the Vipers the channels he hoped to use might be impassable. At high tide there could be local eddies and currents so powerful that they would sweep his vessel on to the coral.

Hector put the worry out of his mind. 'Hold this course while I go down and prepare a copy of the pilot chart for Dan.'

He was adding the final details to the sketch when the cry came that land lay ahead. He hurried up on deck to find Dan waiting for him.

'It's the same pair of islands where we anchored when we were fishing the wreck of the galleon. I'm sure of it!' he said to Hector.

Hector handed the sketch map to his friend. 'I've marked our channel, Dan. In places it's not more than ten paces wide, and there's an awkward dogleg halfway along. Get us to the entrance. After that, use your eyes to con us through. We'll watch for your signals.'

Without a word, the Miskito took the sheet of paper. Moments later he was climbing the shrouds.

At the helm Bartaboa was still uneasy. 'Hector, de Graff's been within cannon range for some time. Yet he's not pressing the chase. He's slowed his ship to match our speed.'

Hector studied the pursuing frigate. The *Sainte Rose* appeared alarmingly close. But he could see that de Graff had reduced sail. 'He hopes that we are ignorant enough to run ourselves aground, do his work for him.' He cupped his hands around his mouth and called up to Dan. 'Can you see the reefs yet?'

'White water, two miles ahead!'

Hector swung round to face Bartaboa. 'Put her head to wind. Act as if we've been taken by surprise, and make a mess of it!'

The sailing master threw his weight on the tiller. The bow swung, the sails began to tremble and sag. Then the wind was from their wrong side and they flapped and clattered in noisy confusion. Sheets and braces went slack, and then creaked and twanged in protest as they came taut at the wrong angle. The blocks slammed and rattled. The *Speedy Return* stopped head to the wind, like a drunk stumbling into a door jamb. Bartaboa timed the recovery to perfection. He waited as the pink wallowed and lurched, then he heaved back on the tiller just in time for the pink to swing round on her previous course and begin to move again.

Aboard the pursuing frigate it must have appeared as if the helmsman on the *Speedy Return* had suddenly seen the reefs, and clumsily tried to turn away from them before his captain had countermanded the manoeuvre.

De Graff pounced. Hector saw extra sails break out on the frigate and she gathered speed, racing down on her victim. He looked ahead over the bows of the pink. As if on cue, the Vipers were showing. Waves burst in a broken arc ahead of the little vessel. Here and there patches of white foam swirled over coral outcrops. In the gaps the sea was lifting in a succession of low, powerful swells as it forced its way across submerged dangers. To the north, as far as the eye could see, an expanse of broken water gave warning that an underwater barrier of rock and sand and boulders extended across the vessel's track. It was a sight to appal any mariner.

He heard a shout from Dan. The Miskito was pointing urgently, his arm rigid, the hand still holding the scrap of paper that was his chart. He must have seen the entrance to the channel.

'Not too fast!' Hector hissed at Bartaboa. 'We must keep de Graff on tenterhooks.' Bartaboa called something to his Coromantee sailors. One of them grinned with pleasure as he and a companion eased out a sheet. Its sail spilled a little wind, barely enough to be noticed. But the *Speedy Return* slowed fractionally.

Another quick look aft, and Hector saw that the *Sainte Rose* was directly behind them now, less than a musket shot away, closing in for the kill. The frigate's entire crew were on deck, gazing at their victim, waiting for the *Speedy Return* either to turn and be boarded, or to smash on to the reefs. De Graff himself was instantly recognizable, a tall figure in blue and white, standing by himself at the windward rail.

'Another two cables!' Dan shouted down. 'Then hard to starboard.'

Hector felt the swooping change as the *Speedy Return* passed over the hidden outer fringe of the reef. The hull rose and then dropped swiftly as a gathering swell passed beneath her keel. Now there was no time to look back at the frigate. He concentrated on what lay ahead. The colour of the sea had changed. Once a pure bright blue, it had turned insipid beige. They were running over sandy shallows. All of a sudden a darker patch flashed by to starboard, clearly visible – a large coral head, its jagged crest inches below the surface of the sea. It would punch a hole into the hull of any ship that ran on to it at speed. In the next few moments more coral heads appeared on either hand. The *Speedy Return* was thrusting headlong into the coral maze, seeking her hidden, crooked path.

He heard Bartaboa let out an oath, and one of the Coromantees ran past him and flung his weight on the tiller to assist. The pink heeled and shot off on a new course. Looking up at Dan, Hector saw that the Miskito was beckoning, indicating a change of direction. Out of the corner of his eye Hector noticed a dark patch in the water beside the ship. At first he thought it was more coral, but the black shape was keeping pace with the ship, racing alongside her. It was her shadow on the sea floor. The water was less than a fathom deep.

The pink dashed onward, deep among the breakers. White water tossed and tumbled on either side. Both helmsmen kept their eyes fixed on Dan at the masthead.

The Miskito pointed another change of direction, and the pink heeled as the rudder came over again. Bartaboa was swearing steadily in a low voice. Hector found himself gripping the rail fiercely, his knuckles white. One of the Coromantee sailors, standing by the starboard main brace, flashed him a grin of pure delight as he enjoyed the madcap ride.

'De Graff's decided to follow you,' said a calm voice. Hector had forgotten all about Anne-Marie Kergonan. She was standing close to the stern, dressed in a white shirt and a dark brown dress, her hair held back by a crimson and white scarf. She seemed utterly composed, staring aft. Hector swung round to follow her gaze.

It was true. The *Sainte Rose* was also entering the area of white water. De Graff must have grasped that the *Speedy Return* knew of a channel through the Vipers and was using it to slip through his fingers. He was relying on staying directly in his quarry's wake. But he was taking a terrible risk.

'He's more of a fool than I thought,' murmured Anne-Marie to herself, just loud enough for Hector to overhear.

Next came an awful thump followed by a grinding sound as the hull of the pink scraped against coral. Hector's heart leapt into his mouth. He waited for the sickening crash as the vessel came to a halt, gashed open by the reef. But there was only a brief tremor through the hull, the speed scarcely dropped, and then she had slithered past the obstacle and was moving freely again.

'Good Dutch shipbuilding,' joked Bartaboa, in an attempt to relieve the tension. But his face remained taut with apprehension.

'How much farther to go?' Hector yelled up to Dan.

'Less than two cables. Then we're through the worst.'

Hector allowed himself a brief moment of hope. Perhaps the *Speedy Return* would wriggle through the reefs with only a few feet of planking scratched and gouged by the coral. But then what? If de Graff managed to follow the same channel, the pursuit would resume. This time there would be no escape. As soon as they were back on the open sea, the frigate was sure to overtake the smaller vessel. He could picture the outcome: half a dozen round shot to disable the pink, then de Graff's ship alongside and grappled fast, his men, vastly superior in numbers, dropping on to the deck of their quarry to take possession. Any resistance would be futile. Hector decided that when that moment came, he would order Dan, Jezreel and the others to surrender. He would accept sole responsibility for enraging de Graff, and hope the filibustier would deal leniently with the rest of them.

A full-throated howl interrupted his thoughts. One of the Coromantees, the same man who had grinned at him when easing out the main sheet, was bellowing with glee. Head thrown back, he was doing a shuffling dance on deck, clicking his fingers and crowing with delight.

Hector looked to see the reason. The *Sainte Rose* was at a dead stop, her bow at a strange upward angle, her hull canted over to one side. Her foremast had carried away and toppled forward. Rigging and sails lay jumbled across the foredeck. A snapped main topmast hung suspended like a broken wing. Her deck was alive with men trying to bring the damage under control.

'She's run on the reef!' Bartaboa burst out, his voice exultant. 'They'll not get her off in a hurry.' He gesticulated excitedly to his crew. 'Throw off the sheets! No hurry now.' Then he remembered where he was, and relayed his orders in their language.

The crew of the *Speedy Return* scrambled to obey their instructions as Hector took in the scope of the disaster that had overtaken de Graff. The *Sainte Rose* was solidly aground. The force of the impact had carried her forward for half her length, the hull sliding up on the coral outcrop. De Graff was helpless.

Hector thought quickly. 'The tide? How's it making?' he demanded of Bartaboa.

The sailing master was still shouting orders. He broke off long enough to take a look at the two small islands before answering, 'Two hours past high water is my guess.'

Hector stepped across to where the Reverend Watson had been observing events. 'Can your sakers reach that far?' he asked.

Watson nodded. 'Easily.'

Hector turned back to Bartaboa. 'Bring her head to wind. We anchor here.'

The sailing master stared back at him in surprise. 'Why don't we sail on for Port Royal and leave de Graff and his men to their fate?'

'I have a debt to collect,' Hector told him.

Shaking his head in disbelief, Bartaboa ordered his men to brail up the sails and drop anchor. The *Speedy Return* drifted to a halt little more than a hundred paces from the spot where the *Morvaut* had fished for the Spanish wreck.

Dan came sliding down the backstay and dropped on deck. 'Be careful, Hector. De Graff's more dangerous than a wounded jaguar. He's got at least a hundred men on that frigate. That's more than we could handle if they get too close.'

'I don't plan on allowing that to happen,' said Hector. He turned to the Reverend Watson. 'If I can bring one of your guns to bear, can you put a round shot into the frigate for me?'

'With pleasure and as often as you like!' the parson answered, his eyes sparkling.

It took half an hour to attach a spring to the anchor cable and haul in so that the pink swung broadside on to the frigate. Meanwhile from the *Sainte Rose* there was the distant thump of axes followed by a number of heavy splashes as de Graff's men cut away the fallen spars and rigging, then heaved some of their guns overboard, trying to lighten the ship. Then they lowered their longboat, and a double team of oarsmen attempted to haul the ship off the coral. But the frigate stayed, stuck fast.

'Time to attract their attention,' observed the parson. With Jezreel's help he had loaded one of the pink's sakers and spent several minutes aiming the gun, making minute adjustments until he was satisfied. 'Here you are, captain,' he said to Hector, handing him a length of lit matchcord. 'You brought us through the Vipers, so you should do the honours.'

Hector touched the glowing tip of the cord to the saker's vent. The gun fired, and there was a triple splash as the cannonball skipped across the sea towards its target. It must have struck the frigate's hull. They saw men thrown to the deck. The dangling topmast broke free and came crashing down.

'Jezreel, be so kind as to swab out the barrel. We'll get ready for a second round,' said the parson.

He was less than halfway through the reload when de Graff's own flag, the privateersman's colours of blue with a white cross and the fleur-de-lis in the centre, was hauled down from the mizzen.

'Now what?' asked Bartaboa.

'We wait for de Graff to come to us,' Hector told him.

'You seem very confident.'

'He plays by his own set of rules. He'll want to come to some sort of agreement,' said Hector.

The frigate's longboat had given up the attempt to pull the *Sainte Rose* off the reef and was alongside de Graff's ship. After a short stay it pushed off and came towards the anchored pink. Someone in the bow was holding up a white sheet.

'Are we going to let them come alongside?' asked Bartaboa nervously.

'Only long enough for de Graff to come aboard. No one else,' said Hector. The tall figure of the filibustier captain could be seen seated in the stern of the approaching vessel. Bartaboa cupped his hands around his mouth and shouted the warning. Jezreel, Dan and three of the Coromantee sailors lined the rail, pointing loaded muskets down at the visitors.

De Graff grabbed for the shroud chains and swung himself on to the main deck. The filibustier captain carried neither pistol nor sword. Nevertheless he had chosen to wear a richly ornamented baldrick across his immaculate dark blue tunic. From the polished toes of his bucket boots to his broad-brimmed hat with its white plume to match his breeches, he cut an elegant figure that Hector knew was designed to impress.

'Mr Lynch,' said de Graff. 'Hector Lynch, isn't it?' His china-blue eyes flicked towards the watching crew. If he was surprised to see how few they were – and that several looked to be former slaves – he did not show it.

'We have some unfinished business,' Hector said bluntly. He was determined not to be overawed by a man he had just out-witted, however formidable the other captain appeared. 'Some time ago you intercepted a pinnace I had chartered, the *Morvaut*, and seized some valuables from me and my companions. I want them returned. If they are no longer in your possession, I demand equal value as compensation.'

The filibustier raised a hand to his luxuriant moustache. 'I am happy to oblige. Is there anything more?' His voice was languid, as if discussing a minor detail.

'Nothing. As soon as we have received the value of our property, the *Speedy Return* will continue on her voyage. You and your crew will be at liberty to continue with your efforts to get your ship off the reef. Should that prove impossible, I'm sure your carpenters can construct additional boats to carry your crew back to Providencia.'

De Graff treated Hector to a patronizing stare. 'You know all about small boat journeys, I seem to remember. To satisfy my curiosity, tell me how you managed to get away from my prize crew on that pinnace and then disappear.'

Listening carefully to the cool, dispassionate voice, Hector had become aware of a pent-up fury behind the disdainful courtesy. He was about to answer when a voice from behind him said, 'They escaped with my help.'

Anne-Marie had withdrawn into the cabin when de Graff came aboard. Now she stepped out on to the open deck and addressed the filibustier captain boldly.

The change in de Graff was startling. The veneer of polite-ness cracked. He rounded on the Breton, his features flushed with anger. 'I thought as much at the time, you bitch!' he spat.

There was no mistaking the venom in his voice. All civility had vanished. De Graff was bitter and ferocious. 'You've been leading me a dance, haven't you? It wouldn't surprise me if you haven't been playing the whore with this young man as well.'

Anne-Marie laughed in his face. 'You fool! I helped this young man escape because he put the woman he loved before all else. He chartered my boat and went fishing wrecks to raise money for his life with her. That appealed to me more than someone who thought of nothing but riches and the luxuries they could buy.'

De Graff's lip curled. 'You expect me to believe that, when you ran away with him at the first opportunity. Doubtless you gloated when you saw the *Sainte Rose* run aground.'

Anne-Marie was having difficulty holding back her temper. Her voice shook. 'Your pride and self-regard led you on to that reef!' she retorted.

'So speaks the daughter of a common prostitute and the widow of a drunk,' said de Graff savagely.

To Hector's astonishment, Anne-Marie took a quick pace towards the filibustier captain and slapped him full across his cheek. 'I demand satisfaction for that insult,' she snapped. Her eyes blazed with anger.

De Graff shook his head in amazement. 'You what?'

'Satisfaction for that last remark. You enjoy acting the gentleman. Now prove it is more than sham.'

'Are you challenging me to a duel?' The filibustier was incredulous.

'I am.' Anne-Marie Kergonan was quivering with fury.

'And what weapons are we to use?' De Graff asked. He was back in control of himself, his voice icily sarcastic.

'The insult was yours, so the choice is mine,' she replied, her jaw set firmly.

'Not pistols, I hope. I heard what you did to that man who disposed of your brother.' Now de Graff's words had a mocking ring.

'No, not pistols.'

'Rapier? Broadsword? I doubt that you have the reach,' said the filibustier. He raised an eyebrow in amusement. He was enjoying baiting her.

'You insulted both my husband and my mother, so I will defend their good name in the manner of which they would approve.'

For a moment de Graff looked baffled. Then his brow cleared. 'You mean a duel with fusils?'

'Exactly,' snapped the Breton. 'Muskets. There is sufficient space on that island over there.' She gestured off to starboard, towards the low islet.

De Graff appealed to Hector. 'This woman has gone out of her wits.'

Anne-Marie seized Hector's sleeve and pulled him round so that they were face to face, barely inches apart. 'Hector, you owe me this,' she said slowly and deliberately. 'That night you and your friends left the *Morvaut* in that cockboat I could have raised the alarm. But I didn't.'

Looking directly into those angry, unblinking eyes, Hector saw how Anne-Marie Kergonan deserved the nickname Tigress. She was single-minded, implacable and fearless. She was also deadly serious that she intended to fight a duel with de Graff.

After the space of a heartbeat, Anne-Marie added in a quieter voice, 'If this goes wrong, look for Maria in Port Royal. That is where I told her to go in search of you.'

She released his sleeve, and Hector found himself saying, 'I will make certain the duel is conducted fairly. Jezreel will be in charge. He knows the customs.'

'Thank you,' said Anne-Marie. Ignoring de Graff, she strode away in the direction of the cabin.

Hector beckoned to Jezreel. The ex-prize-fighter was still at the midships rail with a loaded musket, making sure that the longboat from the *Sainte Rose* stayed well clear. When Jezreel had joined him, Hector said, 'Anne-Marie has challenged de Graff to a duel with muskets. I'm putting you in charge.'

Jezreel took the matter in his stride. 'Who is to fire first?' he asked de Graff.

The filibustier captain shrugged. 'My opponent's sex gives her precedence.'

'Do you have your own fusil aboard your ship?'

'An ordinary musket should do just as well.'

'You can take this,' said Jezreel, handing over his musket. 'It shoots straight, though it doesn't have much range.'

De Graff accepted the gun and looked towards the island. 'That won't make much difference. I doubt there's enough room for a full ground. Let's get this over with.'

Anne-Marie reappeared, carrying the long hunting gun she had brought aboard. Jezreel beckoned her forward so that both she and de Graff could hear what he had to say.

'My task is to remind you of the rules so there are no mistakes. The three of us will be set ashore on that island over there. Each will carry a gun of their choice, a powder flask and a bag of bullets, but only my musket will be loaded. I will stay at the landing place. You will walk in opposite directions until you are separated by a distance which I calculate is not less than fifty paces. When I call upon you to stop, you turn to face one another. Is that clear so far?'

Both his listeners nodded. De Graff had a bored expression on his face as if he did not need the lecture. Jezreel continued. 'The challenger, Anne-Marie Kergonan, will then load her fusil, take aim and shoot at the challenged, Captain Laurens Cornelis de Graff. After the first shot, it will be the turn of the captain to fire. The exchange of shots will continue until one or other of the duellists is killed or wounded. Is that clear?'

Again, de Graff and Anne-Marie nodded.

'One more thing – whoever is receiving fire is obliged to remain absolutely still. That is the custom. If either party attempts to evade the bullet or distract the opponent's aim, it will be my duty to shoot him or her out of hand. Is that clear?'

Again his listeners nodded.

'Good. Then let us go to the island,' said Jezreel. He went to the rail and beckoned to the longboat to come alongside.

✳

HECTOR WATCHED THEM go ashore on the island. Too far away for him to make out the details, he could see Jezreel take up his place at the water's edge, then the longboat rowed clear. Anne-Marie and de Graff began walking off in opposite directions. He counted the number of their paces. It was between thirty and forty, and the distance between them was at least seventy yards when Jezreel must have called a halt. He saw the two duellists turn and face one another. He wondered if Anne-Marie had the strength to hold the long-barrelled hunting gun steady. What followed would require skilful marksmanship. That was why men like her dead husband, the cattle hunter, had chosen this strange way to settle their quarrels. They prided themselves on accuracy with a gun.

De Graff was standing very tall, his back straight. He held his musket cradled in his arms and looked directly at his opponent. He had not deigned to turn side on and present a narrower target. Even at that distance his posture was one of boredom, not fear. Facing him, Anne-Marie was taking her time. Hector saw her place the butt of her hunting gun on the sand, pour in a measure of powder, drop in the musket ball, and ram it home. Deliberately she slid the ramrod back into its slot. Then she raised the weapon to her shoulder. Legs braced, she seemed to pause for a long time, the gun levelled. De Graff was like a blue and white statue. He had taken off his hat and placed it on the ground beside him. A whisper of breeze lifted his yellow hair.

There was a puff of smoke as Anne-Marie pulled the trigger, followed by the hollow report of the musket shot.

For a brief moment de Graff stayed standing. Then his own musket slipped from his arms and, very slowly, he toppled over to one side, fell to the sand, and lay without moving. Jezreel was running forward to assist him. Anne-Marie had dropped her fusil, and she too was running along the strand towards her victim.

Hector had to squint against the glitter of the sunshine off the bright sea. Jezreel had knelt down beside de Graff's body, presumably to check the extent of the wound. Anne-Marie joined him, and from her movements he guessed that she was tearing a strip from her dress to use as a bandage.

Then Jezreel stood up and came striding back down the beach to the water's edge. He waved to the waiting longboat, beckoning it closer. Three or four of the oarsmen jumped into the shallows and ran up the beach. They picked up their captain, carried him back and put him in the longboat. Jezreel and Anne-Marie scrambled aboard and then the boat sped off towards the stranded frigate.

'He's badly hurt by the look of it,' observed Jacques. He had come to stand alongside Hector at the rail. They watched the longboat reach the *Sainte Rose* and the wounded captain being hoisted aboard.

'Let's hope they have a competent surgeon,' said Hector. He held no real dislike for de Graff.

'De Graff runs that ship more like a buccaneer than a royal vessel. There should be a good sawbones aboard,' said Jacques. It was common practice among buccaneers and privateers to club together before a voyage and hire their own surgeon who could deal with shipboard illness and battle wounds.

'I think I ought to go across and see if I can help,' said Hector. He had been a surgeon's assistant at one time and had dealt with gunshot wounds.

'Hello, it seems that they're coming to us for something,' observed Jacques not long afterwards. The longboat had again put off from the frigate and was rowing rapidly towards them. When the boat was within earshot, a man stood up and began shouting urgently.

'What's he calling for?' asked Hector.

'He's asking for a priest. Anne-Marie must be a crack shot,' observed Jacques dourly.

Hector ran in search of Watson. He found him seated on a cannon, hat on head and Bible in hand. He was reading passages from Scripture, first in English, then consulting a slip of paper and mouthing the translation to his audience of two of the Coromantee sailors. 'Reverend, the frigate is calling urgently for a priest,' Hector told him.

Watson looked up. 'If it's to administer the last rites, then Graff will want a Papist, not me.'

'I doubt he'll care very much what sort of clergyman he gets. I'll go with you,' said Hector brusquely.

Watson closed his Bible with a snap and accompanied him to where the longboat had already pulled alongside. Moments later they were being rowed towards the *Sainte Rose*. 'Is your captain badly hurt?' Hector asked one of the oarsmen in French.

'In the heart,' came the reply, and the man bent to his next stroke.

A boarding ladder had been lowered, and an impatient-looking naval officer was waiting to escort them. As Hector was hurried across the deck, he noted that de Graff's crew had already got on with making good the damage to their ship. Men were splicing broken cordage, a team of carpenters and their mates were busy with drawknives, shaping a new topmast, and from below came the sound of hammering. Doubtless the hull planking was being repaired. The crew were rough, ill-disciplined and often tipsy, but in an emergency they were good seamen.

They stopped before a handsome door of carved mahogany set under the break of the poop deck. Their escort knocked discreetly and stood aside for Hector and the parson to enter.

After the poky accommodation of the *Speedy Return*, the frigate captain's cabin was palatial. It extended across the full width of the ship. A broad stern window let in bright sunshine that lit up every corner of the room. On the floor was a fine carpet patterned in red and black. The bulkheads were hung with paintings. An inlaid writing desk stood beside a glass-fronted cabinet containing books and rolled-up charts. There were half a dozen gilt chairs of the type Hector would have expected to see in a salon.

Seated on one of them was Anne-Marie Kergonan. She was dressed with particular care. Her fringed petticoat and silk gown were in green and gold, and she had tied matching bows in her hair. From a ribbon of green watered silk around her throat hung a heavy gold man's ring set with a large green gem.

Hector was lost for words. He could scarcely recognize the fierce duellist who had gone ashore dressed soberly and carrying a fusil. He came to the conclusion that de Graff must have kept an entire wardrobe for her on his ship. Anne-Marie's hands were demurely folded on her lap, and she gave him an enigmatic, self-assured look.

An even greater surprise was de Graff. Hector had expected to find him on the point of death. Instead, the filibustier captain was very much alive. Propped on cushions, he was sitting up in a sea cot suspended by ropes from the deck beams. His uniform coat was draped over his shoulders. Opened at the front, it revealed a thick swathe of bandages covering his bare chest. He looked alert and healthy apart from a slight pallor that Hector put down to loss of blood.

'Thank you for bringing a churchman, Monsieur Lynch. I'm glad to see he has his Bible with him.'

Watson was looking equally taken aback.

Hector recovered his composure. 'Captain, I am pleased to see that you are not badly hurt. And I trust that honour has been satisfied.'

De Graff grinned. 'More than satisfied. You might say that honour has been retrieved.'

'I'm afraid I don't follow you.'

De Graff shifted, easing his position in the cot. 'My wound is painful but not fatal and it has made me see things differently.'

Hector allowed himself a quick glance at Anne-Marie. She had one hand up to her throat and was fingering the ring on the ribbon. She was looking mildly triumphant.

'I never thought I would encounter a woman who would challenge me to a duel nor aim a fusil so well,' said de Graff. 'Such a woman is beyond compare.'

Hector waited for the filibustier to go on.

'So I have asked Anne-Marie to be my wife. She has agreed.'

Hector felt his mouth drop open with shock.

De Graff attempted a small bow in his direction. 'I am in your debt, Monsieur Lynch. Thanks to you I have come to realize that my recent actions were unthinking. They were driven by jealousy. In my business jealousy is a dangerous weakness. Marrying Anne-Marie Kergonan will mean I need no longer be swayed by it. I will think clearly again.'

Hector looked from him to Anne-Marie. The ring on the neck ribbon must be a token from de Graff.

'Let me be the first to congratulate you,' he said to the Frenchman.

'Not until the priest here has solemnized our vows. Mr Lynch, I would be glad if you would act as one witness. Lieutenant DuBois here will act as the other.'

The Reverend Watson had recovered from his astonishment. He took off his hat, opened his Bible and cleared his throat. He was about to begin reading when, suddenly, he paused, looked up and said to de Graff, 'Captain, you do know that it is customary for the minister to receive a marriage fee.'

'Yes, yes, we'll deal with that later,' de Graff answered brusquely, waving his hand dismissively. 'Please get on with it.'

It took Watson no more than five minutes to perform the ceremony and pronounce Captain Laurens Cornelis de Graff and Anne-Marie Kergonan to be man and wife.

'Well, that calls for a celebration,' said de Graff as the parson closed his Bible and replaced his hat on his head. The naval officer went across to a walnut cabinet and took out half a dozen crystal glasses and a bottle of fine cognac. He poured and handed out the drinks and the assembled company toasted the marriage.

De Graff was in an expansive mood. 'Mr Lynch, I will give instructions that goods to the same value of those taken from the *Morvaut* are placed aboard the longboat taking you and the minister back to your ship. I hope you will excuse me if I don't escort you, but my wound is too fresh to allow me to walk.'

Hector had turned to leave the cabin when he was brought to a halt by Watson saying loudly, 'Captain de Graff, there is still the matter of my fee.'

A wave of embarrassment swept over Hector. He was ashamed at the parson's naked greed as he waited for Watson to name his price. Fortunately de Graff seemed not the least put out. 'Of course, Monsieur, tell me what you want. I count myself lucky that a priest was so close to hand.'

'I would like the longboat,' announced Watson.

There was a bemused silence.

'My ship's longboat?' asked de Graff.

'Yes. I would be obliged if the boat could be handed over to me. That will be my fee.'

De Graff looked completely baffled. 'But I need the longboat to set the anchors when we attempt to pull the *Sainte Rose* off the reef by her capstan.'

Watson was adamant. 'It will be enough if the longboat is delivered to the *Speedy Return* after the anchors have been set.'

De Graff looked across at Hector. Both men were disconcerted.

'Reverend, we don't need a longboat,' Hector interjected. 'It's too big to carry on the *Speedy Return*. We'd have to tow it all the way to Port Royal. We already have the cockboat as a tender and that is sufficient.'

'The longboat is not for us,' said Watson.

'Then for whom?' asked Hector. He could not imagine why the parson wanted a thirty-foot open boat equipped with mast and sails.

'You are forgetting our Coromantee crew. We cannot take them back to Port Royal. They would be treated as runaways, branded or chained, perhaps both. Certainly they would be whipped.'

'And what good would the longboat be for them?'

'I've been talking with Dan. He tells me that his people are partly descended from men from Africa wrecked on their shore.

The Miskito might look favourably on a boatload of black sailors who reach them. You have seen that they are prime seamen. I propose giving them the longboat and enough water and food to see them safely to the Miskito shore. There they can take their chances.'

Hector looked at the parson. Watson had removed his hat once again, and he was passing his hand through the last few long strands of lank greasy hair. His eyes were pleading.

Hector knew that he owed a debt to his African sailors. The *Return* could make it back to Port Royal without their help. A skeleton crew could handle the pink.

'If Captain de Graff agrees to provide you with the longboat, I will let the Coromantees leave. Will you go with them?'

The minister shook his head. 'No. My work is still among the oppressed. I will return to Port Royal with you and somehow get myself to another island where I can continue my ministry.'

Hector caught de Graff's eye. The filibustier captain spread out his hands in a gesture of resignation. 'So be it. If you and Mr Lynch will return directly to your ship, I will have the boatswain arrange for all my ship's anchors to be carried out, ready for hauling off on the height of the next spring tide. Once the anchors are properly set, the longboat will be handed over to you.'

'Can I have your word on that?' said Watson.

'You don't need my word,' answered de Graff with a gallant nod towards Anne-Marie. 'My wife will make sure that I keep the bargain.'

THIRTEEN

IN PORT ROYAL THE WEATHER had turned very peculiar. Thunderclouds billowed and massed over the town, their undersides dark and swollen. But they never released rain. The sea breeze which normally cooled the town by day failed. The air trapped under the cloud blanket was stiflingly hot and oppressive. Drawn into the lungs it felt as if it had already been breathed twice over. Everyone suffered. There was a general run of headaches and fevers and the lowering sky produced a widespread sense of foreboding. The evenings drew dark almost the moment the sun went down, and at that early hour many townsfolk took to their beds and hammocks. They lay sweating, unable to sleep, listening to the hum and whine of the flying insects that multiplied and thrived in the sultry conditions. In the front room of his town house, Captain Blackmore, planter and council member, could feel the sweat trickling down his back and pooling in the little hollow at the base of his spine. Although only a short while after sunset, it was already so dark that he had called on the servants to light the candles. He sat at a table and watched a beetle cautiously explore the wooden surface. The insect was the size, shape and colour of a roasted coffee bean.

The planter leaned forward and picked up a candle holder from the table. He held it over the beetle and carefully tilted the light so that a runnel of melted wax dripped down and landed on the insect's back. The splash of molten wax caused the beetle to turn and scuttle for cover. The planter quickly laid his arm on the table, blocking the insect's escape. The beetle turned back. As it did so, the planter dripped a larger splash of liquid on to its carapace. The beetle raised its wings, trying to fly away. But it was too late, the wax was congealing, holding it down, trapping it. A third cascade of the wax and the beetle died, entombed like a fly in amber.

Captain Blackmore put down the candle and looked across at Maria seated opposite him. They were alone. 'I gather that you spend much of your free time on the waterfront,' he said.

'I can assure you, sir, that I am not neglecting my duties to your children,' answered Maria. The planter had called her unexpectedly to the interview after finishing his supper. The three children in her charge were asleep upstairs, and the planter's mother, Mrs Blackmore, had not yet returned from a visit to friends for gossip and a game of whist.

'Quite so. Señor Pimiento tells me that they are making fair progress in learning Spanish.'

'The little girl in particular.'

'It is not fitting for the governess of my children to frequent the waterfront. It gives the wrong impression.'

The planter looked at Maria pensively, his fingers toying with the base of the candlestick. His brooding gaze unsettled her. She looked down at her hands clasped on her lap, and strained her ears hoping to hear the footsteps of Mrs Blackmore returning to the house. She wished fervently for some sort of interruption to the interview. The planter allowed the silence to drag out before he said quietly, 'I'm told that a pirate by the name of Lynch was sent here by the Spanish authorities in Cartagena to be tried for piracy. But he seems to have disappeared. Would he be a relation of yours?'

Despite the heat in the stuffy room, Maria felt as if someone had thrown a bucket of ice water over her. Her stomach muscles tensed. She wondered how Blackmore had come by his information and whether it was correct. Struggling to keep her voice steady, she said, 'It is true that I am married, and that my husband is a seafarer. But he is no pirate. There must be other Lynches serving at sea. It is a common enough name in the Caribbees.'

'I expect to have a hand in the man's fate when this particular Lynch is back in custody,' said the captain. He paused to allow the significance of his remark to sink in.

Maria forced herself to sound meek. 'Forgive me, sir, but if he is accused of piracy does he not face trial before the chief justice?'

'He does, and if the chief justice finds this Lynch guilty of piracy – as he surely will – he will condemn him to be hanged and his body put on show at Gallows Point. But first the Governor must approve the death sentence.'

'And the Governor will seek your advice?' said Maria cautiously. She sensed that Blackmore was approaching the crux of the matter, and she knew that it would be unpleasant.

'Governor Inchiquin is not well. This oppressive weather has made his illness very much worse. He has taken to his sickbed and delegated all his official duties to a council of three nominated by the Assembly. I am one of those who were selected.'

'I congratulate you and hope that the Governor recovers his full health in due course,' said Maria flatly.

'More likely the Governor will never recover.' Blackmore's gravelly voice held no trace of regret.

Maria shifted slightly in her chair as if about to rise.

Captain Blackmore deliberately allowed his gaze to drift downward from her face and linger on her bust. 'If this pirate Lynch does turn out to be your husband, you can come to me for help.' His tone left no doubt how he expected to be rewarded for his assistance.

Climbing the stairs to her room, Maria felt a tightening knot of fear as she wondered if Hector knew the danger he faced on his return to Port Royal – and how she could possibly warn him. More practically, when she reached her bedchamber, she closed the door and wedged a chair under the handle.

*

ABOARD THE *Speedy Return* the leaden colour of the sky was worrying Jacques. He was easily seasick and he feared that he could be called upon to handle the rig on a heaving, slippery deck.

'You don't think that a hurricane is on the way, do you?' he muttered to Hector. The two men were sharing the afternoon watch. Despite the ominously overcast sky, the north-west wind was holding steady and they had been able to lash the helm, and as a result had very little to do.

'Wrong season,' came the brief answer. Hector had been in a half-trance, daydreaming of what he would say to Maria now that he knew she could be waiting for him in Port Royal.

'It'll be a pity if bad weather keeps the crowds away when we sail into port flying de Graff's own flag upside down. It'll spoil the effect,' said Jacques.

'That's not a storm sky. The clouds are too stationary,' Hector reassured his friend. He had insisted that de Graff surrender his personal ensign. The white cross on a blue ground with a single large fleur-de-lis at its centre would be proof of his mission's success. He intended to hand it to Governor Inchiquin as a trophy.

Jacques stifled a yawn. 'I'm looking forward to spending some of the compensation that de Graff paid for stealing our salvage from the Spanish wreck.'

'And what will you do after sampling the delights of Port Royal?' asked Hector. His happy anticipation of seeing Maria was tempered by the knowledge that he and his friends would soon be going their separate ways. Dan had already left. He had volunteered to go with the longboat and the Coromantee sailors to the Miskito coast. There he would introduce them to his own people, and plead their case before the council of elders. At the last moment the Reverend Watson had changed his mind and decided to accompany them, as had Allgood and the other two men Jezreel had recruited. Now there were only Hector, Jezreel, Jacques and Bartaboa to handle the pink, a sufficient number if the weather did not break.

Jacques grinned. He was cheering up. 'Depends how much money remains after I've had my debauch.'

'We don't yet know how much there is to begin with,' Hector cautioned. 'De Graff promised goods to the value of our salvage. But I haven't had time to check the chests and bags that his men put aboard.'

Jacques was not to be discouraged. 'Port Royal is a den of thieves. I'm sure we'll find someone willing to take everything off our hands, no questions asked.' He broke off and squinted forward over the bows. 'I think I see high mountains dead ahead.'

Hector followed the direction of his gaze. Far in the distance appeared a faint irregular line, about a hand's breadth above the horizon. Against the gloomy backdrop of the sky the line was difficult to make out but it could be the crest of a mountain ridge. There seemed to be a darker solid patch beneath it, possibly a land mass. Hector wished that Dan were still aboard. The Miskito's keen eyesight would have settled any doubt.

'If that's Jamaica, we should reach Port Royal before noon tomorrow.' His heart beat a little faster at the knowledge that he could be very close to Maria.

From the main deck below them Jezreel had noticed the sudden air of activity. He put aside the rope he was splicing and came up the companionway to join them.

'Jamaica!' exclaimed Jacques, pointing.

'Can't be absolutely sure yet,' Hector warned.

Jezreel studied the horizon and as he did so a shaft of sunlight broke through a cleft in the clouds. For a moment it lit up a patch of sea midway between the *Speedy Return* and the land. Sailing in that circle of light was a vessel. Hector knew her instantly. She was the *Swan*, the same elderly naval frigate which had brought him and his friends from Cartagena to face justice in Port Royal. She was heading towards them.

Jezreel also recognized the warship. 'That's Jamaica all right. The *Swan* must be on patrol, watching out for any French attack on the coast.'

'Can't we ignore her and sail past?' Jacques suggested. He was still not sure about the coming weather and wanted to be snug in port as soon as possible.

Hector thought for a moment. 'That would be easy enough. *Swan* is a slow sailer as I recall. But it would give the wrong impression, as if we had something to hide. Best if we report to her captain.' Privately he was disappointed that their arrival in Port Royal and his chance to locate Maria would be delayed, if only for a few hours.

They watched the *Swan*'s lumbering approach. It was obvious that her captain wanted to intercept the pink. When still a mile away he fired a windward gun, the signal to call a halt. Dutifully, the *Speedy Return* let fly her topsail to show that she understood the command, and Hector and his three shipmates began to douse the brig's sails. The pink lay waiting as the larger vessel closed the gap and lowered a boat.

'That's the same lieutenant who handed us over to the provost marshal in Port Royal,' said Jezreel. A fat, yellow-haired young officer could be seen in the stern sheets of the boat as it rowed towards them with the boarding party.

Hector felt a faint prickle of alarm. He had a premonition that something was about to go wrong. He should not have stopped for the *Swan*, but headed directly for Port Royal.

A sailor from the boarding party swung himself nimbly up on to the deck of the *Speedy Return*. He turned and held out an arm to help his more clumsy officer. Hector remembered the young lieutenant's name. It was Balchen, George Balchen. He was a plodder, a little lazy and lacking in imagination and – from what Hector could recall from conversations on the voyage from Cartagena to Port Royal – had an uncle on the Navy Board in London. That was probably how Balchen had got his comfortable posting on the Jamaica station.

With a grunt the lieutenant heaved himself on to the *Return*'s deck and straightened up, catching his breath as he looked about him. Hector noticed for the first time that the lieutenant's eyes were pale grey and very close-spaced. They came to rest on him and Balchen's expression of astonishment was rapidly replaced by one of suspicion. He frowned, trying to recall exactly what had been said when he left Hector and his friends after the meeting with Secretary Reeve at King's House in Port Royal.

'What are you doing here!' he exclaimed. 'Broke your parole, did you? I should have made sure you were locked up.'

'My friends and I were released on the orders of the Governor,' said Hector stiffly.

The lieutenant gave a snort of disbelief. He turned to the men of his boarding party. 'Search this ship! Find out what she's carrying,' he ordered.

He faced Hector again. 'The last time I set foot on this vessel it was to seize her as a smuggler. I see you've changed her to a brig, hoping she won't be recognized.'

Hector tried to sound reasonable. 'We adapted her rig because she sailed better that way. We were chasing French filibustiers.'

Balchen guffawed. 'With what crew? I see only four of you. Hardly enough to go tackling the French.'

'It's complicated . . .' began Hector.

'I'm sure it is,' snapped Balchen. One of his sailors was coming forward, carrying a small canvas sack. Hector recognized one of the bags put aboard by de Graff. Judging by the way it bulged, it contained a variety of hard-edged objects.

'I think you should look at this, sir. Found it tucked away in the forepeak,' said the sailor. He opened the mouth of the sack and pulled out the topmost item – a two-handled silver bowl. It was a valuable piece, about eight inches high, its rim ornately decorated with a scrollwork of flowers. It would have graced a very rich man's table.

'Christ alive! Not even smuggling. That's loot!' exclaimed Balchen. He took the bowl from the sailor and inspected it closely. 'Some sort of crest, Latin inscription. Don't know what it says.' He turned the bowl upside down and looked at the base. 'Hallmark is a lion, so it must be English-made, though no knowing who owned it before this gang of villains got their hands on it.'

'Another three bags, sir, much the same. Bowls, jugs, some plate, jewellery too,' said the sailor.

Hector decided that matters were getting out of hand. 'Lieutenant, those items are legitimate prize. I have a privateer's commission from the Governor.'

Balchen raised a sceptical eyebrow. 'Let's see it then.'

Hector hurried to find the parchment that Mr Reeve, the Governor's secretary, had provided. He handed it to the lieutenant, who read through it slowly. When he had finished he looked up at Hector with a triumphant smirk. 'This document is a fake.'

'It is genuine, prepared by Mr Reeve the Governor's secretary and signed by Lord Inchiquin himself,' objected Hector.

The lieutenant sneered. 'Lynch, you've picked the wrong man to try to hoodwink. I happen to know that the Navy Board has banned the practice of giving out privateering commissions. They are no longer issued. They encourage piracy.'

'I can assure you this one is genuine,' Hector repeated.

'If this were a French commission I'd say you purchased it.' Like everyone else Balchen had heard tales of how the governors of the French-held islands made money by selling privateering commissions with the names left blank, to be filled by the purchaser.

'Could be he's working with the French, and all,' said another sailor who had joined them. He held up de Graff's flag.

Balchen's eyes bulged with shock. 'So you're a traitor as well as a pirate!' he burst out.

'That flag is not mine. It is intended as a gift for Governor Inchiquin.'

Balchen swung round on his heel and shouted to his men, 'We're taking charge of this ship right now. Put this lot under arrest and take them across to the *Swan*.'

Hector made one last attempt to retrieve the situation.

'Lieutenant, you're making a mistake. Lord Inchiquin sent us to locate a French ship that had been raiding shipping. We are on our way back to Port Royal to report that we have found the vessel. She is commanded by Sieur de Graff and, when last seen, was hung up on the Vipers Reef. If the Governor acts quickly, he or our Spanish allies may be able to send a naval force to intercept de Graff and deal with him.'

A slow, knowing grin spread over Balchen's face. 'Lynch, if you were a better liar, you wouldn't make such extravagant claims and you would make sure of your facts. Lord Inchiquin is gravely ill. He has placed the government in the hands of a committee of planters. They couldn't care less about de Graff. When we reach Port Royal, I will hand you over to the provost marshal, properly this time, and make sure you are locked up, even if I have to turn the key myself.'

*

THE LIEUTENANT WAS as good as his word. Forty-eight hours later Hector was seated on a rough bench in a small box of a room, some three paces by two, with a brick floor and a single, small barred window high up in one wall. The provost marshal of Port Royal had put him in a cell by himself after Balchen warned that he was the ringleader of what the lieutenant called a gang of damned, bloody pirates. Jacques, Jezreel and Bartaboa were somewhere in the same gaol, but communication with them was impossible. The Marshalsea prison was one of the best-built structures in the town. The walls were three feet thick, the doors iron-plated, and the roof was strengthened with double beams to deter anyone from escaping upwards.

Hector rose to his feet and banged on the door, calling for the warder. After a delay a small hatch built into the thick door slid back, and he found himself looking into the pimply face of a boy who must have been no more than thirteen or fourteen years old. Hector guessed that he was the son of a regular prison guard, standing in for his father. 'What do you want?' said the lad. He blushed as his adolescent voice broke awkwardly, one moment high, the next low and croaking.

'Will you carry a message to Government House for me, to Mr Reeve, the Governor's secretary?'

'Why should I do that?' asked the lad. His eyes shifted nervously, and he brought up a hand to wipe his nose.

'For payment,' said Hector.

The boy looked interested but doubtful. 'Have you the money with you?'

'I've money hidden away. I can get it later.'

'Not likely.' The tone was dismissive.

'You know that my friends and I were caught with loot from piracy?' said Hector. The lad's expression told him that rumours about their arrest had spread. 'There's more hidden away. Some of it could be yours.'

The youthful eyes were shrewd and calculating. 'All right. I'll carry your message when I'm free to do so, after my father comes back on duty.'

'First I need paper, pen and ink,' said Hector.

The hatch slid shut and Hector paced up and down patiently until once again the hatch opened, and a hand thrust in a sheet of paper torn from a school exercise book, pen and ink. Hector sat on the bench and hurriedly scrawled a note to Reeve while the boy waited. When the note was ready, Hector handed the paper back.

'The ink and pen as well,' demanded the youth.

Hector obeyed. The hatch was shut, and he sat down to wait.

❋

ANOTHER FULL DAY dragged past. It was not until close to sunset that the door to his cell swung open, and Mr Reeve walked in. The change in the secretary's manner and appearance was a shock. He looked wan, untidy, his wig askew and – for some reason – shamefaced. His air of bustling efficiency was gone. Now his manner was both hesitant and demoralized.

'Mr Reeve, thank you for coming to see me,' began Hector.

Over the secretary's shoulder he could see a warder, a man this time, standing at the open door and supervising the interview.

'I came as quickly as I could,' said Reeve. He glanced about him, looking for a chair on which to sit down. But there was only the single bench.

'My friends and I have been arrested for piracy, for joining the French. I hope you'll be able to set matters straight,' said Hector.

The secretary held up his hand to stop him. 'Sadly, I'm no longer kept informed of what is going on.'

Hector blinked in surprise.

Reeve's shoulders seemed to sag a little. 'Lord Inchiquin is very sick and has gone to stay in the countryside. This oppressive weather in town only makes his illness worse. His day-to-day duties are now being performed by a select committee of the Assembly.'

'So I was told,' said Hector, 'but surely your office still functions.'

Reeve shook his head. 'I am passed by. My appointment is as secretary to the Governor. Technically, if he is not in post, I have no authority.'

'Surely you will be able to verify that my commission as a privateer is genuine. You drafted it,' said Hector.

The secretary looked embarrassed. 'Indeed I did, and in good faith.'

'So why can't you consider it now?'

'Because to do so would injure Lord Inchiquin.' Reeve saw Hector's puzzled expression. 'As I explained at the time, a privateer's commission is exceptional.'

Hector was so baffled that, without meaning to, he spoke sharply, 'Nevertheless you wrote out a commission, took it to Lord Inchiquin to sign, and arranged for me to have the *Speedy Return* and provisions from government stores.'

The secretary looked pained. 'That is the problem. Lord Inchiquin should have waited for your commission to be approved by London. Instead he acted hastily and allowed the *Speedy Return* to sail.'

Hector felt as if the walls of the cell were closing in around him. 'I don't see how that affects matters now.'

Reeve adopted an apologetic tone. 'Please, Mr Lynch, you have no idea to what lengths the planters will go to be rid of Lord Inchiquin. They hate and resent him. If they can show that he issued an illegal commission and allowed government stores to be used, they could hurt him badly. Even get him dismissed.'

Hector glared at the distressed man so fiercely that Reeve dropped his gaze.

'I'm sorry,' said Reeve. 'My loyalty is to His Lordship.'

'So you cannot help me?' said Hector bitterly.

'Not at this time. Maybe when His Lordship has recovered his health and taken up the reins of government again.'

'But that may be too late! Here they have a short way of dealing with pirates,' Hector burst out.

Reeve flinched. 'If there's anything I can do in a private capacity, please tell me.'

Hector thought furiously. He and his companions were now friendless and abandoned in Port Royal. No one would even know they were being held in gaol. 'There is one thing you can do,' he said sourly. 'I'm told that there is a young woman recently come to Port Royal. She's in her early twenties, good-looking, with dark chestnut hair, and speaks with a slight Spanish accent. If you could try to trace her and tell her where she can reach me, I would be very obliged.'

The secretary looked relieved that there was something he could do to ease his conscience. 'This woman, does she have a name?'

'She is called Maria. If she is using her married name, it is Lynch. She is my wife.'

Reeve was looking even more penitent than before as he moved towards the cell door.

'Stop!' said Hector. A last-minute thought had occurred to him.

The secretary turned and lingered, though the look on his drawn and weary face told Hector he could see no point in staying any longer.

'Mr Reeve, there is someone else who might be able to assist if you could contact him on my behalf.'

The secretary raised an eyebrow enquiringly, without any enthusiasm. Clearly he thought that it was unlikely that anyone could help Hector.

Hector chose his words carefully. 'When I was in Cartagena, an important merchant assured me that he knew someone here in Port Royal who would intervene on my behalf when I came to trial.'

'An implausible claim,' observed Reeve, regaining a touch of his old rigour.

'I had been of assistance to the merchant, saved his son, and he felt that he was in my debt. He said someone in Port Royal owed him a favour. This man would know when to help me. Do you have any idea who that might be?'

Reeve pondered the question before he answered, speaking cautiously. 'My first thought would be that he was referring to Señor Pimiento, the asiento representative here. He oversees the purchase and shipping of slaves to the Spanish colonies under licence and is in regular contact with Cartagena. But Señor Pimiento could hardly be able to fill the role as your mysterious benefactor. He has no power in the colony.'

'It would be someone of importance, someone capable of influencing a judge and sentencing.' Hector tried not to sound desperate, but he had to follow up any possible lead that might result in his release and that of his friends.

Reeve spread his hands in a gesture of surrender. 'This unknown person will be keeping his connection with Cartagena a very close secret. If his relationship with your friend in Cartagena is so firm, then it must have been built up over many years, from a time when the Spanish were our enemies. That was treason.' He gave a thin smile. 'What you claim is interesting. At one time

I thought I had my hands on all the levers of power in Jamaica, and knew all that went on. But it seems that I was mistaken.'

✳

CAPTAIN BLACKMORE was strolling beside Maria as he and his family returned from Sunday service. The Blackmore townhouse was only a five-minute walk from St Paul's, the church favoured by the wealthier citizens of Port Royal. To an observer it would have seemed that the planter was being courteous, falling in step beside the governess of his children and chatting to her casually as they returned home along the seafront. His mother and three children were a few steps behind, out of earshot. The little group was passing the battery of a dozen cannon known as Morgan's Line in honour of the late Governor.

'This pirate Lynch is back in our custody,' said Blackmore conversationally, though keeping his voice low. 'He and his accomplices were caught with sacks of loot, taken out of English and Spanish ships. He even used a French privateer flag.'

He gave Maria an enquiring sideways glance. 'He's of average height, fair complexion, dark brown hair, and has hazel eyes. In his late twenties. Does that sound familiar?'

When she said nothing, he added, 'He's a fluent Spanish speaker, with a trace of a Galician accent. Surely that should place him if he is your husband.'

Maria kept her head down, struggling not to let her emotions show. Hector was in Port Royal but in terrible trouble. She had to make contact with him, discover if there was a way to help him. She was very conscious of Blackmore's gaze. To some it might have seemed kindly and avuncular. But it made her skin crawl.

She avoided answering Blackmore's question directly. 'Have the authorities dealt with him severely?' she asked.

Blackmore smiled grimly. 'Not yet. He's in the Marshalsea prison, along with his accomplices. I expect the trial will be held within a week. No question about the verdict. After that my colleagues and I will decide what's to be done.'

Maria paused in her stride and looked to her right, out across the glassy sea, as if to admire the view. It had the advantage of turning her face away from Blackmore, and it meant that the three children and their grandmother would catch them up. There was no point in continuing the conversation.

Blackmore lowered his voice still further. 'If that man is your husband, I can arrange for you to have a meeting with him.'

Maria resisted the temptation. She knew it was a trick. If she admitted that Hector was her husband, Blackmore would take advantage of the fact. It was better to lie to him. 'My husband speaks no Spanish. This Lynch must be a stranger.'

She could tell by his cold stare that he did not believe her. There was just time for him to murmur one last comment. 'Nevertheless I think it would be better if you met him. My information may be incorrect in some details.' He turned to address his mother, who had joined them. 'I'm arranging for you to go back to the plantation tomorrow. I have little confidence in our manager there. The children can stay on with me for a couple of days. There's a meeting of the Assembly tomorrow and it will be a chance for them to see their father at work. Their governess can bring them to the public gallery when I am speaking.'

It was neatly done, Maria thought. Blackmore had reminded her of his importance and at the same time got his mother safely out of the way. She decided that for the next few nights she would move into the children's room, in case the captain came knocking at her bedroom door.

THE WEATHER BROKE on Tuesday. The day dawned with no trace of the overcast that had blighted the town for more than a week. In his cell Hector could see the patch of blue that had replaced the sullen drab in the single window and hear the voices of passers-by, more cheerful now the sun was shining. He had worked out that the chief warder liked to spend his afternoons in the tavern. He always smelled of drink in the evening, and it was in his absence that his son ran the prison. Hector had no way of knowing if his conversation with Secretary Reeve would produce news of Maria or some sort of message from Señor Corbalan's mysterious contact in Port Royal. There was nothing he could do but wait and, being accustomed to the need for patience during long sea voyages, he was able to spend most of his time stretched out on the bench in his cell, dozing.

The lad's creaky voice roused him. 'You have a visitor.'

Hector sat up so sharply that he nearly fell to the brick floor. He swung his feet to the ground and turned. Maria was standing in the open doorway. He felt giddy for a moment as if about to faint. Then in two quick strides he was across the room and had thrown his arms around her. He hugged her so fiercely to him that he felt her struggling to draw breath. But she had her arms locked around him and the two of them stood there, without the need for words. Looking past her he saw the warder son standing in the open doorway and watching them open-mouthed. The lad had prob- ably never seen such a display of emotion. With his eyes Hector beseeched the boy to leave them alone. The lad understood. Without a word, he stepped back and gently closed the door.

'Let me look at you,' said Maria finally. He slid his arms lower until they were around her waist and she could lean back and see him. Her face was radiant, filled with love and relief. He bent for- ward and kissed her hungrily, feeling her body curve forward again against his. It was the sensation that he had craved. They stayed like that, the whole world distilled into the space around them. Finally Maria pulled away, though she still kept her arms around his neck. Neither of them was able to give up the other's touch.

'Thank God, I've found you,' she said. Her voice was husky with emotion, and a single tear rolled down her cheek.

'No need to cry over it,' said Hector softly. With his thumb he wiped away the tear. 'How long have you been in Port Royal?'

Before she could answer, another surge of emotion ambushed him and again he had to hug her close. For several more minutes they simply stood and held one another.

Eventually Maria, holding his hand, moved towards the bench. 'I need to sit down,' she said. She produced a small handkerchief from the sleeve of her dress and dabbed her eyes. 'I came as soon as I knew where you were. All that matters is that you are alive and well.'

She put away the handkerchief, stroked the back of his hand, and then rested her head on his shoulders. He could detect a faint perfume in her hair. Without raising her head, she murmured, 'There must be some way to get you out of here.'

'There is,' he answered firmly. 'I've told Mr Reeve that there is someone who can help me, someone influential who can get the charges quashed and arrange my release. I've asked Mr Reeve to find this man.'

She looked puzzled. 'Mr Reeve? Who's he?'

It was Hector's turn to be bemused. 'Lord Inchiquin's secretary. The man who told you where to find me.'

She frowned. 'I found you for myself. My employer told me.'

There was a silence and then Hector said, 'Perhaps I should start at the beginning. Jacques, Jezreel and I – and a man named Bartaboa – have been arrested for piracy, and accused of working with the French.'

Maria nodded. 'That's what I was told.'

'But it is a mistake. Lord Inchiquin issued me with a commission as a privateer. Unfortunately he is no longer in charge in Jamaica, and cannot vouch for me. Nor can his secretary, Mr Reeve. He's the man I thought had found you.'

'But what about this person who may be able to help you?'

Hector rubbed his chin. 'The trouble is, I don't know who he is. If I did, I would get word to him.'

'How do you know he exists?'

'It's a long story, but a Spanish merchant in Cartagena promised that he would arrange for this man to help me because this man owes him a favour.'

'But your friend in Cartagena didn't tell you his name?'

Hector shook his head. 'No. Maybe you could find out who he is more quickly than Reeve. You seem to be good at making enquiries. You found me here.' He gave her hand an affectionate squeeze.

'That was nothing. The man I work for told me about you. He knew a great deal about you and where to find you. Even suggested that I visit you.'

'What's his name?'

'Captain Blackmore. He's a wealthy planter and member of the Assembly. I have a job teaching Spanish to his three children.'

Hector looked down at the floor. A thought had occurred to him. It was a coincidence, but worth following up. 'This Blackmore. Does he have any contact with the Spanish?'

'He sees Señor Pimiento often. Señor Pimiento is the agent for the asiento in Port Royal.'

'And you say that Blackmore knows all about me?'

'Yes. He described your appearance, the colour of your eyes, even that you speak Spanish with a Galician accent.'

'That's odd,' said Hector slowly. 'As far as I know, I've never met this Captain Blackmore.'

He turned to her, his eyes lit up with hope. 'He has to be the man Señor Corbalan was speaking about!' He jumped to his feet and began to pace up and down the small cell. 'Maria, think for a moment. Is there any reason why Blackmore would have commercial contact with Cartagena?'

Maria thought back to her days in Jamaica. Then she remembered the morning she had first come ashore from Petit Goâve and watched the furtive loading of the casks of rum from the isolated beach, rum that came from Captain Blackmore. Then there was the odd remark from the mulatto overseer who had helped her. When he had heard her Spanish accent and that she was looking for work, he had suggested that he take her to see Captain Blackmore. How had he put it? 'He's in thick with the Spaniards.' It all added up.

Maria's heart sank as she looked into Hector's excited face and said, 'Hector, you're almost certainly right. Blackmore is heavily engaged in smuggling. He probably has been dealing with the Spaniards for years.'

Hector was triumphant. 'Oh, Maria!' He seized her hand. 'This is the stroke of fortune that we needed. The man who employs you is the man who Corbalan spoke about. It will be the easiest thing in the world to work with him, and organize my release.'

Maria looked at him, a flush rising to her cheeks. Her voice trembled as she said, 'Hector, this man is the last person in the world who would help you.'

He saw her distress, and his eyes searched her face. 'What do you mean?'

'Captain Blackmore would prefer to see you hang rather than help you. He risks being exposed as an accomplice of the Spaniards.'

The light in Hector's eyes began to dim. 'That's what Reeve said might happen.'

Maria was twisting the scrap of cloth in her hands. She summoned up her courage before she looked Hector full in the face and told him, 'There is another reason why I cannot ask Captain Blackmore to use his influence to help you. He has made it clear that he will only do so if I sleep with him.'

Hector went white. He felt dazed and angry, strangely detached from his surroundings. It was as if someone had punched him in the stomach. He could not trust his emotions and dropped his gaze, staring at the floor, trying to gather his thoughts. The bricks in the floor seemed to ripple as if a wave had passed through them.

Time stood still, and then the world was tilting and shaking in the strangest, most unnatural way.

The bench on which Maria sat rocked a couple of times. Then it tipped over and she was thrown to the ground. Hector had already lost his balance and was sprawled on the floor. He tried in vain to get to his feet but everything was moving from side to side and there was nothing solid or firm which he could hold on to. Maria was staring about her wildly.

Then they heard the rumble and crash of falling masonry.

FOURTEEN

'EARTHQUAKE!' BLURTED HECTOR. Without thinking he was crouching over Maria, trying to protect her with his body. Another tremor shook the ground, and several lumps of plaster cascaded down from the ceiling. The air was filled with a fog of swirling dust. Dimly he heard the first screams float in from the outside world, then another rumbling crash as somewhere in the distance another wall fell. He looked around for better shelter, but there was none. The bench was the only furniture in the cell.

'We must get out of the building,' he shouted into Maria's ear. Her hair was powdered with brick dust. She had sustained a cut to her cheek, and there was a smear of blood. But she appeared unharmed, though numbed by the suddenness and severity of the earthquake.

Still on hands and knees, Hector forced himself to take a long slow breath to calm himself. Then he rose slowly and cautiously, and made a dash for the door. He grabbed the heavy iron handle just as another tremor rocked the building. He clung on, lurching to one side and managed to stay upright. There was a splintering crack close above his head, and he looked up to see that the heavy doorframe had been twisted out of shape by the movement of the building. He wrenched at the handle and, to his relief, the door pulled a third of the way open before it jammed on its distorted hinges. He turned back and helped Maria to her feet. The ground had stopped shaking, though he dreaded that another tremor could come at any time. Holding her by the hand, he began to squeeze through the narrow gap, praying that the building would not shift, crushing him between the door and jamb. He burst free, and a moment later Maria followed him.

They found themselves in a narrow corridor. A pile of slumped rubble blocked any movement to their left, but in the opposite direction the way was clear. Hand in hand they staggered forward, breathing in the fog of dust. 'I must find the others,' Hector wheezed, coughing to clear his throat. They passed several more doors that led into cells, for each had a shuttered window. Then they were in a room where the warders spent their time. It was deserted. Three or four chairs lay on their sides, a table still upright but streaked with spilled beer, a couple of leather tankards had tumbled across the floor. The door to the street was wide open. Clearly the warders had fled into the safety of the open air. Hector looked to see if they had abandoned the prison keys. Lying under the table he saw them – a bunch of heavy metal keys on a ring. 'Maria, get outside and wait for me. I'll find the others,' he said. She hesitated. 'Go!' he shouted. 'I'll be out in a moment.'

She turned and ran.

He tried to get his bearings in the unfamiliar surroundings. Two doors led off into the interior of the building. He opened the nearest of them. Another corridor, very like the first, more iron-plated cell doors on either side. 'Jezreel! Jacques!' he shouted. To his relief he heard an answering shout. It came from the second door along. He ran to it and slammed back the shutter. Jezreel, Bartaboa and Jacques were all inside and on their feet. None of them looked to have been harmed. 'Hang on! I'll get you out,' Hector called. He tried the keys in the lock, one after the other. On the third attempt he felt the levers turn. 'That's it!' he called, and pushed on the door. It did not move. He stepped back and threw his weight on the door. Still it did not budge. 'It's jammed. Try pulling it open from your side!' he shouted. He slammed his shoulder against the metal panels, ignoring the jolt of pain. He felt the door move a fraction. He heard Jezreel's deep voice say calmly, 'Take your time, Hector. On my count, One, two, three . . .' And this time the door banged open.

His friends stepped out. 'This way!' Hector hustled them back the way he had come.

'What about the other prisoners?' asked Jacques.

'There's no time! If there's another quake, the whole building may come down,' Hector snapped irritably. He was thinking of Maria waiting outside. To have found her, only to be crushed beneath a collapsing building would be stupid.

'You've done your bit. See you shortly,' said Jezreel. He took the bunch of keys from Hector's hand, and strode along the corridor, sliding open the shutters of the cell doors and peering in.

Hector found Maria hovering anxiously by the main prison entrance. With her were half a dozen strangers, local worthies by the look of them. They were nervously watching the prisoners coming out of the gaol although they were doing nothing to stop them. There was no sign of any warder nor of the boy. Hector supposed that they had gone to their homes to see what damage had been done.

'Thank God you're safe,' said Maria hugging him. She was half crying with relief.

'We must wait for Jezreel,' Hector told her. He looked about him. The scene of devastation came as a physical shock. Inside the prison there had been no way of knowing what was going on outside. The prison lay at the eastern, poorer end of town, and possibly two-thirds of the houses had collapsed. Their brick and plaster walls had fallen into the roadway, their roofs caved in. The houses that still stood were the humbler structures lightly built of wood, though several of these were askew and looked dangerously unstable. In several places the ground had split into jagged, random cracks, several feet across. Several large holes had appeared, as if the surface had suddenly fallen into underground caves. There were surprisingly few people about.

Most were standing in shock, though a few were clawing at the rubble and fallen stone, trying to get back into their shattered houses. Whether they were searching for their families or merely to recover their possessions, was impossible to tell.

It was when he turned and looked in the opposite direction that Hector understood the full force of the tremor. The building adjacent to the Marshalsea was the courthouse. It had been designed to look imposing, with tall windows, a broad flight of steps leading to a door flanked by columns, and faced in imported stone. It was a total ruin. Beams and rafters stuck out of piles of rubble.

'Looks as though we won't be standing trial in there, at least for a while,' said Jezreel. He, Jacques and Bartaboa had finally emerged from the prison. Behind them were five or six men, fellow prisoners. These were looking about themselves with a mixture of disbelief and optimism.

'Come on!' one of them muttered to his companion. 'Let's get out of here.' The two of them scurried away.

Bartaboa was distraught. 'I must go to see how my family are.'

'Your family?' said Jacques.

'My sister and her children live above the Three Mariners.'

'We'll go with you in case you need a hand,' said Jezreel.

The little group set off past the wrecked courthouse and turned out on the waterfront. They had not gone more than a few paces when they stopped short, unable to believe their eyes. It was Hector who first voiced what all of them could scarcely credit.

'The sea! Where's it gone?' All along the docks, the water level had dropped far below anything that was natural. Vessels normally tied up with their decks above or level with the quayside, were now sunk almost out of sight. Gangplanks which had once sloped downward from the ships to the dock were now tilted the other way.

'What's going on?' murmured Jacques in awe.

As they watched, the row of ships continued to sink downward. Gangplanks clattered and slipped. Mooring lines grew taut and snapped, or wrenched the bollards from the quays. The sea was disappearing beneath them, sucking backwards, recoiling from the land.

Suddenly there was a slithering, grinding crash, and a large section of the parapet of Fort Carlisle, the nearest harbour bastion, broke away and fell, landing into water now less than a foot deep, where once an ocean-going ship had been able to moor.

'What makes the tide do that?' asked Jacques.

'That's not the tide, but something else,' said Hector. Puzzled, he was staring up at the outer wall of the fort. It appeared to be leaning outwards and at the same time sinking downwards. He dragged his attention back to the harbour. The water had ebbed so far that they were beginning to see patches of stinking mud, slime-covered boulders, the blackened ribs of old wrecks. Farther out, from where the merchant ships were at anchor, came shouts and cries of fear. The ships were grounding, touching the bottom with their keels. There was not enough water to keep them afloat. Their crews were scrambling to abandon their vessels or keep their footing on sloping decks. Several of the vessels began to heel over on their sides.

'I've never seen anything like it,' breathed Jezreel.

They stood transfixed, unable to comprehend what was going on. Before their eyes, fish wriggled and flapped in the damp mud, stranded by the receding water. Gulls and cormorants came wheeling down from the sky, calling and shrieking, to pick up easy meals. There was something uncanny and frightening about their gleeful bursts of gluttony in a harbour that was draining away and vanishing. All along the quay astonished observers stood and gaped at the sight. It was so extraordinary that even those who were salvaging goods from a shattered warehouse turned and watched.

Through the soles of his feet Hector felt a distant trembling. It was a very faint shivering. Something made him look at Fort Carlisle again. This time there was no doubt. The seaward wall of the fort was definitely leaning at an angle. The massive rampart, made of stone blocks weighing several tons, was tilting towards the sea as if the foundations had been undermined. Yet there was no water to gnaw away the foundations.

The vibration underfoot increased and, before his eyes, the massive structure of the fort began to slide slowly and unstoppably into the empty harbour. It was an appalling yet majestic sight.

He seized Maria by the arm. 'We must find a refuge, a sanctuary, before the water returns,' he blurted.

'What do you mean?' asked Jacques, his voice sharp with alarm.

'I've a feeling that the sea will come flooding back. And I fear the consequences.'

'First I have to save my family,' insisted Bartaboa. He began to run, heading full pelt along the quay towards the ferry landing. The Three Mariners stood nearby. Hector and the others followed.

As they ran, the shivering of the ground grew stronger. It was accompanied by a low vibrating hum, which seemed to rise up into the bones. It was difficult to keep on a straight line and not weave from side to side. They were like drunkards in a tipsy foot race. An entire section of the quay ahead of them slid sideways, breaking away from the road. Sailors, longshoremen, potboys, serving women, who had already scuttled out from the buildings fearing their collapse, now looked about them in alarm. A nearby warehouse, a rope store, dropped downwards as if the ground had opened up beneath it. Farther along the waterfront two buildings tipped forward. A stack of large barrels which had somehow survived the initial shock disintegrated. The hogsheads tumbled, then rolled in all directions.

The trembling continued.

They ran on desperately and reached the Three Mariners only twenty paces behind Bartaboa. He dashed inside, calling for his family. They heard his voice, deep within the building, shouting frantically. Then, without warning, the entire tavern fell in on itself, burying everyone who was inside.

They pulled up short, out of breath and horrified. Jezreel was about to continue towards the ruined tavern when Hector shouted at him to go no farther. 'There's nothing you can do. There's worse to come. Remember what happened when the hurricane hit us in Campeche.'

Hector turned to face the others and explain. 'The sea ebbed away, and then came back over the land in a terrible flood that nearly drowned us. I fear that is about to happen here, only far worse. We have to get somewhere high enough to be safe when the sea returns.'

'We should take refuge in one of the forts,' suggested Jacques.

'The forts aren't safe,' Hector told him. 'You saw how Fort Carlisle fell, so can the others.'

'I still don't understand why it collapsed,' insisted Jacques.

'Nor do I,' Hector admitted, 'but we must leave the waterfront. It is too exposed.'

Cautiously they made their way into the town and along the High Street. Here they saw the first looters. A gang of toughs was scrabbling through the wreckage of a jeweller's shop. The passers-by ignored them. Most of the townsfolk had glazed looks on their faces as they wandered aimlessly or stood in the middle of the street, well clear of the standing buildings. Women clutched their children to them, and on one corner a number of injured had been laid out on the ground and a black-clad surgeon was attending to their wounds. Most of the injuries seemed to be head wounds and broken limbs.

Hector racked his brains, trying to make sense of what was happening. He was beginning to detect a pattern in the trail of destruction. The waterfront had suffered the worst, and the poorer part of town. By contrast, fewer of the buildings near the central marketplace were damaged. There had to be a reason for the difference. But there was no time to stop and think. He was sure that the worst of the calamity was yet to come. The surface of the ground was still vibrating. It put him in mind of a great beast gently twitching its skin, as it prepared to rid itself of biting insects with a major spasm. Sooner or later that paroxysm would occur.

They were halfway along Main Street when the next strong tremor came. The ground shook violently, and several buildings on the side closer to the harbour began to disintegrate. Tiles slid off their roofs and thumped to the sandy ground. Their upper floors began to sway. A three-storey building which had a bakery on the ground floor collapsed in on itself. Hector felt a jelly-like sensation on the spot where he was standing. He looked down and saw a faint ripple disturb the surface of the ground. Water oozed to the surface as if squeezed from the depths. Before his eyes the ground on which Port Royal was built was turning to a substance like thick gruel. In a moment of gallows humour he wished that the Reverend Watson was still with them. The pastor would have appreciated the biblical explanation for the disaster destroying the city.

'A house built on sand will not stand,' Hector quoted out loud.

His companions gaped at him.

'Port Royal is built on sand,' he shouted at them. He understood now. 'The sand under the foundations has become soggy and unstable. It slips away from underneath the city each time the earth shakes.'

'How can the sand be wet when the sea is retreating?' asked Jacques.

'I don't know. Maybe it has become saturated deep down, over the years.'

'So what are we to do?' asked Maria.

'Go where there is rock, not sand, beneath us,' he answered.

All of a sudden an image came into his mind: on a seaman's chart the city appeared as a long thin curve extending out from the land. The curve finished in a hook on its seaward end. Strip away the buildings, and any mariner would recognize it as the outline of a reef seen from above.

'Port Royal stands on the spine of a reef. We have to go where the reef is made of strong coral, not weak sand.'

Jacques frowned. 'How do we know where that coral is? We haven't got time to dig down and find out.'

Hector was very clear in his own mind now. 'Remember the Vipers, and where we found the first salvage from the Spanish wreck? Downwind and downcurrent. That's where the sand builds up, in the lee of a reef. Under Port Royal it should be no different. The coral will be on the side which faces the prevailing wind.'

He started to lead them away from the High Street, down Tower Street that led to the south shore. 'The windward side of Port Royal is in this direction.'

Jacques was looking doubtful. 'Surely that puts us into danger. When the sea comes rushing back in, we'll be swept away.'

'We must find somewhere that is higher up, but also strong and well protected.' Even as he said it, Hector wondered if that would be possible.

Unexpectedly Maria spoke up. 'There is a place. I was there on Sunday morning after church service. It's right on the shoreline but quite high, and very strongly built.'

'We have to hurry!' said Hector.

'It's no distance – a high stone platform built for guns, called Morgan's Line.'

They set off at a run and turning a corner they saw the fortification. About fifteen feet high it was solidly built from sizeable blocks of cut stone. On the flat top stood a row of heavy cannon, their muzzles jutting through the embrasures of a parapet on the seaward side. There was no sign of a guard or any artillerymen. They must have gone to either their barracks or their homes, or perhaps to loot. Morgan's Line was deserted.

They climbed the stone steps to the top of the platform and Jezreel walked over and looked out through one of the embrasures in the parapet. 'Hector, I hope you're right in thinking that this is the place to be.'

Hector joined him at the embrasure. They could scarcely be closer to the shore. The high-tide mark was no more than ten paces from the base of the gun platform. Farther out was the same extraordinary sight that they had witnessed at the harbour. The sea had gone. It had retreated for at least a mile, leaving behind a dreary expanse of rounded boulders and hummocks of worn coral divided by narrow channels.

'When is the sea going to return?' asked Maria wonderingly. She had come up to stand at Hector's shoulder, looking out at the eerie sight.

'It's returning already,' said Jezreel quietly. There was awe in his voice, and fear.

Far, far out a thin white line extended right across the horizon. For a little while the line appeared to be stationary, but soon it became obvious that the line was advancing towards them. In another minute it was close enough to be revealed as a wall of water surging forward.

'Oh my God!' breathed Maria. Her eyes were wide with shock.

Hector threw an arm around her. 'When the wave strikes, shelter behind a battlement and hang on as hard as you can. Remember that the backwash may be as dangerous as the first onslaught,' he said.

The wave appeared to accelerate. It was moving as fast as a horse could gallop, and growing taller. Where once it had been less than the height of a man, now it was double or treble that height. It was roiling and tumbling forward on itself, the leading edge smashing down on the coral shelf in a welter of foam, only for another wall of water to rear up and rush forward.

Maria stood, transfixed. 'Get behind a battlement!' yelled Hector and dragged her into shelter just as the giant wave roared up the foreshore and struck the base of Morgan's Line.

A dirty white curtain of foam, spray, debris and solid water climbed the face of the battery and rose high above their heads. Then it toppled forward and came crashing down on them. They cowered, feeling the whole gun platform shake. A moment later the water was swirling around their feet and legs, threatening to sweep them away. They grabbed for the nearest cannon and clung on as the water plucked and pushed at them. Then the tidal wave reversed direction and began draining away almost as fast as it had arrived.

'It didn't overtop the battery!' crowed Jacques, standing up. His shirt and breeches were soaking wet. He looked as if he had been thrown bodily into the ocean. They noticed a strange sound, a roaring, swirling noise like a great river in flood. They moved across to the landward side of the platform and looked down. The sea was pouring steadily into the town. Three or four feet deep it was swirling along the street, carrying everything before it. No longer the clean blue of the sea, the flood water was a dirty brown, stained with sand and slime, and covered with dingy scum.

Hector was staring across the town, towards the harbour. 'Something terrible has happened,' he said. It was difficult to be certain but Port Royal in that direction seemed different. The city skyline had changed. He could no longer make out the roofs of the taller buildings near the harbour. The great warehouses were gone. He remembered the bell tower of a church but it had disappeared. Oddest of all were the masts of several ships. They seemed to be much closer than before, almost as though they protruded from the houses.

The gun platform heaved up under their feet as another earth tremor struck. The surface of the flood below them leapt and pulsated in thousands of short, steep waves which slowly subsided.

'This can't go on! It feels like the end of the world!' gasped Jacques.

They waited fearfully, silently counting the minutes, expecting another after-shock. But instead there was an uncanny stillness as if the earth had expended all its energy and lay exhausted. Very slowly the flood water began to recede.

'We should go down and see if we can help out in the town,' said Maria.

Hector shook his head. 'We must wait a little longer. I think the earthquake has disturbed the sea floor. It's like a basin of water which has been shaken. The ripples slop back and forth until they settle.'

Scarcely had he spoken than the sea began to rise again. This time there was no wall of water suddenly crashing across the foreshore, but a steep swell that heaved in from the sea. The flood water in the street rose again.

It was mid-afternoon, three hours later, when they finally decided it was safe enough to leave the safety of the gun platform. By then they were hungry and fiercely thirsty. In search of something to eat they made their way down the steps of the gun platform and waded through water that came up to their knees. They found that the nearest houses had survived remarkably well. Many had cracks in their walls and ugly gaps where the plaster had fallen away. Window frames were out of true, and what glass remained was nearly always shattered. But as structures they were still intact. Householders who had taken refuge on the upper floors were emerging from their front doors. They treated Hector and his companions to suspicious glances, fearing them to be looters. Some ostentatiously fingered pistols and blunderbusses until they considered the danger past. Then they returned to taking stock of the damage or comparing stories of their woes. A few set their slaves and servants to the dreary task of salvaging furniture that had been inundated.

Crossing York Street, Maria caught sight of Captain Blackmore. He had managed to obtain a small dug-out canoe from somewhere and with the help of a servant was pulling it along. His three children were riding in the canoe and looking about themselves in wonder. Maria drew back into a doorway and waited until they were out of sight.

Hector had noticed her reaction. 'Who were they?' he asked.

'The children I was teaching Spanish to, and their father,' she replied.

Hector glanced at her sharply. 'The same Captain Blackmore who's been pestering you?'

'Yes.'

'You've too kind a heart, Maria. It's a pity the sea didn't take him. Covetous swine like that always seem to float to the surface.'

Maria said nothing. She doubted she would ever see the captain again, and was relieved and glad that the children were safe.

They turned out on to the High Street and Maria let out a gasp of dismay. Nothing could have prepared them for the sight on the far side of the road.

A great swathe of Port Royal had vanished. Where once had been a long frontage of shops and dwelling houses, only two blocks remained upright, and even they were battered and damaged like the stumps of broken teeth. Much more shocking was what lay immediately behind them: the sea itself. The High Street was now part of a new waterfront. The flood had advanced right into the city, drowning everything in its path, and had not retreated. Here the city resembled the victim of an accident left lying face down in the shallows. Partly submerged buildings were all that was left of what had once been the commercial district. Some still showed their upper floors, but many were reduced to nothing more than a buckled roof or the jagged edge of a broken wall sticking up from the water.

For a long moment they stared, too appalled to react. Finally Jacques spoke. 'How could the tidal wave have done this?' he asked.

'With the help of the earthquake,' said Hector soberly. The tops of larger structures were still discernible – King's House, the courthouse, even the Marshalsea prison. But dozens of warehouses, workshops, taverns, sheds and lodging houses had been engulfed. So too had the Three Mariners where Bartaboa had perished. The ruins of Fort James and Fort Carlisle, the two massive bastions that had once guarded the harbour, were now two small stone islands a hundred paces from land. The tidal surge had wreaked havoc with the shipping. Sloops, wherries and merchant ships lay where they had been dumped when the water retreated. Some had been carried inland and left stranded on top of buildings now under water. Hector recognized the shattered remains of the *Speedy Return*, lying over on her side. A little farther on was the *Swan*. The frigate was upright, her spars intact. It must have been her masts he had seen from the top of the gun battery. She had been carried a good fifty yards into the town and deposited on the remains of a government storehouse. The venerable ship had broken her back as she settled. The *Swan* would never sail again.

Human scavengers were picking through the flotsam along the edge of the water. Maybe they were searching for food, but more likely they were looking for valuables washed ashore and stripping corpses if they found them. Hector felt a pang of revulsion, but then he remembered that when he and his friends had fished the Vipers they too had profited from a calamity.

A familiar figure caught his eye. A man dressed in a black coat and wearing an old-fashioned wig was standing at the water's edge with his back to him and looking out over the scene of desolation. Hector recognized Mr Reeve, the Governor's secretary. He went over to speak to him.

'How many people lost their lives?' he asked.

Reeve turned, and the sadness in his face was replaced by a look of pleased surprise. 'Mr Lynch, I had not expected to see you alive.' He noticed Maria standing with Jacques and Jezreel. 'And that must be the lady you were talking about. I'm glad you've found her. It is wonderful that you were spared.'

'The Marshalsea is well built. It saved us from the initial shock. Afterwards we found refuge from the flood on Morgan's Line.'

'You were lucky. The prison is now under ten feet of water.' Reeve passed a hand wearily across his face. 'No one would have imagined this nightmare.'

'What happened to produce such havoc?' asked Hector.

'The land gave way. It slid sideways and downwards and the sea swallowed it up,' said Reeve. He made it sound so simple and so inevitable.

'I saw the sand in the High Street turn to gruel.'

'People are fleeing in whatever boats still float.' There was despair and resignation in the secretary's tone.

'Is no one staying on to organize some relief? asked Hector.

The secretary shrugged his shoulders. 'You can't blame them. There is no food, little shelter, and as you can see from those vultures over there –' he indicated the looters – 'there is precious little law and order.'

Reeve treated Hector to a conspiratorial look. 'Let us derive some satisfaction from the appalling calamity. As far as I am aware you and your companions drowned when the Marshalsea prison slipped under water.'

Hector took the hint but still hesitated. 'Eventually the authorities will catch up with me. They have long memories.'

'Not this time, Mr Lynch. All the files and records kept in King's House have been lost. Even poor Mr Balchen who arrested you is dead. His body was taken out of the wreck of the *Swan* less than an hour ago.'

Mr Reeve held out his hand in a gesture of farewell. 'I suggest you and your friends find yourselves a small boat capable of making the crossing to another island – I wish you and Maria a happy life together.'

Hector gazed out over the desolation that had once been Port Royal and the broken remains of the *Speedy Return*. Her jolly boat was still chocked on deck amidships. The pink lay at an angle, and it would be easy enough to slide the jolly boat into the water. It was large enough to carry the four of them away from Jamaica. He could salvage his charts and navigation instrument from the cabin, and sail away just as he had done when he fled from de Graff. He shook hands with the Governor's secretary, turned and made his way towards Maria and his companions. The spring had come back into his step. He would carry his luck with him, the same luck that had brought him and those closest to him through the catastrophe of Port Royal. Already he was thinking about wind directions, currents and sea distances, calculating the best course to steer to a port where a larger ship would take them onward. As for a final destination, that was for each one of them to decide. Perhaps in the American colonies in the north, or perhaps on the shores of the Indian Ocean where, it was said, flourished a new Utopia, a free country called Libertalia, honestly governed by resourceful men.

HISTORICAL NOTE

The first shakings of the Great Earthquake of Port Royal were felt shortly before noon on Wednesday, 7 June 1692. It was described as a rolling, rippling motion of the ground. Residents of 'the wickedest city in the world' were not unduly alarmed. They were accustomed to the occasional earth tremor. But this first shock was followed by two more tremors of greater magnitude, now estimated at 7.5 on the Richter scale. The packed-sand surface of the streets rose and fell 'like the waves in the sea'. Great cracks opened and closed in the ground. Pedestrians were thrown off their feet. People slid into holes and fissures. Famously, a merchant named Lewis Galdy slipped into one crack in the ground, was washed out by the following tidal wave, picked up by a boat in the harbour and brought safely to land. Others were not so lucky. Some two thousand people – about a third of the population – perished. They were crushed under collapsed buildings, drowned, or entombed alive. A gruesome aspect of the flooding was that the shallow-buried bodies in Port Royal's cemetery were dislodged. These decaying cadavers were found floating alongside the fresh corpses in the harbour. There was huge structural damage. The entire waterfront of Thames Street with all its wharves and taverns slid into the water. Forts collapsed as their foundations gave way. Row upon row of commercial and residential buildings, extending for several blocks into the town centre, either fell or were submerged by an inrush of the sea. The tsunami effect capsized or wrecked ships in harbour, including HMS *Swan*, a naval frigate carried into the town and dumped there. At first the sea had retreated, up to a mile in places, then came surging back as a six-foot wall of water. Like the fictional Hector Lynch, the

Anglican rector of Port Royal, Dr Emmanuel Heath, hoped to find refuge by climbing up on to the battery at Morgan's Line. He ran towards it and was shocked to see the tidal wave bursting over the fortification.

The date of death of Lord Inchiquin, the Governor, has been changed to add colour to Hector's predicament as a prisoner in the Marshalsea at the time of the earthquake. William McMurrough O'Brien, second Earl of Inchiquin, had in fact died in January of that year. But it is correct that he had once been a prisoner of the Barbary corsairs, like Hector (see my novel in the Pirate series, *Corsair*). The future Earl was ransomed on a payment of 7,500 dollars.

The colourful Laurens de Graff was real. It would be difficult to dream up such a swashbuckling figure. Contemporaries and historians describe him as tall, handsome, blond, courteous, gallant, a good duellist, and sporting splendid sweeping moustaches. He also had a vicious temper. By the time Hector encounters him, de Graff would have been a buccaneer–filibustier for some twenty years. A constant irritant to both the Spaniards and the English, he seized and robbed their ships, led daring raids on coastal towns, and evaded or outfought all the naval forces sent to capture him. Henry Morgan, well qualified to judge, described de Graff as 'a great and mischievous pirate' and sent a ship to hunt him down – also with no success. When the Nine Years War (1688–1697) spread to the Caribbean, both France and England courted de Graff, wanting him on their side as the guerrilla leader par excellence. De Graff favoured the French and was rewarded by Louis XIV with a commission in the colonial forces under Governor de Cussy based in Saint-Domingue. About this time, de Graff took a ship on an expedition to fish for a Spanish wreck on the Serranillas, part of the coral reef system then popularly known as 'the Vipers'. In 1693 de Graff launched raids on the coast of Jamaica. How or where he ended his days is not known. One source claims that he was a pilot for Pierre d'Iberville on his 1699 expedition to Louisiana.

Inevitably such a larger-than-life figure attracted numerous legends. Of his gallantry it was said that he sent his personal physician to tend the wounds of a Spanish captain he had defeated in a running battle. On another occasion he allegedly put a stop to an impending massacre when a force of buccaneers captured a coastal town and, finding no loot, were about to slaughter the inhabitants. The most romantic story concerns his second marriage (he was married firstly to Petronilla de Guzman in the Canaries). The tale recounts that de Graff insulted – or perhaps killed – the husband of a French woman of Saint-Domingue. In a fury she challenged him to a duel. De Graff was so impressed with her spirit that he proposed marriage instead. The name of the woman was Marie Dieuleveultor 'Mary God Wills It'– not Anne-Marie Kerganon as in Hector's tale. Like Anne-Marie, de Graff's second wife is said to have been a daughter of a 'fille du roi', one of the female gaolbirds or orphans shipped from France to Saint-Domingue to boost the population in the colony.

The 'Island of Salt' where Hector and his friends are marooned is an uninhabited island off the coast of Venezuela, now known as Salt Tortuga. In May 1687 eight runaways, thirsty and suffering from exposure, landed there from a small open boat. They were indentured servants on the run from Barbados and hoping to reach Curaçao. One of them, an English surgeon named Henry Pitman, wrote a book about the adventures that followed: a gang of pirates already on the island burned their boat and made off, leaving them stranded; they learned to survive on turtles, shellfish and wild plants; and eventually escaped from the island by capturing a vessel from another crew of sea brigands who had quarrelled among themselves. Daniel Defoe drew upon Henry Pitman's experiences when he wrote the story of Robinson Crusoe – Defoe's publisher lived in the same house in London as Henry Pitman – and I have done the same for the adventure of Hector Lynch.

SAXON

THE POPE'S ASSASSIN

Rome, 799 AD. Pope Leo is viciously attacked in the street, by unknown assailants. Sigwulf, a Saxon prince who has been banished to the court of King Carolus in Frankia, is sent to Rome as a spy to discover who was responsible.

There, he discovers a web of lies – the only clue to the attackers' identity is an intricate gold buckle, which Sigwulf links with a mysterious gold warrior flagon he finds in the home of the Pope's chamberlain. Could the attack have its source in the highest levels of the church? Pope Leo had made enemies among the nobility on his rapid ascension to St Peter's Throne, and there are many who would see another in his place.

Returning to Paderborn Palace in Frankia to report his discovery, Sigwulf learns that the flagon has been stolen, and he is tasked with tracing it. His journey takes him deep into dangerous territory, to the notorious stronghold of the pagan Avars . . .

The first two chapters follow here.

Chapter One

The cut-throats lurking in the alley were typical of Rome's gutter class. Lank, greasy hair, sallow complexions and a sour smell of sweat-soaked clothes marked them as slum dwellers from the grimy tenements near the bend in the Tiber. Cheap to hire, they were notoriously unreliable. Their employer, standing with them, was taller by a head. His bulky fur hat was more suitable for a cold winter's day than a bright spring morning in the Eternal City and he had knotted the laces of the ear flaps painfully tight under his chin. The intention was to make his face less easy to recognize. It gave him a pinched and resentful look.

'Reminds me of a hedgepig with gut ache,' whispered one of his hirelings to a companion.

The tall man was listening to the sound of a choir on the steps of the church of San Lorenzo a couple of streets away to his left. It was a last-minute rehearsal of their psalms for that morning's solemn procession. Now, very faintly, he heard the sound of horses' hooves approaching from the opposite direction.

'Get ready. Here he comes,' he warned. The men edged further back into the dark shadow cast by the high side wall of the monastery church dedicated to Saints Stephen and Silvester.

Gradually, the sound of hooves grew louder. A sparse crowd of spectators lined the Via Lata, the ruler-straight main thoroughfare in front of the church, and now they craned their necks to get a first glimpse of the approaching riders. The choir fell silent, and a large and heavy wooden cross, painted white and yellow, was hoisted in the air above them. It swayed unsteadily, held up by one of the poor from the local hospital, who had been selected for his role. Smaller, more ornate crosses sprouted, their gilded poles spiralled with coloured ribbons. They were the stationary crosses to be displayed as the procession walked out of the city by the Flaminian Gate. On the way they would stop to celebrate the stations at the Church of St Valentine, then cross the Ponte Milvio to arrive at their final destination – St Peter's Basilica and the ceremony of the Greater Litany.

The tall man in the winter hat took half a step out from the shadows so that he could see over the heads of the spectators. He noted that the onlookers were mostly women, with a sprinkling of older men and idle bystanders, and a few of the foreign visitors who came to Rome on pilgrimage. The latter were the only ones gaping with real curiosity, anxious to identify which dignitaries were coming. He could see no soldiers, no guards, no watchmen, and that was very satisfactory.

The horsemen came into view. They were in a small group of just seven riders. All but two were beautifully dressed in elaborate church vestments. Their planeta, the long flowing gowns of dark silk, were edged with bands of gold embroidery that glittered in the sunshine. Their leader, a middle-aged man with a podgy, pale face, had a high white headdress and wore a voluminous tent-like garment of patterned brocade. The others had purple skullcaps, ribbed with silver cord. The two more plainly dressed riders were bare-headed and in simple tunics of undyed linen.

The tall man watched as the riders came to a halt, only a few yards away, and began to dismount. He waited until all of them were on their feet, and their grooms had led away their mounts.

'Now!' he shouted, and his gang of ruffians burst out from

cover. No one had been looking in their direction. The surprise was complete. There were screams as the ruffians pulled knives and clubs from under their clothing and flourished the weapons at anyone who got in their way. The crowd scattered in panic. In a few strides the attackers reached their target, the man in the white headdress. His feet were kicked from under him so he fell heavily to the flagstones. He lay there, winded. The cut-throats turned on his companions, yelling abuse, slashing at the air with their blades. Their victims fled, holding up the skirts of their gowns to prevent themselves from tripping. Only one of them hesitated. A blow in the face from a club sent him staggering back, his nose streaming blood. A hand snatched the jewelled cross dangling on his chest, snapping the gold chain. Then he, too, beat a retreat. In moments the Via Lata was empty of spectators, leaving only the attackers and their hapless victim, who was sprawled on the ground.

The tall man in the fur hat stepped up and kicked him hard in the stomach. Tangled in his vestments, his victim could only curl up in a ball and bring up his arms to protect his head. He had lost his black slippers and costly cloak, and the silk gown had rucked up to his knees, revealing long white linen socks. 'For the love of God,' he gasped.

'Deal with him,' ordered the tall man.

Two of the ruffians grabbed their victim by the shoulders and hoisted him up onto his knees. A third attacker, knife in hand, placed himself in front of the terrified man. The white headdress had fallen off, revealing a scalp spotted with large dark freckles, a rim of thin, greying hair around his tonsure.

The man with the knife hesitated.

'Get on with it!' snapped Fur Hat. When there was no response, he moved around behind the kneeling man, seized him by both ears and held his head steady. 'Do as you were told,' he ordered.

The knife man drew a shallow breath, took a half-step forward and jabbed the point of the knife at his victim's left eye. The kneeling man jerked his head to one side in terror. The point of the knife missed. The edge of the sharp blade cut a long gash in the flesh above the cheekbone.

'Try again!' snarled the man in the fur hat.

The knife-wielder made a second stab, and again he missed the eye. Another gash appeared. Now the face of the kneeling man was streaming with blood.

'Clumsy fool!' cursed the tall man. He let go of his victim's ears, and reached up to suck a cut in his hand. The knife blade had gone past the cheek and sliced him across the knuckles. The men holding up the victim released their grip. The bleeding man in the clerical garb fell forward on his face on the ground, whimpering.

'Time to get out of here,' muttered one of the hirelings. His colleagues were already leaving. One of them was bending down to scoop up the valuable cloak that had come loose during the fracas. The thief who had snatched the pectoral cross had long since disappeared. A little distance away small knots of people were beginning to gather on the Via Lata, gazing nervously to see what was going on. Gang warfare in Rome was commonplace, but the brawls seldom happened so publicly.

'Get the bastard out of sight!' commanded the man in the fur hat. He looked around him. His squad of a dozen had dwindled to just three, the knife-man and two more. Fur Hat leaned down, seized his victim by the collar of his gown, and began to drag him bodily towards the door of the church.

His hired men hurried to assist him. They pushed open the door and dragged their bleeding victim onto the marble floor of the atrium within.

'You were also meant to cut out the tongue,' Fur Hat snarled at the knife man once they were inside.

'Not as easy as it looks,' came the surly response.

'We have no time to waste.' Fur Hat caught his breath and flexed the fingers on his hand that had been nicked. The injured man lay at his feet, groaning pitifully.

Fur Hat nodded towards the door that led from the atrium into the adjacent monastery. 'Put him in there for now.'

Watched by their employer, the three cut-throats manhandled their battered victim through the door and into the monastery, then down a corridor. A door to a cell stood open and they heaved their captive inside; they dumped him on the floor, then shut him in. Returning to the church, the leader of the three men held out his hand, waiting until the man in the fur hat gave him a leather pouch. Then all four slipped out through a side door and back into the street outside. Their employer hurried towards the hill called the Ceolian. His accomplices headed in the opposite direction, back towards the slums.

'We should have asked for a lot more money, Gavino,' said their leader, hefting the pouch to feel its weight. His two companions watched him closely, suspicious, in case he was about to run off with it.

'Underpaid, were we?' said the man called Gavino. He had wielded the knife. The dark stubble of his beard failed to hide the rash of pockmarks that marred his lower face. 'We could find out who that fur-head is, threaten to report him to the authorities unless we get more money.'

'Too risky. Those churchmen run this city and the justices dance to their tune.'

'Bloodsuckers, all of them. From top to bottom,' said his colleague. He hawked up a gob of phlegm and spat into the gutter.

'Well, you missed your chance to put your boot into the boss man.'

'You mean that old fart we just gave a going-over?'

The leader looked at his companion pityingly. 'Of course, you oaf.'

'Who was he?'

'He calls himself Christ's Vicar on Earth – His Holiness the Pope.'

Chapter Two

I was squinting through the iron bars of the palace's leopard enclosure when the bishop's messenger tracked me down.

'You are Sigwulf?' the courier asked politely. The armpits of his brown woollen tunic were soaked with sweat and his face was flushed crimson from the early summer heat. From his accent I judged him to be from somewhere in West Frankia and a stranger to Paderborn. Someone must have told him that I took an interest in the royal menagerie.

I nodded and accepted the folded paper he held out to me.

The flap was held down with a blob of pale yellow wax into which the sender had pressed a simple mark: a plain cross of four arms of equal length enclosed in a circle. I cracked the seal with my thumb and opened the single sheet. There was just one line of neat, church-like script:

> *Sigwulf, I have recommended you to Archbishop Arno of Salzburg.*
> *Alcuin.*

That explained the cross. Alcuin was now the Bishop of Tours though I had known him when he was political advisor and private tutor to the family of our supreme overlord, Carolus, King of the

Franks. Eight years earlier it was Alcuin who had chosen me to take a selection of wild animals – including two ice bears – to Baghdad as a gift to the Caliph from Carolus; hence my continuing interest in the king's collection of beasts.

It was common knowledge that Alcuin still dabbled from a distance in affairs of state and corresponded regularly with members of the king's council. But I felt a tremor of disquiet that he should have written to me directly. I was an insignificant member of Carolus's vast household, a *miles* or courtier-soldier. I held no rank, even if, from time to time, I had been called upon for special duties and had carried them out with moderate success.

The bearer of the letter wiped his sleeve across his brow and stood waiting for my response.

'Did Alcuin provide any oral message?' I asked.

'No, sir. He only said that I was to bring you to meet with Archbishop Arno.'

'You know where to find the archbishop?'

'Yes, sir. I just delivered another of my master's letters to the archbishop. He's in his office.'

I glanced one last time into the leopard enclosure. I had been hoping that the May sunshine might encourage the mother leopard to show her twin cubs, born two weeks earlier. There was still no sign of them. 'Then please take me there,' I said.

The messenger – his name, he told me, was Bernard – led me through the muddle of buildings that formed the royal precinct. Paderborn was only one of Carolus's capitals – he had others at Aachen and Ingelheim – and the king had established it on Saxon territory as a symbol of his victory over their federation. That feat of arms had extended his enormous realm until it now covered half of Europe. The king regarded the Saxons as chronically untrustworthy so a high rampart of wood and earth enclosed Paderborn, and its buildings were crammed inside, higgledy piggledy. It was not always clear which were barracks, storehouses, accommodation or administrative offices. Even Carolus's palace, where Bernard brought me, was part residence, part audience hall and part basilica.

The ten-minute walk gave me time to compose myself before a meeting with Archbishop Arno. His reputation as a hard taskmaster was formidable. Not so long ago, Carolus had picked him for the thorny task of turning the fiercely pagan, horse-riding Avars into Christians. The Avars were another of the king's recent conquests. They had plagued Eastern Europe for generations, raiding and demanding tribute. Even the Emperor in Constantinople paid them off. Carolus's army had finally crushed them and now he expected their mass conversion. Doubtless the king judged Arno to be sufficiently ruthless to see the job done, and, if necessary, done at sword point.

The archbishop's physical appearance when I was shown into his presence matched his notoriety. Arno was as rough-hewn as the broad, scarred campaign table at which he was seated. Everything about the man was blunt and square, from his powerful hands with their stubby, thick fingers and hairy backs to his hefty muscular shoulders and a face whose heavy features were framed by a close-clipped iron grey beard. Dressed in a plain woollen shirt and leggings, he looked like a bricklayer.

I put his age at about forty-five – some ten years older than me – and the keen grey eyes that scrutinized me from under bushy eyebrows held no trace of friendliness.

'What do you know about politics in Rome?' he demanded brusquely. His doorkeeper had withdrawn after introducing me. The only other person in the room was a secretary seated at a writing desk in one corner, taking notes on a wax tablet. The archbishop's voice suited his appearance – it was a pugnacious growl.

'A snake pit, my lord. I spent the winter there some years ago, with a delegation from King Carolus to the Caliph of Baghdad.'

'This time the snakes have stuck in their fangs.'

I waited for him to go on.

'Pope Leo has been attacked in the street by a gang of toughs and beaten up. His eyes were gouged out and his tongue removed.' Arno presented the details without emotion.

My face must have shown my shock. During my time in Rome I had observed Pope Leo's predecessor, Pope Adrian. Crude violence would have been unthinkable against Adrian. People feared him and he had been well guarded. I struggled to imagine how anyone would seek to mutilate the man who had followed him on St Peter's throne.

'Who attacked him?' I asked.

'That is what I want you to find out.'

I goggled at him.

The archbishop was speaking again. 'Alcuin writes to me that you have a useful contact in Rome, inside the Church.'

I knew at once who he meant.

'Paul the Nomenclator,' I said. 'His office dealt with requests to the Pope for meetings and grants. He helped me greatly. But he must have retired by now.'

'Anyone else?'

I shook my head.

Arno took a paper from his desk. The writing was the same as on the message I had received, and the content covered the entire page. 'Find out what really happened, and do it discreetly and fast,' he said.

'I'm not sure if my earlier visit to Rome equips me—' I began.

He cut me off abruptly. 'The king's council wants to know who is behind the attack. The safety and well-being of the Holy Father is a matter of state importance. You may take it that this mission is by command of Carolus.'

I pulled myself together. I had no business to question the wishes of Carolus.

'Is there any background information that might help with my inquiries?' I asked meekly.

Arno's eyes flicked to the letter in his hand. 'Alcuin mentions certain rumours about Pope Leo. Complaints about his private life.'

'What sort of rumours?' I prompted, this time making sure to sound respectful.

'That he has been selling lucrative Church appointments.'

There was nothing new in that, I thought to myself. Paul the Nomenclator had regarded simony as a perfectly normal activity within the Church and had profited from it himself.

Arno had not finished. 'There's also a rumour of adultery,' he said.

I made the mistake of smirking. 'Attacked by a jealous husband, perhaps?'

The archbishop scowled at my levity. 'Don't treat this lightly, Sigwulf.' He laid a spade-like hand on a nearby pile of documents. 'These are all letters received from Rome, written anonymously or by certain senior members of the Church, full of complaints about Leo and his shortcomings.'

'Am I to investigate those letter-writers as suspects for the assault?' I asked.

Arno dismissed the suggestion. 'Their turn will come if and when the king's council decides to launch a formal investigation into Pope Leo's behaviour. Right now, your job is to discover who was responsible for the attack and report back to me – and only me – without further delay.'

It seemed that my interview was over.

'My lord, I'll start for Rome at dawn tomorrow,' I said, standing a little straighter. It was obvious that the archbishop preferred his underlings to obey him instantly and without question.

'On the way you can interview an eyewitness to the attack.'

'On the way, my lord?'

'Your shortest route passes through Ratisbon. You'll meet a large party of travellers coming in the opposite direction. They are heading here from Rome. The snowmelt is early this year so they should be through the Alpine passes by now. One of the travellers is a man by the name of Albinus.'

'How will I know him?'

The archbishop gave a grim smile. 'He's got a freshly broken nose. He's chamberlain to Pope Leo, and took a clout in the face from a cudgel, trying to defend his master.'

'Then I take it that Pope Leo himself is amongst the travellers.'

The archbishop nodded. 'After what happened, Leo is frightened for his life. My informants tell me that he is coming here to meet Carolus and seek his protection. The Duke of Spoleto, one of Carolus's most loyal vassals, is accompanying him with an escort of soldiers.'

'Should I interview the Pope as well?'

Arno made a gesture as if brushing off a fly. 'Leo's version of events is not to be trusted. He'll try to implicate his enemies, not tell the truth.'

'What about this man Albinus? He could be a liar too.'

Shrewd eyes held my gaze. 'Alcuin says in his letter that you're no fool. I expect you to know a lie when you meet it.'

The archbishop was already reaching for another document on his table. 'Send me a preliminary report of whatever you manage to learn from his man Albinus,' he grunted. 'My secretary will provide you with money for travel expenses and essential costs. Keep any bribes to a minimum.'

I made my way out of the office, silently cursing Alcuin for landing me in this predicament. Rome was more than two thousand miles away and the troubles of Pope Leo did not concern me. I was perfectly happy to go on spending my days in the undemanding routine of a *miles*. It meant little more than showing up for the occasional muster of the household troops, some arms drill on horseback while being shouted at by a sergeant-instructor, and generally pottering about on the fringes of the king's retinue. It allowed me plenty of spare time to help out the keepers of the royal menagerie at feeding times. I had no wish to be the archbishop's spy.

*

Arno's staff provided me with credentials as a *missi*, an envoy travelling on royal business, so I would be able to commandeer horses as I rode to Ratisbon and beyond. On the fifth day, I came across Pope Leo's entourage resting up in a monastery in the Alpine foothills after they had trudged through the mountain passes. The monastery was a modest enough establishment situated on a spur of high ground that overlooked the road. Its chapel was the only stone-built structure. All the other buildings were made of local timber and roofed with wooden tiles that had weathered to a sombre grey that blended with the drab, rocky countryside. I arrived shortly before noon and the guesthouse was already full to bursting, but royal edict obliged the hosteller to provide food and shelter to a *missi*. Muttering under his breath, the harassed monk found me a corner where I could sleep on a straw palliasse. Then he brought me into the refectory building, explaining that, with so many members in the papal party, he had been forced to arrange two sittings for every meal. Entering the long narrow room with its low ceiling, I quickly recognized Albinus with his broken nose and a face that was covered in large greenish-yellow bruises. He and his companions had already taken their places at table. Apologizing for my late arrival, I made for a gap on the bench beside him, and sat down.

'Some for you?' I asked, reaching for the loaf of rye bread on the table and tearing off a chunk.

'Thank you, no. I have some recently broken teeth and the crust is somewhat hard,' he answered, before sucking gingerly at his spoonful of turnip soup.

'How did that happen?' I enquired cheerfully, as if to make conversation. Albinus was of ordinary height, stoop shouldered and diffident. In company he was the sort of person who would be easily overlooked.

'You'll have heard about the attack on the Holy Father, I suppose,' he mumbled between sips.

'Only rumours. I've been away in the Northlands,' I lied. 'Tell me what happened.'

'It was monstrous. A crowd of villains burst out from the spectators on the Via Lata, right in front of the Church of Saints Stephen and Sylvester. In full view they knocked down His Holiness just as he was about to take his place in the procession of the Great Litany. Quite appalling.'

In telling his story, Albinus had become much more animated. He sat up straight and looked me in the eye. I guessed that he had told the story many times before.

'Is that when you got injured?' I asked him.

'It was.' He paused. 'But not so dreadfully as His Holiness. The attackers gouged out his eyes and cut out his tongue. He was lucky to escape with his life.' Albinus's battered face registered horror with almost theatrical exaggeration. By contrast his voice, though it had become stronger, remained strangely flat and unemotional, as if he was describing something at second-hand.

'You saw all this? It must have been a nightmare,' I said, coaxing him to continue.

'No. I was half-unconscious and driven away by those brutes.'

'What happened to the Holy Father?'

'He disappeared. When I came back with the papal guards, there was no sign of him. Just smears of blood on the pavement where he had been so savagely mutilated.'

'What did you do?'

'I was frantic. I made inquiries, and the next day there came word that the Pope was not dead but being held prisoner in a monastery up on the Caelian Hill.'

This was something I had not heard about from Arno, and the information would have a direct bearing on my investigation. 'How did he get there?'

Albinus turned down the corners of his mouth and simultaneously raised his shoulders in a gesture that I recalled was how the Romans expressed bafflement. 'His attackers must have taken him there. Naturally, as soon as we knew where he was, we organized a rescue. I went there with a party of papal guards and several of my colleagues.'

He looked around us as if to encourage those sitting nearby to listen to his tale.

'We got word into the monastery, to someone there who was as appalled as we were by what had happened. Late that evening, Pope Leo was lowered from a window on a rope. We were waiting in the street below, and brought him back to safety.'

'A miracle,' I said fervently. 'The angels must have been watching over the Holy Father. To lower a blind man, with no tongue, out of a window must have been near impossible.'

Albinus had laid down his spoon. Now he leaned across and gripped me by the wrist. 'But that was not the only miracle. When the Holy Father was incarcerated within the blackness of his prison, the angels came to him. They replaced his eyes and his tongue grew again.'

I sat absolutely still, waiting for him to go on.

'When we received the Pope, he was bruised and sorely wounded, but he could see and speak!' the chamberlain added dramatically.

'Is he here now in this monastery?' I asked, hoping that I sounded suitably astonished.

Albinus let go of my wrist. 'He dines with the Duke of Spoleto in the abbot's private quarters. His Holiness prefers seclusion. He prays that his enemies may be forgiven.'

'A truly amazing tale,' I said fervently. A monastery servant had placed a bowl of soup on the table in front of me while Albinus was talking. I put my face down towards my meal to hide from the chamberlain the doubt in my eyes.

Later that evening I wrote a full account of Albinus's story and left it with the Duke of Spoleto's staff. I gave instructions for it to be handed to Archbishop Arno when the papal party reached Paderborn. Doubtless, the duke's people would open and read my report, but that would do no harm. I repeated the tale exactly as I had heard it from Albinus and I relied on the worldly and sceptical archbishop to wonder at the truth in the recital.

www.panmacmillan.com